WOLF

SWAT: SPECIAL WOLF ALPHA TEAM

TROUBLE

PAIGE TYLER

sourcebooks
casablanca

Published by Sourcebooks Casablanca, an imprint of Sourcebooks, Inc.
P.O. Box 4410, Naperville, Illinois 60567-4410
(630) 961-3900
Fax: (630) 961-2168
www.sourcebooks.com

Printed and bound in Canada
MBP 10 9 8 7 6 5 4 3 2 1

With special thanks to my extremely patient and understanding husband. Without your help and support, I couldn't have pursued my dream job of becoming a writer. You're my sounding board, my idea man, my critique partner, and the absolute best research assistant any girl could ask for.

Love you!

Prologue

Khaki Blake slowly steered her patrol car along the dark service road behind the Grace Park apartment complex. She angled her cruiser's spotlight toward the collection of Dumpsters and trash heaps, trying to find the source of the reported screams on the 911 call that had come in thirty minutes ago. It was dark as hell behind the apartments, and she couldn't imagine why anyone would be messing around back here, but the person who'd called said there was something "bad going on" so the police had to check it out. And since she was in the area, that meant she was the one to check.

Just because she hadn't seen anything yet didn't mean there wasn't something "bad going on." Lakefront, along with several other cities along the I-5 corridor in Washington State, had been dealing with a growing gang problem, and the Grace Park complex was a hot spot of crime activity, with four different gangs claiming some part of it. If trouble was going to happen during the late-night shift, it would be here. Which was why dispatch was sending another cruiser for backup. That was standard procedure for this part of town. You didn't want to be a cop left on your own around here if something went wrong. Unfortunately, her backup hadn't showed yet, so until then, she was going to keep looking for what had prompted the call. Although if it was gang related—a beat down, an initiation, or any other crime—everyone involved was probably long gone by now.

She was just about to turn around and make another pass when she caught a flash of movement near one of the Dumpsters. She stomped on the brakes, angling her spotlight toward the area. It was tough to see around the piles of garbage around the Dumpster, but she swore she'd seen a woman's high-heeled shoe poking out from behind it. Khaki inched the cruiser forward, hoping to get a better view, but didn't see anyone. That didn't mean there wasn't a person to go with that shoe.

Khaki grabbed the radio and thumbed the button. "Dispatch, this is 3C-04. I'm 10-23 at Grace Park. Exiting the vehicle to check the scene. Possible assault victim. Stand by for ambulance request. What's the ETA on that backup?"

There was silence on the other end for so long that Khaki thought her radio was down. Then dispatch finally answered. "3C-04, backup delayed by traffic. Recommend you remain in your vehicle until they arrive."

Khaki frowned. Traffic—at three o'clock in the morning? She'd just reported a possible assault victim and dispatch wanted her to wait?

She swung the spotlight around again but still didn't see anyone. *Crap.* If someone was behind that Dumpster, that person wasn't moving very much, and that couldn't be good.

"Negative, dispatch. I have a visual on a possible victim. I'm exiting the vehicle at this time."

Flipping on her mobile radio, she stepped out of the

car. She was just pulling out her flashlight when she saw the shoe move—this time for sure. The edge of the high heel drummed against the ground a few times, as if the person was trying to attract her attention. Khaki pulled out her Glock, checking every dark corner as she worked her way toward the Dumpster and the person behind it as fast as she could without losing awareness of her surroundings.

She rounded the Dumpster and grimaced. There was a woman lying there all right, and she looked bad. She had olive skin and dark hair, but it was hard tell anything beyond that because she had been beaten. There was no mistaking the blood on the torn red dress she wore. It looked like whoever had used her as a punching bag had tried to kill her.

Khaki quickly looked around, then crouched down and put two fingers to the woman's neck, checking for a pulse. It was weak, but it was there.

The woman groaned, trying to push Khaki's hand away.

"Ma'am, I'm with the Lakefront Police Department. I'm here to help, but you have to hang on."

The woman dropped her hand. It was a wonder she was even still alive.

Khaki reached up and thumbed the mic attached to her shoulder. "Dispatch, this is 3C-04. I need an ambulance on the north side service road of the Grace Park apartments."

"Roger, 3C-04. Status of victim?"

The woman was still breathing, but Khaki wasn't sure for how much longer. "Victim is critical."

"Roger, 3C-04. Medical services are on the way,"

the dispatcher said. "ETA less than ten minutes. Is the scene secure?"

Khaki was about to give the affirmative on that, knowing the EMTs sure as hell wouldn't come into this neighborhood if she didn't. But before she could, a door slammed and three men came out of an apartment. They were silhouetted by the light coming through the doorway behind them, so Khaki couldn't make out their features, but they were big and half-dressed, and at least two of them were carrying weapons that glinted in the faint light.

"That bitch is mine, and I'm not done with her."

At least that's what Khaki thought the man said. His accent was so thick, it was nearly impossible to know for sure. But the menace in his voice was unmistakable, and it wasn't very hard to figure out how the poor woman ended up the way she had.

Khaki lifted her Glock as the two armed men raised their weapons. Training demanded she shout, "Police! Freeze!" but she didn't bother. These men weren't going to care that she was a cop.

A bright flash of light lit up the night, followed by a loud boom as one of the men fired a shotgun in her direction. Pellets hit her right shoulder and chest like white-hot bee stings. Her vest stopped the ones that would have pierced her heart, but her shoulder wasn't protected, and she winced at the pain as she fired multiple rounds at the men. She dropped one man where he stood and sent the other two running back into the apartment.

That didn't stop them from shooting at her, and Khaki leaped to cover the nearly unconscious woman as bullets dotted both the ground in front and the metal Dumpster behind them.

Khaki thumbed her mic with one hand as she returned fire with the other. "Dispatch, this is 3C-04. Officer needs assistance. Shots fired. Repeat, officer needs assistance. Shots fired. Need immediate backup!"

Dispatch might have replied, but Khaki didn't hear it. The gunfire was getting closer, and she knew that sooner or later, it was going to hit her or the injured woman.

"I have to move you," she told the woman. "It's going to hurt, but I don't have a choice."

The woman's eyes fluttered open, then closed again. Khaki hoped that meant she understood. Not that it mattered—Khaki had to get them out of there.

Holding her Glock with one hand, Khaki shoved her other arm under the woman's shoulders and dragged her across the pavement. The woman cried out in pain, but Khaki ignored it. She just kept moving and firing random shots at the apartment, praying the two shooters would stay there until she reached her cruiser.

Khaki made it to her cruiser just as her magazine ran out. She didn't bother reloading. Instead, she holstered her gun so she could slip her other hand under the woman, then heaved her into the front seat. It was a tight fit with the steering wheel, radio rack, and computer console, but Khaki didn't have time to be gentle. She maneuvered the woman until she got her in the passenger seat, then climbed in herself.

She was just putting the car in gear when gunfire erupted from beside the Dumpster. The side and front windows of the cruiser shattered as a hail of bullets smashed into the glass. The car rocked as both tires on the driver's side blew out and the engine died. Pain lanced through her left thigh, but she ignored it as she yanked out her Glock and quickly reloaded. Opening the door, she rolled out of the car onto the ground, and returned fire at the two men trying to kill her.

Time slowed. All Khaki remembered was thinking that the woman in her cruiser would be dead if the men got through her. She vaguely remembered changing out another magazine, and then everything went still.

The two men who'd been shooting at Khaki lay unmoving by the Dumpster. Khaki twisted around, checking every shadow for another shooter, but didn't see anyone else. Heart pounding, she holstered her weapon and grabbed the door handle to pull herself up, intent on checking the woman in the car. So many shots had been fired, she was sure the woman had been hit.

As she crawled to her feet, Khaki realized she was the one who'd been hit. In the thigh and maybe her shoulder again—it was hard to tell. She'd thought getting shot would hurt a lot worse, but she barely felt it. Did that mean she'd been hit bad and was going into shock?

Khaki found the woman curled up tightly against the passenger door, staring at her with wide, tear-filled eyes. Miraculously, the woman hadn't been shot at all.

Khaki eased herself into the driver's seat and reached over to grab one of the woman's hands in hers. Pain shot up her arm. She'd been hit in the right shoulder for sure. But she didn't let that stop her from squeezing the woman's hand.

"It's going to be okay," she said.

The woman slowly nodded, then started crying. Khaki pulled the woman against her injured shoulder, keeping an eye out as the sounds of sirens approached from a distance. *About time.*

As the sirens got louder, Khaki wondered again why she wasn't in more pain. And why the hell had it taken backup so long to get here?

Chapter 1

Three Months Later

XANDER RIGGS SHIFTED IN HIS CHAIR, WONDERING why the hell his boss had asked him to come to this meeting. Gage Dixon knew Xander hated rubbing elbows with the brass down at police headquarters. Other than Deputy Chief Mason, everyone else at headquarters was a waste of space. It had been so long since some of them had carried a weapon, Xander wasn't sure how they could still call themselves cops.

"What's this meeting about anyway?" Xander asked the commander of the Dallas SWAT team. They'd been left stewing in this small conference room for fifteen minutes, and Xander couldn't wait to get out of there.

Gage shrugged, which was his way of saying he didn't know, but Xander didn't buy it for a second. His boss never did anything without a plan.

Xander was tempted to pull out his phone and check his email while they waited, but he resisted the urge.

"I noticed Mac was moving a little slow yesterday at the compound," Xander said instead. "Is her knee still bothering her?"

Gage's jaw tightened. Even though Gage had killed Walter Hardy, the man who'd kidnapped and come close to killing his fiancée, reporter Mackenzie Stone, he still held himself responsible for the fact that she'd hurt herself while trying to get away from the bastard in the first place.

"Only when she goes running," Gage muttered. "Every time she does, her knee swells up; then it's sore as hell the next day. Her doctor told her to stay off it for a while and take a break from running, but Mackenzie refuses to listen."

"That sounds like her—stubborn to a fault. Maybe you should hide her running shoes."

Gage snorted. "Trust me, I thought about that. But then she'd go running in her bare feet and her knee would probably be even worse. I need a better plan."

Xander lazily swiveled back and forth in the fancy leather chair. "Talk her into taking a week off with you and refuse to let her get out of bed. That should do the trick."

"I thought about that too," Gage said. "But I'm saving up vacation days for the honeymoon."

Seriously? Xander couldn't remember the last time his boss took leave. Not unless you counted the few days he'd taken off after they'd all almost gotten blown up in that meth lab, courtesy of Walter Hardy.

"Gage, you haven't taken a vacation in what, five years? You have plenty of leave. Take a week off and spend it with Mac."

If Xander was ever lucky enough to stumble over that one-in-a-billion woman who was perfect for him, he sure as hell wouldn't think twice about taking off to be with her.

Gage opened his mouth—probably to say he was too busy—but then he grinned. "You know, that might actually work. She's been after me to take some time off since we got engaged so we can go house hunting."

"House hunting, huh?" Xander grinned. "What's next, a minivan?"

"Now that you mention it, I have had my eye on one of those."

Xander did a double take. "Seriously?"

Gage just looked at him.

That was a relief. It'd be a shame if Gage traded in that Charger of his.

"Speaking of Mac," Gage said. "She has a friend she wants you to meet."

Alarm bells went off in Xander's head. "Tell Mac thanks, but no thanks. I don't do blind dates."

"You sure? This friend of hers could be *The One* for you."

The One—capital *T*, capital *O*. *The One* soul mate every werewolf supposedly had. A soul mate like Gage had found in Mac.

Xander had always been on the fence about soul mates. Part of him wanted to believe it was true, but his pragmatic side—okay, his cynical side—told him it was nothing more than silly folklore, no different than all the legends about moonlight, silver bullets, and werewolf hunters. Even after seeing Gage and Mac get together, he still wasn't convinced. There was no denying they were amazing together, and Xander could admit he'd gotten caught up in the whole idea, but at the moment, he was more ready to believe it was random luck than cosmic werewolf destiny.

"The odds are probably greater that she's a serial

killer who got chased off Craigslist and is looking for her next victim the old-fashioned way," Xander said drily.

Gage's laughter was interrupted by the sound of voices in the hallway.

Xander gave his commander a sharp look. "I thought we were just meeting with Mason."

"I thought so too."

Gage stood as Deputy Chief Hal Mason walked in, so Xander did too. The chief was accompanied by two men and a woman. Xander recognized one of the men as the Dallas Chief of Police, Randy Curtis. That was weird. Curtis never got involved in the day-to-day police operations.

Xander saw Gage stiffen. *Shit.* That just ratcheted up his own concern another notch.

"Sergeant Dixon, Corporal Riggs." Mason gave him and Gage a nod. "You know Chief Curtis, of course." Mason gestured toward the other two people. "This is Janet Hayes, one of the department's human resource managers, and Mitchell James, one of the lawyers who serves as an advisor to the city council."

Xander said nothing as he shook hands with Curtis, then the other two people. He was already getting a bad feeling about this. What the hell did a human resource manager and a city council lawyer want with SWAT?

James smiled at Gage as they all sat down. "I've been looking forward to meeting you for some time now, Sergeant Dixon. I've followed SWAT's work since I arrived in Dallas a few years ago. Your team's record is truly amazing. But I have to tell you, I was especially impressed by how you handled Walter Hardy and kept him from fleeing the country."

Xander almost laughed. The department's official reports had downplayed the part of the story where Hardy had kidnapped Mac and tried to kill her. While they hadn't lied, they'd left out certain critical details about what had happened at that private hangar where everything had gone down and let everyone assume the rest. Luckily, none of the local and national media had dug too deeply. That was a good thing, considering the SWAT team had pretty much torn Hardy and his men to shreds in the fight. The medical examiner's office had concluded the bodies had been savaged by coyotes postmortem, and even though no one had ever seen any coyotes hanging around the Dallas/Fort Worth airport, that became the official story.

"I'm just glad that none of our own got hurt," Chief Curtis continued before Gage could say anything. "You back that many desperate criminals armed with automatic weapons into a corner, and you usually end up with a bloodbath on your hands."

"That's just a testament to the quality people that Sergeant Dixon has brought onto his team over the years, and his commitment to demanding, rigorous training," Mason said sharply.

Had Xander imagined it, or had Mason just snapped at his own boss? If he didn't know better, he'd think Curtis was about to reprimand Gage and the team for something. If that was the case, Mason wasn't on board with it—whatever *it* was.

Curtis frowned but didn't respond. Instead, he exchanged looks with James. The lawyer offered Mason a smile that just oozed bullshit. "I think everyone would agree with you, Deputy Chief. But I'm sure even

Sergeant Dixon would admit we can make the SWAT team even better."

Better? Their team was already the best in the state of Texas, if not the whole United States.

Xander slid his boss a sidelong glance to see Gage taking part in a staring contest with Curtis.

"Sir, maybe you should just tell me what this meeting is about," Gage said.

The chief nodded, then looked at the woman from human resources. "Janet?"

The HR manager's eyes widened. Did she think they were going to bite her?

"Of course, Chief." She swallowed nervously, smoothing back her graying hair as she turned to address Gage. "Sergeant Dixon, I'm sure you're aware of the police department's goals with regard to diversity. We pride ourselves on having a department that's as broad and varied as the population we serve."

Xander frowned. Where was she going with this?

"What Janet is trying to say is that several members of the police union, as well as those from local civil rights groups, have raised concerns over the fact that there aren't any women on the SWAT team," James said. "You may not realize this, but your unit has developed a reputation as being something of a boy's club. Since I'm sure that was never your intent, I've approached the chief with a plan to rectify that and improve the department's image."

Xander felt like he'd been punched. This was what he and the rest of the Pack had dreaded for years—that a regular, average human cop would get assigned to the team. If that cop were a guy, it would be bad enough.

But if that cop was a woman? It would be a catastrophe. Having Mac around the compound those first few days had thrown the whole team into a tailspin. He couldn't imagine how much worse it would be with a female cop, a person trained to be suspicious and notice things that others dismissed. He and the other werewolves in the Pack would never be able to use their supernatural abilities. They'd have to go back to acting like regular cops again. Everything Gage and the rest of them had worked so hard to build would be gone. And at some point, it would end up getting someone killed.

"Is this some kind of a joke?" Xander demanded. He knew he should probably keep his mouth shut, but he'd never been very good at that. "You come in here and blow sunshine up our asses about how impressed you are with our performance, then tell us you want to add someone to the team for no other reason than you think it will improve our image?"

James lifted a brow. "Are you implying that women aren't good enough to be in SWAT?"

Xander bit back a growl. This jerk had reached into his bag of tricks and pulled out the male chauvinist card rather than admit the truth.

"Don't even go there. You don't know a damn thing about me," Xander said. "As far as I'm concerned, if someone is qualified for SWAT, they're qualified— male or female. But if we were talking about qualified candidates, we wouldn't be doing it in a conference room, and we sure as hell wouldn't need a lawyer in the room with us."

On the other side of the table, Curtis and Mason refused to look Xander in the eye. That was when it all clicked into place, and the sinking feeling he'd been getting in his stomach got worse.

"That's what this is about, isn't it?" Xander demanded. "You want to put someone on the team, but bypass all the normal qualification requirements, don't you?"

Xander didn't even realize his claws were out until Gage put a hand on his arm. *Shit.* Thank God his hands were under the table, where no one else could see them.

"That's enough, Xander." Gage's voice pulled him back from the edge as only an alpha werewolf's could. Xander retracted his claws and took a deep breath, clenching his hands into fists in his lap, so he wouldn't be tempted to reach across the table and choke the crap out of the idiot across from him.

"Mr. James, there's a reason SWAT has a demanding selection process," Gage said. "It ensures the police officers we bring in can do the job that's required. Anything less puts everyone else on the team at risk and, ultimately, the people we're supposed to serve."

The lawyer nodded. "I'm aware that it's a difficult job, Sergeant, but I'm sure there are a few positions on the team that can allow someone with less experience to contribute?"

Beside James, Hayes nodded in agreement. Xander ground his teeth to keep from saying something he shouldn't. *Clueless bureaucrats.*

Gage, on the other hand, didn't look as if he was going to be nearly as successful at keeping his anger in check. In fact, his face darkened so much that Xander thought his boss might actually launch himself across the table at the talking ass with feet who was trying to screw up the perfect team he'd built. Xander wasn't so sure he'd try and stop Gage if he did. Hell, he might just help.

Gage swung his gaze at Mason. "When I took over the team almost nine years ago, you assured me I'd be able to handpick the personnel. Has that changed?"

The deputy chief's mouth tightened into a thin line. "Dammit, Gage. This isn't my doing. The city is worried we're exposing the department to a discrimination lawsuit. My hands are tied here."

James leaned forward, holding up his hands in a placating gesture. "Gentlemen, please, let's not be dramatic here. There's no reason this has to come down to a discrimination case or a lawsuit. I already have a list of suitable candidates. All you have to do is pick the best of the best."

James took a piece of paper from his briefcase and slid it across the conference table. Gage scanned the list, then passed it to Xander without a word.

Xander didn't know everyone on the list, but the names he recognized scared the hell out of him. Instead of cops from narcotics, homicide, or any other division that dealt with high-stress life-and-death situations on a daily basis, they were from internal affairs, the training academy, and community outreach. Xander didn't hate cops who did those jobs—they were important and needed doing—but that kind of work simply didn't prepare you for the SWAT team.

It didn't make sense. If the department seriously wanted to put a woman on the team, there were a lot of them out there with better résumés. Xander knew that for a fact because he'd worked with many of them.

What was this dumbass lawyer trying to do, destroy the SWAT team from the inside out?

Xander was ready to tell all of them where they could stick their stupid list, but Gage beat him to it.

"There's no one on here who's even remotely qualified to work on my team."

"Your team?" James snorted. "Forgive me, but I was under the impression that the SWAT team worked for the city of Dallas and that it answered to Deputy Chief Mason, who answers to Chief Curtis. They'll decide who's qualified to work on the team."

This time it was James who initiated the staring contest, and Xander knew that the only reason Gage looked away first was so he could glare at the deputy chief. "You'll have my resignation before the end of the day."

"Gage—" Mason started, but James cut him off.

"I'm sorry you feel that way, Sergeant," James said. "I'm sure Senior Corporal Riggs will do an outstanding job in your place."

Xander would have laughed if he wasn't so damn pissed. "Thanks, but no thanks. And before you ask why not, it's because I'll be turning in my resignation along with Sergeant Dixon. I'm pretty sure the rest of the team will do the same."

Xander liked Dallas and his job, but protecting the Pack was the only thing that mattered to him. And he knew every other member of the Pack felt the same way.

"All fourteen of them?" James countered.

"All fourteen of them," Xander confirmed. "But look on the bright side. Then you'll be able to fill your new SWAT team with as many people as you want."

"Gage, let's talk about this," Mason said.

"Let them go," James said. "They're bluffing. There's no way the entire team will quit just because their commander wants to take his ball and go home."

Mason shot James an irritated look. "Do me a favor and shut the hell up. You couldn't even comprehend why cops get out of bed in the morning, much less how they decide who they're willing to work—and die—for." Mason turned to Curtis. "I told you this would happen. If there's one thing the incident with Hardy should have taught us, it's that every one of those men on the SWAT team live and breathe for Sergeant Dixon. If he leaves, I have absolutely no doubt they'd all leave with him. And trust me, another city like Houston, Austin, or San Antonio will scoop them up in ten seconds flat."

Xander had always liked Mason—well, as much as he could like a man who was closer to being a politician than a cop. While Mason might back Gage, Xander doubted Curtis would do the same. The chief's job was purely political.

Curtis worked his jaw as he looked from Gage to Mason and back again. "Gage, we're in an impossible position here. Your team is the best in the country, but the city is going to get its way on this whether you and your men like it or not. And I'm with Deputy Chief Mason when I say we don't want that to be at your expense. We need to put a woman on your team. How do we make that happen?"

Gage leaned back in his chair and folded his arms. "You let me pick the woman from a list of candidates I put together."

Xander stared at his boss. Gage had to be shitting him. But his commander looked completely serious.

James opened his mouth to say something, but Chief Curtis silenced him with a glare.

"You have a deal, Sergeant," he said to Gage.

Xander didn't know whether to be relieved or not. He and the other guys in SWAT might not have to walk away from their jobs, but he didn't see how they could stay focused if they added a woman to the team.

———

"You're not serious about putting a woman on the team, are you?" he asked Gage as they walked out of headquarters. "You just needed time to figure out a way to get around this, right?"

Gage gave him a sidelong glance. "The chief was pretty damn clear. He wants a woman on the SWAT team, so I'm putting a woman on it. I've been thinking of doing it for a while anyway."

That was news to Xander. He stopped, sure he hadn't heard right. When Gage kept walking toward the team SUV, he jogged to catch up.

"Putting a woman on the team would be a nightmare. You know that," he said as he started the engine and put the SUV in gear. "We're werewolves. How the hell do you think we're going to be able to hide that from her and do our job at the same time? And don't even get me started on the whole pheromone thing."

They might be men first and wolves second, but if there was one thing that could bring the whole Pack to its knees, it was the scent of a woman.

"We won't have to hide what we are if the female cop I bring in is a werewolf," Gage said.

Wait. What?

Xander had been hit over the head before, shot a few times, even blown up once, but none of those things had ever knocked him for a loop like that announcement.

He glanced at Gage as he turned onto the street and headed toward the SWAT compound. "Female werewolves exist?"

Gage chuckled. "What, did you think all werewolves were men?"

"Well…yeah."

Which was rather stupid now that he thought about it. But he'd never heard of a female werewolf, much less seen one.

"They exist," Gage said. "And I know where to find one I think will be perfect for the team."

"Where?"

Gage pulled out his cell. "Washington State."

"How the hell—?"

But his boss was already on the phone, making reservations for a flight to Seattle. Xander didn't really have to ask. He knew Gage had set up Google alerts for anything related to cops, firefighters, EMTs, and people in the military who seemed to do amazing things after experiencing a traumatic event. It was how Gage had found most of the guys on the team, including Xander. His boss had gotten really good at spotting werewolves trying to hide who they were.

But a female werewolf? It was going to take a while to get his head around that. What would she look like? Would she be big and muscular like all the guys on the team? Would she be overly aggressive and prone to fighting—again like the guys in the unit?

Worse, would she get facial hair when she partially shifted? He shuddered. Damn, that wasn't a pretty image.

The bigger question was how the team was going to react when they heard Gage was bringing her in to SWAT. A female werewolf would satisfy Chief Curtis's demand, but it had the potential to create even bigger problems.

And as hard as he tried, Xander couldn't quell the feeling of dread from building in the pit of his stomach as he pulled into the parking lot of the SWAT compound.

The scent hit Khaki the moment she climbed out of her patrol cruiser. She didn't have a clue what it was, but it seemed both familiar and unique at the same time. Lately her nose had been doing that, picking up a scent so strongly she had no choice but to pay attention to it until she figured out what it was. She'd tried ignoring the urge when it first happened, thinking it would go away. But it never did, not until she'd identified and filed the knowledge away for safekeeping in a head that was becoming scary good at remembering smells. She was like a walking card catalog, but instead of being stuffed full of the Dewey decimal system, it was filled with scent samples. If it wasn't for the fact that this new talent scared the hell out of her, she would have been amazed by it. But of all the smells she'd cataloged, none came close to this one. Instinct told her she should recognize it, but the source of the scent was just out of reach. Maybe that was why it intrigued her so much.

She was still trying to figure out what it was when a man stepped into her path. At first she thought it was her ex-boyfriend and current pain in the ass, Jeremy Engler. But the tall, muscular man standing in front of her definitely wasn't Jeremy. Her ex was pretty big, but this guy looked like he could smash Jeremy flat as a beer can with one punch. That should have made her cautious, but she'd long since stopped being wary of people and things—just one more thing about her that had changed since the night she'd been shot three months ago. Plus, they were standing outside the Lakefront Police Station. If this guy was up to no good, he wouldn't be stupid enough to do it here.

"Officer Blake?" The man held up a badge. "I'm Sergeant Gage Dixon from the Dallas PD SWAT team. I'd like to talk to you for a few minutes, if I may?"

Khaki stared at him, so caught up in his unique scent she almost didn't see the hand he extended for her to shake. Telling her nose to quit it, she reached out and took his hand.

"Sergeant," she said. "You're from Dallas, you said? What brings you all the way to the Pacific Northwest?"

"That's what I'd like to talk to you about. Do you have time to get a cup of coffee?"

It was late and all she wanted to do was go home and fall into bed, just so she could get up and start her personal groundhog day routine all over again. Working third shift sucked, but if a sergeant from the Dallas PD SWAT team had hung around until she got off duty, whatever he wanted to talk about must be important.

She smiled. "It's been a long night, but I guess I can spare a few minutes."

The twenty-four-hour diner next to the police station was empty except for two fellow police officers there to grab breakfast before starting their shift. They gave her a nod, eyeing Gage Dixon curiously as she led him to a booth on the far side of the old-fashioned diner.

"So, what can I do for you, Sergeant Dixon?" Khaki asked after the waitress took their orders.

Considering they were in a diner full of food, including a pair of apple pies fresh out of the oven that were sitting on the counter a few feet away, his scent shouldn't have been so distracting, but it was making it hard for Khaki to concentrate.

Dixon rested his forearms on the table and clasped his hands. "I know you're tired, Officer Blake, so I won't make this complicated. I'm here to offer you a job."

Khaki blinked. "In Dallas?"

"In Dallas," he said. "On my SWAT team."

A tremor of excitement rippled through Khaki. She'd been looking for a way out of the Lakefront PD for months and Sergeant Dixon was handing her the perfect opportunity. Then again, maybe she was dreaming. Why would a SWAT commander offer someone with no tactical training a job on his team?

Khaki waited until the waitress dropped off their coffee before asking Dixon that same question.

Dixon glanced at her as he added sweetener to his coffee. "Because you have other skills that outweigh your lack of experience and training."

Khaki considered that as she added sweetener and milk to her own coffee. Now she was even more curious. Obviously, Dixon knew something about her that she didn't.

"What kind of skills?" she asked.

Dixon lifted his dark eyes to hers. "For one thing,

you keep your head and do your job when things go south. I've read about what you did during that firefight behind the Grace Park apartment complex. There are a lot of cops who would have abandoned that woman to save their own asses, but you stayed and you got her out alive. That says a lot about the kind of person you are."

Yeah, it said a lot, but Khaki wasn't so sure what. People she knew, people whose opinions she'd always respected, told her she'd been an idiot to risk her life for that woman. But she was a cop. It was her job to risk her life for other people.

She sipped her coffee. "Okay, but that doesn't really answer my question. Why come all the way up here from Dallas? It can't just be the fact that I risked my life that night to save someone else."

"But it wasn't just that one night, was it?" His eyes locked with hers. "How many commendations have you received since then?"

Khaki's head rocked back. "How did you get a look at my files? They're private."

"I've never seen your files," Dixon said. "But I've seen your name mentioned in the Tacoma papers a lot in the past few months. It wasn't hard to put two and two together and figure out that your actions would garner you some commendations. So, how many?"

She stared down at her coffee. "Three."

She couldn't tell him the reason she'd been given those commendations was because she'd become a pariah in her own department and that any request she put in for backup went unanswered—just like that night behind the Grace Park apartments. And if she couldn't tell Dixon that, she definitely couldn't tell him that with all the strange things that had been happening to her since that night, she preferred dealing with dangerous situations by herself anyway.

Khaki picked up her mug and took a swallow of coffee, not because she needed the jolt of caffeine, but because she wasn't quite sure what to say.

She'd worked for the Lakefront PD for eight years and had always been considered a good cop with a good reputation and a lot of friends on the force. Then she'd started dating Jeremy—a well-liked cop from a family of cops who had made a name for themselves in the community. He had friends in high places, so he was on the short list for sergeant, then lieutenant. Everyone thought they made the perfect couple—until she decided to break it off with him.

Everything had gone downhill fast from there. Jeremy had handled her rejection like the arrogant, conceited asshole he was—which meant poorly. When he couldn't convince her to take him back, he stalked her and harassed her at work, telling outrageous lies about her to other cops, and screwing with her reports. Almost no one in the department believed anything she said about him, and those who did wouldn't do anything about it. Jeremy was the big man on campus as far as everyone in Lakefront was concerned. No one in the city would look at him sideways.

She'd found out later that was why her backup had been late that night three months ago. She'd been blackballed. Thanks to Jeremy, her fellow cops were never going to lift a finger to help her ever again.

"Was that the night that everything changed for you?"

Dixon's question pulled her out of her reverie. "What?"

"Is that when you gained your new abilities?"

Khaki's heart began to beat like crazy. She darted a look at the two cops on the other side of the diner to see if they'd heard what Dixon said, but neither man looked her way. "What new abilities?"

Dixon's mouth edged up. "Relax, Khaki. No one can hear us. There's just you and me talking about what's been happening to you over the past three months. Assuming that's when it started."

Khaki's first instinct was to immediately deny everything. Her second instinct was to get up and run out of the diner. But Dixon looked so calm and relaxed sitting across from her that it was hard not to trust him. The internal sensor she'd come to trust so much recently was telling her the SWAT commander wasn't a threat. In fact, he might be the only person she could confide in.

"How did you know?" she asked softly.

"That the change was happening to you, or that it started three months ago?"

"Both, I guess."

He smiled. "It's not so hard to recognize the signs indicating a person has changed since I went through it myself."

Khaki stared at him. "You're like me? You can…do things you shouldn't be able to do?"

"You mean, can I run way too fast? Can I hear and smell things I shouldn't be able to? Am I stronger than I should be? The answer to all those questions is yes. And yes, I can heal from things a lot faster than I should, too, which is probably the first thing you learned after you were shot that night."

Khaki's hand tightened around her coffee mug. She'd finally found someone who'd dealt with the same things she was dealing with now. Or, more accurately, he'd found her.

When she'd been hit in the shoulder with a cluster of shotgun pellets and a 9 mm, not to mention another round in the thigh that night at Grace Park, the doctors had patched her up and put her on two weeks of bed rest, saying she was dealing with the wounds incredibly well. Only they didn't know how well. In the middle of the night two days later, she'd gotten up to hobble to the bathroom and discovered she wasn't hobbling anymore. Panicking, she'd torn the bandage from her leg to see that the wound was completely healed. The shoulder wound, which had been much worse, was nearly healed as well.

She'd never gone back to the hospital for her final checkup, worried the doctors would realize she was some kind of freak. When they'd called to check on her, she told them she'd already been cleared by another doctor on staff. They'd assumed the paperwork had been lost and let it go.

Since that night, she'd been wounded twice more, once with a knife and once with a small automatic. The wounds had healed so quickly she hadn't even bothered to tell anyone about them.

"Do you know why this happened to me…to us?" she asked.

"Yeah, I do." His mouth twitched. "But it might be a little hard for you to believe it."

Khaki let out a short laugh. "Hard to believe? Sergeant

Dixon, last week, a drugged-out factory worker stopped beating his kid just long enough to shove a seven-inch-long hunting knife through my stomach. I pulled it out and threw him through a wall, then carried the little boy down three flights of stairs so we could wait for child services out on the curb. There's nothing that I wouldn't believe at this point."

He nodded. "That's good to hear because that makes it a lot easier to say this next part."

She leaned forward, eager to hear what he had to say.

He sipped his coffee, then set down the mug. "You're a werewolf, Officer Blake, just like I am. I run an entire SWAT team full of people just like us down in Dallas. And I want you on the team too."

Okay, maybe there were some things she wasn't quite ready to believe yet.

"We're *what*?"

Khaki didn't realize she'd said it so loud until the two other cops in the diner looked her way. She lowered her voice.

"Want to run that by me again? Because I could have sworn you said we're werewolves."

"That is what I said." Dixon sighed. "Look, I know it sounds crazy, but from what I've been able to figure out, there's a gene in some of us that gets tripped when we experience a traumatic, life-threatening situation—like what happened to you at that apartment complex."

She shook her head. "It doesn't just sound crazy. It is crazy. There has to be some other explanation. We can't be werewolves. If we were, we'd only be able to do the things we do when the moon is full."

Dixon laughed. "That's only in the movies. Which is

a good thing since the incidents my team and I go out on don't follow the lunar cycle. And before you ask, no, silver won't kill us. But a regular bullet will if it hits something vital, like the heart."

Khaki ran her thumb over the diner's logo on the mug, trying to wrap her head around what Dixon had told her. It still sounded crazy. But it would explain why she was suddenly superhuman. And as insane as his claim was, she needed something to help her make sense of things right now.

"And you said the entire SWAT team is made up of…werewolves?" she asked.

He nodded. "All sixteen of us."

"Sixteen," she echoed. "Wow. It sounds like you've already got a full unit. Why recruit me?"

"Human resources said we need to add a woman to the team to fill our diversity quota," he said, then quickly added, "but that's not the only reason. I was going to offer you the job regardless. HR's demand just moved up the timetable. You're a good cop, one I'd be honored to have in the Pack."

"Pack?"

His mouth curved up in a smile. "As in wolf pack."

Right.

Dixon regarded her in silence. "I know this is a lot to take in, and I don't expect you to give me an answer now." He dug his wallet out of the pocket of his jeans and took out a business card, handing it to her. "At least think about it."

Khaki glanced down at the card, then looked at him. "What about HR? Aren't they going to expect you to hire someone pretty quick?"

"Don't worry about them. Take whatever time you need."

She studied his business card again. She'd been a little disappointed when he told her he was offering her the job because human resources thought it would be good PR to have a woman on the team. But she believed him when he said he'd already planned to recruit her regardless. Ultimately, she didn't care what had brought the commander of the supposedly all-werewolf SWAT team to her figurative front door. Dixon was here and he was giving her the perfect opportunity to get away from her ex-boyfriend and a job where no one liked her or had her back. As far as she was concerned, it was a dream come true. She might not believe she was a werewolf, or that he and his SWAT team were either, but they were freaks like her, and that was good enough.

"I'll take it," she said.

Dixon paused, his mug of coffee halfway to his mouth. "Are you sure? I don't mind if you want to take a few days to think about it."

She nodded. "I'm sure."

"Okay." He took another swallow of coffee. "In the interest of full disclosure, I should let you know that you're going to have to earn the respect of the Pack before they fully accept you, and that might not be easy. The guys are all alpha werewolves who have never seen, much less worked with, a female werewolf before. There's no handbook on this. We're going to have to figure it out as we go. If they treat you like every other newbie on the team, they'll probably be tough on you until you prove yourself."

"I can handle tough," she said and meant it.

If there was anything these past few months had taught her, it was that she was stronger than she'd ever given herself credit for.

Even though Dixon told her she didn't have to report for duty right away, she told him she'd be able to start work in a few days. Now that she'd made the decision to quit her job, there wasn't any reason to hang around Lakefront. Her parents and sisters still lived in Chicago, so she had no family in the area. And thanks to the debacle with Jeremy, she didn't have any friends here anymore either. As far as her apartment went, the lease was coming due, so all she'd lose was her deposit. The place had come furnished and whatever didn't fit in her two big suitcases, she'd mail to the SWAT compound down in Dallas.

Maybe the fact that she had so little attachment to this place explained why it felt so right to accept Dixon's job offer.

Now the only thing to do was make it official. By that, she meant telling her boss at the Lakefront Police Department she was quitting. In one way or another, she'd worked for Sergeant Aaron Silver the whole eight years she'd been on the force, and other than the fact that he seemed oblivious to what had gone on between her and Jeremy, she'd always liked him. She almost felt bad telling him she was leaving, but even he knew it was time for her to have a fresh start somewhere else.

She was just thinking she might be lucky enough to get out of there before Jeremy showed up when he stormed into the bull pen. *Crap.*

Khaki pretended not to see him as she put the last few knickknacks from her locker in the box she was packing, but she saw him coming toward her out of the corner of her eye.

"What the hell is going on?" he demanded. "Carpenter called on the radio and said you're quitting to take a job at the Dallas PD. Is that true?"

She carefully tucked her favorite coffee mug into the box before meeting his gaze. Anger flashed in his gray eyes. How had she ever mistaken this arrogant jerk for a nice guy when he was demeaning to the other cops, abusive to suspects, disrespectful to his superiors behind their backs, and most telling of all, controlling when it came to her?

"I'm packing up my locker," she pointed out. "What do you think?"

He clenched his jaw so hard she thought he might break something. "So you're leaving me, just like that?"

"I left you a long time ago, Jeremy." Months ago, actually. But clearly it hadn't sunk into that thick skull of his. "Today, I'm leaving Lakefront."

"To go to Dallas with that cop you had coffee with the other day," he sneered. "Are you screwing him now?"

Khaki wanted to smack him so badly that her hands hurt. She balled them into fists. "I'm not even going to answer that."

Giving him a cold look, she picked up the box of knickknacks and brushed past him. Jeremy grabbed her by the arm and spun her around.

"Don't walk away from me when I'm talking to you," he ground out.

Khaki's blood pounded in her ears. Jeremy was in

a room full of cops, but he didn't seem to give a damn about manhandling her—not that any of them were likely to do anything about it. Well, she wasn't afraid of him like they were. Jeremy had never been dumb enough to put his hands on her before, and he was never going to do it again. She'd make sure of that.

One minute he was gripping her arm, and the next her box of stuff was on the floor and she had Jeremy facedown beside it, one hand on the back of his neck and the other twisting his arm behind his back. She shouldn't even have been able to physically overpower him like this considering he had at least a hundred pounds on her, but her newfound strength made it easy.

She squeezed with both hands, knowing she could crush him like a bug if she wanted to. And God, a big part of her wanted to. She'd enjoyed working in Lakefront before becoming involved with the jackass. She'd been a good cop, with a good reputation and a lot of friends on the force. Now, her reputation in this town was crap because of him.

Jeremy tried to push himself up and twist out of her grip, but she only squeezed harder, shoving his face into the floor and cranking down harder on his wrist until she could hear the sounds of bones about to snap. He let out a pitiful yelp of pain. *It would be so easy to teach this stupid jerk a lesson.*

Sensing someone beside her, she glanced up, barely repressing a growl. Aaron stood there, a mix of shock and horror on his lined and weathered face. Khaki slowly looked around the station and saw every officer looking at her the same way. They actually seemed scared of her.

She turned back to Aaron. He shook his head slowly,

his eyes full of understanding and what looked like pity behind his wire-rimmed glasses.

Khaki felt her anger slowly disappear, replaced with revulsion. She hated it when she lost control like this—another side effect of that night three months ago. She let Jeremy go and stood. Jeremy was smart enough not to get up right away. If he came at her again, she wasn't sure she'd be able to stop herself from doing some real damage.

Bending down, she collected the few possessions that represented her only remaining ties to this place and put them in the box. Her favorite coffee mug was in pieces—just like her life here. Taking a deep breath, she walked out of the station without looking back. Her mother had always told her she should never burn any bridges. Well, this bridge was totally toasted.

Next stop, Dallas.

Chapter 2

XANDER HAD TO PICK HIS JAW UP OFF THE FLOOR OF the training room when Gage introduced the newest member of the SWAT team. He didn't know what to expect, but it sure as hell wasn't Officer Khaki Blake. Tall with an athletic build and just enough curves to fill out the SWAT T-shirt, she had the biggest brown eyes and softest-looking lips he'd ever seen. She had her dark hair back in a bun, so he couldn't tell how long it was, but he'd bet money it fell past her shoulders. She smelled way too good to be believed, too—like a slice of frosted spice cake in a uniform.

Shit. He was practically panting. If he didn't get a grip soon, he was going to start drooling.

He gave the other guys a covert glance to see how they were dealing with her scent and was stunned to see that none of them reacted at all. Why not? His nose wasn't that much better than theirs. He knew for a fact that several of the other guys—Cooper Landry and Jayden Brooks specifically—could smell a hell of a lot better than he could.

Maybe everyone was so mesmerized by finally getting to see a female version of their kind that the rest of their senses had stopped working.

Gage had left it up to Xander to fill the guys in on what had gone down at the meeting with Deputy Chief Mason while he'd headed home to get ready for his trip to Washington State. While the guys had been pissed that the top brass was playing politics with the team, they'd been intrigued at the idea of adding a female werewolf to the Pack.

They'd bombarded him with dozens of questions, none of which he could answer. Was she as fast and strong as they were? Did her abilities manifest themselves in completely different ways? Would she be as aggressive as they were and able to handle herself in a fight? Were there more like her out there, or was she the only one?

Not all the questions were so general. Brooks wondered what she would look like, Max Lowry wanted to know if she would smell like them, and Eric Becker... Well, Becker just wanted to know if she liked to wear yoga pants. God, that kid had an obsession with those things.

Xander had told them what he knew—that no one except Gage knew a damn thing about female werewolves. And Xander wasn't so sure how much their commander knew either.

While Xander was lost in thought, Gage turned the floor over to Khaki, who was currently explaining how much she appreciated the opportunity to be in SWAT.

"I know I won't be handed anything, but I look forward to proving to every one of you that I belong in the Pack and on the team." She spoke in a light, lilting voice that, surprisingly, filled the large classroom. Xander could definitely pick up the Midwest accent, so she probably wasn't originally from the Pacific Northwest. "I'm not asking for anything from you but a chance to prove myself."

Xander surveyed the room again, trying to read expressions and body language. Some of the younger guys, like Becker, Cooper, Max, and Remy Boudreaux, seemed ready to accept her. And while the others were projecting a cautious wait-and-see attitude, no one appeared to oppose her yet.

That was a relief. From what Gage had told him about Khaki, she seemed like a good cop. But getting accepted into the Pack was an uphill battle for anyone new. Just ask Max and Becker—the two most recent additions to the team. It would be near impossible if some of the guys were already opposed to a female on the team before she even started.

Khaki's scent wafted across the room and teased his nose again, more insistently this time. Xander took a deep breath through his mouth, hoping to clear his head. It seemed to work, until she and Gage walked over to him.

Xander pushed away from the desk he was leaning against to stand up straight. Being this close to Khaki, he could see that her brown eyes had little flecks of gold in them too. He had no doubt she'd look even more amazing when she shifted and her eyes turned completely gold.

"I'm giving Officer Blake the afternoon off to go apartment hunting, so you won't be able to start training right away," Gage said. "But I wanted to make sure she got to meet her squad leader before she took off."

Xander was so busy figuring out how to breathe without overdosing on her scent that it took a minute for Gage's words to register. When they finally did, he had to lean back on the desk again to keep from falling over.

He'd just assumed Khaki would be assigned to Mike Taylor's squad. Which was stupid, he realized. Xander had one less team member than Mike, so now they'd be even. But Mike was more patient than Xander, and less brusque. Or it only seemed that way because Mike thought before he spoke, whereas Xander blurted out the first thing that came to mind. Regardless, Xander felt he wasn't the best person to train Khaki.

Even if he was, he couldn't. She smelled too damn irresistible. He'd never be able to concentrate for more than a minute at a time, much less be objective about anything.

Khaki smiled and held out her hand. Xander shook it, trying to ignore how smooth and warm her skin felt in his rough mitt.

"Sergeant Dixon told me a lot about you, Corporal," she said. "I'm looking forward to learning from you."

Xander returned her smile, unable to help himself. "Welcome to the team."

Thank God the rest of his squad came over or he might have stood there gazing into her eyes for the rest of the day. He released her hand and stepped back as Max, Hale Delaney, Becker, Cooper, Alex Trevino, and Trevor McCall crowded around Khaki, asking her where she was from and how long she'd been a werewolf. That was when reality kicked back in and reminded Xander that the woman he'd just spent the past fifteen minutes mentally undressing was going to be in his squad, and that he was going to be her supervisor.

He was in so much trouble.

There was no way he could be her boss. It wouldn't be fair to her or his team, and it sure as hell wasn't something he could handle. He'd end up spending all his time gazing at her like a lovesick puppy instead of training her on weapons and tactics. He'd probably get her or someone else on the team killed because he would be too distracted.

As Becker explained their rotating physical fitness program to Khaki, pointing out that she was more than welcome to put them through any kind of session she wanted when it was her turn—like yoga, for example—Xander caught Gage's eye and jerked his head toward the door.

"What's up?" Gage asked as they moved down the hall, stopping outside the indoor basketball court.

"You can't put Khaki on my squad. It won't work."

Gage's brows furrowed. "Why not?"

"It just won't." He folded his arms across his chest. "My squad is already set up and running like a well-oiled machine. I don't want to screw that up by adding an unknown into the equation."

Gage didn't say anything. *Damn.* Xander should have known his boss wasn't going to buy it. He'd have to come up with something better if he wanted to convince Gage to put Khaki on Mike's team.

But what else could he say? It wasn't like he could admit he was in lust-at-first-scent with the newest member of the team.

"You saw the way Becker was mooning over her," Xander said. "You know that kid isn't going to be able to work with Khaki without being distracted. He'll end up getting himself killed."

Xander hated throwing one of his teammates under the bus like that, but if it kept Khaki off his team, he'd live with the shame. It would be best for everyone involved.

"Yeah, I saw," Gage said. "But I'm pretty sure you can keep Becker under control, and if you can't, don't worry. I have no doubt that Officer Blake will have no problem dealing with Becker on her own."

That was probably true, but still…

"Gage, I'm serious about this."

"I'm serious too," Gage said curtly. "It's in everyone's best interest that Khaki does well in this unit. Not only will it keep HR out of our business, but it will also give us another person with a unique skill set that we can tap into to get the job done. I have no idea how high the ceiling is on her potential, but my gut tells me it's up there in the clouds. That's why I picked you to be her squad leader. You have more experience working with female cops than Mike does. I have no doubt you'll be able to mold her into the best SWAT officer she can be. And regardless of Becker and his endless infatuations, I think your team will be the best fit for her."

"But—"

"But nothing, Xander," Gage growled. "I've already made my decision, and if you'd been listening, you would know she's already fitting in with the guys on your squad. Besides, you've been one person down for a while now. Having Khaki on your squad will even everything out."

Xander clenched his jaw. He wasn't going to get out of this, so he might as well save his breath. And while he appreciated all the sunshine his boss was blowing up his ass, he was sure Gage was going to regret his decision. But until then, Xander was going to have to keep his raging hormones in check and train Khaki as best he could.

This had the potential to turn into a catastrophe of epic proportions.

Sometimes having really great hearing sucked.

Khaki was fielding questions from her new team-mates about her background—where was she from, did she have any family, how long had she been a cop, how long had she been a werewolf—when she heard Riggs tell Sergeant Dixon that he didn't want her on his team.

Crap. And here she thought her first meeting with her supervisor had gone well.

She thought it had gone better than that. Dixon had told her about Riggs when he'd picked her up from the airport, filling her in on his background and training methods. He'd sounded like the real deal, and someone she could definitely learn from. As soon as Dixon had introduced her to the man, she'd known he was some-one special. She couldn't really say why, but all of her newly discovered werewolf senses told her that she and Corporal Riggs were going to mesh perfectly. He exuded confidence, yet he didn't come off as arrogant or cocky. Not like that jackass ex-boyfriend of hers.

It probably didn't hurt that he was so damn attrac-tive. In a room full of Adonis-class hunks, Xander Riggs stood head and shoulders above the rest. He wasn't nec-essarily taller or better built. And it wasn't that he was more handsome than the other guys. It was simply that the combination of dark hair, chocolate-brown eyes, and kissable lips really did something for her.

Then there was his scent.

The moment she'd set foot in the compound, she realized that the unique scent she'd picked up from Dixon back in Lakefront wasn't actually that unique. It turned out that what she'd smelled was werewolf scent. She confirmed that when she walked into the training room and was assaulted with sixteen different versions of that same smell. Each one was subtly different, which meant she'd be able to identify each man on the team easily from now on, but in general, all of them smelled like a werewolf.

But then Riggs had walked into the training room, and snap! The scent coming off him was so tantalizing she'd almost leaned forward to get a better sniff. She controlled herself—barely. Shoving your nose into your new supervisor's neck and snuffling at him like a pig probably wasn't the kind of first impression she wanted to make.

She'd still been appreciating every subtle nuance of her squad leader's scent when they'd shaken hands. And when he'd smiled…she'd gotten all warm and fuzzy fast.

She was just thinking her biggest problem was going to be not crushing on her new squad leader—a problem she was more than ready to live with—when she'd heard Riggs say she wouldn't work on his team.

Worse, everybody else in the room heard it too. Most of them tried to hide it, but she saw the surprise on their faces as they heard Riggs saying anything and everything to get out of having her on his squad. Becker looked pissed when Riggs tried to pin the blame on him, saying he would be so distracted by her presence that he'd get himself killed.

She turned back to the guys, wishing she could crawl

off somewhere to hide. This introduction had gone from perfect to craptastic in less than five minutes, and she didn't have a clue why. But she knew what would happen next. She could already see it in her new teammates' eyes. They were wondering what Riggs knew about her that they didn't. Was she some kind of screwup? A troublemaker? She'd seen those same looks before, and she knew she was going to come out on the short end of the stick. Nobody was going to give her the benefit of the doubt over a senior cop like Riggs.

Why had she come here? The cops back in Lakefront might have disliked her, but at least she'd been able to do her job, even if she had to do it without backup. That wasn't going to work here. You couldn't be a loner on a SWAT team. She was wondering if she should leave when the team's resident explosives expert, Cooper, and the hugely intimidating mountain of a man, Brooks, each took up a position on either side of her and casually leaned back against the table while Becker spun a chair around backward in front of her and straddled it.

She tensed, bracing herself for whatever they were going to throw her way.

"So," Cooper said conversationally. "You got hit with a shotgun blast. What's that like?"

Khaki stared at him, not sure she'd heard right. Then she looked around the room. The other guys were either sprawled in their chairs or leaning back against tables, regarding her thoughtfully.

She turned back to Cooper. "Well…um…it hurt. Like really big bee stings on crack."

Cooper laughed. "Bee stings, huh? Well, then you

don't ever want to get hit with a MAC-10 at close range because that hurts a hell of a lot more than bee stings."

Pushing away from the table, Cooper pulled off his T-shirt, showing off an impressive amount of muscles and almost a dozen well-healed scars along his chest and left shoulder.

"Nine .45 caliber rounds at less than twenty feet," he said, motioning at his scars.

Brooks snorted. "You call those scars? And here I thought they were mosquito bites. Now this is a scar."

Giving Khaki a grin, Brooks pulled up his T-shirt to show a long, thin scar that ran all the way across his chocolate-brown abs and around his side to the middle of his back. "This was from a coked-up junkie with a machete. He thought I was trying to steal his stash."

She winced. The long, faint scar must have come from one hell of a wound. Although the scar was impressive, it wasn't nearly as impressive as those spectacular abs of his.

"Notice how most of that scar is on Jayden's back," Mike quietly pointed out from across the room. "That's because he was running away at the time."

The other guys laughed. Khaki laughed too. The next thing she knew, the men were flashing all kinds of skin, showing off their scars and telling outrageous lies about how they'd gotten them. At least she was pretty sure they were lies. Khaki laughed so hard, she thought she was going to cry. But she didn't. She didn't want anything blurring the mind-boggling view of the perfectly chiseled bodies on display in front of her. If someone from HR walked in, they probably would have lost their minds, but as far as Khaki was concerned, this was the team's way of telling her they wanted her in SWAT, regardless of what Riggs said.

"What about you?" Becker asked her. "Don't you have any scars you want to show off?"

She almost shook her head no, but then stopped. As odd as it sounded, showing off scars and swapping stories was their way of bonding as teammates. If she didn't do the same, she knew they wouldn't pressure her, but it would be silly of her not to show them the one on her stomach. Unlike them, though, she wasn't going to take off her T-shirt.

She pulled her shirt out of her pants and lifted it up enough to show them the long scar three inches above and to the left of her belly button. "A suspect knifed me last week."

"Shit," Alex breathed. "Was that a serrated blade?"

He got up and moved closer, leaning in to get a better look at the puckered skin. As one of the team's medics, he was probably used to seeing a lot of really nasty wounds, but he seemed particularly impressed with hers.

"Yeah," she answered. "The knife hurt worse coming out than going in."

"I bet." Becker flashed her a boyish grin. "That's going to be a cool scar in another week or two."

Khaki wouldn't normally take that as a compliment, but from these guys, it was.

"I have a scar on my thigh from a bullet too, but it happened the night I..." *What had Dixon said it was called?* "Changed," she finished.

"Yeah?" said the youngest guy on the team, Max. Maybe it was the glint in his blue eyes or the mischievous smile tugging at the corner of his mouth, but of all the guys, he seemed to be the one who had a bit of bad boy in him. "Show us."

To do that, she'd have to push her pants down, and she wasn't about to do that. Khaki opened her mouth to tell them as much, but a woman's voice interrupted.

"What are you trying to do, drown this poor woman in werewolf testosterone?"

Khaki turned to see a pretty, dark-haired woman coming into the room, a smile on her face. While the woman wasn't a werewolf like them, all the guys greeted her warmly. One sniff of the scent on the woman and the engagement ring on her left hand told Khaki why they gave her such a warm reception.

Mike made the introductions. "Officer Blake, meet Mackenzie Stone, Sergeant Dixon's fiancée," he said, confirming what Khaki already knew.

Khaki smiled. "Nice to meet you."

Mac ignored Khaki's outstretched hand and hugged her instead. "Call me Mac. Nobody calls me Mackenzie but Gage, and he does it just to be stubborn."

Khaki laughed. "Mac works for me. And call me Khaki."

"Will do." Mac smiled again. "Gage said he gave you the rest of the day off to look for an apartment. I thought you might like some help."

"Aww, Mac," Becker complained. "Khaki was just about to show us the scar on her thigh."

Khaki's face turned three shades of pink.

"Then I got here just in time," Mac said.

Khaki laughed and opened her mouth to agree when her nose picked up the delectable scent that could only belong to one man on the team. Riggs stood in the doorway, his arms crossed over his broad chest and a frown on his face.

"In time for what?" he asked.

"To take Khaki out to look for an apartment," Mac answered.

Riggs's frown deepened, but he didn't say anything. Khaki refused to let his sour mood affect her. Thanks to the other guys on the team, things were back on track, and if Riggs didn't like it, too bad. She didn't need him to like her for this new job to work out. She had teammates who were willing to give her a chance, a new friend in Mac to help her get settled in, and a chance to be part of something special—a pack of werewolves who were just like her.

Who cared what the glowering, sinfully handsome, yummy-smelling Corporal Xander Riggs liked or didn't like?

Chapter 3

KHAKI YAWNED AS SHE FOLLOWED COOPER, MAX, and Hale out of the admin building to the sandbox where the team gathered for physical training—or PT as Becker called it. "Sandbox" was a good term for it. About thirty feet square, it looked like a kid's sandbox, only bigger. Khaki wasn't exactly looking forward to doing sit-ups and push-ups in there, but it was better than exercising on the scrub grass that made up most of the compound.

When Becker had told her they did PT, Khaki had gotten excited. Like most police departments, Lakefront expected their officers to exercise on their own time. Even though she loved working out, doing it before or after the graveyard shift made going for a run or heading to the gym a chore.

But apparently Sergeant Dixon was serious about PT. The team did it together three times a week. And according to the other guys in her squad, it tended to be intense. Becker, who would be running this morning's session, was still inside ironing out a few last-minute details with Corporal Riggs.

Khaki yawned again as she took her place in the loose circle the team had formed in the sandbox. Beside her, Cooper glanced at her.

"You sure you're up for this? It looks like that jet lag thing is seriously kicking your butt."

It was nice to have a coworker express some concern

about her well-being—even if Cooper was essentially saying she looked like crap. It had been a while since anyone had bothered to care.

"Mac and I looked at nearly twenty apartments until we found one she thought was both a good deal and in a good part of town," she said. "Then she kept me up half the night decorating the place and meeting all my neighbors. I don't know how she does it—I'm exhausted."

Not that Khaki was really complaining. She'd enjoyed hanging out with Mac. It was always difficult to make friends in a new place, but after spending five minutes with Mac, Khaki felt as if she'd known her for years. She still couldn't believe that Mac knew about the SWAT team's superhuman abilities and accepted them. Khaki broke out in a cold sweat when she even considered the idea of telling her parents and sisters about what had happened to her.

"Yeah," Cooper agreed. "Mac is a bundle of energy when she's focused on something. You could have taken the day off to get moved in. I'm sure Sarge wouldn't mind."

Khaki shrugged and started loosening up like everyone else. "Sergeant Dixon told me to skip PT this morning, but I didn't think that'd be a good way to start my first real day of work here."

Cooper nodded as if he understood, but before he could say anything else, Dixon, Riggs, and Becker came out to join them. Dixon made a few quick comments concerning the day's work schedule, then mentioned something about equipment that needed to be shipped out for repair, before turning the session over to Becker.

Eric Becker had struck her as something of a goofball

the day before. An attractive, muscular, and hunky as hell goofball, but definitely not a guy who liked to be taken too seriously. Becker started them off with fifty wide-arm push-ups, followed by fifty crunches, followed by fifty more push-ups—close arms this time—and suddenly Becker seemed a lot more serious than he had the day before. Within minutes, everyone was sweating, including Khaki. Then the guys pulled off their shirts, and the serious workout started.

Khaki decided she should probably keep her T-shirt on, though she certainly didn't mind looking at all the sweaty, rippling muscles on display. Among all the fabulous examples of male perfection available for her to feast her eyes on, the one guy that kept drawing her gaze the most was Riggs.

Yesterday, she'd told herself she was going to ignore anything and everything Riggs did and said that didn't relate to work. That had seemed the most mature way to deal with him. Let him be a jerk if he wanted. She'd show him that she didn't care.

Yet five minutes after seeing him whip off his shirt, she was having a hard time looking at anything but him. She had to force herself to stare at the ground just so she wouldn't get caught ogling his sculpted pecs.

While Becker led them through an exercise he called "prison cell push-ups," which involved a combination of traditional push-ups with squat thrusts in between, she mulled over why she was so attracted to Riggs. Well, for one thing, he was sinfully good-looking. He also had a really great smile. Not to mention a deep, husky voice and a killer body. And he smelled amazing too. So, okay, she could see why she was attracted to him.

But why did the guys she was attracted to have to be such assholes? What did that say about her?

She pushed the question aside and focused on the push-ups. Becker wasn't playing around, but as he progressed from one demanding exercise to the next, Khaki realized that she was hanging tough with the guys. As well-muscled as they were, she harbored no delusions that she was anywhere near as physically strong. They all looked like they could bench-press a car. But she was strong as hell for her size—another gift after that night she'd gotten shot. She was also willing to bet that when it came to agility and speed, she might be able to give most of these hunks a run for their money. The notion made her forget all about Riggs and how late she'd stayed up last night thinking about him.

She expected Becker to lead them through some kind of cool down after all those sit-ups and push-ups, but instead he told Cooper and Max to take off. Khaki frowned as they jogged away to make a complete circuit along the compound's fence.

She glanced at Hale. His dark blond hair was standing straight up like he'd just run his hand through it, and he was popping his neck from side to side so hard she could hear the bones cracking. "What's up?" she asked.

"Rabbit." He must have seen her confused look, because he laughed. "It's kind of like follow the leader, except it's for werewolves. Becker is going to be the rabbit. He'll run around the compound, leaving a scent trail that we have to follow precisely. If any of us catch him, we win."

That sounded kind of…juvenile. "What do we win if we catch him?"

Hale grinned, blue eyes dancing. "Bragging rights. What else?"

Khaki laughed. These guys might be SWAT cops, but they were still just guys. And guys could turn anything into a competition, even a game of chase. She was about to ask what Cooper and Max were up to when they came jogging back.

Cooper nodded at Dixon. "The perimeter is all clear. Nobody around for miles."

Khaki didn't have a clue what that was about, but she lined up with the others as Becker took his position out in front.

"How long of a head start does he get?" she whispered to Hale.

"Ten seconds." Riggs's silky voice was so close that his warm breath brushed her ear. Pulse skipping, Khaki turned to see her squad leader standing beside her. Even if Riggs was a total jerk, she still had to admit that he smelled amazing. The scent coming off his sweat-soaked body was so delicious, it was hard not to lean closer so she could breathe in more of it.

She licked her lips and got a handle on her out-of-control sniffer. "Ten seconds doesn't seem like a very long time."

Riggs's mouth twitched. "Becker is really fast. Ten seconds is more than enough time for him. No one's going to catch him without some serious shifting."

Since the squad leader seemed to be in a talkative mood, she was about to ask him what the heck he meant when he said "serious shifting," but Dixon gave the word to start the game. She turned just in time to see Becker take off running for the far end of the SWAT compound.

Wow. Becker wasn't just fast. He was wild-animal fast. A wild animal with two-hundred-and-some pounds of muscle and a set of six-pack abs. He made it to the far end of the compound in eight seconds. She knew, because Dixon was standing in front of everyone with his hand up, holding them for the ten count.

She turned to ask Riggs if that was even possible, just to make sure she wasn't seeing things. That was when Khaki realized she wasn't in Kansas—or Washington—anymore. Half the guys on the team had...changed. Some a little, some more than a little. Right beside Riggs, Cooper was standing there with a feral grin on his face, long canines protruding from both his upper and lower jaws. Farther down the line, Max's upper canines were even longer, and as she watched, she swore she saw the bones of his lower jaw broaden and push out like they were making room for even more teeth.

All along the line of shirtless SWAT officers, eyes were flashing yellow-gold, claws were coming out the tips of fingers, and deep low growls were filling the air.

Oh, crap!

Adrenaline surged through her body, demanding she go into fight-or-flight mode. When Dixon had told her they were werewolves, she'd thought it was simply the SWAT team's way of coming to grips with their super-human abilities. Like saying they had Spidey senses. She never imagined they were real-life werewolves—or that they would be scary as hell.

Dixon suddenly dropped his hand and she got to see what a dozen werewolves looked like as they tore after their prey.

And that was pretty damn scary too.

Instinct made Khaki race after them. She sensed Riggs fall in behind her. Maybe she was faster than he was. Or maybe he was hanging back to see how she handled this first challenge. Either way, he didn't pass her.

Khaki's keen sense of smell told her that Becker had already turned left through the obstacle course and was headed for the climbing tower. Her instincts screamed at her to angle that way to cut him off. But those weren't the rules of the game. They had to follow the path Becker set.

Her teammates' growls got louder as they neared the obstacle course. Her nose, which thankfully worked just fine without her having to go all werewolf, pointed her toward a series of telephone poles mounted horizontally at various heights above the ground. She was impressed. Becker had selected an obstacle that would force the guys chasing him to slow down and go single file. As competitive and fired up as they were, she could only imagine what a cluster that was going to turn into.

Khaki glanced to either side of her as she neared the poles. Almost all the guys had shifted now, and while she didn't have a clue how to do the shifting thing herself, her inner werewolf—she couldn't believe she was thinking that—allowed her to keep up with them. How much faster would she be with all the fangs, claws, and growling?

But that wasn't going to happen right now, so she pushed herself as hard as her body would let her and was surprised when she was rewarded with a burst of speed that got her ahead of more than half the team. She couldn't beat all of them to the logs, but at least she wasn't stuck behind the bigger guys. They would have slowed her down.

She raced across the logs behind Remy, Cooper, and Connor Malone, jumping from one narrow telephone pole to the next as easily as if she were running down a sidewalk. It was exhilarating to move so fast across something that was less than twelve inches wide and ten feet off the ground. It was also terrifying, especially when she thought about how much it would hurt if she fell off moving at this speed.

The last log had to be at least fifteen feet above the ground and she automatically slowed down. She immediately chided herself for being a coward, but it turned out that being careful was a good idea. Up ahead, Cooper threw an elbow back at Connor, disrupting his stride just enough to send the big sniper tumbling off the telephone pole. Connor hit the ground with a thud, which was immediately drowned out by the howl of triumph that Cooper let loose.

Khaki almost slowed to drop off the log to check on Connor, but the man was already on his feet, circling back to go through the obstacle again. If she didn't know better, she would have sworn he was running with a broken arm. She realized there was another part of this game that Hale hadn't mentioned—catching Becker might be the ultimate object of Rabbit, but apparently, making sure no one else caught him if you couldn't ran a close second.

Footsteps thudded behind her. She stopped worrying about Connor and started hauling ass. She didn't know if one of these guys would toss her off the log from behind, but she didn't want to find out.

She launched herself off the end of the log and hit the ground rolling, surprised she was so comfortable with a move like that. She'd never done anything this crazy before, but it seemed to come naturally.

She chased Remy and Cooper to the next obstacle, then to the climbing tower after that, but she couldn't make up any ground. Mostly because she wasn't trying too hard. After watching Jayden practically shove Max right through a plywood wall, she decided keeping her head on a swivel might be the best way to do well at this game. As hard as some of them were going at each other, she might actually win—if she could just avoid being taken out by her teammates.

She followed Remy and Cooper through several fake building facades, jumping through empty window frames and running up stairs, then climbing down from roofs. She didn't catch sight of Becker the whole time. Then again, none of them probably ever would. He was that damn fast.

She cleared the last building and turned for the finish line—the PT sandbox—where Becker was standing with a smile on his face. She was only ten feet behind Remy and Cooper, who were still battling for the lead. She might be able to catch up and pass them if she picked up the pace. Then she heard footsteps pounding fast behind her. She threw a quick glance over her shoulder and practically stumbled when she caught sight of Riggs on her tail. Like the other guys, he'd gone werewolf too, and his gold eyes glinted in the early morning sun.

How the hell *had* he caught up to her? She hadn't seen him since the start of the chase. She pushed harder, trying to pull away, but Riggs closed the distance between them again. She might have been more agile on the obstacles, but she simply couldn't run as fast as the guys when they shifted. All it would take was a shove from her squad leader to send her tumbling head over heels through the finish line like an idiot. As fast as she was going, she wouldn't stop tumbling until she reached the parking lot.

What a way to make a first impression.

Khaki was so sure Riggs was going to take her out that she almost backed off and let him pass her. But something inside her refused to give in, and she pushed even harder.

She tensed, sure the shove was coming, but it never did. Her squad leader stayed right behind her the whole time. Werewolf or not, she was breathing hard and fast by the time she crossed through the sandbox and slowed to a walk on the far side. She resisted the urge to lean over and gasp for air and instead glanced at Riggs as he walked it out beside her. His fangs had retracted, as had his claws, and there was a light sheen of sweat coating his bare chest. It was all she could do not to reach out and run her hands over all that glistening muscle.

She bit her lip and dragged her gaze away from all that tanned perfection to find Riggs watching her. Had he seen her checking him out?

If he had, he didn't call her on it. Instead, he regarded her with those dark, enigmatic eyes, then turned and walked back to the sandbox.

What the heck was that about? Khaki had a sinking feeling that her squad leader could have blown past her to the finish line if he'd wanted to, then gloated about

it afterward. She couldn't understand why he hadn't.
Maybe he wasn't a complete asshole, after all.

Reaching up to push back the hair that had come loose
from her ponytail, Khaki slowly walked over to join the
guys in the sandbox. Cooper and Remy were about to
come to blows as they argued over who had cheated
more in order to gain the second-place finish. Remy's
Cajun accent came out more when he was angry, and
it was hard catching everything he said, but she got the
gist of it. These guys were even more competitive than
she expected. Riggs stepped between the two men.

"Knock it off," Riggs growled.

Khaki felt the hair on the back her neck stand up at
the power in those deep, rumbling tones. It must have
had the same effect on Cooper and Remy because they
stepped away from each other, teeth and claws retracting.

"Okay, everyone," Mike said. "Hit the showers."

That sounded good to Khaki. She was covered in so
much sand, she felt like a sugar cookie. Considering the
guys were just as sweaty and dirty, she thought they'd be
as eager for a shower as she was, but they were all standing there staring at her with weird looks on their faces.

"What?" she asked.

Hale rubbed the back of his neck, clearly uncomfortable. "Um, we only have one set of open bay showers."

Khaki frowned. Open bay showers? What the hell
were those? Then it hit her. "There's no way in hell I'm
showering with all of you."

Cooper's mouth twitched. "Oh, come on. Think of it
as a team-building exercise."

"Yeah," Becker agreed with a grin, then added, "We
promise not to stare."

Khaki doubted any of them would be able to keep that promise, especially Becker. And while the idea of seeing all the guys naked was definitely interesting, she'd never seriously consider it.

Out of the corner of her eye, she saw Riggs studying her. "Not gonna happen," she said firmly. "I'm all about team, but I draw the line at showering with a dozen men at once."

"We can break up into groups of three or four if that'll make you feel better," Remy told her in that sexy Cajun accent of his.

She shouldn't laugh at their juvenile teasing, but she couldn't help it. "Forget it."

"Bummer." Jayden let out an exaggerated sigh. "So what do we do, play rock, paper, scissors to see who gets to shower first?"

Khaki was willing to gamble for the first shot at the showers, but Riggs stepped in and put an end to the negotiations before they even started.

"Blake, you're showering first. And since Becker's game obviously didn't tire out the rest of you, how about we try a couple more laps around the obstacle course?"

The guys grumbled but fell in behind Riggs as he led the way.

"Don't take all morning in there," Hale called over his shoulder.

"And don't use up all the hot water," Cooper added.

Khaki laughed as she jogged to the admin building and ran upstairs. She grabbed her toiletry bag, then stripped off her T-shirt and shorts, and hurried into the open shower. Riggs would probably keep the guys running laps until she finished, but she didn't want to take any chances. As she squeezed shower gel onto her pouf, her mind wandered to all those sweaty, hunky guys outside. They might be her teammates, and so full of testosterone that they were literally a danger to themselves and each other, but God, they were hot. She was looking forward to more of these early-morning PT sessions, especially if it included the aforementioned guys running around with their shirts off.

But as she ran the soapy pouf over her naked body partaking in a little harmless daydreaming about her studly teammates, she found herself thinking less about all the guys and more about one of them—Xander Riggs.

She tried to make sense of that, wondering if it was just a werewolf thing because he smelled so damn good and her nose was so freaky keen. But that didn't make sense. She wasn't fantasizing about his scent. She was fantasizing about his naked body all covered in sand— and her.

That made even less sense. It was obvious Riggs didn't think much of her and she really wasn't too fond of him, but thinking about her squad leader was doing crazy things to her pulse. Not to mention other parts of her anatomy. Her fingers dug into the pouf as she caught a whiff of her arousal. That was new. She knew she was excited, but she hadn't realized her scent was so strong she could smell it.

If she hadn't been in a rush, she would have touched herself.

Definitely not a good idea. All she needed was for one of the guys to come running upstairs to see what was taking her so long to find her bringing herself to orgasm in the showers.

Khaki turned the shower to cold and tried to immerse herself in as many nonsexual thoughts as she could.

It didn't take long to come up with something. All she had to do was remember what it was like seeing the guys shift. That had been freaky. And amazing. The guys were fast, strong, and fearless as all hell in their human form. But when they shifted like they had, it was as if they turned into some kind of superheroes.

She frowned as a thought struck her. What happened if she had to play the rabbit next time and they found out she couldn't do what they could do? Because in the three months she'd been like this, she'd never once sprouted fangs or claws, and she was pretty sure she would have known if her eyes had started blazing like theirs. Maybe female werewolves didn't display the same kind of attributes that the males did.

Worse, what if they expected her to be able to do that werewolf stuff as part of her job? She'd done well keeping up with them this morning, but she'd seen the way they'd navigated the obstacle course. They used their werewolf talents to move in ways she couldn't. What happened when they found out she wasn't the same kind of werewolf?

Oh, crap. She was so screwed.

Khaki leaned back against a table in one of the training buildings, trying not to let her nerves show. Looking at all the chemical jars, glass beakers, Bunsen burners, and plastic baggies scattered around, it was obvious the place had been set up as a mock drug lab. And an impressive one at that. But she and her squad weren't here to talk about taking down drug dealers. Riggs had brought them here to talk about integrating her into the SWAT team—and more importantly, what was expected of her.

Riggs grabbed a dusty wooden chair and spun it around, then straddled it, draping his muscular arms over the back and fixing his gaze on her.

"I'll give you the same speech I give everyone when they join my squad," he said. "When it's just us working together, you can call me Xander. When Sergeant Dixon, other cops, reporters, or the brass is around, I go by Corporal Riggs."

She nodded. "Understood."

"Gage said you had some issues with your last job," Xander continued. "He didn't give me any details, and I don't want them. I don't care about any of that, and neither do the other guys. You bust your ass and lay it on the line for the rest of us, and every one of us will take a bullet for you."

Khaki wasn't quite sure how to respond to a speech like that. Should she growl or grunt…or something? In the end, she went with what came natural for her—being honest.

"Thanks. I'll do my best not to let any of you down."

Xander nodded and looked at the other guys. They all lifted their chins in a sign of approval that all men seemed to know how to do from birth.

"Okay, now that we've got the pleasantries over with, let's get to the real reason we're here." Xander was the kind of guy who got right to the point. "As of now, our squad is on limited-duty status until we get you up to speed and off probationary training status. And we need to do that as quickly as possible."

Trevor, the SWAT team's armorer, frowned, his brown eyes wary. "How quick is quickly?"

"Gage wants Khaki ready for limited field ops in a week, fully qualified in two," Xander said.

Khaki didn't know much about SWAT, but that sounded a little ambitious.

Cooper must have thought so too, because he let out an expletive. "That's bullshit. How the hell does Sarge expect us to get her trained that fast? The rest of us got a month to reach limited ops status. It's like he's setting her up to fail."

"He's not setting her up to fail," Xander said. "He handpicked Khaki for the job against the wishes of people who have their own agendas and the power to make life hell for all of us. Gage has to prove he made the right decision, and he needs to do it fast."

Great. No pressure or anything.

"What if I can't get trained in time?" Khaki asked.

Xander fixed her with a look. "Then Gage is going to be in a tough position."

Meaning Dixon might have to transfer her out of SWAT to make way for another female cop—one who wasn't a werewolf. Despite just getting here, her stomach clenched at the thought of transferring out of the unit.

Xander must have seen the worry in her eyes because he shook his head. "I know what you're thinking, Khaki, but don't even go there. We don't care about any of the political crap or the what-ifs. The boss wants you ready to go in a week, so you're going to be ready to go in a week." He leveled his gaze at her. He had really nice eyes. "To make sure you're ready, I have to know what you're good at and what your weaknesses are."

Khaki hesitated. The idea of admitting how little she really knew about SWAT procedures to her squad leader was awkward enough, but saying it out loud in front of everyone was even worse.

"We've all been where you are, Khaki," Xander said when she didn't answer. "Gage found us, brought us in, and trained us. You can't be any worse than the rest of us were when we got here."

Khaki wasn't so sure of that. But she'd have to own up to it sooner or later. Besides, it wasn't like they weren't going to figure it out when they saw all the things she couldn't do.

"I've been a patrol officer for eight years, and while I can handle myself on the street, I don't know the first thing about SWAT, other than what the acronym stands for," she admitted.

Trevor leaned back in his chair, propping the sole of his boot on the edge of the table in front of him, his gaze approving. "Don't sell yourself short. Eight years on the street is pretty damn good. And now that you're a werewolf, you might have some skills you haven't realized."

"Ever done any rappelling or climbing?" Max asked. "Even if it was just for recreation."

She shrugged. "I climbed around the rocks a couple times up near Mount Rainier. Does that count?"

"What about weapons?" Alex added. "Anything beyond your standard sidearm?"

She gave him a sheepish look. "A shotgun."

"Hand-to-hand combat, wrestling, or martial arts?" Hale asked.

"Only what I learned in the academy."

She braced herself for the grumbles she was sure were coming. But none of the guys seemed concerned about her lack of skills.

"Hell, I think you're further along than I was when I started, Khaki," Becker said.

"She's further along than you are *now*," Cooper said.

Becker flipped him the bird, chuckling while he did. Even though Khaki laughed along with the guys, she couldn't resist glancing at Xander to see what he thought of her answers. But he didn't look annoyed that they had to teach her most of those things. He was still sitting there with his arms casually draped over the back of his chair, regarding her with interest.

"We'll start with the basic skills, then," he said. "Pistol and M4 carbine qualification, then move on to rappelling, urban climbing, entry procedures, and basic hostage tactics. Those areas are our bread and butter. You get them down, and you'll be ready for limited operations."

Khaki's head was already spinning. It sounded like she'd need a month just to get all that stuff down—and she had to pick it up in a week.

"What else do I have to learn to be fully qualified?" she asked.

"Hand-to-hand combat and takedown techniques, picking locks, bypassing security systems, first aid, demolitions, and hostage negotiations. Not to mention honing any specialty skills you have," he said matter-of-factly. "But none of those things are as important as how we operate as a team. When we show Gage that we can all work together, then you're fully qualified."

Khaki was about to ask how Dixon would know when that happened, but Xander had already stood up and was handing out assignments.

"Trevor, you start her on our standard issue Sig 9 millimeter. She's already qualified on a .40 caliber Glock, so it's just a matter of getting used to a new weapon. Alex, you get to introduce her to the M4." Xander looked at her. "After that, Becker will teach you urban climbing, then Max will show you how to rappel."

Did he mean all today? Apparently he did because five minutes later, Khaki was standing on the firing line of the small pistol range, a loaded Sig in her hand. She took a deep breath and spread her feet wide in a shooting stance. She was skilled with a handgun, but that was a Glock. A Sig felt completely different. Besides that, there was the little issue of the seven huge guys standing there watching her, with Xander off to her right, his arms crossed over his chest and his eyes locked on her like a pair of laser beams.

Time to show the guys on the SWAT team that Dixon had made the right decision in hiring her.

Khaki sighted in on the target and squeezed the trigger slowly, punching a hole through the center of the man-shaped silhouette at fifteen yards. Then she adjusted to the target half-hidden behind a fake door a little closer in and popped that one too. More confident now, she picked up speed, transitioning from target to target rapidly and hitting all of them. At least here was one thing she knew how to do well.

When she'd emptied the magazine, she lowered the gun and threw a glance in Xander's direction to see him scowling.

"Stop screwing around with all the close targets and pick up the pace," he growled. "Then give me a couple magazines' worth of rounds with your left hand."

Her left hand? She'd done that once, about three years ago. Khaki sighed. Maybe it was going to be even harder to impress her squad leader than she'd thought it would be.

Chapter 4

XANDER WAS DOG-TIRED BY THE TIME THEY FINISHED the last PT drill and headed for the showers. For Khaki's benefit, Gage had them doing PT every day this week. Xander wanted extra PT time whenever he could fit it in, but the last two days of training with Khaki had gone long, and all the guys on his squad were dragging to some degree.

It probably didn't help that he hadn't slept worth a crap the last two nights. But every time he closed his eyes to try, all he saw were images of Khaki running in her form-fitting PT gear, growling sweetly as she hit the obstacle course with wild abandon, or sweating as she climbed up the side of a building, then laughing as she rappelled down the other side way too fast for his liking. Since she'd arrived, Khaki had been bouncing around like a pixie with a caffeine addiction. You'd never know that he was doing his best to push her to within an inch of her life during every training session. She just kept smiling and coming back for more.

As he jogged upstairs, he yawned so hard his jaw cracked. He really needed some sleep. But that wasn't going to happen, at least not anytime soon. Because Khaki had gone beyond invading his dreams. She'd taken possession of most of his waking thoughts as well. She had climbed into his head and he couldn't get her out, no matter how hard he tried.

And now he braced himself for the hardest part of the day—walking into the locker room and the adjoining open bay shower after Khaki had been in there.

Xander felt his cock harden the moment he reached the top of the stairs and her scent hit him. God, it literally made him weak in the knees. For the life of him, he couldn't understand why he was the only one being affected by it. It wasn't like this was just a passing scent lingering around the locker room either. It permeated every corner of the ten-by-twelve space, and it was overwhelming. Every time he breathed it in, his body responded in a way that was impossible to ignore.

The worst part? Knowing that her scent was so much stronger in the locker room because she'd been prancing around up here naked.

He tried to slam the door on that thought, but it didn't work. The moment he let his mind wander even a few feet in that direction, his imagination took over and he was bombarded with images of Khaki standing in the shower with warm water streaming down that incredible, fit body of hers.

His cock's reaction to those images was instantaneous and intense.

"Damn it to hell," he muttered, checking to make sure none of the guys were around to see him fighting his way out of his own shorts.

Thankfully, the rest of the team had finished cleaning up and were already downstairs. As their voices drifted upstairs, he heard Mike's guys talking about all the extra ops they'd been running the last few days while his squad had been off rotation getting Khaki up to speed. Hopefully they all stayed down there, at least until he turned on the cold water. Otherwise, he was going to look funny walking into the community shower with his dick leading the way.

Khaki's scent was even stronger in the tile-enclosed space of the showers, and Xander forced himself to breathe through his mouth instead of his nose as he twisted the cold water on full blast and stepped under the icy spray. The frigid temperature helped a bit, allowing him to think about something else—like what kind of training the squad was going to do with Khaki today.

He'd spent a good portion of last night thinking about it. He sure as hell hadn't spent it sleeping, so why not? His original plan had been to spend the week going over the basics—shooting, climbing, rappelling, and individual tactics. But Khaki was doing well enough in those areas for them to do team stuff now. It was probably a good idea to see what she could handle anyway. Even though Gage had promised that his squad would be on limited duty until Khaki was ready, they couldn't depend on that. If something too big for Mike's squad to handle on its own came up, Gage would be forced to put Xander's squad back to work. Normally, that wouldn't be a big deal. Xander could usually find a way to get the job done without putting the newbie in a bad position. But he wasn't sure he'd be able to do that with Khaki. When she went out on a call with them, everything she did would be put under a microscope. He had to make sure she was ready for the spotlight when the time came.

Unfortunately, that meant pushing her harder than he already was. He didn't like to do it, but he couldn't see any other way around it.

He turned the water off and reached for his towel. At least his hard-on had gone down.

In the locker room, he put on his uniform, then sat to lace up his boots. A sweet scent immediately engulfed him. He jerked his head up to see if Khaki had come upstairs without him hearing her, but the room was empty. There was only one way to explain why her scent was so concentrated on this part of the bench. She'd sat in this exact same spot. The fact that she might have been naked at the time wasn't lost on him. His body's reaction was immediate and obvious.

"Damn it to hell," he growled.

How the hell was he supposed to go downstairs like this? Worse, how the hell was he going to focus on training Khaki with his cock doing its best impression of a two-by-four all day?

Xander tugged his boot laces tighter, silently reciting baseball stats and hoping it would be enough to distract him. He spent an extra ten minutes upstairs, just to be on the safe side.

When he got downstairs, Mike and his squad had already taken off on an incident. Khaki was telling the other guys about a domestic violence call she'd gone on in Washington State. Her voice drifted off when she saw him.

"What's on the agenda today, boss?" Becker asked.

"You'll find out soon enough," Xander said. "Follow me."

He led them outside and down to the training structure closest to the admin building, the one they affectionately called the House of Doors. The windowless concrete block building was nothing more than a maze of rooms, hallways, and stairwells, separated by lots and lots of doors—hence the name. The place was a nightmare to maneuver through and search quickly, so they usually used it for hostage-rescue training. But today, Xander had another use for the haphazard collection of rooms—team movement drills.

Xander stopped at the entrance and flipped on the lights inside. When Khaki was ready, they'd do the exercise in complete darkness.

He turned to her, careful not to let himself focus on her big brown eyes and lush lips. He'd already learned how quickly he could become distracted when he did.

"You've done well with the individual skills so far, which means it's time to move to the next level—small team tactics," he told her.

Khaki nodded but didn't say anything. He didn't have to hear her heart rate pick up to know she was nervous. The look on her face said it all. He wanted to say something comforting, but was worried it might come off the wrong way. If she were a man instead of a woman—one he was seriously attracted to, at that—he sure as hell wouldn't coddle the guy. Of course, if she were a man, he wouldn't be having these thoughts in the first place.

Xander forced himself to ignore her racing heart and concentrate. "The hardest task for a newbie to learn in SWAT is how to move as part of a team. There are a lot of theories on how a three- or four-person team is supposed to move through a building, clearing each room in a schematic manner, covering each other's blind spots and making sure you don't miss anything, but they're just that—theories."

"And crappy ones at that," Alex added. "Most of the people who claim to know how it's done have never had to actually do it."

Xander couldn't disagree with that, but he still silenced Alex with a glare.

"The typical way a SWAT unit works a new member into the team is to train a lot," Xander continued as he turned back to Khaki. "But even with weeks of hard training, you can still end up with a collection of individuals instead of a team. Luckily, you have an advantage that the average SWAT newbie doesn't have."

She thought a moment, then her lips curved. "I'm a werewolf."

Her smile provoked a powerful response in him he hadn't anticipated. Any attempt to maintain his stern, detached demeanor failed miserably and he found himself grinning.

"Yeah, you're a werewolf. But more importantly, you're a member of a pack of werewolves. You're genetically designed to mesh perfectly into a pack. All you have to do is let it happen."

Her smile faltered, which confused the hell out of him. He'd essentially told her she didn't have to do anything other than simply let loose and be a werewolf.

"Trevor, Becker, Max, and Hale, you guys'll play suspects and hostages." He gave them a nod. "Go ahead and take up positions inside. Just basic stationary threats to start with."

They went inside, leaving him, Khaki, Alex, and Cooper. Normally, he'd pair Khaki with a senior member of his team, like Diego Martinez. But Diego wasn't in his squad anymore. The idiot had gotten into a brawl a while back and Gage had transferred his stupid ass to Mike's squad as punishment. That was how Xander had ended up with Max, which was a crappy swap. Not that there was anything wrong with Max, but the guy was young, with less than a year in SWAT. Losing somebody with Diego's experience and getting a pup who was barely more than a newbie himself was tough to deal with. And to make matters worse, as part of that same brawl, Gage had also partnered Max up with Hale, another senior guy. It probably wouldn't be a permanent situation, but for now, those two were tied together at the hip.

That left Trevor as the only senior team member left, and right now Trevor still had his hands full with Becker. Becker was a good cop, but he had his own way of doing things, and sometimes he liked to color too far outside the lines for Xander's liking.

Xander glanced at Alex and Cooper, watching as they showed Khaki how to operate the paintball guns they'd be using for the exercise. He briefly debated the pros and cons of pairing Khaki up with one of them, but decided against it. While both men had the experience and patience to train Khaki, Xander's gut told him neither one would be a good fit with her.

And he would be?

"Khaki and I will take the right side of the house while you two guys cover the left," he told Alex and Cooper before he could change his mind. "We'll start at a crawl and speed up when she's ready."

Xander took the paintball gun Cooper held out. If he stayed focused, he should be able to pull this training off without a problem. After all, he'd trained all the other members of his squad. But then Khaki stepped closer and her scent gently wafted over and punched him in the gut.

He clenched his jaw as he loaded paintballs in the gun, then slipped it into his thigh holster. "Here's how this is going to work, Khaki. I'm going to be at your right shoulder as we move from room to room, guiding you the whole way. Just relax and let your wolf senses guide you."

She nodded. Her face might be calm, but her body vibrated with excitement.

"Ready?" he asked.

She nodded again, then turned to face the heavy wooden door, leaving herself enough room to rear back and get a good kick in. Cooper and Alex moved in close, and Xander could feel the hair on the back of his neck stand up as he felt all the energy pouring off the three other amped-up werewolves.

Xander placed his left hand on Khaki's back, as Cooper did the same to Alex. Xander almost jumped from the electrical shock that coursed through him from the contact. He covered it by tightening a strap on her vest, but he had to shake his head to refocus.

"The moment you go through the door, stay low and clear the area just inside the door to the right," he instructed, trying not to breathe in her intoxicating scent. "I'll cover everything farther into the room. Cooper and Alex will worry about everything to the left of twelve o'clock. No matter what threats you see in the room, you have to clear your sector. You have to trust that everyone else will do their jobs. You have to trust us with your life."

Xander rested his hand on her back again. He felt the
tingle but was prepared for it this time.

"On my mark," he said. "Go!"

— w —

As Xander'd expected, Khaki was a fast learner. And
as expected, he found it difficult to focus on the task at
hand, especially when he spent so much of the time with
his body in contact with hers.

Schematically clearing a building typically required a
lot of body contact between team members, with every
instruction being communicated almost entirely through
hand signals and taps on the other person's shoulder or
back, a gentle nudge here or there, a brief touch on the
arm. Then there were the moments when all four of them
were pressed close together, as they initially moved into
a room or headed up a stairwell. Then his whole body
was touching hers, and he was practically on fire.

Xander didn't know how it was possible, but being
this close to Khaki for so long had made him more aware
of her then he'd ever been aware of another person—or
werewolf. It was beyond picking up her unique scent.
Now, he swore he could literally smell her emotions.
She was so excited as she moved through the building
that she bordered on being giddy. He'd never experienced anything like it in his life, and it was freaking
him out.

Then there was her heartbeat.

All werewolves had good hearing, and picking up
someone's heartbeat when they were excited wasn't
all that special. But he wasn't only hearing the rapid
thud-thud of her racing heart; he was feeling it as well.

Right there in his own chest, almost as if he had a second heartbeat.

Xander shoved the thought aside before it completely distracted him and concentrated on the only thing that really mattered—Khaki's training. Moving through buildings like this was SWAT's bread and butter. She had to get good at it, and she had to do it fast.

But he had to admit, she *was* good, and she *was* fast. After only a few minutes of instruction, Khaki picked up how their werewolf SWAT team cleared a room. A few minutes after that, she had their four-person team moving through the building nearly as fast as they'd ever moved. He could practically feel her confidence grow as she used her nose, ears, and werewolf intuition to figure out where people were before she even entered a room.

Khaki also proved very adept at quickly distinguishing who was playing the good guys and who were the shooters. Time after time, she slipped quietly into the room and put a paintball right in the middle of the bad guy's chest before they even got off a shot of their own.

At this rate, Khaki would be considered a "go" at this task before lunch.

"Okay," Xander said after they'd completed the exercise for the tenth time. "Let's do it with the lights off this time."

Xander cut the lights, then got in position behind Khaki and put his hand on her back. Her heart thudded beneath his palm as hard and fast as it had the first time they'd entered the house. He didn't know why she was so nervous. Werewolves could see in the dark.

But when Khaki kicked in the door and entered the

house, she didn't move with the same confidence as before. Instead, she slowed down, working her way through the rooms at half speed. She was still new to all this, so it wasn't surprising they'd finally stumbled over something she had a problem with. Even as slow as she was, she navigated the house much better than a regular SWAT officer equipped with night vision goggles would.

Despite knowing that, Xander still ground his jaw in frustration when she came to an abrupt halt outside one of the rooms. He took a deep breath, trying to get a grip on his sudden irritation when he realized he wasn't the only one who was tense. The strange scent-slash-emotions connection he'd developed with Khaki told him that she was just as frustrated as he was. The anxiety and embarrassment was practically rolling off her in waves.

He didn't realize how much it was truly affecting him until he heard himself growl under his breath.

What the hell? This had gone beyond picking up on Khaki's emotions. Now it was as if he was experiencing them himself. The worse she did, the worse he felt.

He tried to fight his way through the feelings and emotions, but it was tough, like swimming upstream through fast-moving water. If he could just understand what had changed when he shut off the lights, maybe he could help her calm down. Which would hopefully calm him down as well.

It didn't make sense. Werewolves could see in the dark just as well as they could in the light. There was absolutely no reason for Khaki to be having so much trouble.

Xander was so focused on what was tripping up Khaki that he didn't realize they'd moved into another room. Off to the right, Trevor was standing behind the hostage tied to the chair—in this case, Becker—with his paintball gun pointed at Becker's head. This was a standard training scenario for them. Step into a room, make an instantaneous assessment of the situation, then take out the shooter before he shot the hostage.

Even though Cooper and Alex were in the room with them, neither of them would take the shot. This was all about Khaki.

But when she swung her paintball gun in Trevor's direction, her pistol was aimed too low. Either she didn't know Becker was there, or she didn't know he was playing the part of the hostage. Regardless, she was about to pop Becker in the head.

Xander reached out to signal a cease-fire by tapping her shoulder, but it was too late. There were two clicking hisses from the pressurized air gun and it was over. Xander couldn't determine if the spike of adrenaline he felt had come from him or Khaki. Regardless, he ended up yelling a lot louder and harsher than he'd planned.

"Lights, dammit!"

Someone hit the switch outside, lighting up the room. Becker was tied to the chair with a shocked look on his face and a line of orange paint streaking the side of his head.

The emotions Xander had been feeling boiled over and finally broke through the wall he'd put up around them. He caught Khaki's arm and spun her around. "What the hell just happened? You killed the frigging hostage!"

The words came out so fast and so furious that it was as if someone else was saying them. Khaki opened her mouth to say something, but then closed it again. Face red, she dropped her head and stared down at the floor. The emotions that flooded Xander now weren't anger or anxiety. They were shame.

Fuck.

Xander wanted to howl in frustration, but he couldn't do that in front of his team. They'd think he was losing it, although it was probably too late for that. Cooper, Alex, Trevor, and Becker looked at him like he'd already lost his mind. Shit, with the way things were going right then, maybe he had.

But there was no way to explain his outburst. He growled and pointed at the door.

"Everyone downstairs. We'll run it again with the lights on, then with the lights off. And we'll keep doing it until Khaki gets it right."

"So, how's Blake working out?"

Xander practically jumped at Mike's question. He'd been so lost in thoughts of Khaki that he hadn't even heard the other squad leader come into the showers. That woman had him so messed up, he wasn't even aware of his surroundings anymore. Someone could have ridden through the compound on an elephant and he wouldn't have noticed.

Hopefully talking to Mike would get his mind off Khaki and all the crap that had happened in the House of Doors, at least for a little while.

Xander dumped half a bottle of soap in his hand and

started washing the sweat and grime from that day's training off his skin. "A lot better than I'd thought she'd be doing at this point."

"You sound surprised." Mike glanced at him as he lathered up a bar of soap. "You know if Gage went to all the trouble of bringing her here as the first female on the team, she had to be good."

Xander shrugged as he reached for the shampoo. He squirted some on his head and let it run down his face, thankful when the stuff blocked the scent Khaki had left lingering in the locker room.

"She's raw as all get-out, but she has a natural instinct for anything related to cop work," he said as he washed his hair. "She'd never even held a Sig until two days ago, and I'd already put her up against almost any guy on the team. She's picking up the M4 faster than anyone I've ever seen, and she can climb and rappel like a frigging monkey."

Xander cringed as he rinsed the shampoo out. Shit, could he gush any harder? But he was being honest. Outside of the little issue she had navigating the House of Doors in the dark, Khaki was turning into one hell of a SWAT officer. Now if he could just get used to being around her without feeling like his body was in sexual overdrive. Maybe with a little more exposure, she wouldn't have such a drastic effect on him.

"Glad to hear she's doing so well," Mike said.

Xander didn't miss the glance his friend threw his way. Next to Gage, Mike was his closest friend in the Pack, but Xander'd already had a really shitty day and he wasn't in the mood to wait for the guy to get to the point he was so obviously trying to make.

"What the hell does that mean?" he demanded.

Mike shrugged as he turned off the water and walked out of the shower. "Nothing. It's just that some of the guys think you're pushing Khaki too hard."

Xander bit back a growl. Obviously someone on his squad had told Mike about what had happened in the House of Doors. That bothered the shit out of him. If someone didn't like the way he was doing things with Khaki, he should have the balls to tell him to his face, not tattle to someone outside the squad.

He turned off the water and stormed out of the shower, grabbing his towel and angrily scrubbing it over his chest.

Mike glanced over his shoulder at him. "Take it easy. You're starting to shift."

Xander hadn't realized his claws were out until he looked down at his hands. He quickly ran his tongue over his teeth to see if his fangs were out and damn near cut himself on their sharp tips. He took a deep breath and forced himself to relax. A moment later, he felt everything retract back to where it was supposed to be.

What the hell was wrong with him? He hadn't lost control like this so many times in a single day since he'd been a freshly changed pup.

"I guess I hit on a sore subject, huh?" Mike said as he pulled on his jeans. When Xander didn't say anything, he continued. "So, have you been pushing her too hard?"

Xander opened his mouth to ask who the hell had told him but then shut it again. Who it was didn't matter. Why they'd done it did. And he already knew the answer to that. Because they knew it was time someone talked to Xander, and they knew that Mike was the best one to do it.

He shoved his towel in his duffel bag and thought about the way he'd been treating Khaki, not just this morning, but the previous two days as well, and he cringed. When he hadn't been scowling at her, he'd been shouting at her to go faster, or be more aggressive, or stop thinking like a cop and start acting more like the werewolf she was.

Doing those things wasn't out of character for him— he always wanted the best from his guys—but the way he'd gone about it was. Standing here now, he couldn't remember even one time he'd told Khaki she'd done something well, not even when she'd done it better than anyone else in the squad ever had. And then this morning? Yeah, he'd crossed the line.

"Shit," he muttered. "I suppose I have been."

"Mind telling me why?" Mike took his shirt out of his locker and shrugged into it. "Because it isn't like you to be an ass."

Xander started getting dressed too, mostly to give himself a chance to figure out what to say. How the hell could he explain to Mike why he'd been such an ass to Khaki when he barely understood why himself? He wanted to teach her to be the best SWAT officer she could be, but if he didn't maintain some distance between them, every guy in the Pack would figure out how attracted to her he really was. He didn't understand it and it scared the hell out of him—especially the part where it seemed like he wasn't in control of himself when she was around.

Of course, he couldn't say any of that to Mike. They

were best friends, but Mike was also about as by-the-book as it got. If Xander admitted what he was feeling for Khaki, Mike would definitely tell Gage. No matter what else was going on, the thought of Gage transferring Khaki to Mike's squad almost made Xander's heart stop beating.

But Mike was waiting for an answer.

"I'm just feeling the pressure to get her trained as fast as possible," Xander said.

"Bullshit," Mike said. "There's more to it than that. I know for a fact that you thrive on impossible challenges. What's really got you going?"

Why couldn't Mike simply let it go? Xander grabbed a T-shirt from his locker and pulled it on, trying to come up with something that would satisfy his friend's curiosity. He couldn't lie. Mike'd pick that up in a hot second.

"Shit, Xander. Don't you think Khaki deserves the best training you can give her?"

Xander's head rocked back like he'd been punched. Where the hell had that question come from?

"You know I do," he growled. "Why the hell would you even ask me that?"

Mike finished lacing up his sneakers and stood. "I was wondering if the reason you're being such a dick is because you don't want a woman on your team."

This time Xander felt his claws and fangs come out. But Mike stood his ground, his eyes turning golden and his fangs sliding out too.

"Are you frigging kidding me?" Xander shouted, clenching his hands into fists to keep from ripping Mike's head off—literally. "After all the years we've worked together, you pick now to start having such a low-ass opinion of me? How could you even think I'd pull something like that—treat Khaki like shit—just because I didn't want her on my squad?"

"Then look me in the eye and tell me you're not trying to punish Khaki because Gage put her on your team," Mike shot back, his elongated canines inches from Xander's. "Then maybe I'll believe it."

Xander didn't feel like going through a werewolf lie detector test at the moment. He would have much preferred giving in to his animal instincts and letting the claws fly. With all the stress he'd been under since Khaki'd arrived, a good brawl would make him feel better.

Although Mike hadn't been a werewolf as long as Xander had, he fought in a much more controlled manner compared to Xander's more instinctive style. If it came down to a brawl between the two of them, they'd be evenly matched and get equally bloody.

By some miracle, Xander controlled himself and retracted his claws and fangs millimeter by millimeter.

"I'm not trying to punish Khaki," he rasped, his gaze not wavering from Mike's. "I want her on my team. And I sure as hell don't have anything against her because she's a woman."

Mike regarded him in silence, undoubtedly listening for an increase in Xander's heart rate, a hitch in his breathing, a tensing of the core muscles, or the scent of his sweat spike—or any of the dozen other signs that would tell him Xander was lying.

But Mike wouldn't pick up any of those signs because they weren't there. Xander might have one hell of an unhealthy attraction to Khaki, and he might have yelled at her more than he should have, but he never intended to mistreat her.

After a moment, Mike nodded, his claws and fangs retracting, his gold eyes returning to their normal dark brown. "Sorry, buddy. I had to ask."

Xander dropped his head in exhaustion, feeling the sleep deprivation he'd been experiencing over the last two nights suddenly catching up to him all at once. "So now you know I'm not some kind of male chauvinist pig out to railroad Khaki off the team because she's a woman."

"Yeah, I do." Mike leveled his gaze at him. "The more important question is, does Khaki know that?"

Chapter 5

KHAKI COULDN'T PULL OUT OF THE SWAT COMPOUND and head home to her new apartment fast enough. There was a bubble bath and a spy novel with her name on it. She could really go for a beer too, but she hadn't picked up any when she went grocery shopping the other day, and she didn't have the energy to stop for some.

God, what a crappy day.

She sighed. Okay, maybe it hadn't been all bad. On the upside, she'd picked up the team's room clearance techniques faster than she thought she would. Regardless of that hiccup when it came to doing it in the dark, she'd earned big points with every guy on the squad except Xander. She knew because they'd told her so over lunch. She'd appreciated their support, more than they would probably ever know, but when Cooper told her to just keep doing what she'd been doing and they had her back, she'd just about lost it. She'd actually had to go to the ladies room to "freshen up" so they wouldn't see the tears in her eyes.

Khaki hadn't felt that kind of support in a really long time, and she hadn't realized how much she'd missed it.

She only wished she'd impressed her squad leader as much. No matter how hard she worked, or how well she did something, it was never good enough for him. Worse, there'd been times over the past few days when it seemed like he couldn't even stand to be in the same room with her. It was like he thought she had cooties. Or smelled funny.

Khaki stopped at a light, tapping the steering wheel of her new Mini Cooper in time to the music on the radio and thinking about the other problem she had with Xander—one that had nothing to do with him and everything to do with her.

Regardless of how hard she tried to fight it, she'd developed a weird werewolf obsession with her squad leader.

She'd been attracted to Xander the moment she laid eyes on him. She liked the way he looked and loved the way he smelled. But since that first meeting, her attraction had turned into something that could only be described as obsessive. And since she'd never felt this way about any other man, she could only assume the source of the problem was her inner werewolf.

Hence, werewolf obsession.

She hadn't slept through the night since arriving in Dallas despite falling into bed exhausted at the end of every long day. But no matter how tired she'd been, she'd fantasized about her hunky squad leader instead of sleeping. And she'd had some vivid fantasies.

A car's horn jolted her attention back to the traffic light. *Crap.* How long had the light been green? She punched the gas, and her Mini surged forward with a squawk of rubber.

A big SUV zipped past her in the fast lane, a woman old enough to be her grandmother behind the wheel. Khaki barely noticed, her thoughts on Xander again.

Having these thoughts about her squad leader was stupid, especially considering her previous experience with workplace romance. Why was she so attracted to him anyway? All the guys on the team were gorgeous, so why was he the only one she was drawn to?

Being near him made her heart beat so fast, it felt like she was running a race. And when he had put his hand on her back during the training exercise today, it had felt like electricity coursing through her body.

But the thing she was having the hardest time dealing with was his scent. He didn't just smell nice, or yummy, or even delicious. He smelled intoxicating. When they were working close together, especially in tight spaces, breathing in his scent had her thinking some really crazy stuff. Like how much she wanted to throw him down and jump him like a wild animal. More than once she'd felt her hands trembling as they'd itched to reach out and touch him.

It was scary how bad she had it for him—and frustrating to know he obviously couldn't stand her.

Khaki turned into the parking lot to her apartment complex. As crazy and frustrating as her obsession with Xander was, she could control it. It would take willpower, but she had willpower to spare.

What had her most worried was what had happened in the House of Doors today when Xander had turned off the lights. Because she didn't think that any amount of willpower was going to be able to help her deal with her inability to shift.

Over the three days she'd been with SWAT, she'd seen every member of her squad shift to some degree. And they were able to do it like it was nothing. She'd seen claws popping out and retracting like they were controlled with a switch. Max had gotten in a tussle with

Alex over something stupid, and she'd watched in fascination as his jaw had actually widened to make room for a scary number of really long teeth. There'd even been scruff starting to grow in along his jawline as he and Alex faced off against each other.

She'd thought he might go all the way until he turned into a real honest-to-goodness wolf with four paws and a tail. Becker had implied that some of the guys could do that. But before that could happen, Xander had stepped in and slammed Max against a concrete wall so hard it had cracked some of the blocks. Max's claws and fangs had immediately retracted, and Xander had let him go, as if it was no big deal.

She'd seen enough to know that this shifting thing was really important. She also knew she was screwed because she couldn't do it.

She'd successfully covered up that fact since she'd arrived, using her smaller size, natural speed, and greater agility to make up for what the others could do when they shifted. But when those lights had gone out, her speed and agility hadn't helped her one bit. She'd looked around and seen all the glowing eyes and known she was in trouble. They could all see while she couldn't. She could make out basic shapes and outlines, but she sure as hell didn't have enough clarity to move like she'd been before the lights had gone off.

She'd tried to force her eyes to change so she could see in the dark like them, but she just got a headache. None of the guys had ever met a female werewolf before. What if it turned out that female werewolves couldn't shift like the males did? She didn't give a crap about the claws and the fangs. She didn't need those to be a good SWAT officer. But what if she could never see in the dark like they did?

With her heart beating like mad, she'd wanted to stop the training, to admit it was something she couldn't do. But her pride wouldn't let her. So instead, she'd used the only talents she seemed to have developed—she'd closed her eyes and used her nose and intuition to figure out where walls, doors, obstacles, and targets were. Even though she'd moved slower than before, it had worked. Until she'd shot Becker in the head with orange paint.

The memory made her cringe.

Khaki knew she could use her nose to navigate, given time. But she wasn't going to be able to fool Xander and the other guys forever.

She was still thinking about how horrible that moment was going to be when she pulled into her assigned space in front of her apartment and saw Jeremy standing there holding a bouquet of roses.

Khaki stomped on the brakes and got out of the car, slamming the door behind her. "What the hell are you doing here?"

Her stomach churned. She'd moved halfway across the country to get away from this jackass and he'd followed her?

Jeremy held out the roses but didn't answer. Was he crazy? Were roses the in thing this season to buy a woman after you'd harassed her to the breaking point?

"I don't want your damn flowers," she said. "I want to know what you're doing here."

His jaw tightened, and she half expected him to toss

the flowers on the ground and grab her instead. But he didn't.

"I came to say I'm sorry," he said slowly, as if the words were a steel wire attached to his testicles that tightened as he spoke.

"Yeah?" She folded her arms and glared at him. "Well, you should have saved your money because I'm not interested."

The muscle near the side of his eye jumped like it always did when he was trying to control his temper. There had been a time when she would have backed down from a fight with him, but not anymore.

"Khaki, please. Don't give up on us."

"Us?" She snorted. "There is no us. There never was. There was just you. I was simply the woman you thought looked good standing at your side. And when you decided I wasn't playing my part like I was supposed to, you made it your mission to destroy my life."

Jeremy's upper lip curled, but instead of lashing out, he gave her a cool smile. "Khaki, sweetheart, that can all be behind us. Come home with me. I'll take you back and we can act like this never happened."

Take her back? Khaki's vision blurred as anger swept through her. Who the hell did this jerk think he was?

"I'm not going anywhere with you!" She knew she was shouting, but she didn't care. Jeremy had chased her out of her home in Washington. He wouldn't chase her from this one. "My life is here now and it doesn't include you."

He glanced down at her uniform and sneered. "Your life is here? In SWAT? Please. What the hell made someone think you would ever be qualified to do that kind of work?"

She opened her mouth to tell him that he didn't have a clue what she could and couldn't do because he'd never taken the time to find out, but Jeremy's harsh laugh cut her off.

"Oh, let me guess," he said. "The big knuckle-dragger Carpenter saw you with at the diner is SWAT, isn't he? Where did you meet him? Did he put you on the team so he'd have you nearby whenever he needed to knock off a piece? What'd you have to do to get the job, send him naked pictures of yourself, or was there phone sex involved too?"

Khaki thought she'd been angry before, but that was nothing compared to how furious she was now. Her whole body was practically vibrating with rage. Before she knew it, she'd ripped the flowers out of his hand and shoved him backward—hard. He had no idea how badly she wanted to tear him to shreds. Her fingers flexed as she imagined how good it would feel to dig her nails into him. Her teeth ached at the thought of sinking into that scrawny throat of his. If he hadn't been too cheap to buy a vase to go with those dumb-ass flowers, she could have beat him with it.

Maybe it was because she had something worth protecting now, or maybe it was that she simply didn't want to get Jeremy's blood all over the sidewalk in front of her apartment, but either way, she resisted the urge to do any of those things.

"You need to get the hell out of here," she growled. Really growled. "Or that little takedown move I showed you back at the station in Lakefront will seem like a love pat compared to what I'll do to you now."

For a minute, Jeremy looked like he might test her. But then his true cowardly nature took over and he backed away.

"I don't know what I ever saw in you, you crazy bitch," he ground out. "But trust me, you're going to be sorry you let me get away."

Khaki suppressed another growl. "More likely I'll be sorry I didn't kick your ass when I had the chance," she muttered as he got in his rental car and drove off with a squeal of rubber.

"Did he hurt you?"

The woman's voice was soft behind her. Khaki took a moment to gather herself before turning around to see her neighbor Emma Sutton with a concerned look on her face. The redhead was clutching the strap of her shoulder bag so tightly her knuckles were white.

"No," Khaki said. "He never touched me."

Emma eyed her skeptically. "If he didn't touch you, why are your fingers bleeding?"

Khaki looked down to see drops of bright-red blood dripping off the tips of every finger. It looked like a demented manicurist had gone after her cuticles with a razor blade. *What the hell?*

"Did that son of a bitch smash your fingers in his car door?" Emma grabbed Khaki's hands before she could stop her, trying to see how bad her injuries were. "Screw him. I'm calling the cops."

Khaki fought the urge to yank her hands out of Emma's grip, knowing that if she did, it would only alarm the woman even more. But she didn't want her neighbor getting a good look at her fingers. She had no idea what was going on, but she was afraid it had to do with being a werewolf, and she didn't want Emma to see something she shouldn't. But Emma let go first, and only so she could dig in her purse for something—most likely her cell phone.

"You don't need to call the cops," Khaki said. "I am one, remember?"

Emma shook her head as she pulled out her phone. "I'm not letting that jerk get away with doing something like that. If you don't press charges, I will."

Khaki appreciated Emma's resolve, but she was too freaked out to deal with this right now. She wanted to get inside and take a closer look at her hands, but she had to deal with her neighbor first.

"Emma, it's nothing. Really." She forced herself to give the woman a smile. "The thorns on the roses stuck me when I grabbed them out of his hands."

Emma didn't look so sure, but she stopped dialing.

Khaki held up her hands. "See, they're not even bleeding anymore. Just some scratches."

Well, they were still bleeding some, but not as profusely.

Emma looked closer, then frowned. After a moment, she lowered the phone. "Okay, maybe it's not as bad as I thought. But you should still tell somebody. You can't let that guy get away with showing up here and yelling at you like that. Who was he anyway, your ex?"

"Yeah." Khaki breathed a sigh of relief. Thank God her new neighbor wasn't going to push the issue. "I'll call my boss as soon as I get into my apartment, okay?"

Emma nodded. "Okay. But you have to promise that you'll call me after you talk to him. I want to know you're all right."

"I will."

Khaki hurried up to her apartment and immediately ran into the kitchen to wash the blood off her fingers. Once the worst of the mess was gone, she stared at her fingernails, hoping to see…well, something that would explain what happened in the parking lot. But there wasn't any sign of werewolf claws peeking out from under her regular nails. Beyond a thin line of blood under her nail tips and around the cuticles, there wasn't much of anything to see at all.

She pulled a paper towel off the roll and dried her hands. Just because she didn't have claws now didn't mean they hadn't come out during her argument with Jeremy. It was the only thing that explained why her fingers had been bloody.

Had Jeremy seen them? She'd been so focused on the thought of hitting her ex with a flower vase that she hadn't noticed what he'd been looking at. But the more she thought about that, the less likely it seemed. If he'd seen claws coming out of her fingers, he would have said something. Subtlety wasn't his strong suit.

So she was safe there, but it still left her with an even more pressing question. Why had her claws come out, and why wasn't she in control of them?

She held up her hands and stared at them, silently willing her claws to pop out. But not a damn thing happened. Her hands stared back at her, as if saying, *What do you think you are, a werewolf or something?*

Khaki clenched her fingers, then flipped them down and open—like Wolverine did in the movies.

Still nothing. She felt stupid.

Khaki sighed. She shouldn't be surprised her claws

didn't work right. Why would they? She couldn't control her eyes in the dark, so why should her claws be any different?

Khaki pulled out her ponytail holder and ran her fingers through her hair as she walked through the living room and into her bedroom. She needed to talk to someone about what the heck was going on with her. If the issues she had with today's training hadn't convinced her, what just happened had. If she didn't get a handle on this werewolf thing quick, she would end up getting booted off the SWAT team. Worse, she might accidentally reveal herself to someone like Jeremy.

But who should she talk to? She sat on the bed and unlaced her boots as she considered that. She could call Cooper or Becker. She'd hung out with them the most. But she dismissed the idea just as quickly. Becker wasn't much more experienced at this werewolf thing than she was, and Cooper struck her as the kind of guy who simply *was* a werewolf without thinking too much about it. Neither one would be able to teach her what she needed to know. Plus, she wasn't sure if they'd keep her secret from the rest of the Pack. She didn't want everyone knowing she was a deficient werewolf.

Who could she trust? She went through the list of names of the other guys in her squad as she took off her uniform and pulled on jeans and a tank top. Although she might trust them to have her back in a shoot-out, she wasn't sure she could confide in any of them. In fact, the only person she felt comfortable enough to talk to was Mac, and she wasn't even in the Pack—not technically, anyway.

Khaki grabbed her cell and called Mac before

she could change her mind. Mac answered on the second ring.

"Hey, what's up?"

"Not much." Khaki winced at the lie. But she couldn't very well spill everything on the phone. "I could use some advice about something though. Would it be okay if I came over to your place?"

"I didn't mean to chase you out, Sergeant Dixon," Khaki said as Mac shooed her big, tall fiancé toward the door.

"Don't worry about it," Mac said, glancing over her shoulder at Khaki. "He was already heading out to the store to pick up more pita chips for me anyway."

Outside in the hallway, Dixon turned to give Mac an amused look, his dark eyes twinkling. "You have four bags in the pantry."

Mac went up on her toes to give him a quick kiss on the lips. "But you can never have enough pita chips. And you know how much I love them."

Giving him a grin, she made a shooing motion with her hand again, then closed the door and turned to Khaki.

"What can I get you to drink?" she asked as she walked into the kitchen. "We have water, iced tea, soda, or beer."

"Iced tea is fine," Khaki said, then added, "You really don't need to go to any trouble, you know."

Mac smiled at her again. "It's no trouble. Grab a seat on the couch. I'll be right in."

Khaki took a seat and looked around. Though small, the apartment was nice. While it was definitely decorated with a woman's touch, Dixon's presence was obvious in some of the framed pictures on the wall and the automatic weapons coffee-table books.

"So, what's going on?" Mac set two glasses of iced tea on a pair of coasters, along with a bowl of pita chips, then sat cross-legged on the other side of the sectional couch. "Are the guys in the Pack being jerks? If so, tell me who, and I'll set them straight."

Khaki almost laughed at the image of Mac laying into Xander while the squad leader stood there nodding politely. But having someone fight her battles wasn't the reason she was here.

"It's not the guys," she said. "They've been great."

Mac's eyes narrowed suspiciously. "Right. So if everything's so wonderful, why are you here looking for advice?"

Khaki picked up her glass and sipped her iced tea. Now that she was here, she wasn't quite sure what to say. On the other end of the sectional, Mac was waiting patiently.

Here goes nothing.

"I'm hoping you can give me a few tips about…how to be a werewolf," she said.

Mac raised an eyebrow. "O-kay. Maybe I'm missing something here. You're already a werewolf. Right?"

"Yeah, but…"

Khaki hesitated. Maybe she'd better start at the beginning. So in between pita chips, she told Mac about what had happened that night she'd gotten shot behind the Grace Park apartment complex, about how quickly she'd healed, and about all the crazy things she'd been able to do afterward, admitting that she didn't even know she was a werewolf until she'd seen the guys on the team shift. With as few embarrassing details as possible, Khaki then went on to describe the problem she'd had in the House of Doors and what happened with her ex-boyfriend tonight.

"Your ex is here in Dallas?" Mac asked.

Khaki nodded. "I guess Sergeant Dixon told you about him, huh?"

Mac shook her head. "Not very much, though I'm glad to hear you dumped him. Gage just mentioned that you'd been in a relationship with another cop and that it didn't end well."

Understatement there. It was nice to talk to a woman who listened to her without judging or trying to fix things, like men always seemed to do. She wanted to tell Mac about Jeremy, but right now, she needed to get her inner werewolf under control.

"Back to the werewolf thing," she said. "I've seen the guys do it often enough to know that I should have claws and fangs and be able to see in the dark, but I can't do any of those things."

Mac's eyes widened. "Wait a minute. Are you saying you've never shifted at all? No claws, no fangs, no night vision, no…fur?"

Khaki shook her head. Although to be honest, she wasn't too upset about not sprouting fur. She had no interest in excess body hair.

"Never," she admitted. "My nose works really well, and I'm faster and stronger than any woman I've ever seen, but I just figured that maybe female werewolves couldn't do what their male counterparts could. Then I started arguing with my jerk of an ex-boyfriend and…" She held up her hands and wiggled her fingers. "My fingers started bleeding. I think my claws came out without me even knowing it. Can that really happen?"

"All the time."

"Really?"

Mac nodded. "You've been around the guys long enough to know that they shift when they get pissed, excited, or hyped up, right? Trust me, most of them don't even realize it's happening either."

"But it's never happened to me before."

"It did tonight." Mac smiled. "You're pretty new to this whole werewolf thing. Maybe you just had to get angry enough to let the shift happen."

Khaki supposed that made sense. She'd definitely been angry with Jeremy. But while some of the guys shifted a little when they got mad, they could do it when they weren't angry, too.

"But how do I control it?" she asked Mac. "How do I get the parts of the werewolf that I want while keeping the other parts hidden? And how do I keep it from coming out at the wrong time?"

Mac shrugged. "I can't help you with that. Gage has told me about what it's like when he's shifting, and I've seen him do it a lot. But we've never gotten into the how-to part of it. You're going to need to talk to one of the guys, preferably one who's been a werewolf for a while. Gage, maybe?"

Khaki shook her head, embarrassed at the thought. "There's no way I can tell him that I don't know the first thing about being a werewolf. It's why he hired me. I don't want him thinking I'm incompetent." She gave Mac a stern look. "You can't tell him either."

Mac held up her hand. "I won't, I promise. But you need to talk to someone, sooner rather than later."

Khaki took another sip of iced tea as she ran down the list of guys on her squad again. Other than Cooper, Trevor was the only other werewolf with a lot of experience. While she definitely got along with him, she wasn't sure he'd be very good at teaching her how to be a werewolf. There were several experienced werewolves on Mike's team, but she didn't know any of them well enough to ask.

"Have you ever considered asking Xander?"

Khaki almost choked on her iced tea.

"I'm serious," Mac said. "I know he can be a bit brusque sometimes, but he's a really good guy. He's your squad leader and you can trust him to keep anything you tell him in confidence. If you ask, I know he'd help you."

Khaki wasn't too sure of that. She opened her mouth to tell Mac there was no way in hell she'd ask her squad leader for help, but the words wouldn't come out. Maybe it was her inner werewolf trying to tell her something. Or maybe it was because she knew she had nothing to lose—Xander couldn't possibly think any less of her than he already did.

Chapter 6

KHAKI STOOD OUTSIDE XANDER'S APARTMENT, TRYING to work up the courage to knock. This had seemed like a great idea when she'd left Mac's place, but now she wasn't so sure. Was it too late to chicken out?

Coward.

She lifted her hand and knocked. He might not even be home. Maybe she should have called first.

She was just about to knock again when the door opened. She blinked, the speech she'd rehearsed on the way over disappearing at the sight of Xander. He was wearing jeans and a T-shirt that showed off his well-muscled biceps. They were so mesmerizing, she could barely take her eyes off them.

"Khaki. What are you doing here?"

While the words weren't exactly harsh, they were enough to snap her out of her stupor.

She reached up and nervously pushed her hair behind her ear. "Can I come in?"

He didn't say anything for so long, she thought he was going to make her say whatever she'd come to say right there in the hallway. But then he stepped back.

"Yeah, sure."

His apartment had bachelor written all over it. There was little in the way of décor unless you counted the monster TV mounted on the wall in front of a sectional that while not shabby definitely had that lived-in look.

There was a baseball game on, but the sound was muted. All of that faded into the background as the smell hit her. It was like being immersed in a bottle of Xander-scented cologne. It actually made it hard to breathe—without drooling at least.

"What can I do for you?" Xander asked.

He'd closed the door but hadn't moved away from it. He wasn't making this very easy on her.

She glanced at the couch. "Would it be all right if we sat down?"

He gestured toward the sectional, then sat as far away as he could. Maybe she should have taken a shower before coming over.

Khaki wet her lips. "I know you don't like me very much, but—"

He frowned, his brows drawing together. "What makes you think I don't like you?"

Had he seriously just asked her that? She let out a snort. "I might be new to this werewolf thing, but my ears work just fine. I heard what you told Sergeant Dixon the first day I arrived about not wanting me on your squad. Since then you've made your feelings pretty obvious."

Xander had the good grace to look ashamed. He leaned forward to rest his forearms on his knees. "Um… about that—"

She held up her hand. "Let's just agree to not get into that right now, okay? I didn't come here to talk about why you hate women cops or whatever your issue is with me. I came because I need your help."

His eyes clouded in confusion. "Help with what?"

Khaki knew it would be easier to just come out

and say that she needed him to teach her how to be a werewolf, but instead she found herself telling Xander about Jeremy and the argument they'd had in front of her apartment.

"Did he hurt you?" Xander interrupted before she could get to the part about her nails bleeding.

Khaki did a double take at the vehemence in Xander's voice. He looked so furious, he probably would have snapped Jeremy's neck if her ex had been there.

"No," she said. "And Jeremy isn't why I'm here anyway."

When Xander gave her another confused look, she explained about her bleeding fingernails and that Mac had told her it sounded like an uncontrolled shift brought on by her anger.

"Has it ever happened before?" he asked.

She shook her head, then gave him a sheepish smile. "I've never shifted before."

His eyes went wide. "Never? You've been a were-wolf for over three months and in all that time, you've never shifted, not even by accident?"

"No." She shrugged. "Since I couldn't do it and you and the rest of the team could, I thought that maybe female werewolves didn't shift."

Xander shook his head. "I'm not the authority on female werewolves, but from what Gage has told me, you can do anything a male werewolf can."

She didn't know about that. "I can't even see in the dark, much less cut loose with all the claws and stuff like you and the other guys can."

He stared at her. "Why didn't you tell me this sooner?"

Khaki lifted a brow.

He flushed under his tan. "Okay, stupid question. Sorry. But if you can't see in the dark, how were you able to get through the training in the House of Doors today?"

She cringed. She didn't want to admit she'd been breaking the rules, but he'd asked.

"I used my nose to mentally map out the walls and doors. It took a while though, which is why I was so slow moving from room to room."

Xander regarded her thoughtfully. "You can actually pinpoint a person's precise location in a room purely by sense of smell—enough to shoot them, I mean?"

She gave him an embarrassed look. "Obviously not very well. I did hit Becker."

"Barely, and it doesn't really matter anyway. At least not when you're using a paintball gun," he said. "We all have good noses, but none of us can smell our way through a dark room. It's frigging incredible."

If Khaki didn't know better, she'd think Xander had just complimented her. She would have thanked him, but he continued.

"Are there any other special things your sense of smell allows you to do?"

It should have been a simple question, but it wasn't. How did she know what special things she could do with her nose when she didn't know how the guys used theirs?

"Well, I can pick up every scent around me and remember it," she said slowly. "Forever."

"Seriously?" When she nodded, Xander let out a low whistle. "That's even more in-freaking-credible than sniffing your way through a dark room."

Khaki felt a silly sense of pride at the words. "You really think my sense of smell is that special?"

"Hell yeah." He shook his head. "I'm not sure exactly how to capitalize on it yet, but I have no doubt it will be a benefit to the team."

She had visions of the guys running her around like a bloodhound. "I'm okay with that, as long as you teach me how to shift like the rest of the squad."

He flashed her a grin that made her pulse trip over itself. "Deal. You want to start now, or would you rather wait until tomorrow at the compound?"

"I kind of hoped we could start now," she said, then added, "And that we could do the lessons in private. I don't want the guys knowing how inept I am."

He nodded. "That's fine with me, but you really don't have to hide this stuff from the Pack. We've all been through it to one degree or another."

She wholeheartedly doubted Xander or any of the other guys had a problem like hers, but didn't say so. "I'd rather keep this between us."

"Okay," he said. "Then the first thing you need to do is relax and get comfortable."

Khaki was almost afraid to ask what his definition of "relax and get comfortable" was. From what she'd seen at the SWAT compound, the guys didn't seem to ever relax and get comfortable.

Xander grabbed the remote for the television and turned it off. "Let's sit on the floor."

Khaki sat cross-legged between the coffee table and the television. Considering Xander had kept his distance until now, she was a little surprised when he sat down facing her barely a foot away. This close, it would be so easy to get lost in those beautiful brown eyes of his.

"Ready?" he asked.

She nodded.

"Close your eyes."

She obeyed.

"I want you to picture yourself running barefoot through the forest."

Xander's deep voice was soft in the silence of the apartment. His low, rumbling tones caressed her skin, making her feel more relaxed than she'd felt in a long time.

"Imagine the wind in your hair. The soft ground under your feet. The sun on your skin," he said. "It's just you and the trees. There's no one around for miles."

Sitting here in his living room, Khaki could almost imagine her feet slapping against a trail, the dappled sunlight touching her face as she ran in and out of the shadows created by the trees.

"Now feel yourself fall forward onto all fours," Xander told her. "You're running crouched over, speeding along the path as your fingers dig into the earth."

Khaki's mind instinctively rebelled. Running on all fours didn't feel natural. "I can't."

"Yes, you can," Xander said, his calm voice soothing away the resistance.

She tried again, and this time she rejoiced in the bizarrely strange sensation of running on four feet.

"The sun is going down now," Xander whispered, his mouth only inches from her ear, and she didn't know if the shiver that ran through her was from the sudden lack of imagined sunlight or his warm breath caressing the sensitive skin of her shoulder and neck.

"The shadows are growing longer, the darkness under the branches deeper," he continued. "Imagine yourself opening your eyes wider, letting every flicker of light in to fill the darkness."

Khaki never would have dreamed that the brusque, demanding squad leader she knew could make her feel so relaxed. But the more he whispered in her ear, the less he resembled her preconceived image of him.

"It's dark now, but you can see as clearly as if it's bright daylight. You're running through the dark, able to see every tree and rock and leaf around you, and it's amazing."

She smiled a little, unable to help it. In her vision, she was sleek and fast, running tirelessly through a pitch-black forest, leaping over downed trees, big rocks, and small streams. Xander was right. It *was* amazing.

"Open your eyes, Khaki," he entreated in that same soft voice.

She obeyed.

Xander was sitting in the same spot he'd been before, a smile on his handsome face. As hard as it was to tear her gaze away from his, she couldn't resist looking down to see if her claws had come out. But her nails were the same.

Disappointed, she opened her mouth to ask why it hadn't worked and realized that the overhead lights weren't on anymore. Xander must have turned them off when she had her eyes closed.

The room should have been completely dark, but it wasn't. She could see everything, from the subtle colors in the rug she was sitting on to the finest features of the hunky guy who seemed to be regarding her with amusement twinkling in his gold eyes.

"I can see," she breathed in wonder. "How is that possible? I didn't do anything."

Xander chuckled, the sound deep and sexy as he leaned back on his hands. "No, you didn't *do* anything. But you did *let* something happen. That's the key. You can't make it happen. You have to let it come out naturally. Because that's what it means to be a werewolf—giving yourself up to the animal inside you and allowing yourself to become what you really are."

She got up and ran around the dark apartment, laughing like a kid on Christmas. When she found herself in his bedroom, her laugh turned into something lower and more animalistic as the overwhelming scent coming from his big bed told her that Xander Riggs slept in it completely naked. Nothing else would explain how completely his scent blended with the sheets.

Ignoring the urge to bury her nose in their softness, Khaki turned and ran back to the living room before she could think too much about Xander's naked body, his bed, and what it would be like to get wrapped up in both.

He was still sitting on the floor, grinning.

"Do my eyes look different?" she asked.

He didn't say anything for so long, she began to wonder if something was wrong. But then he grinned even broader. "Yes, they look different. A green-gold completely unlike any other werewolf's eyes I've ever seen."

That alarmed her a little. "Do you think they're okay?"

"Of course they're okay. They're just unique—like you. Sit down and I'll show you how to back out of the process."

She plopped down in front of him eagerly. Over the

next two hours, he taught her how to get her night vision to disappear, then how to bring it back again. Sooner than she ever would have thought possible, she could make her eyes shift in and out of night-vision mode without even thinking about it.

Giddy because she'd learned something like that so quickly, Khaki grabbed Xander's hand to give it a squeeze. His hand was warm and slightly callused compared to hers, and her breath hitched at the tingle that surged through her. His gold eyes flared brighter for a second, like he'd felt it too. She wanted to hold on longer to see if the tingle might get even stronger, but then reminded herself that he was still her squad leader and that she shouldn't be holding his hand. But the moment she let go, her hand itched to reach out and touch him again.

"Teach me something else," she said excitedly.

His mouth twitched. "Okay, but just one more little thing. We don't want to push it too hard. This stuff can take a lot out of you when you're new at it."

She opened her mouth to tell him that she could spend the rest of the night doing this, but realized she was a little tired. It had been one hell of a long day.

"Okay, you're probably right," she admitted. "But do you think you can show me how to make my claws come out?"

He frowned. "Claws are a few rungs up the ladder from night vision. They can be tough if you're tired."

Khaki tried not to let her disappointment show, but Xander must have seen it because he shook his head with a laugh.

"Okay, we can try it. Just don't get your hopes up too high."

She scooted closer to him on the floor, promising that she wouldn't.

Xander had her close her eyes and imagine running in the forest again, except this time he had her focus on her fingers.

"Dig your fingers into the soil—deep," he said. "Think of your claws gaining purchase as you push to get up the hill."

As he continued in that soft, honeyed voice of his, Khaki wondered if part of the reason she'd wanted to continue the lessons was simply so she could keep hearing him talk. He did have a really nice voice, and she'd be lying if she didn't admit she liked feeling his breath on her skin.

Khaki didn't know how long she sat there with her eyes closed, but when Xander finally told her to open them, she found herself looking at a set of long claws extending from her fingertips.

"Your claws are a part of you, just like your eyes," Xander told her. "You can't *make* them come out any more than you can make your legs longer or your hair turn blue. But if you *let* them come out, they'll be there every time for you. It's the basic rule for all werewolf abilities. You have to be calm and relaxed and allow your inner wolf to come out. Sometimes, claws and fangs will come out if we're angry, but then that's not control. It's just rage."

Khaki held her hands up, transfixed by her long claws with their slight curves and sharp tips. She looked closer at the nail beds to see that they weren't bloody at all. Maybe letting her claws come out naturally was less traumatic on them.

She took a deep breath and imagined her nails the way they always were—oval shaped and just slightly longer than her fingers. She didn't try to force her claws back into their other shape, but simply saw them that way.

As she watched, the claws slowly retracted. It felt strange, but it wasn't painful. How could they possibly hide themselves in her slender fingers? What was she thinking? She was a werewolf. None of this was logical.

"That was perfect," Xander said. "Very smooth."

Khaki laughed. "You think so?"

"Yeah, but I think we should call it a night."

She was getting tired. She'd probably crash as soon as the adrenaline rush wore off. But she was having so much fun, it was tough to stop. It wasn't just the were-wolf lessons she was enjoying either. She was having fun being with Xander. That was crazy, considering just a couple of hours ago, she was sure he hated her guts. She didn't know what had changed or why he was being nice to her now, but she wasn't going to complain. He was a gorgeous guy with a great voice, apparently infinite patience, and a rocking body that would make any female werewolf growl.

Khaki pushed those thoughts aside and remembered her manners.

"Thanks for taking the time to teach me all this stuff," she said as she stood up. "I know it's not in your normal duty description, but I really appreciate it."

He grinned as he got to his feet. "Don't worry about it. Training you, no matter the subject, is my most important job. I'm glad you decided to trust me enough to tell me you needed help. I know we haven't exactly hit it off very well."

"You were here when I needed you. That's what matters." She picked up her purse and slung it over her shoulder. "But I think it goes without saying that I'll need some more lessons. I hope we can do this again?"

"Of course," he said. "We can do your next lesson here or your place. Wherever you're comfortable."

Wow. Xander seemed not only willing to teach her more, but almost eager. She hadn't expected that.

As he walked her to the door, Khaki tried to come up with some reason not to leave. She had this crazy urge to stay and talk. She didn't know why she thought he'd even be interested. It was getting late and he probably wanted to get back to TV and his game.

At the door, she turned to look up at him. She wasn't sure what she'd been going to say, but anything that she might have said disappeared as Xander's eyes caught and held hers. Why did he have to be her squad leader? He was so unbelievably hot, and he smelled divine. In fact, the longer they stood there, the better he smelled. Then her nose picked up another smell that almost made her knees give out. Xander's scent was blending with something completely different and so masculine, but so sweet at the same time, that her nose tingled and her mouth watered. *Crap.* She was literally starting to drool over her boss.

She wanted to kiss him so badly. Actually, she wanted to do a lot more than that. But she wasn't that stupid. He was her squad leader, and if her little run-in with Jeremy had reminded her of anything, it was that workplace romances with fellow cops always ended badly.

Besides, she'd promised Emma she'd call to let her know everything was okay. She couldn't do that if she was throwing herself at Xander.

Not that he was likely to reciprocate.

"Thank you again," she said as he opened the door for her.

"You're welcome again," he said in that same deep, sexy tone that sent waves of warmth right through her. "Good night, Khaki. See you tomorrow."

Khaki nodded, not trusting herself to say anything else. She felt very proud of herself for being able to walk away from a situation that had "bad idea" written all over it. But that didn't mean she wasn't kicking herself at the same time.

"Hey, Khaki."

She turned at the elevator, her pulse skipping a beat. Xander stood in the doorway of his apartment, one hand on the jamb, the thumb of the other hooked casually in the front pocket of his jeans.

"I know I can come off like a jackass sometimes," he said. "But if you think that means I don't like you, you're wrong."

Khaki stared. Had she heard him right? Xander disappeared inside before she could decide.

She stood there in the hallway long after his door clicked shut, half of her wanting to knock on it again and the other half telling her to get her ass back in her little car and go home.

Common sense finally won out, but the decision was a lot closer than it probably should have been.

Chapter 7

SO MUCH FOR LIMITED-DUTY STATUS.

Xander lay facedown on the roof of a three-story building downtown, slowly sweating in the afternoon sun. It wasn't very hot for this time of year, but the way the rays were heating up the flat tar roof, it felt like the middle of summer.

He looked through his binoculars at the bank they were supposed to be covering, but it was over four blocks away and almost impossible to see with all the other buildings that were in the way. It made him wonder again what the hell they were doing here. Oh, yeah. Playing nice.

Gage had pulled him and the rest of his squad out of PT that morning, saying he had a job he needed them to cover. When Xander had reminded him they were on limited-duty status, the Pack alpha had given him a shrug.

"Sorry, but this one came out of nowhere. The FBI has a task force that's been tracking a group hitting banks all through the Southwest. They've asked the DPD for assistance, and Deputy Chief Mason offered them SWAT."

Xander had tried his best to weasel out of the job, mostly because he wasn't too fond of working with the feds. "FBI has their own SWAT team. What the hell do they want with us?"

"They probably just want to have you available for perimeter work or something stupid like that," Gage told him. "But they made the request officially through Mason, and he wants us to play nice."

"So why can't Mike's team handle this? You know I still need more time training Khaki."

His boss had stopped looking amused at that point, which told Xander the conversation was pretty much over.

"Because this job has the potential to turn into a recurring gig," Gage told him flatly. "The task force isn't exactly sure when the bank robbers are going to strike next, but they do know they don't have the time to keep briefing support people every time they need to call them in. That means whoever I put on this will be subject to short notice recalls, and if your squad is going to be on limited duty anyway, I'd rather it be you."

Xander checked in with his squad again. The senior agent in charge of the FBI taskforce, Philip Thompson, had said he didn't want any of the locals using their own radios because there was too much chance of compromising the operation, but Thompson could kiss his ass. Xander was monitoring the FBI channel through one radio and earpiece while talking to his squad on a completely different radio and frequency. Who said men couldn't multitask?

"Nothing here," Trevor reported over the internal SWAT channel. "Not surprising since we're so far from the bank that someone could have stolen the whole building and we wouldn't know it."

Xander swore silently. In theory, Trevor was covering the northern side of the perimeter with Becker and

Cooper. But in reality, he was sitting on his ass just like
Xander was doing here to the south of the bank with
Hale and Max. Neither group would be in a position
to do much when—make that if—the bank robbery
actually went down. But that was the way the FBI had
wanted it.

Khaki checked in from the western edge of the perimeter where she and Alex were maintaining a sniper and
observation post nearly six blocks from the target. It
wasn't much of a sniper outpost since Alex didn't have
a better visual on the bank than the rest of them.

Xander had known this operation was going to be
a soup sandwich the moment they met Thompson.
Talk about a clusterfuck. Even the people in the local
FBI field office didn't like the way this new agent in
charge had come in swinging his weight around. Xander
couldn't blame them. No one liked outsiders coming in
and trying to run the show as if everyone else were a
bunch of idiots.

Apparently, these particular bank robbers had hit
nine banks in three months without leaving a single
usable clue. That was Xander's first indication these
guys weren't a bunch of amateur smash-and-grab types.
Nobody could hit nine banks without leaving evidence
behind unless they were serious professionals.

Thompson had spent some time explaining the crew's
MO in the briefing, saying they spent nearly a month
conducting surveillance and planning in a particular
city, then hitting three banks all in the span of a week.

"They're disciplined, organized, and almost certainly
have some kind of military or even law enforcement
background. They come in heavily armed and have

shown that they won't hesitate to shoot if they have to. They've already killed three people. In two months of working this case, we've come up with next to nothing."

"If these guys are so good, what makes you think they're going to hit banks here in Dallas?" Xander asked.

Thompson could have tried to bullshit his way through a lie about the FBI's amazing investigative skills, but instead he was completely honest. "We've been chasing hunches and rumors for weeks and haven't come close to identifying anyone in the crew, much less where or when they're going to strike next. Then, out of the blue, a woman contacted us who claimed to have information on the next bank the group was going to hit. She indicated the target was here in Dallas."

"How reliable is the source?" Xander asked.

"We can't really say at this point," Thompson said. "All we know for sure is that the woman knows details about the previous jobs that weren't released to the press. We think she's one of the robbers' jilted girlfriends and that she's looking for retribution. She gave us intel on the next job, down to the address. We have to act on it because it'll likely be our only shot to get these guys."

After that, the rest of the briefing came down to one simple directive aimed specifically at the Dallas PD support personnel—don't get in the way of our FBI operation.

Thompson had told Xander in no uncertain terms that he and his squad, along with the other local assets, were there for backup, contingency, and crowd control purposes only. Xander would have raised the bullshit flag, but Deputy Chief Mason wanted them to play nice. And with all the backing Mason had given Gage when

it came to hiring Khaki, Gage was more than ready to
support that request. The squad wasn't happy about it,
but they agreed to go along with the plan.

In reality, Xander wasn't as pissed off as he normally
would have been. With Khaki so new to SWAT, he
wasn't keen to get them involved in a serious shoot-out
so soon anyway. At least this would give him a chance
to see how she operated in a field environment without
the threat of actual gunfire. It might be a good training opportunity.

Even though he doubted the robbers would show,
Xander still kept his eyes glued to the bank—what he
could see of it anyway. While he did, he replayed the
events of last night.

On the one hand, he was thrilled that Khaki had
trusted him enough to ask for help. But on the other
hand, his whole damn apartment was so thoroughly
saturated with her incredible scent that he was probably
going to have to move if he ever wanted to sleep again.
It was like he'd discovered some new form of torture.
Lie in bed all night with a hard-on that wouldn't go
away, inhaling the overwhelming perfume of the most
beautiful woman on the planet.

And the funny thing was, he'd put up with it forever
if it meant having a chance to spend more time alone
with her like he had last night.

When Khaki had shown up at his door in those curve-
hugging jeans with her long hair free of its usual ponytail or bun, he thought for sure she was going to lay into
him about being such an ass, so he'd been stunned when
she admitted she needed help learning how to shift.

Being alone with her and the alluring scent she put

off was hard enough at work. Getting hit with it up close for hours as they sat there together on his living room floor had been maddening. Then there was that sexy little way she pursed her lips when she was concentrating. It had taken all of his strength not to kiss her when she did that.

But the cherry on top of the cake had to be those eyes of hers. When she'd finally figured out how to control her night vision, those beauties, which were amazing even before the shift, had glowed with the most vivid green he'd ever seen. They were so mesmerizing it nearly stopped his heart. And the pure joy on her face as she ran around his apartment had made him so happy.

Afterward, he'd been sorely tempted to ask her to stay—for a beer, or dinner, or even to watch the game. He didn't really care what they did as long as she stayed. But if he had, his control would have slipped, and he would've done something stupid. Like bury his hands in her silky hair and kissed her. They'd just gotten to a place where she might not hate him completely. He decided to count himself lucky and just leave well enough alone.

Xander was still daydreaming about getting together with Khaki for another werewolf lesson when he heard alarms ringing.

He immediately refocused his attention on the bank below him only to realize the sound wasn't coming from that direction.

"What the hell is happening?" Thompson demanded over the radio. "Someone give me a status report."

"You're sitting on the wrong bank!" Khaki's voice was angry in Xander's earpiece. "They're hitting the one in the building we're set up on. The bank on Jackson Street."

Thompson swore, then ordered his people to move in while at the same time yelling at the local PD to seal off the perimeter and demanding Khaki give him more info. But Xander was already getting a sinking feeling in his gut. A feeling that told him the FBI and everyone else had been royally played.

"Khaki, figure out what the hell is happening and give me a sitrep," he said into his mic.

Even though his first instinct was to stay out of this and let the FBI go down in flames, Xander was up and running toward the far side of the roof. As he raced across it, he gave hand signals to the other guys with him— converge on the new target. Max and Hale were catching up to him before he even reached the edge of the roof.

As he neared the low wall that ran around the perimeter of the roof, Xander shifted, thrilling at the surge of power racing through him as his leg and core muscles twitched and thickened. His boot hit the edge of the wall and he propelled himself forward as hard as he could, ignoring the height he was leaping from and how far he needed to go to make it to the other building. He'd scouted the surrounding rooftops before settling into position earlier and knew that he could make this jump, even with all the tactical gear he was wearing.

From his scouting, he also knew that this was the fastest way to get where they needed to be. Three blocks west by rooftop, followed by a quick scramble down the fire escape would put him on Jackson Street. Then it would be a straight shot to the bank on the back side of the building where Khaki and Alex were set up.

Xander sailed over the matching low wall on the adjacent building and hit the roof in a tumbling roll, cradling his M4 to his chest to protect it. He was on his feet within seconds. He had five hundred feet of rooftop to cover on this building before reaching the next gap he had to leap over. He hadn't gone more than twenty or thirty feet when he heard Max and Hale make their jumps. One of them—Max probably—shouted just before he hit the graveled roof. At any other time, Xander would have been worried about someone looking up and seeing three big-ass guys in full tactical gear jumping across a twenty-foot gap between buildings, but with a bank robbery in progress, he didn't think that'd be a problem.

The robbers must have figured out someone leaked their plans to the FBI. Yet, instead of abandoning Dallas completely, they'd switched to another bank positioned just outside the textbook perimeter of the first target. Not only were these guys smart—that prior military-slash-law enforcement background theory was looking better by the second—they were ballsy. There was no other reason to hit an alternate target so close to the first one other than to show the FBI that they could.

"The suspects have reached the street," Khaki reported over the FBI frequency. "There are six men that I can see, all heavily armed. Two black SUVs are moving in from the end of the street to pick them up."

"I have agents converging on your location," Thompson told her. "Sniper, can you engage? I need the suspects pinned down for a few minutes."

"Negative," Alex replied. "The target zone is full of civilians and it's chaos down there. I do not have a clear shot."

"Dammit!" Thompson swore. "Take the shot anyway. Shoot the SUV's tires. Just slow them down."

It was Xander's turn to curse. He opened his mouth to countermand Thompson's order, but Khaki beat him to it.

"We can't do that. Even if we hit the target, the chances of a through-and-through ricochet hitting a bystander is too high."

Max and Hale had caught up with Xander and all three of them cleared the alley and hit the next rooftop in perfect sync. Xander sped up and pulled ahead of his teammates, wanting to be the first one on the fire escape. He had to get eyes on the situation, because something told him it was going bad really fast.

Thompson was ordering Alex to shoot just as tires squealed nearby.

"One SUV is away. DPD cruiser in pursuit," Khaki reported. "The other one is still on the curb. Looks like they're waiting for someone. Additional cruisers are blocking either end of Jackson."

"I'll have agents on the scene in ten seconds," Thompson told her. "Whatever you do, don't let that second SUV out."

Xander hit the top of the fire escape so hard he almost flew right off of it. He took the steep metal stairs three at a time, leaping the last fifteen feet into the alley rather than using the drop-down ladder. He raced out of the alley and sprinted up Jackson, pushing his way through the crowd of terrified people running in the opposite direction. He was still two blocks away when he heard gunfire.

This was going to be a bloodbath.

"Dammit, Thompson!" Khaki yelled. "Tell your people to stop shooting. There are at least twenty civilians behind the same row of cars the suspects are using as cover, and your agents are punching holes right through them."

But no orders to cease fire ever came. Xander put on more speed, or at least as much as he could with all the people running away from the scene and blocking his path.

Xander heard Alex curse.

"Two of the suspects are using kids as shields. I can't get a shot at them, and the frigging SUV is armored and has solid run-flat tires. Without armor-piercing rounds, I'm not going to be able do a damn thing to stop these guys."

"The feds are going to hit the kids," Khaki ground out in exasperation in his SWAT earpiece. "I'm going down there to get them."

"Negative. Stand down." Xander's heart shoved so hard up into his throat he almost had to stop running. "That's an order!"

Khaki didn't answer. Xander hoped it wasn't because she was doing something she shouldn't, but as he reached the DPD cruisers barricading Jackson Street, he saw her rappelling down the side of the bank building from five floors up.

What the hell was she doing?

The answer to that was obvious as she dropped down behind the bad guys—and right into the FBI's target zone. Luckily, some of the feds realized she'd entered the fray and stopped shooting. But others seemed completely oblivious.

Xander sped toward her, shouting for a cease-fire, watching in terror as bullets continued to rip through the line of cars in front of Khaki. Werewolves were tough as nails, but a lucky shot could kill them just as easily as it could a normal human. For all they knew, female werewolves might not have the same healing powers as their male counterparts.

Khaki ignored the hail of bullets. She lashed out with a well-placed kick to knock one suspect to the ground, then grabbed the other one and threw him half a dozen feet into a brick wall. Xander could hear her rumbling growl all the way from here. He only prayed she didn't lose control and pick now as the time to finally shift completely.

But the moment the suspects were out of play, she reached down, scooped up the two little kids in her arms, and started running, herding a group of other children and women in front of her as she went.

Xander couldn't help but admire Khaki's actions under pressure even as he shouted at the few agents still popping off rounds to cease fire. The level of chaos only increased with the lull in shooting, as the civilians who'd been hugging the pavement and were pressed up against cars left their hiding places and ran in different directions.

The next thing Xander knew, the two suspects had jumped in their SUV and crashed through the police barricade at the end of the block. The heavy-armored vehicle smashed the two cruisers aside like they were toys. The few lucky shots that hit the SUV as it sped away didn't do much more than knock divots in the damn thing.

Xander rounded the row of shot-up cars along the sidewalk, heading for Khaki just as Thompson strode up to her from the other direction with fire in his eyes.

"You had them and you let them get away," the fed shouted. "What the hell is wrong with you?"

An animalistic rage like he'd never felt before crawled up Xander's back and he let out a low growl. He wasn't the only one. Hale's fangs had elongated ever so slightly and his fingers flexed around his M4. Trevor, Becker, and Cooper came running at full speed from the same direction Thompson had approached, looking equally pissed. And Max? The team's youngest werewolf looked like he was ready to shift and rip Thompson to shreds.

Xander was going to have a full-scale werewolf riot on his hands at any second.

Khaki rose to her feet from where she'd been kneeling beside a little girl and rounded on the FBI agent with her own brand of fire in her eyes. She advanced on him with so much fury that Thompson took a step back.

"What's wrong with me? What the hell's wrong with you?" Khaki demanded. "There were a hundred civilians on this street and you decided it was a good idea to pin the suspects in here and start shooting?"

She jabbed a finger at the row of cars parked on the street. "There were kids hiding behind those cars you just shot the crap out of. Why did I let the suspects get away? To save those kids—from you."

Thompson opened his mouth to say something, but Khaki cut him off. "Save it! You screwed up here— not us."

Brushing past him, she walked over to the kids she'd

just rescued and knelt down beside the little girl again to gently brush her blond hair out of her tear-streaked face.

"Damn straight," Max said softly. "Dropped his ass like a dirty toilet seat. That's what I'm talking about."

The other guys in his squad let out low chuckles. Xander could understand why. Khaki had just put Thompson in his place like a seasoned pro. They hadn't caught the bad guys, but she'd saved lives. That was a win in his book.

But while he was proud of Khaki, he was damn pissed she'd thrown herself into the middle of that firefight.

Xander swore under his breath. Talk about a double standard.

If Khaki had been one of the guys on the team, Xander would have expected whoever it was to jump in and save those kids. So why hadn't he demanded the same of Khaki? Because he'd been scared as hell she would get hurt.

Xander turned to see Alex jogging down the street. He must have used the stairs instead of rappelling like Khaki. Despite admitting his judgment was seriously impaired when it came to Khaki, that didn't stop him from snarling at Alex.

"Why the hell didn't you stop Khaki from coming down that rope?"

"You're kidding, right?" Alex snorted. "Khaki has a mind of her own. Maybe you've been too focused on the details to see the big picture, but she's as alpha as any of us. If she thinks something needs to be done, she's going to do it. I couldn't have stopped her—not without knocking her out cold. I doubt you could have stopped her either. She's getting her feet under her damn fast.

In a few more weeks, she'll be ready to stand toe-to-toe with Gage."

Xander stared at Alex, dumbfounded. He knew Khaki got along well with the guys, but he'd thought that was simply because she was…well…a woman. If Alex was right, she'd vaulted to the top of the Pack's testosterone-laden pecking order in less than a week without ever having to snarl, punch, or body slam anybody. That didn't happen in the Pack.

"Seriously?" he asked.

"Yeah." Alex grinned. "You better watch out, or she'll take over your squad before you know it."

─── ∾ ───

It was after six by the time they got back to the compound. Xander had hoped to knock out his required paperwork and go home, but Deputy Chief Mason had called Gage and said he wanted a full report before the end of shift. That dashed any possibility of getting out of there early. So while the rest of his squad was upstairs laughing, joking, and getting cleaned up, Xander was stuck at his desk writing out a detailed report on absolutely everything that had happened that day.

Nobody was blaming Xander and his squad for the way things had gone down. In fact, due to the magic of YouTube, their SWAT team, especially Khaki, had come out smelling like roses. But a bank had been robbed, the suspects had gotten away, and more than one lawyer was already in front of the cameras talking about suing the city. The chief and deputy chief wanted details, and they wanted them now.

Gage had called Xander into his office the moment they'd walked in. Not to talk about the possible lawsuits, but about what Khaki had done. Xander had admitted he was pissed she'd disobeyed his orders, but more than impressed by her willingness to put saving a life ahead of anything else.

Gage grinned. "Yeah, I saw the videos. Pretty impressive stuff. Look, I know there's been friction between the two of you, and I've heard what some of the guys have been saying, but keep riding her hard. It's paying off."

Thankfully Gage let Xander go to finish his report. Considering the image his commander's order had left seared into his mind, that had probably been a good thing.

It was nearly eight o'clock by the time Xander finished. So much for getting home early enough to catch up on some sleep. Not that he expected to get much rest with his place smelling like Khaki. Maybe he'd shower and sleep here instead. Like that would help. Her scent filled every corner of the compound too. It was so strong he couldn't smell anything else but her anymore. Why the hell did it affect him so much?

He was so busy trying to figure out the answer that he didn't even realize anyone was upstairs until he got to the top of the landing and saw Khaki wrapping a towel around her very wet, very naked body.

Xander stared at the towel-draped piece of perfection in front of him, unable to breathe. His heart was pounding nearly as hard as his cock.

Khaki looked up, her eyes locking with his. He expected her to run back into the showers or turn her back, but she merely stood there holding his gaze as she slowly tucked the towel more tightly around her wet body. The move made her breasts squeeze together, giving him an enticing glimpse of cleavage.

He forced his gaze away from her breasts only to find himself ogling her long, sexy legs instead.

Shit.

Xander jerked his head up to find her regarding him with those big, dark eyes of hers. *Oh God.* He needed to get out of here before he completely lost it.

Mumbling an apology, he turned and stumbled back down the stairs, practically falling over his feet. It wasn't his fault. Walking down steps with a hard-on was nearly impossible. Not to mention the fact that his head was no longer functioning properly.

How could he not have known Khaki was up there? He'd just walked in on her half-naked, then stared at her like a perverted Peeping Tom. What the hell had he just done? More importantly, what was Khaki going to do about it? Call her union rep? Human resources? Get her gun?

Soft laughter drifted down the stairs, stopping him in his tracks. If Xander thought his heart was beating fast before, it was nothing compared to how it was racing then. *Holy fudge monkey.* She had the most beautiful laugh he'd ever heard.

Then it struck him.

He'd walked in on his one and only female teammate, gawked at her almost-naked body for who knew how long, and she didn't seem the least bit upset.

What the hell?

Khaki was surprised to find Mac waiting for her when she got home. The dark-haired journalist was leaning against the wall reading something on her iPhone. Khaki quickened her step.

"Hey," she said. "Everything okay?"

Mac pushed away from the wall with a smile. "Everything's fine. It's you I'm worried about. I heard about that shoot-out you and the guys got into downtown. I just wanted to make sure you were okay."

She could have just called, but Khaki was glad she hadn't. She liked hanging out with Mac. Khaki unlocked the door to her apartment and pushed it open.

"Come on in." Khaki glanced at Mac over her shoulder as she led the way into the apartment. Comparable in size to Mac's place, it had the same open floor plan and a great view of downtown from the picture window in the living room. "Want some iced tea?"

"Thanks." Mac flopped down on the couch, then hooked her arm over the back of it so she could look at Khaki. "The videos of you rescuing those kids are all over the Internet. I still can't believe the way you came down the side of that building. My heart was in my throat just watching you."

Khaki shrugged, embarrassed. She hadn't done anything that any of the other guys on the team wouldn't have done.

She poured two glasses of iced tea and carried them into the living room, handing one to Mac as she kicked off her flip-flops and sat down on the other end of the couch.

"I don't even remember making a conscious decision to rappel down," she admitted. "I saw those poor kids and let instinct take over."

Mac laughed. "Well you should let your instincts take over more often because you looked awesome coming down that rope. I bet there's a ten percent jump in women joining the Dallas Police Academy based on those videos alone."

Khaki didn't know about that, but it would be great if Mac was right. It was way easier to follow your dream of becoming a cop when you were a little girl if you had a female role model to look up to.

"How did your talk go with Xander last night?" Mac asked as she sipped her tea. "Was he able to help you?"

"Yeah, he did." Khaki was still surprised how well last night had gone, even with all the issues Xander obviously had with her. "I can't believe how much I learned from him in just a few hours."

Of course, she didn't mention the fact that one of the things she'd learned last night was that it was dangerous to be alone with Xander. He made her think about doing things she really shouldn't.

Mac grinned. "I told you he could help. All you had to do was get past his rough exterior. How's it going with the rest of the guys? They don't know about you and Xander, do they?"

Khaki almost spilled her iced tea. She quickly set it down on a coaster. "Know about what?"

"That he's giving you lessons on how to be a werewolf."

"Oh." Whew. For a minute there, Khaki was worried Mac had figured out she had a thing for her squad leader. "No. Xander told me they wouldn't have a problem with it, but I made him promise not to say anything."

Mac nodded. "I can understand that. He's right about the guys though. They're a good group."

Khaki smiled. "Yeah, I know."

After the shoot-out downtown, everyone on the squad—including Xander—had made it a point to let her know she'd done a hell of a job. She hadn't even been here a week and it already felt like this was the place she was meant to be.

"Everyone on the team is absolutely amazing," she added. "I couldn't ask for anything more."

Well, that wasn't exactly true. She wouldn't mind asking for a better relationship with her squad leader. But she supposed she couldn't have everything. No need to be greedy.

On the other end of the couch, Mac regarded her thoughtfully. "Why do I get the feeling there's a really big *but* at the end of that sentence?"

Khaki forgot that Mac was a reporter—apparently a damn good one. She didn't miss a thing.

"It's just that it's tough working around a team full of sexy men," Khaki said, trying to sound casual.

Mac laughed. "I can imagine. I love Gage like crazy, but I'd be lying if I didn't say I'm with you on that. Those guys aren't hard to look at, are they?"

You have no idea. "The hardest part to deal with is the scent he puts off. It smells so damn good."

Mac paused to give Khaki a questioning look, the glass of iced tea in her hand halfway to her lips.

"What?" Khaki asked.

"You said, the scent *he* puts off," Mac said.

"I did?"

"You did."

Crap. She'd stepped right into that one. What the heck was wrong with her? She never got this easily rattled—because she'd never been around someone like Xander before.

Was that why she hadn't said anything when she heard him coming upstairs earlier that evening?

She could have hidden behind the tiled wall, but she hadn't tried to cover up or even look like he'd caught her by surprise. She didn't have a clue what she'd been thinking. All she could say for sure was that she'd been as aroused as hell. If Xander had taken one step closer, she might have dropped that towel to the floor and jumped him right there on one of the wooden benches.

A smile curved Mac's lips. "There's one guy on the team in particular who smells especially nice, huh?"

"I didn't say that." Khaki uncurled her legs from under her and went into the kitchen. "Do you want something to snack on? Because I, for one, am starving."

Mac followed on her heels. "Uh-uh. You're not getting off that easy. I know all about you werewolves and your noses. I also know how a scent can get you going. So, tell me, who is it?"

Khaki opened the fridge and stared at the shelves of yogurt, skim milk, fruits, and veggies. Part of her didn't want to tell Mac. She was Sergeant Dixon's fiancée after all. How likely was it that Mac wouldn't say anything to the man she was going to marry? Especially when she found out that the team member Khaki was lusting after was one of Gage's squad leaders? A squad leader who was Khaki's supervisor?

But another part—the bigger part—told her that she could trust Mac.

Khaki closed the fridge and turned to face her. "It's Xander."

If Mac was surprised, she didn't let it show. "Xander, huh? I can't say I blame you. He's more than a little attractive and a really amazing person. Well, once you get past all the perimeter defenses. But that kind of complicates things, doesn't it?"

That was an understatement. "I can't help it. I know it's wrong. He's my squad leader, for heaven's sake. But he's so hot, I can't stop myself. When I'm around him, it's hard to even think straight."

Mac tilted her head to the side, regarding Khaki thoughtfully. "Do you think Xander feels the same way?"

Khaki let out a short laugh. "Good Lord, no. He tolerates me, that's about it."

"You sure about that?" Mac asked in surprise. "I find it hard to believe he's not attracted to you. Heck, probably half the guys on the team are. You're the only female werewolf they've ever met."

"I get what you're saying, but none of the guys act like that around me," Khaki said. "They treat me more like their sister. And Xander isn't attracted to me at all. I'm sure of it."

Which hurt more than it should have. Her head might have known it was a good thing that Xander wasn't attracted to her, but right then, with nobody but her and Mac around, she could be honest enough to admit that her heart, and a few other parts of her anatomy, really wished he was.

"Are you?" Mac asked. "Sure, I mean?"

"I'm sure." Khaki opened the fridge again and took out whole wheat bread, sliced turkey, cheese, and a tomato, then gave Mac a questioning look. "Want a sandwich?"

Mac shook her head. "I'm going to have dinner with Gage when he gets home."

Who said anything about dinner? This was more like an appetizer. That was another perk that came with being a werewolf. She could eat whatever she wanted and not have to worry about extra calories ending up where they shouldn't.

Khaki set everything on the counter. "I asked Xander flat-out when I went over to his place last night. He insisted he liked me just fine, but I knew he was lying. I could tell he was really uncomfortable around me. He was tense and on edge the whole time. Which is nothing new. He's like that all the time around me. I think he finds me irritating and a nuisance."

Mac gave her a dubious look. "If you say so. But either way, you'd better be careful. If being with Gage has taught me anything, it's that werewolves are extremely affected by certain pheromones. If you go walking around lusting over Xander, he's going to pick up on it—and so is every other guy on the team. Then things will get really complicated. I learned that the hard way. Those guys can pick up on arousal like it's barbecue and they aren't shy about letting you know it."

Khaki groaned as she grabbed a plate from the cabinet. "Oh God. I never thought about that."

"Yeah. And it gets worse." Mac shook her head. "If I'm even slightly aroused and Gage picks up on it, he gets crazy horny—like he-can't-control-it horny. What do you think is going to happen if all the guys on the team pick up on the fact that the one and only female werewolf on the team is aroused? You'll find yourself getting chased by fifteen out-of-control, horny werewolves going crazy with lust. And while there are some women who might find that entertaining, something tells me you wouldn't."

Khaki set the plate on the counter with a thud. "Oh crap. What the hell am I going to do?"

Mac offered her a small smile. "Take a lot of baths?"

Chapter 8

THE MERE THOUGHT OF FACING KHAKI AFTER WALKING in on her in the shower was enough to make Xander almost call in sick the next morning. There was only one problem—werewolves didn't get sick.

Last night had been tough on him. Khaki's scent was still just as strong in his apartment as it had been the previous night, only now he had a visual to go along with that scent. He'd lain in bed the whole night, staring up at the ceiling and dreaming about that shower scene he'd walked in on. If he didn't know better, he'd have thought she was toying with him, trying to drive him crazy. Of course she hadn't been. That was just wishful thinking on his part. But still, the look on her face, the way she had that towel wrapped around her body, the way she'd laughed—it was seared into his mind forever.

He hated having these kinds of thoughts about Khaki. She was one of his team members. It was flat-out wrong. But it seemed the harder he fought against his feelings, the stronger they became.

When Xander finally rolled in for PT, the guys were still talking about the shoot-out with the bank robbery suspects the day before, especially how Khaki had come down off the roof and saved those kids—and how she'd torn into the FBI agent. The story was already getting exaggerated. They practically had Khaki tearing poor

Thompson to pieces. Max swore he saw the guy crying by the time Khaki was done.

Xander didn't mind his squad exaggerating Khaki's exploits. That meant she was becoming one of them and they wanted to brag about her like they would have done with any other member of the squad. Of course, Khaki wasn't any other member of the squad. That became blatantly obvious about ten minutes later when she showed up wearing a pair of tight yoga pants with flared bottoms and carrying a whole box full of rolled-up rubber mats, then led them outside for PT.

"Cooper pulled a hamstring running yesterday during the bank robbery, so he asked me to fill in as PT instructor today," she said as she handed out the mats. "Pulling a muscle like that is a perfect example of why we need to start working flexibility into our fitness program. And the absolute best way to do that is yoga."

"You've got to be shitting me," Jayden muttered to no one in particular. "I'm a two-hundred-and-sixty-pound werewolf. I don't do yoga."

Cooper gave Jayden a sidelong glance. "Today you're doing yoga. Your hamstrings will thank you."

"Thank you, Cooper," Khaki said sweetly. "Now, if everyone will unroll their mats and stand with their feet shoulder-width apart with their hands in a prayer position like so, I'll show you how to breathe properly. And, Cooper, take it easy on that hamstring, okay?"

Xander rolled his eyes. Pulled hamstring his ass. Werewolves pulled muscles just like anybody else, but even a serious tear would heal in an hour or so. No, if Xander had to guess, Cooper was doing someone in the squad a favor. And judging by the appreciative look

Becker was giving Cooper, Xander knew exactly who it was.

Xander shook his head as he put his hands together in the prayer position, palms together and fingers pointing up. Becker's plan wasn't a bad one. Khaki looked really hot in those pants. And if there was one person who could get these guys to work on their flexibility, it'd be Khaki. If any of the guys had tried to come in here and pull this off, they would have been dog-piled by now.

Even so, most of the guys were eyeing Khaki dubiously as they mirrored her position. This was going to be…different. Some relaxing stretching would be a nice break from the ordinary.

Xander had to admit, watching Khaki bend and twist in those tight pants as she led them through various poses definitely made the wasted PT session worth it. He could finally see why Becker thought so much of those yoga pants. Though if Becker didn't stop staring, Xander was going to walk over and punch him in the mouth.

Xander pushed the thought aside with a barely suppressed growl. As long as he didn't leer or act like an ass, Becker had just as much right to look as he did. That didn't quell the jealousy surging though him though.

After a few minutes of the gentle stretching, Khaki put them into positions that weren't quite as relaxing. That's when Xander really started to feel the workout. Damn, some of these things were hard.

"Get a little deeper in bound side angle, Alex," Khaki called out. "Really reach under your leg and grab the other wrist."

"Shit, I've got too many muscles to be bending this

way," Jayden grumbled. "I'm going to damage something important down here."

Max snorted. "You don't use it anyway."

The other guys laughed, including Xander. But if they were like him, it was probably more to cover up the fact that they were having problems with bound warrior. It was like being a pretzel. The next pose was even worse. Something about a crow or a chicken. Either way, yoga was tougher than he'd thought. Props to whoever did it regularly because he was sweating like crazy.

He wasn't the only one. Every guy on the team was grunting and swearing as Khaki led them through moves that stretched parts most of them hadn't even known existed. Even she was sweating.

That was when he noticed something that almost knocked him out of his twisted triangle pose—a scent so strong he had to bite down on his tongue to keep from growling. *What the hell?*

Xander took a deep breath, trying to identify where it was coming from. When he did, he almost howled. That delectable scent hitting him so hard was coming from none other than Khaki's glistening, sweat-slicked body. He was downwind of her, so as she led them from twisted triangle into a straight-legged hamstring stretch, the aroma kept getting stronger and stronger. She always smelled good, but for some reason, today her scent was even more powerful than normal.

Stopping his hard-on from uncomfortably filling his shorts wasn't even an option. But this was more than simply an arousing scent. It was as if he'd been struck by lightning. Every cell in his body was tingling and alive. If his heart had stopped beating right at that moment, he wouldn't have been surprised. But as agonizing as it was to stand there and inhale Khaki's pheromones without pouncing on her, the thought of walking away was too painful to even consider.

He tore his gaze from Khaki and looked around, trying to see how everyone else was dealing with this mind-numbing sensory assault. But other than some swearing and complaining about how long Khaki was keeping them in this last pose, it didn't seem like any of the guys noticed the scent rolling off her like a tidal wave.

How was that possible? It was the most amazing thing he'd ever smelled in his life. There was no way the other guys couldn't smell it.

But obviously they didn't or they'd have gone nuts. What the hell was happening to him?

Then, as he knelt there trying hard to breathe through his mouth and not his nose, the answer came to him. There could be only one reason he was affected by Khaki's scent like this. And that one reason scared the hell out of him.

Khaki Blake must be *The One*—capital *T*, capital *O*—for him. If Xander hadn't been kneeling right then, he would have fallen over.

As he watched Khaki flexing and twisting in mind-boggling grace, he realized that every single legend about *The One* was true. He may have found his soul mate.

But then a far more painful truth hit him. While he might have found his soul mate, she was one of his squad members. She'd also just gotten out of a crappy workplace romance that had blown up in her face and driven her out of her last job.

He wasn't too intoxicated by her pheromones to know what both of those things meant. Khaki, and all that could be, was out of his reach.

Suddenly, that amazing scent of hers didn't seem so sweet. In fact, it seemed more like a kick in the balls.

Khaki had no idea what she'd done during PT to piss off Xander, but when the rest of the squad headed down-range to get in some target practice, he'd announced he was staying in the admin office to write some reports. But from the way he'd avoided her gaze as he said it, she knew he was lying. Clearly, he didn't want to be around her any more than he had to be.

She tried to forget about Xander and his issues as she walked down to the shooting range with the guys. She laughed with them, even when they called her "yoga wolf" and ribbed her about this morning's PT session. She knew their teasing was just good-natured fun. She was part of the Pack now. The change from the previous day was subtle, but she could feel it. Between yesterday and today, they had become a family. It was nice to be part of something so special.

But no matter how much she laughed and joked with her teammates or how secure she felt with her new place within the Pack, she still wrestled with her relationship with Xander. The sense of disappointment welling up inside her when he stayed in the admin building instead of joining them was overwhelming. The worst part was she didn't even understand why it bothered her so much. She'd known she wasn't Xander's favorite person since day one. Heck, she'd said as much to Mac last night.

But after how well her werewolf lesson at his place had gone, not to mention the way she'd handled herself yesterday during the bank robbery, she'd thought she and Xander were in a good place.

Obviously, she'd been wrong.

She knew it was juvenile to get caught up in trying to understand Xander and whatever problem he had with her, but it was hard to pretend it didn't matter when he acted like he'd rather be flossing his teeth with barbwire than spend even five minutes in her company. It physically made her chest hurt if she thought about it too much. It was like she'd lost something she'd never even had.

Khaki wished she could talk to another female werewolf about it. Mac was great, but there was stuff going on that Mac couldn't understand or explain. Khaki knew in her gut that her werewolf nature had something to do with these feelings she was having. This wasn't just a matter of being attracted to Xander. She'd been attracted to men before enough to know that what she felt now wasn't normal. No man had ever taken hold of her soul the way Xander had. Even now as she was busy loading magazines for her M4, her head was somewhere else—like remembering how good Xander had smelled this morning during PT. The urge to walk over in the middle of the workout and rub her body up against his had been almost impossible to resist. If the other guys hadn't been there, she probably would have done it—then thrown him down on his yoga mat and jumped him.

The image made her fingers tingle and her gums throb. She knew from last night what that meant and she quickly glanced at her fingertips to see if her claws were out. They weren't, which meant her fangs weren't either. But she carefully ran her tongue over her teeth just to check. How the hell would she have explained that, by saying loading 5.56 mm magazines got her excited?

What was wrong with her? How could thinking about Xander make her want to shift when she didn't even know how to do it yet?

—∾∾—

Khaki was on her fourth magazine when Trevor's cell phone rang. Just when she'd finally gotten Xander out of her head and was able to think about something other than her squad leader.

Trevor had been putting them through a wounded-dominant-arm scenario with their M4s, making them go through the process of shooting, clearing a jammed weapon, and reloading—all with their nonshooting hand. Doing those things with an M4 was tough enough with both hands. With just her left, it was challenging as hell. Which was why it had required all her attention.

"We've got an incident," Trevor said as he hung up.

Khaki grabbed her M4 and followed the guys, jogging to keep up with their long strides. She got to the admin building just in time to hear Xander asking if Gage was sure he wanted to do this.

"After how she handled herself during the bank situation and what you've been telling me about her training, I think she's ready," Gage said. "Don't you?"

Khaki held her breath. She didn't know exactly what they were talking about, but she'd come to expect the worst.

Xander didn't even hesitate. "She's more than ready."

She hadn't expected that. Just another indication that she didn't have a clue what went on in Xander's head. Then again, what woman could understand men anyway? Their logic rarely made sense to anyone but themselves.

Khaki quickly put on her tactical gear and pulled the straps snug, then climbed into the SUV with Cooper, Becker, and Alex. All they knew was that a little girl had been kidnapped and the DPD wanted their help with the rescue.

The on-scene commander, an older lieutenant named Matthews, filled them in as soon as they got to the subdivision.

"The girl's name is Melissa Kincaide. She was taken a little over an hour and a half ago," he said as they all gathered around the back of the SWAT operations vehicle.

Well, not all of them. Trevor was in the operations vehicle with one of the city's civilian negotiators, trying to establish communications with the man who owned the house they were parked down the street from.

"The mother and two other neighbors were with their children waiting for the bus to take them to school this morning," Matthews continued. "As they were getting on the bus, the suspect drove up and grabbed Melissa, then sped away."

"Any chance they misidentified the suspect?" Xander asked.

The lieutenant shook his head. "No. All three of the adults and half the kids recognized Clete Reynolds. They've seen him around the neighborhood."

Khaki didn't miss the worried looks that passed

between her teammates. She hadn't dealt with a lot of hostage situations, but it couldn't be good that the man hadn't even tried to hide his face during the abduction, hadn't cared if someone recognized him.

"And before you even ask, there isn't any family connection between the little girl and Reynolds," the lieutenant added. "It's as if he simply wanted to grab one of the kids at the bus stop and Melissa was the one he ended up with. When a patrol car showed up, he shot at them. My guys pulled back and set up the barricades, then got the nearby houses evacuated. One of the officers slipped around the back of the place and peeked in a few windows. He never saw the girl, but the suspect is in there with an arsenal of weapons."

Xander continued talking to the on-scene commander while she and the guys got their weapons. Even though Khaki was new to all this, she had a feeling this wasn't going to end well.

Trevor came out of the operations vehicle as Khaki was double-checking her M4, worry etching his brow.

"We've been trying to talk Reynolds into coming out, or at least letting the girl go, but the guy isn't exactly rational," he said. "I can't even confirm the man has the girl, much less where he's holding her. One second he's telling me he hasn't done anything wrong, and the next he's shouting that he'll die before he lets us take away what's his. I'll keep trying, but this guy has a hair trigger. He could snap at any second."

Xander nodded, then turned to her and the rest of the guys. "We don't have time for a detailed plan, so we'll just keep it simple. We have a one-floor ranch with a basement. Since the patrol officer didn't see the girl when he looked in the windows, there's a good chance she's in the basement. Max and Hale, I want you two on the back, right side. Alex and Khaki, you have the back side left. Max, the power box is on your corner, so you'll kill the power on my word."

"Roger that," Max said.

"Cooper, Becker, and I will be at the front of the house," Xander continued. "Hopefully, we'll be able to lure Reynolds there while the rest of you find the girl and get her out. We'll try to take Reynolds alive, but Melissa Kincaide is our first priority. Everyone stay alert. We go in on my command."

Khaki's heart raced as she and the guys approached the house. Out of the corner of her eye, she caught sight of the terrified people lining the police barricades at the end of the street. Lieutenant Matthews was standing off to one side trying to comfort a woman who was probably Melissa's mother. The woman was holding on to a little girl's Hello Kitty book bag and a pretty pink cardigan sweater for dear life. The moment the woman saw them moving toward the house, she broke loose from the lieutenant's hold and dashed around the barricade, running straight to Khaki.

"He took my little girl," the woman sobbed, clutching Khaki's arm. "You have to bring her back to me. Please."

Khaki opened her mouth to reassure her, but the woman didn't give Khaki a chance.

"Take this," she beseeched, shoving the little pink sweater into Khaki's hand. "Lissa dropped it. She's going to need it when you find her. She gets cold so easily."

Tears misted Khaki's eyes and she blinked them

away as she gently put the sweater back in the woman's hands. "We're going to bring your little girl out of there safe and sound, and when we do, you can give Melissa her sweater, okay?"

The woman nodded, fresh sobs racking her body as she clutched the sweater to her chest. Then Matthews was there, securing the woman in a firm but gentle grip. The lieutenant gave Khaki a nod before leading the woman back toward the barricade.

Khaki turned to catch up to the team to find them waiting for her.

"You ready for this?" Xander asked in that same soft voice he'd used when he taught her how to shift enough to see in the dark.

She nodded. "I'm ready."

"Good." The corner of his mouth edged up. "Be careful, huh?"

"You too."

She and Alex used the neighborhood houses as cover as they moved around to the back of the suspect's house. In broad daylight like this, it would be hard to sneak up on this guy, but they had to try.

As they got into position, she heard Trevor giving status updates to Xander in her earpiece. It didn't sound like it was going very well. According to Trevor, the kidnapper was starting to lose it.

Khaki dropped to one knee near the window closest to her and peeked through the blinds into the bedroom. Alex motioned with his hand, pointing at himself, then the window, then her. He'd go through the window first while she covered him. She nodded.

Her hand tightened around her M4 as she waited

for Xander to give the order to move in. This was her first real SWAT mission. She didn't count the bank job because that hadn't been a planned situation and there hadn't been a hostage. This was different. There was a little girl in there who would likely die if they screwed up.

Khaki took a breath and let it out slowly, forcing herself to relax. If they ended up in the basement, she had to be ready to let her eyes shift. She replayed Xander's words from their lesson.

Picture yourself running barefoot through the forest. Now imagine yourself opening your eyes wider, letting every flicker of light in to fill the darkness.

Khaki felt her eyes start to shift when she heard a man yelling from inside the house quickly followed by gunshots, breaking glass, and the clank of bullets hitting the cars along the street. Her first thought was of Xander and the guys who'd been heading through the front, and she sagged with relief when she heard him give the order to kill the power and enter the house.

Alex launched himself through the window, taking out the glass, most of the framework, and the curtains on the other side. Khaki leaped in after him, covering him as he got to his feet and tossed the curtains aside.

Khaki heard other windows breaking as she and Alex headed out of the bedroom and down a long hallway toward the center of the house. The other members of the squad would be moving in the same direction soon enough.

They'd just reached the end of the hallway when a middle-aged man with a beard and a shotgun came running. He glanced at her and Alex, eyes wide and crazy as he pivoted and headed down another hallway. No wonder Trevor thought Reynolds was losing it. The guy didn't only sound insane; he looked it.

She gave chase, putting on speed when she realized he was heading for the basement. Dammit!

"He's going to the basement," she yelled, following Reynolds down the stairs.

Khaki let her nose lead her until she felt her eyes shift. The sound of a trigger being squeezed made her slam on the brakes, and she threw herself backward as the roar of a shotgun filled the tight stairwell.

Behind her, Alex must have sensed what she was about to do because he jumped back at the same time. The shotgun blew a ragged hole about the size of her head in the sheetrock wall beside her. Luckily, Reynolds missed her by a figurative mile. The debris from the sheetrock hadn't even hit the floor before she was on her feet and running again, Alex right behind her.

She reached the basement only a few steps behind Reynolds. Unable to see as well as they could in the dark, he seemed more interested in not running into anything than in shooting at her and Alex again. That was okay with Khaki.

Unfortunately, she didn't see the little girl anywhere. But they'd caught Reynolds. It would just be a matter of time before they rescued Melissa.

Khaki reached out to grab Reynolds by the shirt when he simply dropped out of sight. She skidded to a halt just in time to keep from falling into a ragged hole in the concrete floor.

"What the hell?" Alex muttered as he came around from behind her to see why she'd stopped.

She didn't have an answer. All she knew was that it was so dark she had trouble seeing anything in it—even with her eyes shifted.

Boots echoed on the stairs. A moment later Xander was beside her.

"What have we got?" he asked.

Cooper squatted beside the hole. "We got a tunnel rat, that's what we got."

Then, without another word, he hopped into the hole.

Khaki didn't think. She simply let her eyes open as wide as they would go to let in as much light as possible, and dropped into the blackness after Cooper.

It was a short trip to the bottom. She looked around, trying to get her bearings as she moved away from the hole so the other guys could join them.

"Holy crud," Becker whispered. "It's a freaking maze down here."

Khaki silently agreed. They'd landed in the central hub of a network of tunnels that Reynolds had dug under his house. From where she was standing, she could see five main tunnels running off in different directions with smaller tunnels branching off from the main routes. Sheets of plywood and four-by-four beams shored up the ceiling and walls, and little trickles of dirt drifted from every gap.

"What the hell is that smell?" Max asked, covering his nose with his gloved hand.

Khaki didn't blame him. Her nose had started to burn the moment she'd hit the ground. She'd never smelled anything like it, which was saying a lot. She'd spent her time in a lot of drug dens and meth labs out in Lakefront, and while the odor down here was similar, it definitely wasn't the same.

"I don't know," Xander said. "But let's not spend any more time down here than we have to. Spread out in teams of two. We need to find Reynolds before he gets to that little girl."

Khaki paired up with Cooper, thanking God over and over that Xander had taught her how to shift her eyes. If she had to use her nose in here, she wasn't sure she could do it. The place reeked.

She and Cooper had only gone about twenty feet when they heard gunfire. She turned and raced back the way they'd come, tracking the sounds of a scuffle down one of the other main tunnels, Cooper on her heels.

They got there along with everyone else, just in time to see Hale pinning Reynolds to the ground, a zip tie already on the man's wrists, the shotgun lying in the dirt about ten feet away.

When Hale hauled the guy to his feet, Xander flipped on his flashlight and shined it in the man's face "Where's the little girl? Is she down here?"

Reynolds squinted against the light, babbling incoherently and shaking his head from side to side. Whether he was freaked out because he'd just gotten his ass kicked by a group of cops with glowing eyes or simply spent too much time down here inhaling these fumes was anyone's guess. Regardless, they weren't going to get anything out of him.

"What the hell is this stuff?"

Khaki turned to see Max holding up a mason jar of honey-colored liquid. He angled the jar toward Xander's light, shaking it as he tried to figure out what it was. Beside him, there were several pallets of the jars, stacked high on top of each other.

"You think he was making moonshine down here?" Max shook the jar again. "If it is, what're all these sparkly things floating in it?"

Cooper brushed past Khaki. "Stop shaking the jar, Max."

Max frowned down at the jar in his hand and shook it some more. "Why? What is it?"

"Stop shaking the fucking jar, you moron!" Cooper growled so loudly that a sprinkle of dirt from the roof of the tunnel rained down around them.

"I finally figured out what this smell is," Cooper said, glancing over his shoulder at the rest of them. "It's nitric acid. This crazy son of a bitch has been trying to make his own explosives. Those sparkly things are nitric salts. You treat them too rough, and we're gone. Hell, with all the jars on those pallets, a good portion of the neighborhood is gone with us."

The tunnel went dead quiet. Even Reynolds stopped babbling.

"What do I do with it?" Max asked softly.

"You put it down," Cooper advised. "Slowly."

Outside, Matthews must have heard every word Cooper said through his mic because the lieutenant told them he wanted them out of there ASAP.

"We need to get Explosive Ordnance Disposal down there to clear those tunnels before we look for the girl," Matthews added.

"Lieutenant, as bad as the air is down here, that girl will be dead long before EOD can get through this place," Xander said into his mic. "It might take days."

"Dammit," Matthews swore. "Clear out as many members of your team as you can. I want essential personnel in there only. And find that little girl—fast."

Khaki expected Xander to say that everyone on his team was essential, but he pointed at her and Cooper. "You two are staying. Everyone else out."

The guys looked at Xander as if he were crazy. Khaki could imagine what they were thinking. Cooper was former Army Explosive Ordnance Disposal. But what the hell did Khaki bring to the table? She had to admit, she wasn't sure either.

"Max, Hale, Alex, Becker—out," Xander ordered. "Now."

Khaki could tell from the looks on their faces they didn't like it, but they went, dragging a dazed and confused Reynolds with them.

Xander turned off his radio, then motioned for her and Cooper to do the same. "Khaki, I need you to find that little girl."

She blinked. "What? How can I do that?"

"You can pick up her scent."

Of course. Xander thought that with her exceptional sense of smell, she could track the girl despite the reeking, burning chemical odor permeating every inch of the tunnels.

"Maybe," Khaki agreed. "If I knew what she smelled like, but I don't."

Xander's golden eyes were bright in the dark. "Yes, you do. I know for a fact that you got a whiff of that little girl's pink sweater when her mom shoved it into your hand. You smell, and remember, everything. You just have to find her scent in that head of yours."

Cooper's brows furrowed. "What the hell are you

talking about? No werewolf could smell a damn thing in here. We're wasting time. We need to start searching."

Xander gave him a hard look. "She can do this. Her nose doesn't work like ours. It's better."

Khaki vaguely remembered picking up a lot of odors when Melissa's mom had grabbed her. There was the smell of cotton and polyester, laundry detergent, eggs and bacon, some kind of furniture polish, peanut butter cookies, even the salty scent of tears. There were so many scents to shift through. And the horrible chemical smells down here didn't help.

She shook her head. "Xander, I don't think I can do it."

He put his hands on her shoulders and gave them a reassuring squeeze. "We need to find her now. We don't have time to wander around down here searching. You can do this. I know you can."

The confidence in those words almost brought tears to Khaki's eyes. She thought of Melissa's mother sobbing and begging Khaki to find her little girl. Then she thought of Melissa. Wherever she was, she was probably terrified.

"I'll try," Khaki told Xander.

His mouth curved. "That's all I can ask."

Taking a deep breath, Khaki slung her M4 across her back, dropped down to her knees, and closed her eyes. Off to her right, she sensed Cooper move closer. She knew that Xander was keeping him away.

She shut them out and began to sort through the myriad smells down there surrounding her. She forced her nose to dive down under the harsh chemical odor, to ignore it and push it to the back of her mind so she could distinguish other scents.

She smelled dirt, of course. And Xander. Cooper too.

She scrunched up her nose and dug deeper, finding Reynolds's smell—stale sweat paired with booze and urine. Underneath that, she picked up the faint trace of moles and rats that had long since left the tunnels.

And then, when she was about to give up, she found what she was looking for—the scent of peanut butter cookies and little girl tears.

Khaki jumped to her feet and ran toward the central hub of the tunnels, letting her nose lead the way.

Behind her, Xander ordered Cooper to stick tight to her so she wouldn't get herself blown to pieces. Cooper obeyed, running so close to her he might as well have been glued to her side as she ran through the tunnels.

Khaki was so focused on the little girl's scent she didn't even see the tripwire stretched across the tunnel until she heard it break. The explosion echoed in her ears and thumped her in the chest, squeezing every ounce of air out of her lungs and picking her up to throw her down the tunnel.

Surprisingly, she didn't pass out—at least, she didn't think so. When she got her wits back, she was lying on the floor of the tunnel, something heavy pinning her legs. She pushed herself up on an elbow to see what it was and found a muscular arm draped over her. She couldn't tell whether it was Xander or Cooper because the rest of him was buried under a slide of sandy clay soil. *Crap*. The tunnel had collapsed. She looked around and saw Cooper pushing himself into a sitting position a little farther up the tunnel.

She stared wide-eyed at the arm sticking out from

the dirt. It was Xander. He must have shoved her and Cooper out of the way before the explosion brought the tunnel down.

Khaki scrambled to her knees and frantically clawed at the dirt. A moment later, Cooper was at her side, grabbing Xander's arm and pulling on it as she dug.

It probably only took thirty seconds, but it was the longest thirty seconds of her life. She couldn't imagine how someone could be alive under that mess, but as soon as she got enough dirt out of the way, Cooper yanked a coughing, gasping Xander out from underneath.

The urge to throw herself into his arms was hard to resist, and she balled her hands into fists at her side to keep from giving in to the urge.

"Do you still have the girl's scent?" he asked.

It took only a second to confirm that she still did. "Yeah, but I think we may have lost our only way out."

He shook his head. "First, find the girl. Then we'll worry about how to get out of here."

Khaki looked over her shoulder at the collapsed tunnel behind them, not wanting to think too much about how close she'd come to killing them all, then turned and homed in on Melissa's scent. On the upside, the collapsed tunnel had cut down on the chemical odor. It made it easier to follow the girl's scent.

Following her nose got harder when the tunnel dead-ended beside a pile of unused four-by-fours and plywood.

"Oh no," she breathed.

Fear gripping her, Khaki retraced her steps. Melissa's scent stopped about ten feet back—in a pile of freshly dug-up earth.

"Oh God." Tears blurring her vision, she looked at Xander. "The trail ends right here."

Xander and Cooper both dropped to their knees and began digging. Khaki joined in. A moment later, her fingers scraped against metal. She dug faster, uncovering a metal box the size of a footlocker.

Khaki held her breath as Xander and Cooper dragged it out of the hole, then ripped off the hasp and opened the lid.

Inside, curled up like she was sleeping, was a beautiful, blond-haired girl.

Fresh tears welled in Khaki's eyes. They were too late.

But then she heard the unmistakable sound of a heartbeat. She exchanged looks with Xander and Cooper, then reached into the box and carefully pulled the girl out, hugging the tiny body to her chest.

Melissa sighed in her sleep and snuggled into Khaki's neck, her small fingers curling against the straps of the tactical vest she wore. Khaki smoothed the girl's wavy hair.

"It's okay, Melissa," she whispered. "You're safe now."

At the sound of Khaki's voice, the girl lifted her head and looked around in confusion. There probably hadn't been very much air in the box, so it wasn't surprising she was disoriented. Plus, as far as the girl was concerned, it was dark as night down here.

"It's okay," Khaki said again. "You're going to be okay. Your mommy sent us to come and get you."

The girl looked around, her gaze going from Xander to Cooper. Then she turned and looked at Khaki again. "Why are all of your eyes so shiny?"

Khaki couldn't help but smile as she hugged the girl closer. "Because we eat our carrots. You like carrots, don't you?"

The girl rested her head on Khaki's shoulder again. "Not really. They taste yucky. But I'll eat them if they make my eyes shiny like yours."

Khaki laughed, her gaze meeting Xander's over the top of the little girl's head. The look reflected in his gold eyes made her heart flip.

She cleared her throat. "How do we get out of here?"

Xander looked at that pile of wood farther up the tunnel. "Cooper, get a few of those four-by-fours. We're digging our way out of here."

Less than five minutes later, they broke through to the surface and climbed out of the ground to find themselves in the backyard of a house almost three blocks away from Reynolds's. Khaki carried Melissa down the street to the cheers of onlookers, then carefully put the little girl back into her mother's arms.

There were a lot of tears, some of them Khaki's. She was filthy and beyond tired, but when she gave Melissa back to her mother, she'd never been happier in her life. Still smiling, she turned and did something that was probably very un-SWAT-like. She hugged Cooper, then threw her arms around Xander. While the hug she'd given Cooper was all about team and camaraderie and celebrating a job well done, the one she gave Xander was anything but. When that homemade bomb had gone off in the tunnel, he'd saved her life at the risk of his own. He'd believed in her when she hadn't even believed in herself.

Khaki didn't expect Xander to return the gesture,

so when his strong arms went around her, she almost moaned. She settled for burying her face in his neck instead. Even covered in dirt, he smelled ah-mazing. She wasn't sure why or how, but something told her things between them had changed.

Chapter 9

KHAKI AND THE REST OF THE SQUAD STAYED TO HELP with the cleanup operation. Once the DPD realized how bad the mess was, they'd called everybody—EOD, ATF, the fire department, even the state environmental office. It turned out that Reynolds had been brewing up batches of homemade explosives and storing them throughout his subterranean maze. Some of the tunnels had collapsed, trapping sensitive explosives and hazardous waste under hundreds of pounds of dirt. It would take a week to get all the contaminated soil out.

By the time they finished with the worst of it, the sun was setting. Khaki was starting to come down off her endorphin high and was more than ready to fall into bed. But they'd taken the suspect down alive and saved a little girl, getting her back to her mother in one, albeit slightly dirty, piece. Just as important, everyone on the team had made it through with no injuries. Even as new as she was to this SWAT thing, she recognized that today had been a big win.

Khaki was just telling the guys that she couldn't wait to get home when Xander came over.

"No one's going home yet," he said.

"Why not?" she asked. "I thought we were finished here."

"We are." He grinned. "But I just finished briefing Sergeant Dixon on how well you did today and he decided you're ready to come off limited-duty status. That means it's time to celebrate."

Beside her, a smiling Becker fist bumped an equally happy Cooper. On the other side of her, Hale, Max, and Alex were grinning too.

She looked at Xander. "Seriously? But it's only been a week."

"A week during which you've shown that you can do the job. So stop complaining." His smile broadened. "Now let's get back to the compound and clean up before the bars run out of booze."

Khaki rode back with Cooper and Max, listening as Cooper once again related the story of how she'd found Melissa Kincaide simply by following the little girl's scent.

"I couldn't smell anything but dirt, chemicals, and stale sweat down there," Cooper said. "But Khaki led us straight to the girl regardless of the fact that she was buried in a steel box under a foot of earth. That kid would have been dead in another ten minutes if it wasn't for Khaki."

Max glanced over his shoulder at her from the passenger seat. "That's frigging epic."

She felt her face color. "Don't go giving me a medal yet. I probably would have gotten us all blown to pieces if it hadn't been for Cooper and Xander."

Behind the wheel, Cooper's eyes met hers in the rearview mirror. "You did good down there, Khaki, so just accept the compliments—and all the drinks—that'll be coming your way tonight. You deserve them."

Khaki felt a surge of pride. She'd done it. In less than a week, she'd won over her new teammates. The training had been tough, and every day hadn't been enjoyable, but other than the standard teasing, the guys had been amazingly supportive through it all. She still wasn't sure where she stood with Xander, but she was happy with how far she'd come in such a short period of time.

Cooper and Max had gone from complimenting her to ribbing each other over some imaginary mistake the other had made. Ahead, the other two vehicles carrying the rest of her teammates were pulling into the compound's parking lot.

Khaki smiled. Her teammates. That had a nice ring to it.

Inside, they got the gear cleaned and put away, then headed into the admin building to take showers. She let the guys go first, figuring they'd only be standing around at the bottom of the steps complaining if she didn't.

While she waited, some of the guys from Mike's squad stopped by to congratulate her.

"Aren't any of you guys coming with us?" she asked Remy.

She spent so much time with her own squad, it felt like she barely knew any of the other guys on the team. But Remy shook his head.

"Nah. You all trained together to get you to this point, so the celebration should be private too. The rest of us will hang out later."

Khaki could see their point, but she wouldn't have minded if they wanted to join them. She was still trying to convince Mike's team when her squad bounded down the steps. She glanced at her watch. *Crap*, it had taken them only fifteen minutes to shower and change. They'd better not expect her to get ready that fast.

She passed Xander on the way up the steps. He'd changed into jeans and a button-down shirt, and his dark hair was still slightly damp from the shower.

"Don't take all night," he told her. "I don't know how long I can control these guys. They're ready to do some serious partying."

A naughty part of her wondered if Xander would come up and check on her if she took too long. Maybe this time, she wouldn't even bother to wrap a towel around herself.

While that thought was tempting, she dismissed it. It was more likely that Becker would be the one who came up to hurry her along, and having Becker see her naked wasn't as appealing as Xander. *Sorry*, *Becker*.

Khaki forgot to ask where they were taking her to celebrate but figured it would probably by someplace casual. Still, she decided to go a bit sexier with her makeup than she did during the day. It would have been nice if she'd had something dressier to wear too, but she'd have to make do with the jeans and tank top in her locker.

She made it downstairs in thirty minutes—a record for her.

"Damn," Hale said when he saw her. "You clean up nice."

She opened her mouth to say something witty in reply when she caught a glimpse of Xander standing off to the side, his dark eyes practically smoldering. Apparently, he seemed to think she cleaned up nice too.

⁓

They took her to some hole-in-the-wall barbecue place she never would have found, much less stopped at, if it weren't for the guys. But while the decor didn't look like much, the food was delicious. According to Xander, it was almost as good as the barbecue in Kansas City, where he was originally from. Cooper told her that was high praise coming from Xander.

Since this was the first time the whole squad had gotten a chance to talk since rescuing little Melissa Kincaide, most of the conversation centered around Khaki's unique sense of smell. She tried to answer their questions as best she could, but she didn't really know why her nose was so much better than everyone else's. The guys echoed Xander's sentiment about the skill coming in handy on the job.

Khaki expected to call it a night after dinner, but Becker looked at her like she was crazy.

"Hell no." He grinned. "It's time to party!"

By party, Khaki assumed he meant hit up a few clubs, but instead of stopping at any of the half-dozen bars they passed, Cooper pulled up in front of a tattoo shop called Tiny's. Xander and Alex parked behind them.

A bear of a man covered in tattoos practically up to his ears came out of the back of the shop and gave a manly hug to each of the guys. After he'd greeted all of them, he turned to give her an appraising look. As if she was a blank canvas that needed a lot of work.

"Is this her?" he asked.

"Yeah." Xander grinned. "This is her. Tiny, meet Khaki Blake. Khaki, meet Tiny, the SWAT team's personal tattoo artist."

Khaki thought she nodded at Tiny, but she couldn't be sure. Xander was standing so close they were almost touching, and it was distracting. The evening was turning muggy, and the light sheen of sweat on Xander's skin smelled so insanely delicious when combined with his freshly showered scent, it made her want to rub up against him like a kitty.

A completely inappropriate thought for a werewolf, to be sure.

She was so intoxicated by his scent that it took a moment for the rest of his words to register.

"Wait a second," she said, sure she'd missed something important. "He's the SWAT team's what?"

Xander moved a little closer to her. He couldn't possibly know what his presence was doing to her, could he?

"Tiny is the artist who does our wolf head tattoos," he said.

Right. The snarling wolf tattoo that every member of the team had on the left side of his chest. She'd seen some of them up close, and the work was first-class, as were the muscled pecs the tattoos were on.

"He's the only person in town we trust to ink us," Xander added.

Khaki nodded, still thinking more about Xander's well-muscled chest and smooth, perfect skin than tattoos. But as Xander continued to regard her, the implications of why they were here suddenly became clear. She looked around to see the rest of her teammates eyeing her expectantly.

Oh. "You want me to get a tattoo like yours."

It wasn't really a question, but Xander nodded anyway.

She broke eye contact with Xander before it became obvious she enjoyed looking at him way too much, and glanced at the rest of the Pack. "Um, now?"

Alex grinned. "Yeah. It's what we always do to celebrate when someone comes off limited-duty status."

"That makes sense." She bit her lip, hesitating. "I definitely want to get the tattoo, but I'd rather not get it while you guys watch."

"But that's the way we always do it," Max said.

"I get that," she said. "But I'm not getting my tattoo in the same place you guys all have yours."

"Why not?" Becker glanced down at her breasts, then jerked his head up, as if he just realized what part of her anatomy he'd been eyeballing. Was he blushing? "Oh."

She smiled. "Yeah. And to get the tattoo in the place I have in mind, I'll need to take off some of my clothes, and I'm not going to do that in front of you guys."

Becker looked down her body again as if trying to figure out what clothes she'd have to take off. This time, he definitely blushed.

She glanced at the tattoo artist. "Or you either, Tiny. No offense."

Tiny held up his hands in surrender. "None taken. I completely understand. My wife's a tattoo artist too. She can ink you anytime. Her work is probably cleaner and more feminine than mine anyway. Just give me a call and we can schedule it."

That seemed to satisfy the guys. Then all they were interested in was where she planned to get her tattoo.

"You're just going to have to use your imagination," she told them.

Cooper snorted. "Becker is screwed then. He doesn't have any imagination."

Becker punched Cooper in the shoulder hard enough

to send him stumbling backward a few feet. "This coming from the man who reads comic books."

Cooper laughed again, thumping Becker in the chest just as hard. Khaki winced. Both of those shots were going to leave bruises, for sure. Men were so strange.

"Knock it off," Alex said. "If Khaki isn't getting her tattoo tonight, let's go party."

Telling Tiny they'd see him around, Alex and the other guys headed for the door. Khaki turned to follow when she realized Xander was still standing there regarding her with that same glint she'd seen when she came down from the locker room back at the compound. Was he imagining where she was going to get her tattoo? Heat pooled between her thighs, making her sway a little and she quickly turned and hurried to catch up with the guys. She resisted the urge to glance over her shoulder at Xander again—but just barely. Thank goodness he'd driven his own truck. She wasn't sure she trusted herself to ignore him if they were trapped in such a tight space.

The club the guys took her to was loud and the beers were cold, and she settled back in her seat to enjoy both. But she hadn't taken more than a sip of her beer before Becker grabbed her hand and dragged her onto the dance floor. She laughed as he found a space for them.

She never would have thought it, but Becker could dance his ass off. Despite how tired she was, she got into the beat. She hadn't danced in a long time and almost forgot how much fun it was.

Two songs later, Hale cut in. A few songs after that, Cooper did the same, followed by Trevor. When Alex came over to take his turn, Trevor stayed out on the floor with them. Before long, all the guys except Xander were dancing with her at once, twirling her around so many times it almost made her dizzy.

They probably would have kept her out there all night if some other women hadn't been bold enough to move in and join the party. Khaki took the opportunity to escape back to the table for a break.

She dropped into her chair with a laugh as she watched the guys work their moves on their new partners. The women were clearly enjoying it, if the smiles on their faces were any indication. Khaki couldn't blame them. The guys knew what they were doing on the dance floor. Tall, gorgeous, muscular men who could dance had a way of making women smile.

"Tired already?" a deep voice said from beside her. Khaki turned to see Xander claiming the chair across from her, a bottle of beer in his hand. "I thought you'd be out there dancing all night."

"It's been a long day. I'm beat," she said. "How about you? Why aren't you out there entertaining the ladies?"

Xander set his beer down on the table. "None of them really interest me."

Something about the way he said those words, or maybe it was the smolder in his eyes when he said them, made her body hum in a way that had nothing to do with the music. Khaki found it scary that such an offhanded comment could provoke such a powerful response in her.

She tucked her hair behind her ear and took a long swallow of her beer, hoping it would cool her off. It didn't.

Khaki cursed whatever part of her body was responsible for the visceral reaction she had whenever she was around him. She also cursed the fact that Xander was so hard to read. One second he acted like she was nothing but a pain in the ass, the next he was heaping praise on her for a job well done. Other times, like now, her were-wolf intuition told her he was feeling the same things for her that she felt for him.

She licked her lips and tilted her head to look at him. "Who does interest you then?"

Xander's gaze never wavered from hers. "That's a good question."

Khaki stifled a growl of frustration at the blatant non-answer. But it was her own fault for asking such a stupid question. What the hell did she expect him to say, that hot werewolf chicks in SWAT tactical gear did it for him? While that was a nice thought, she knew it wasn't going to happen.

She should have dropped the whole issue and changed the subject, but Xander was still gazing at her with those molten eyes of his, making her insides do slow rolls and flips.

Khaki reached for her beer again, just to have some-thing to distract her. But the intensity of Xander's gaze only increased as he watched her lift the bottle to her lips and take a sip. She probably should have felt self-conscious, considering his eyes were locked on her every move. But she kind of liked him looking at her so intently.

At least he was paying attention to her now.

She took a long, satisfying swallow of beer, then gently placed the bottle back on the table, locking eyes with Xander. He didn't look away, and neither did she.

The eye contact made the quiver in her stomach move

south. She was so wrapped up in his soulful, dark eyes that she almost forgot she had a keen sense of smell until a sweetly masculine scent hit her.

She didn't know what the scent was, but it was the same one she'd smelled at his apartment the other night. Why was it so mouthwateringly delicious? And if it was coming from him—which it was—why didn't she smell it all the time?

Khaki squirmed slightly in her chair, trying to ease the sudden ache between her thighs. If she hadn't been sitting in a crowded bar right now, she would have slid her hand down for a caress or two.

But since she couldn't touch herself like she wanted to, she'd have to be satisfied with a little thigh-on-thigh action and some covert wiggling. Even that slight movement caused the most blatantly sexual scent to waft up from her aroused pussy. She might have had jeans on, but her sensitive nose picked up the uniquely feminine scent with no problem at all.

Xander's eyes momentarily flashed yellow-gold, then darkened again. That had been a partial shift. She'd seen him and the other guys do it dozens of time at the compound. Then he lifted his head a bit, mirroring something she did herself frequently when she was trying to get a better grip on a particularly interesting scent.

That was when it hit her. Xander could smell her arousal too. And it was having an effect on him.

She realized something else. The masculine scent she'd smelled before—the one that was growing stronger by the second—was coming from below Xander's belt. He was just as turned on as she was, and it was because of her.

Before she jumped across the table at him, Khaki

slowed for a second to ask herself how sure she was of that last part. What if his body was responding to the pheromones she was putting off? Mac had said the guys would pick up on it if she kept lusting.

That didn't quite fit. Yes, she'd gotten tingly gazing into those seriously sexy eyes of his, but those scent-laced fireworks of his had started before hers, she was certain of it. Which meant he'd gotten aroused from simply gazing into her eyes. She'd smelled the same thing at his place when he'd been teaching her to see in the dark, then again this morning during the PT session. She just hadn't realized what it was.

The lightbulb that came on was so bright it almost hurt her eyes. Xander had been telling the truth back at her apartment. He didn't have a problem with her being on his squad. And he definitely didn't dislike her. Maybe he'd kept his distance because he was dealing with the same level of primitive attraction she'd been fighting. Like her, he'd been trying to put a wall between them.

Her boss was hot for her, and she was hot for him. What the hell was she going to do about it?

Thoughts of professional behavior, team chemistry, and the greater long-term good all floated through her head. And every one of those perfectly reasonable thoughts disappeared just as fast.

He wanted her as badly as she wanted him. That was all that mattered. And right then, the urge to have sex with Xander Riggs was seriously overwhelming.

~~~

Xander wanted Khaki so badly it physically hurt. Whereas before he'd hoped he could come up with a way to get her to leave the club with him, right at that moment he wanted nothing more than to tangle his fingers in that long, dark hair of hers, drag her across the table, and make love to her right there in front of everyone. Judging from the pheromones coming off her, he suspected she might just let him. But considering the rest of the team was out on the dance floor and would probably notice if he and Khaki started having sex, going somewhere more private would definitely be a better idea.

He'd started the day sure he was doomed to the painful existence of watching Khaki from afar, never getting to tell her how he felt. He was her squad leader and he couldn't see how he could ever be anything else.

But what had happened down in those tunnels had changed all that. When the booby trap had exploded—when he'd thought he was going to lose Khaki—he stopped caring about all the reasons they couldn't, or shouldn't, be together. He'd known deep in his soul that his life would stop having meaning if he couldn't be with Khaki. He normally wasn't prone to dramatics, but he was sure he'd die if they couldn't be together.

When they'd climbed out of that tunnel into the light of day with Khaki carrying the little girl, he knew right then he couldn't hide his feelings from her anymore. She might not feel the same way about him, but she was damn sure going to know how he felt about her.

Although the idea of telling Khaki how he felt had seemed simple and straightforward in the afterglow of their near-death experience, the reality of doing it turned out to be much more difficult than he'd anticipated.

He hadn't been able to talk to her at all during dinner

at the barbecue place, and the episode at the tattoo parlor had come closer to a brawl than a deep, meaningful conversation. It wasn't until Khaki had sat down at the table that he'd had a chance to even say two words to her. And then he'd discovered he had no clue what to say. How did you tell a woman who worked for you, one who barely knew you and was trusting you to train her to be the best SWAT officer possible, that there was some cosmic force out there that meant you and she were destined to be together?

She'd probably call him a weirdo, slap him for getting fresh with her, then storm out of the club.

So instead, he'd gazed into her eyes. But he couldn't stop. She was just so damn beautiful. The way her heart was beating so loud after all that dancing she'd done combined with the incredible scents rolling off her amazing body all came together to arouse him like nothing he'd ever felt with anyone else. It was tough as hell controlling the urge to take Khaki's hand and drag her out of the club and straight back to his place.

Just thinking about it made him rock hard.

That was when a tantalizing new scent suddenly registered. It was so primal and powerful that he shifted involuntarily. It came so fast, he'd barely controlled his body's urge to change.

It took him two seconds to figure out where the scent was coming from—Khaki. A moment later, he realized what the scent was—arousal. And now that he knew what the scent was, its effect on him was that much more devastating. His heart was racing, his body was doing everything it could to shift into its wolf form, and his cock was throbbing so bad, he was sure it was going to start thumping against the underside of the table any second.

There was no way he could ignore his desire for Khaki any longer. And considering how turned on she obviously was, maybe it was time he stopped trying.

He was just about to suggest they leave when Cooper and Becker came back from the dance floor with the rest of the guys in tow. *Shit.*

"This DJ sucks," Becker said. "Too much slow stuff. Let's go hit some other places."

Xander bit back a growl. The six of them had been two-stepping with half the women in the bar for the past hour and *now* they decided to blow the joint?

"So, how about it?" Trevor asked when he and Khaki made no move to get up.

Xander glanced at Khaki. She looked as eager to go club hopping as he did. He turned back to the four other werewolves.

"Another time, guys," he said. "Khaki's pretty beat. I'm going to take her back to the compound so she can grab her car and head home."

"You sure about that, Khaki?" Cooper asked. "This has the makings of a seriously epic night of drinking. And werewolves don't get hungover, in case you didn't know."

She laughed. "No, I didn't know that. Thanks for telling me."

Becker looked at Khaki as if she were crazy, then shook his head with a laugh. "Damn, you really are new to this werewolf thing, aren't you? But okay, go home and get some sleep. Next time, we're partying until we close down the bars."

Xander waited until the guys left before turning back to Khaki. She smiled.

"Thanks," she said.

"No problem." He cleared his throat. "So, you ready to get out of here?"

She hesitated. "We could do that. But it'd be a waste of a good song."

It took a moment to process what she meant, but he had a good excuse. He was too turned on to think straight. When he finally focused, he realized she was talking about the slow country ballad the DJ was playing. Xander had never heard it before, but then again, he didn't listen to a lot of music, country or otherwise.

On the other side of the small table, Khaki was looking at him expectantly. She wanted to dance. He wasn't much of a dancer, but if it meant getting to hold her in his arms, he could fake it.

"You sure you're not too tired?" he teased.

Her eyes sparkled, and for a moment he thought she was shifting. But no, that was just Khaki's natural sexiness shining through.

"I think I can stay awake," she said. "Though I might have to lean on you a little—just for support."

Xander liked the sound of that. But then Khaki's expression suddenly turned serious. "Are you sure it's okay? What if the guys come back and catch us?"

The thought hadn't even entered his mind, but it was a valid concern. Then he remembered what he'd promised himself earlier today, after they had clawed their way out of those tunnels—that he was done worrying about what other people thought was right and wrong. There was something going on between him and Khaki that was bigger than the rules. That wasn't exactly something he was going to say out loud.

"Why should we be worried?" he asked instead. "We're just going to dance, right?"

She considered that, then smiled again. "Right."

Xander got to his feet, praying he didn't have any obvious bulge in the front of his jeans. Luckily, his hard-on was positioned in such a way that it didn't look too blatant, though he was pretty sure Khaki already knew how turned on he was. And if she didn't, she'd sure as hell figure it out when they started dancing.

He could live with that. Like he'd decided, he was done hiding how he felt about her.

As soon as they found a space on the crowded dance floor, he pulled Khaki close, holding one of her hands in his while letting his other hand slide down her back to the top of her jean-clad ass. He moved instinctively to the slow rhythm of the country song, all his attention focused on Khaki.

She felt so right in his arms. But standing this close to her, looking into her eyes and feeling her warm body pressed up against his, he found it difficult to even breathe, much less think. Fortunately, being with her didn't require a lot of thinking.

Her scent enveloped him, making him dizzy with its intoxicating mix of her natural fragrance and the scent of her arousal. It made his cock throb even harder, but Khaki didn't seem to mind. She pressed closer to him, resting her cheek against his chest as she swayed in time to the music. His heart beat a little faster.

"Is it bad that I've wanted to get close to you like this for a while?" Khaki's words were so soft that Xander wouldn't have heard them if he didn't have a werewolf's enhanced hearing. Knowing she'd been feeling this thing between them—and fighting it—as long as he had did crazy things to him.

"Probably, especially since I'm your squad leader," he said just as softly. "But if it makes you feel any better, I've been thinking about doing more than just dancing with you."

She laughed, wiggling against the bulge in his jeans. "I can tell."

That brought a growl to his throat and he dipped his head to bury his nose in the long hair hiding her neck from him. He inhaled deeply, letting his lips move teasingly across the warm skin there as his hand glided down a little lower on her ass. She was the one who growled then, and damn if it wasn't the sexiest thing he'd ever heard.

The song ended and another began, and they didn't even miss a step. Xander trailed his lips up and down her neck, practically getting drunk off the sublime taste of her skin. He could have stayed right there on that dance floor and done that all night, if his body hadn't been screaming that it wanted even more of her.

He was so wrapped up in his blissful fantasy, he didn't realize she was squeezing his shoulder until he felt her claws dig into his skin. He jerked his head up and saw that the claws on the hand cupped in his were extended as well. They might have been more feminine and graceful than any other werewolf's he'd ever seen, but they looked exactly like what they were—claws.

Xander glanced down at Khaki. Her face was still buried against his chest, but he could still see the tip of one fang as it protruded over her lower lip. He wished he could get a better look. On her, he had no doubt that werewolf fangs looked good.

"Khaki, you're shifting."

He felt her stiffen, but her claws didn't retract. He could only assume her fangs were still out as well. It was hard to tell because she pressed her face even more tightly against his chest.

"I can't make it stop," she said.

The panic in her voice made his gut wrench. He held her closer. "Shh…. Relax, I'm right here. I'll take care of you. We're going to walk off the dance floor and slip out of here without anyone noticing."

She trembled against him. "But what if someone sees me?"

"They won't." He turned, keeping his arm protectively around her as he headed for the exit. "Just keep your arm around me and your head down."

She nodded, slipping one clawed hand in the back pocket of his jeans while trying to hide the other in the material of his shirt. It would take more than a casual look to realize they were anything other than extremely long fingernails. He hoped.

They made it out the door and started down the street to where he'd parked his truck. Khaki still kept her head on his shoulder. He sure as hell didn't mind. It felt good.

"Why is my sense of smell suddenly so much stronger?" she asked softly.

"The closer we are to our wolf form, the better our senses work. Your sexual arousal has pushed you to the edge of a full shift. What can you smell?"

She was silent except for the cutest sniffing sounds

he'd ever heard. "I smell everything—people, cars, asphalt, the burgers they're cooking back at the bar. But stronger than any of that, I smell you. Your scent is driving me insane."

He stifled a groan. "Trust me, the feeling is mutual."

They made it to his pickup without freaking out any locals. The moment they got inside, Khaki flipped down the passenger visor and used the mirror to get a good look at her fangs. She kept turning her head, clearly mesmerized at how the city lights glimmered off her long, white teeth.

Xander couldn't help but laugh at the stunned expression on her face. "Yeah, they look pretty frigging awesome, don't they?"

"They're so…sharp." Khaki glanced at him, her brows puckering. "They don't look…freaky, do they?"

He reached out to brush her hair back from her flushed face. "They're beautiful, just like the rest of you."

Unable to resist temptation any longer, he kissed her. It was a first for him, kissing a girl with fangs. But Khaki's soft lips paired with the sharp tips of those teeth were a perfect metaphor for Khaki. She was definitely soft and feminine in some ways, but she came with her fair share of sharp edges too.

Even though it was light and tentative, it was the most amazing kiss he'd ever experienced.

Khaki apparently agreed, bringing up her hand and tangling it in his hair, pulling him close and deepening the kiss. The taste of her mouth was so sweet, it almost pushed him into shifting himself. But he couldn't let that happen, not here in a crowded parking lot in the Entertainment District.

He reluctantly pulled back, chuckling as Khaki protested and tried to follow him into his seat. "Let's get you home before we end up doing something compromising right here."

She looked disappointed but didn't argue. Pushing the center console of the bench seat up, she wiggled in close, putting on her seat belt as he did the same. He cranked the engine and put the truck into gear, then draped his arm over her shoulder and pulled out of the parking lot. She let out a sigh and snuggled close. God, he could really get used to this.

Out of the corner of his eye, he saw Khaki's perfect, pink tongue slip out to trace along the points of those sexy-ass fangs of hers. That was so freaking hot!

"Am I going to have fangs and claws every time I'm aroused?" she asked.

He chuckled. "No. Strong emotions—good or bad— can bring on an uncontrolled shift. You've probably noticed that some of the guys shift during training when they get really fired up. Especially those who are newest to this werewolf thing."

"Like me?"

"Like you." He grinned. "Don't worry. When you calm down, everything will go back to where it's supposed to."

He felt Khaki's hand on his thigh, and glanced down to see her sliding her fingers up to the bulge in his jeans. She started caressing, and he damn near drove off the road.

"So I guess you've been a werewolf for a while," she said in a sexy, laughter-filled whisper. "Getting excited doesn't cause you to shift uncontrollably?"

Xander growled. His gums and fingertips ached with the need to shift, not to mention his cock. "Normally, no. But I'm having to work damn hard to keep it under control right now."

Khaki laughed again, this time in his ear. The feel of her warm breath against his skin had his heart racing.

"That's good to know," she said. "I wouldn't want to think this insane attraction I'm feeling is only a one-way thing."

Khaki nibbled his ear as she squeezed his hard-on through his jeans. Xander tightened his grip on the wheel. He wanted her so badly. The urge to pull over to the side of the road and take her right there was damn near overwhelming. It didn't help that he could smell the excitement pouring off her in waves. She was just as turned on as he was. And even though his truck's cab probably wouldn't be the most comfortable place for their first time together, he knew she'd be up for it. But he forced himself to calm down and keep the truck on the road. No way in hell their first time together was going to be in his truck.

Xander gave himself a mental shake and moved his hand down to stop her playful caresses. "Oh, the attraction is definitely mutual. But if you don't stop that, we're going to end up in a ditch, and that would put a serious dent in the rest of the evening."

Khaki reluctantly pulled her hand away with a sound halfway between a laugh and a low, sexy growl, and rested it casually against his chest. His cock complained, but he told it to shut up.

Khaki behaved herself the rest of the way back to her place. She was so quiet, Xander thought she'd fallen asleep on his shoulder. But the moment they pulled into the parking lot of her apartment complex, she sat up and popped the buckle on her seat belt. In the glow of the overhead dome light, he could see that her fangs and claws had retracted, though her eyes still had that beautiful green glow to them.

"You want to come in?" she asked softly.

He leveled his gaze at her. "You know what's likely going to happen if I go in there, right?"

She didn't blink. "Yeah. That's why I'm asking."

The hunger in her eyes was unmistakable. She could get him rock hard with a simple look. He couldn't imagine what it would be like once they both got naked.

But he was eager as hell to find out.

Chapter 10

XANDER HOPPED OUT OF THE TRUCK AND RAN AROUND to open the passenger door, but Khaki was already waiting for him by the front bumper, her hand outstretched. He took it without hesitation. The time for thinking was long past.

He didn't really remember Khaki unlocking the door. There was just the jangling of keys, then they were standing in the entryway of her apartment gazing at each other.

"Are we really going to do this?" she whispered as he closed the door behind them.

Xander didn't answer. Instead, he tugged her close, slid one hand into her silky, long hair, and kissed her. The taste of her mouth made something hungry and primal rise up, and he wrapped his other arm around her to pull her closer. It was time to claim her completely.

As the kiss deepened, he had to fight his body's desire to shift. He had the insane need to let his teeth slip out so he could nip her here and there—just a little.

But he held back the instinctive need to let the animal out, not wanting to scare Khaki. Then he felt her fangs come out as she captured his lower lip and gave it a not-so-gentle bite. That destroyed any resistance he had left, and the next thing he knew, he had her pressed up against the wall of her apartment, one hand under her ass to hold her off the floor as the other ripped off her shirt.

His mouth descended to her throat, kissing here, tracing his tongue there, slightly sinking his teeth into that warm, pulsing area where her beautiful neck met that strong, sexy shoulder. He didn't bite very hard, definitely not hard enough to break skin, but the soft growl Khaki let out was so wild and passionate that he found it hard to hold back.

Her claws dug into his back as she ripped his shirt off his shoulders. He knew she'd scratched him hard enough to bleed, but he didn't care. He never imagined it could feel so good to have a set of claws buried in his flesh, but it did. Beyond words.

That was when he stopped holding back and let his fangs bite just a little bit deeper.

The sound of pleasure Khaki made probably woke the neighbors three streets down, but Xander was beyond caring about that too.

—⁓—

Khaki growled as Xander pushed her up against the wall and let his sharp canines come down on her shoulder. It shouldn't have felt so good, but the pleasure spreading out from her neck and shoulder could only be described as orgasmic.

She dug her claws into his back and urged him to keep going. She'd never been this turned on before, and everything Xander did, especially the biting, only made her burn hotter.

It was crazy. She'd never been into anything remotely kinky like this, had never even been a fan of rough sex before now. But at that moment, all she wanted Xander to do was rip off her clothes and take her right there against the wall as hard as he could.

And Xander seemed more than willing to do everything she desired, ripping off her shirt, then shredding her bra with his claws. He shoved her higher on the wall and closed his mouth on her tingling nipples, suckling on them. When one of his fangs lightly grazed the stiff peak, she growled and wrapped both arms tightly around him.

Although part of her wanted Xander to pin her to the wall with his hard, muscular body and make her scream for hours on end, there was another part of her that wanted to be the one ripping and tearing clothing, to be the one taking him to the floor and sinking her fangs into him as she climbed on his thick cock and rode him until they both came harder than either of them had ever come.

No, she'd definitely never been into anything remotely this kinky before.

Khaki grabbed a handful of his hair and yanked his mouth from her breasts so she could kiss him—hard. She pushed away from the wall with her other hand, trying to wiggle out of his grasp so she could get him on the floor, but it didn't work. Xander simply put both hands under her ass, picked her up like she weighed nothing, then carried her into the living room. And the most impressive part was that he went back to teasing her nipples as he did it.

The next thing she knew, Xander had her ass planted on the high table behind the couch, knocking a glass vase aside to make room, smashing it to bits on the floor. She'd just bought that vase a few days ago, but she didn't complain. Something told her that vase wasn't the only thing in her house that was going to get damaged tonight.

Xander buried both hands in her hair, bringing his mouth up her throat and across her cheek, then kissing her so hard his fangs nicked her lips. That only made her moan louder and kiss him back just as forcefully.

She was so caught up in the kiss that she didn't realize he'd slid one hand down and unbuttoned her jeans until she felt cool air on her lower belly. She lifted her ass and held on to the table for dear life as Xander yanked off her jeans. They sailed across the room and nearly took out her favorite painting. She briefly wondered if they should dial it down a notch. That silly notion disappeared the moment Xander ripped off her panties and slowly slid his fingers up and down the folds of her very wet pussy.

She couldn't help but notice that his claws were no longer out. Thank God he had more control than she did.

Khaki gripped the edge of the table and leaned back, watching as he teased her. It didn't take long before his fingers were moist and glistening. A deep growl rumbled in Xander's throat and his eyes blazed with fire as the scent of her arousal filled the room. He was in control, but just barely.

At least he was smart enough to stay away from her clit. She was so turned on that even a light touch there probably would have made her explode on the spot. A week of foreplay could do that to a woman.

But soon enough, she found herself growling with frustration. She reached down and grabbed his fingers, pulling them away. "No more teasing."

Without waiting for a response, she sat up on the table and started working his belt loose. It was harder to undo than it should have been. Her claws were still out and she wasn't used to working with them. But with a little help from him, she finally had his belt unbuckled and the buttons of his 501s undone.

A moment later she learned two important facts about Xander. For one thing, he didn't wear underwear. And for another, he had an absolutely perfect cock.

Khaki's pulse quivered at the sight of his long, hard shaft, trying to imagine how good it was going to feel inside her.

Her hunger only got worse as he kicked off his boots and jeans, standing there in nothing but the shredded remains of his shirt, a light smattering of blood running down his left shoulder from where she'd dug her claws into him. But he didn't seem bothered by the scratches. She couldn't bring herself to be too upset either. It was like she'd marked him as her own.

Khaki gazed at him, taking in everything from his beautiful, muscular body to the desire in his eyes to the way a delightfully scrumptious smelling pearl of pre-cum was even now beading up on the tip of his cock.

Conflicting desires warred within her. She wanted to drop to her knees and take him in her mouth right there in her living room. But she also wanted him inside her more than anything she'd ever wanted in her life. It was more than a need for physical pleasure. Something down in the depths of her soul told her she had to be with him, that she wouldn't be whole until she was.

It was a need that couldn't be ignored.

"Take me to bed," she said softly. "Now."

A sexy grin tipped up the corners of his lips, exposing more of his extended canines. She loved his smile—and those fangs.

"We don't have to use the bed," he said. "The back of the couch looks like it might be fun."

Khaki smiled as she sidled past him. "But the bedroom is where I keep the condoms, so we might as well start there." She threw a look over her shoulder as she headed in that direction. "We can try out the couch after that. Then the kitchen table."

———※———

She slowly rolled the condom down Xander's hard shaft, careful to not nick it with her claws and thanking God she'd remembered to throw the box in with her toiletries when she'd packed up back in Washington. Fortunately, they had half a box of the things. They might put a serious dent in her supply tonight.

Xander was lying flat on his back on her bed, exactly where she'd pushed him when he'd followed her into the room. He played nice while she got the condom in place, but as soon as it was ready, he tried to sit up and take charge.

"Uh-uh." She put both her clawed hands on his chest and pushed him back down. "You stay right there."

She let her claws dig in a bit to show him she meant business, but she doubted he even noticed. He probably would have tried to get up if she didn't stop him by throwing one of her legs across his waist and sitting down on him. He stilled the second the heat of her pussy got close to his cock, the glow in his eyes flaring.

Her gaze locked with his, Khaki deliberately reached down and wrapped her hand around his thick length, lining up the tip with her pussy. She wiggled the head around a little, not trying to tease him, but just making

sure he was really wet. Then she slowly took the first
inch or two inside her. Xander grabbed her hips with a
growl and pulled her down all the way.

Khaki gasped as he filled her. She'd never dreamed
having her inside him could feel like this.

She wanted to stay right where she was, with his
cock buried deep inside her. But the werewolf in her
demanded that she move—urgently. With Xander's
hands guiding her, she leaned forward and lifted herself
halfway up, then dropped down hard. Her gasps turned
to growls as she rode him. Every time she came down,
sparkles of light filled her vision, letting her know that
this night was going to be amazing.

Khaki leaned forward even more and pressed her lips
to his throat. She licked, nipped, and kissed, loving the
way Xander's grip tightened on her ass.

She was just feeling the first tremors of an approach-
ing orgasm when he suddenly rolled them over so that
he was on top. She wrapped her legs around him, threw
her head back, and enjoyed the incredible sensations as
he slammed into her wildly.

Now it was Xander's turn to lean forward and lick, nip,
and kiss as he pinned her wrists on the pillow beside her
head. Not that she was complaining. Everything he did,
whether it was with his tongue, fangs, or lips, felt good.
Better than good. Xander knew exactly how she needed
to be touched before she did. Sometimes his touch was
gentle, like when he sucked her earlobe into his mouth and
toyed with it. But other times, like when he scraped his
sharp fangs along her neck and sank them into her shoulder, she thought she might pass out from the pleasure.

The whole time he pounded into her harder than she

thought humanly possible. The slapping sounds of his hips as they smacked into her thighs over and over was the sexiest sound she had ever heard. And the feel of his cock so deep inside her was beyond heavenly.

There was no slow, blissful buildup to orgasm. One moment she was moaning in delight, the next, she was writhing on the bed like a wild animal as her climax ran over her like a truck.

She yanked her wrists out of Xander's grasp, then reached up to dig her claws in his back, urging him to thrust even harder. He definitely understood what she wanted, and he gave it to her, pumping into her so fiercely she knew she was going to feel it tomorrow. But she couldn't care less. She'd never had sex this good—this perfect—before. And if that meant she was going to have to soak in an ice bath tomorrow, then so be it.

The longest orgasm of her life was just starting to ebb before Khaki realized that Xander hadn't come yet. That hardly seemed fair. She clenched her legs around him and squeezed hard, eager to see his face as he came inside her. But clearly Xander wasn't ready to come yet because he reached back, pulled her legs apart, and flipped her over on her hands and knees so fast she barely realized what he was doing. But then he was sliding back into her from behind, pushing her breasts against the mattress as he yanked her back onto his cock.

As Xander began to move slowly inside her, she felt that pleasurable throb that told her that her body was ready for more. That surprised her. In the past when a man had kept going after she'd already climaxed, she had normally been too tender to handle very much stimulation.

Something told her that wasn't going to be an issue with Xander. She was already yearning for him to go faster and harder.

Khaki pushed her ass back, trying to let him know. She would have told him, but she wasn't sure she was capable of coherent speech at the moment.

Xander got the message and started thrusting harder. Maybe it was because she was a werewolf now, but she knew without a doubt that doggie style like this was going to be her favorite position for the rest of her life. The way the tip of his cock thumped into her G-spot with every thrust in this position was driving her insane. She was shredding the blanket and the sheet under it, but there was nothing she could do to stop it. All she could do was hold on and enjoy the ride.

When Xander grabbed her hips tightly with both hands, and started to slam into her so hard it sounded like she was being spanked, she knew he was close to climaxing too.

She threw a look over her shoulder, locking eyes with him. "Come with me."

His gold eyes swirled, glowing brighter. With something close to a howl, he buried his cock deep inside her one more time and found his release.

Her orgasm this time wasn't as hard as the first one, but knowing he was coming with her made it even more special.

Xander collapsed forward, pressing her into the bed as he slipped his arms under her and squeezed her tightly. The feel of his warm, ragged breath on her neck was a perfect way to end the best sex of her life. If they fell asleep like this, she'd be one happy woman.

But less than a minute later, Xander pushed himself up, then scooped her into his arms.

"Where are we going?" she asked, wrapping her arms around his neck.

He grabbed the box of condoms and headed for the living room. "There's a couch I'm dying to see you bent over, not to mention your kitchen table."

———

"That was amazing," Khaki murmured softly as she lay there with her head pillowed on Xander's muscular chest.

Maybe that was the understatement of all understatements, but at that moment, she simply couldn't put into words exactly what the past few hours with Xander had been like. It was quite possible the right words to describe how good the sex had been with him didn't exist. Or maybe her vocabulary was so limited right now because she'd just overdosed on pleasure. All those orgasms were why she was still lying in Xander's arms right there in the middle of her living room floor. Neither of them could summon the energy to get up and go to the bedroom.

There should probably be a law against a man being so good at making a woman scream in pleasure.

"Amazing, huh?" Xander's voice was a deep rumble. "Yeah, I'd go along with that assessment."

She pushed herself up on her elbow to gaze down at him. "Why did it take us so long to get to this place?"

Xander grimaced. "I don't know. I'm sorry I was such a jackass. I thought keeping you at a distance was the right thing to do. I'm your supervisor and you'd just come out of a bad workplace romance. To be honest, the things you made me feel were so powerful, they scared the hell out of me. But I swear, I never intended to hurt you."

She pressed a finger to his lips, shushing him. "That's behind us now. It was a tough wall for both of us to get over, but we're on the other side now and that's all that matters. If it makes you feel any better, I didn't exactly know how to deal with the things you were making me feel either."

Khaki slid her finger off his lips, down his neck, then across his chest and stomach, snuggling against him again. The sex in the bedroom had quite possibly been the best she'd ever had. But then Xander had dragged her out to the living room, reminding her that the night was just getting started. That's when she'd gotten her first inkling of how much stamina a werewolf possessed. And speaking of werewolf abilities she hadn't known anything about, it turned out that she had a few herself. One of those happened to be flexibility, as she'd discovered when Xander had bent her over the back of the couch in a few ways that she hadn't thought were possible. Even now, she shivered when she thought how hard she'd come while he pounded into her from behind. And from the side. And the front. And upside down too, if she remembered right.

Her gaze wandered from the torn couch cushions to the broken chair beside the kitchen table. She didn't remember how the chair had ended up that way, but she definitely remembered riding Xander while he'd been stretched out across the top of her heavy wood-and-tile dining room table. She'd set a nice, slow pace while he laid back and enjoyed the view. She'd done things to her own body on that table she'd never done in front of another man, and it had been the hottest thing ever. Xander must have thought so too. He'd come so hard he left claw marks in the wood.

But the best part of the night had happened right here on her living room floor. That was where Xander had proved to her that sex didn't have to be hard and vigorous to be great. Riding comfortably between her thighs with slow, measured thrusts, the climax he'd drawn out of her had been the longest, most powerful thing she'd ever experienced.

As hard as it was to believe, thinking about all that amazing sex was starting to get her hot again. After all the orgasms she'd had, she should have been good for a month. Any other time, she would have been.

But that was before she'd become a werewolf. And before meeting Xander.

Khaki was toying with the notion of wiggling down his perfect body to see what she could do to encourage him into going one more round when something suddenly occurred to her.

"What time is it?" she asked.

"What?" Xander mumbled in a sleepy voice.

She pushed herself up on her elbow again, trying to get a look at the clock on the wall in the kitchen. It was still dark outside, but it had to be getting close to sunrise.

"What's wrong?" Xander asked.

She bit her lip, turning back to look at him. They'd both made the conscious decision last night to give in to the undeniable attraction that existed between them and sleep together, but that didn't mean he was ready to throw away his career. Neither was she.

"My car is still at the compound," she said. "We need to get there before anyone else gets into work, or they'll know exactly what happened last night."

"Shit, you're right. I didn't even think of that." He sat up, giving her a hard kiss on the lips. "I blame that completely on you, of course."

She laughed. "I thought I was pretty good, but thanks for confirming it."

Khaki stood up and walked into the kitchen to check the clock. Behind her Xander mumbled something incoherent and thumped back down on the floor. "God, Khaki, what did you do to me? I'm so tired I can't even stand up."

Her eyes went wide when she saw the time. She knew they'd been going at it for a while, but four hours?

"Well, you better get it together," she called to Xander. "It's already four fifteen. If we're going to beat everyone else in, we need to be at the compound in an hour."

She turned and went back into the living room to find Xander still lying where she'd left him. He looked so damn yummy, it almost made her resolve crumble. And the scent he was putting off? In-freaking-credible. If they'd had the time, she would have been over there rubbing up against him like a puppy.

He opened his eyes and looked at her sharply. "Stop that."

"Stop what?"

"Stop smelling like you're thinking about walking over here and eating me. If you actually want us to make it to work on time, that is."

She already knew Xander could smell her arousal,

but she didn't realize her body transmitted her desires so immediately. She was going to have to remember that.

Khaki took a deep breath and tried to think of something else besides jumping Xander's bones. The only thing that kept popping into her head was the Stay Puft Marshmallow Man. Her *Ghostbusters* memory must have worked because Xander's eyes went back to their usual brown.

"We need to shower," he said as he got to his feet. "And I mean really shower. We have to get our scents off each other or every guy on the team is going to know what we've been up to."

She hadn't even thought of that. "Do you think showering will help? Is it crazy to think we can hide the fact that we're sleeping together from a pack of werewolves who can smell the slightest trace of scent? What if we slip up and forget to wash behind our ears?"

"It's worse than that," he said. "There are a couple guys on the team—especially Gage and Mike—who are walking lie-detector machines. They can pick up on stress responses, changes in breathing patterns, elevated heart rates, the whole bag of donuts. We'll have to be careful what we say when we talk about each other and what we tell them to cover ourselves when we're together, or they'll catch us that way too."

Crap. She wasn't a very good liar. She ran a hand through her hair. "It is crazy to try this."

Xander put his arms around her, resting his cheek against her hair. "Probably, but I can't see any other way short of us walking away from the Pack. Or each other."

Khaki didn't answer. She wanted to be in the Pack and on the SWAT team more than anything. She'd worked hard to get here, and she wasn't ready to give it up.

But at the same time, she wanted Xander too—with an intensity she knew it would be impossible to ignore. Openly declaring their relationship to the Pack wasn't a possibility, not if they hoped to keep working together.

Xander was right. They'd have to try and keep their relationship secret. It might be impossible and was likely going to blow up in their faces, but they didn't have a choice.

She went up on tiptoe and kissed him. "I'm not walking away from anything."

He smiled down at her. "Good. Then let's get cleaned up."

Chapter 11

"YOU SHOULD KEEP YOUR SHIRT OFF ALL THE TIME," Khaki said.

Xander glanced at her as he turned onto the road leading to the SWAT compound. She was sitting as far away from him as she could, which was too far away for his liking. He would have preferred to have her snuggled up close like she'd been last night on the drive to her place. But they couldn't take the chance of getting their scents all over each other again.

Any thought of wearing the same shirt he'd had on last night had disappeared the moment he'd found it this morning, shredded to pieces on the floor of her living room. He was going to have to remember that in the future or he'd be going through a lot of shirts.

"Maybe I will." He grinned. "If you ask nicely."

"I can think of one or two ways to ask nicely I'm sure you'd appreciate," she said with a husky laugh that did crazy things to his cock.

Down, boy.

Khaki had been quiet for most of the ride, clearly lost in her own thoughts. Xander was feeling a little subdued himself. Not because he was worried about the Pack learning their secret, but because he was completely at peace with the decision he and Khaki had made to be together.

He realized now that he hadn't fully appreciated how

hard his inner werewolf had been snarling at him to say the hell with the rules and give in to his desires to be with Khaki. Now that he'd taken that leap, it was like his conscience was assuring him he'd done the right thing.

While his mind might have been calm, his body was anything but. Even though they'd made love for hours last night, his need for Khaki burned like a flame deep inside him. Every time he looked her way, those glowing embers threatened to grow into a roaring fire. But if they wanted to not only be together, but work together too, they were would have to control their attraction to each other.

It helped that Gage had called Xander's cell phone right before he'd been about to step into Khaki's shower. Nothing like hearing your boss's voice at five o'clock in the morning to banish all those sexual thoughts.

Gage had wanted to let him know that the FBI bank robbery task force was having another big, multi-agency meeting and they wanted SWAT to be there. Another bank had been robbed last night and all the evidence pointed toward it being the same crew that had hit the bank on Jackson.

"It was a big haul and the FBI didn't have a clue it was going down," Gage told him. "I think they're starting to feel the pressure on this one and it's making them more willing to work with the locals."

After the way the last bank job had ended, with Khaki essentially calling Thompson a dumb shit in front of the entire world, Xander thought his SWAT team would be the last people the FBI would want to work with.

"The meeting starts at eight," Gage added. "Who do you want to take with you?"

Xander's gut was to bring Khaki, but he hesitated. He didn't want to single her out and make it look like he was playing favorites.

"Becker and Cooper, I guess," he finally said. "They need the experience working with the feds."

"What about Khaki?"

"I thought that might not go over too well with the FBI agent in charge," Xander said. "Especially after the way Khaki got in his face the other day."

"All the more reason to bring her then," Gage said. "It's time to show the feds we're not going to play nice anymore."

Xander didn't argue. Suddenly, the idea of spending hours sitting in a big conference room listening to boring FBI briefings didn't seem so bad, not if Khaki was there.

Besides, the meeting got him and Khaki out of PT, and for that he was glad. He wasn't sure he could get through a workout smelling the pheromones she put out when she exercised. He'd have to deal with it later, but after the night of earthquaking sex they'd had, he wasn't sure he could survive it.

"Do you think we showered enough?" Khaki asked as they neared the compound.

Xander leaned over and gave her another sniff. While she still smelled as irresistible as ever, there was no scent on her but her own, mixed with the collection of fruity bath soaps she'd washed with.

"No, you're good. You smell like you were hit with a daisy grenade. How about me?"

She laughed and leaned over to take a sniff. Then she sat back, an amused look on her face. "I definitely can't pick up my scent on you. Hell, I can barely smell yours. I can't believe you washed your whole body with a bottle of antibacterial hand soap."

He shrugged as he pulled into the compound. The parking lot was empty except for Khaki's Mini. "It all smells like soap to me."

She shook her head but said nothing as she hopped out of his truck and got in her car to start it. She was smart enough to know that she needed to run the engine to keep the guys from knowing it had been sitting there all night.

While she did that, Xander ran up to the locker room and changed into his spare uniform. He was only half-finished when he heard her on the stairs. He looked up to see her watching him. The hunger in her eyes was unmistakable.

"Is now the best time to be doing that?" he asked.

She smiled. "Doing what? I'm just watching."

He pulled up his uniform pants, having to work them over his growing hard-on. "Right, just watching. Well, you can watch all you want, but don't go getting aroused. The scent is hard to miss."

Khaki put on a fake pout as he pulled on his T-shirt and tucked it in, then started lacing up his boots. "I'll try, but it's going to be hard not thinking about what we did last night."

It took every bit of willpower Xander had to stay where he was. He had to keep a little distance between them because if he got too close, he wouldn't be able to keep himself from kissing her. And if they kissed...

"I know it's hard," he said. "It is for me too. But it's what we're going to have to do if we want to make this work."

"I know," she said softly. "I'll do whatever I have to do to be with you."

———∿∿∿———

Xander and Khaki were at FBI headquarters with a couple of the guys from the squad waiting for the briefing to start when Becker leaned over and asked her what happened last night.

"What do you mean?" she asked.

"I thought Xander was going to bring you back to the compound to pick up your car, but when we stopped by around three to pick up our vehicles and go home, your Mini was still there."

Her gaze darted to Xander. "Um…"

Oh, shit.

"We stopped to grab coffee on the way back from the club, and ended up spending the next two hours chatting about department politics, evaluation forms, and promotion criteria," he said. "By the time we realized how late it was, Khaki was too tired to drive, so I dropped her off at her place, then picked her up this morning."

Cooper slanted him a strange look. "You brought her into work this morning?"

Xander didn't think Cooper had the experience necessary to tell when someone was lying, and he knew Becker sure as hell didn't. He shrugged. "Yeah."

That must have been good enough for Becker because he changed the subject—something about drinking shots out of syringes last night. Cooper, on the other hand, didn't look as satisfied, and Xander knew he and Khaki were going to have to watch out for him. Cooper was probably one of the most instinctive werewolves on the team. He might not be able to read all the signs that Xander was lying, but he had a gut that would tell him something was fishy.

Fortunately, their favorite FBI agent chose that moment to make his entrance and walk straight to the whiteboard at the front of the room.

Thompson slapped a picture of a dead woman on the board. About thirty, she had blond hair and a face that had probably been pretty when she was alive.

"Greta Dobson was found in an alley this morning with her throat slit," Thompson said. "We've identified her as the person who called in the tip about the bank robbery on Jackson. We know it's her because whoever killed her left a hundred-dollar bill stuck to her chest with a knife through it. They figured out she tipped us off and executed her."

Xander cursed. He'd known this was going to happen.

"The bank the gang hit last night rarely, if ever, has more than a hundred thousand on hand, except for twice a year during regional currency exchanges," Thompson continued. "Last night the bank was carrying nearly four times that amount, and the gang knew about it. They were in and out of the bank in less than two minutes, including the time it took them to blow through a sixteen-inch-thick vault door. As usual, they left nothing behind that we can use, and without Greta Dobson, we don't have a clue which bank they're targeting for hit number three."

"You really think they're ballsy enough to hit another bank in this town now that they have everyone's attention?" a DPD officer in the back of the room asked.

Xander knew he should keep his mouth shut since

this wasn't his party, but the way they'd killed that woman, then left a hundred on her, knowing the FBI would find out, pissed him off.

"These guys are arrogant to a fault," Xander said. "They're going to stay and rub this in our faces. You can bet on it."

For a moment, Xander thought Thompson would disagree simply to be an asshole, but the fed nodded. "That's the FBI's position as well. We have to assume the crew will still follow their same MO and hit another bank soon, if for no other reason than to show they can."

Unfortunately, the FBI didn't have a clue where the crew was going to strike next. Which was why they'd wanted everyone at this briefing, including SWAT. The feds needed access to every confidential informant and source the Dallas PD community had available. They knew it was the only way they were going to catch the bank robbers, especially now that their own source of information was dead.

So they spent the rest of the day calling everybody they knew, hoping someone had heard a rumor about somebody hitting a bank. While the tips came in and they started a list of possible targets on the whiteboard, Xander could tell that no one had confidence in any of them. His gut told him the bank robbers were going to hit their next target without anyone knowing about it in advance. These guys just seemed too good.

When they got back to the SWAT compound, Gage asked Xander, Mike, Jayden, and Cooper to come into his office to talk about what bank the robbers might hit next. Xander had hoped to give Gage a quick run-down of the meeting with the FBI, then take off, but he couldn't bail, no matter how much he wanted to. It would be out of character for him and might make the guys suspicious. So he supported his end of the conversation as they discussed possible bank targets and where they might find reliable sources of info on the suspects.

Xander was doing little more than nodding occasionally while he thought about his date with Khaki that night when he realized the guys were talking about everyone's new favorite subject—*The One*.

"What if you don't realize the woman you're with is *The One* and you screw up the relationship before you even have a chance to see where it could go?" Jayden asked.

"I don't think you have to worry about that," Gage said. "When you meet *The One*, you'll know it. She'll latch on to your soul like a dog with a bone and won't let go. No matter what either of you say or do, it won't change the fact that you're destined to be together."

Xander couldn't argue with that. He only wished he would have realized it earlier, so he hadn't wasted time trying to fight it.

"But what if you meet her and the stars don't line up for you," Cooper asked, leaning back in his chair. "What if she's married? Or wants you to leave the Pack? What then?"

Gage shrugged. "There wasn't anything I wouldn't have given up to be with Mackenzie. I would have left the Pack to be with her, if it came to that. Trust me, if you're lucky enough to find *The One* for you—and I hope every one of you are—grab on to her with both hands and don't let go."

Xander felt his heart beat faster. He wondered if Gage would be giving the same advice if he knew Xander had found *The One*, and that she was on the SWAT team.

———

Khaki wanted to hang around and wait for Xander, but she got the feeling he was going to be stuck in Sergeant Dixon's office for a while. It might look suspicious if she sat at her desk with her eyes glued to the door for the next couple hours. She hoped the meeting didn't run that long, because she was going crazy already. Even though it'd barely been more than twelve hours since they'd made love, she was already going insane with the need to be with him again.

So instead, she gave Mac a call to see if she could stop by.

"Definitely," Mac said. "I want to hear how things are going with Xander."

Khaki laughed as she squawked her tiny tires out of the SWAT compound parking lot. Mac was definitely in for one heck of a surprise.

Mac was waiting for her with a glass of iced tea and a bowl of pita chips.

"Okay, what's the scoop?" Mac asked as soon as they sat down. "Is Xander still being his usual abrasive self?"

Khaki sipped her iced tea, then grabbed some chips. She should probably draw out the suspense a little and tease Mac with the truth, but she'd never been very good at playing games. Mac was her friend, and talking about her relationship with Xander was the reason she'd wanted to hang out with her in the first place.

"Xander and I slept together," she said

matter-of-factly, then added, "Although, if we didn't actually sleep, does it still count?"

"You slept together?" Mac's eyes went wide. "Last night?"

Khaki laughed, loving that she had someone she could share this with—someone who wouldn't freak out about the fact that she'd just admitted to sleeping with her boss. A boss who also happened to be a werewolf.

"Last night," she said. "And again this morning."

"Okay." Mac blew out a breath. "Maybe you should start from the beginning because the last time we talked, you were pretty sure Xander didn't like you at all."

Khaki shrugged. "I was wrong about that."

"Obviously." Mac grinned. "Spill. How did everything change so fast?"

Khaki sat back and sipped her iced tea again, then told Mac everything that had happened, starting with what had transpired down in the tunnels when they rescued Melissa Kincaide, detailing exactly what it was like to smell Xander's attraction to her rolling off him in waves, then what it was like finally being with him, and finishing with their decision to keep seeing each other— and hide it from everyone in SWAT.

"You know that's crazy, right?" Mac said. "If Gage finds out, he's going to have a cow—horns, balls, and all."

"I know, but what else can we do? Neither one of us wants to lose our jobs or our place in the Pack, but ignoring this thing between us is impossible. I know it sounds crazy, but sometimes it seems like I need Xander more than I need air."

"It's not that crazy. Gage went through the same

thing, so I've seen firsthand what it's like when a werewolf finally meets *The One* he's destined to be with."

"What do you mean, 'when a werewolf meets the one he's destined to be with'?"

Mac looked up in surprise, a pita chip halfway to her mouth, but then shook her head. "Xander didn't tell you, did he?"

"Tell me what?"

Mac sighed. "Men can be so dense sometimes. Well, if you could get them to talk about it, I'm sure the guys would do a better job of explaining this, but basically, there's this folklore that says there's one, and only one, perfect mate out there for every werewolf. You know, like a soul mate. When a werewolf finds this one-in-a-billion person, the feeling is supposedly something akin to getting hit by lightning and cupid's arrow at the same time."

Khaki almost laughed at how crazy that sounded until she realized that Mac had just described how it had felt when she'd met Xander.

"You don't really believe in that stuff, right? I mean…soul mates? Seriously?"

Mac lifted a brow. "Khaki, you're a werewolf. You can grow claws and fangs, see in the dark, shake off getting shot like it's nothing, and at some point you'll probably be able to shift completely into a wolf. As amazing and insane as all that sounds, you've accepted it without doing much more than batting an eye. But when I tell you that werewolves can sense when they're around the person they are meant to be with forever, that you have a problem with?"

Khaki didn't say anything. When Mac put it that

way, everything that had been going on between her and Xander made complete sense. There was more to her attraction to him than some out-of-control werewolf hormones. She'd been essentially bonded to him since the moment they'd met. Deep down, she knew he was the man she was meant to spend the rest of her life with.

"Yes, he is," Mac said with a smile.

Khaki thought she'd missed something while she'd been daydreaming, but then she realized she'd said that last part out loud and that Mac was simply agreeing with her.

Suddenly, the obstacles she and Xander were facing didn't seem so impossible to deal with. "It makes the prospect of losing our jobs if we slip up and give ourselves away not seem quite so bad now."

"True." Mac reached for a pita chip. "But why don't we figure out a way to make sure you get to have your cake and eat it too by coming up with a plan on how you're going to keep anyone from finding out about the two of you?"

When Xander opened the door of his apartment, it was hard not to pounce on him, but Khaki resisted the urge, instead sidling past him and walking inside.

"I was a little worried you'd still be at work," she said.

Xander closed the door, his smoldering gaze sliding down her body like a caress. "I was a little worried about that myself, but fortunately, Gage has a fiancée to get home to. I stopped by the store after I left and picked up some things I thought you might like—in case tonight's training runs long."

She smiled. "Hope you picked up something for breakfast too. Because I think training might run a really long time."

His eyes flashed gold. "As a matter of fact, I did."

Khaki was just wondering if whatever he bought could be eaten in bed when Xander closed the slight distance between them and kissed her. She twisted her hands in the fabric of his T-shirt, pulling him closer. She felt her teeth elongate and her claws come out as his tongue slipped into her mouth. This time, she didn't worry about them. Instead, she relaxed and enjoyed the sensation of teasing him with her sharp canines.

Xander groaned, weaving his fingers in her hair and urging her back against the wall, his mouth, and fangs, sliding down her neck. She loved when he did that. The combination of his soft, warm lips and those hard, cold fangs really did it for her.

She thought about asking him to take her to bed but decided she couldn't wait that long. The entryway to his apartment would have to do.

Khaki dug her claws in his T-shirt, ripping it the rest of the way off. Always more in control, Xander took care with her tank top and bra. They continued kissing and nipping at each other as he unbuckled her belt and pushed her jeans over her hips, then dropped to his knees and helped her get completely naked.

She'd been ready to yank him back to his feet, but he put his hands on her hips and pushed her back against the wall, apparently deciding he liked being down there just fine—level with her pussy.

She leaned back, growling as he kissed his way down her stomach. She knew exactly where his mouth was going to end up and she wasn't sure she could handle that. She'd never been licked standing up like this. Could her legs even hold up once he started?

Xander didn't give her a chance to voice her concerns. One moment he was kissing and nibbling around her belly button, the next he put his right hand under her left thigh and spread her wide, forcing her to balance on one leg. The position was so sexy she started to tremble. Then he dragged his tongue up and down the folds of her pussy. He was doing a good job of holding her upright because she thought for sure she was going to lose it.

She reached down to bury her fingers in his hair, careful not to scratch him. Xander's nimble tongue immediately zeroed in on her clit, alternating between little circles and broad licks.

"That's so perfect," she breathed. "Right there."

Xander growled deep in his throat. Between the rumbling sound and the flicking of his tongue, Khaki thought she might come before he even got started. Not that she was complaining. This first orgasm had been building up since they'd left her place to go to work that morning, and she was more than ready to let go.

She rested her head back against the wall, held on tight, and enjoyed it.

Since she didn't want Xander's neighbors to call the cops, she did her best to keep her hand over her mouth and stifle the screams when she came. It worked—at first. But then Xander pushed her back against the wall even harder and lifted her off the floor as he licked her.

She said the hell with it then, and screamed.

Only after the last tremors of her climax faded did he finally set her down on the floor again. Her legs were so wobbly she had to reach down and put her hands on his shoulders to keep from falling.

Xander slowly straightened to his full height, grinning like he knew exactly how wicked he was. "I love hearing you scream like that."

She smiled up at him. "I love that you can make me scream like that."

The chuckle he let out was more of a growl. "Maybe we should take this to the bedroom before you fall down."

He took her hand and turned to lead her toward the back of his apartment, but she tugged him back. "Not so fast. You don't think you can make me come like that and just walk away, do you?"

Xander frowned in confusion, but when she pressed him up against the same stretch of wall she'd just been leaning against, he got the idea. And when she started kissing her way down his hard, muscular chest toward his belt, he definitely did.

Khaki dropped to her knees and wrestled with his belt, then the buttons on his pants. She was getting used to working with her claws. She'd just gotten her hand around his rock-hard cock when Xander's soft, deep voice interrupted her work. "You might want to watch out, you know—for those fangs."

Khaki laughed as she leaned forward and moved her lips slowly across the tip of his penis. "Don't worry. I'll be very careful down here."

As she flicked her tongue across the broad head of his thick cock, they both let out a low growl of appreciation. She slowly moved her hand up and down his shaft, using only her tongue to tease the most sensitive parts.

He had given her one hell of an orgasm, and she wanted to return the favor.

She established an easy rhythm, taking her time and working her mouth in counterpoint to the motion of her right hand. She let her left hand roam freely up and down his muscular thighs, then across his abs.

Xander buried his fingers in her hair, not to control her movements, but merely encouraging her. She didn't need any encouragement. She could do this the rest of the night. Although she had to admit she was aching to taste him. If it was like everything else about him, she knew it was going to be amazing.

When his cock started to throb and swell under her touch, she realized she wasn't going to have to wait long. He was getting close, which only made her go faster.

Xander growled and reached down with his other hand to cup her shoulder, trying to get her to stand up so he could drag her off to the bedroom or take her right there against the wall. She resisted. She knew what she wanted, and she wanted him in her mouth.

When he came, it was the most amazing thing she'd ever tasted, combined with the most rewarding and primal sensation she'd ever felt. It was hard to understand exactly why having Xander come so hard like this meant so much to her, but it did. It must have had something to do with the special bond between the two of them that Mac had described. It was like his pleasure was more important than her own.

Even once he was done, she kept him pressed against the wall with one hand. Nibbling. Kissing. Tasting. She couldn't get enough of him. She wanted to keep going just so she could taste him again.

But Xander decided that enough was enough. He reached down and hauled her to her feet. His eyes blazed yellow-gold and his teeth were fully exposed.

"Are you going to walk to the bedroom?" he growled. "Or do I have to carry you?"

Khaki went up on tiptoe and kissed him. For all the intense passion filling the room, the kiss was soft, but she could feel the energy inside him waiting to explode at any minute.

She draped her arms around his neck, slowly and deliberately wrapped one leg around his waist, then the other. His hands immediately cupped her ass to support her.

"Take me to your bed, Xander," she whispered huskily. "And do anything you want."

His eyes flared even brighter at that, a long, low growl rumbling through his body and into hers.

Xander kept his eyes locked with hers as he headed to the bedroom. She was going to enjoy whatever he had in mind for her.

———

"How long before I can get my shifting under control, at least enough so that I won't sprout claws and fangs every time I think about you naked?"

Khaki snuggled against him, her head on his shoulder. The scratches she'd given him healed even as she watched.

When Xander didn't answer, Khaki wondered if he'd finally given in to exhaustion and fallen asleep. But then she realized his heart was beating too fast for that.

"It's different for every person," he finally answered.

"But I wouldn't worry about it. You're learning exceptionally fast. I wouldn't be surprised if you have it under control in a couple of weeks."

She let her fingers trace around the wolf head tattoo on the left side of his chest. "But it seems like I don't have any control over it at all when I'm excited or aroused."

He chuckled. "I seem to remember you having pretty good control over it when you were giving me a blow job. Trust me, I noticed."

She scraped her nails—completely human now—across his tattooed chest and told him to shush. "That's only because I was completely focused on you at the time and not thinking about anything else."

"Which I appreciate," he said. "But I should also point out that you pretty much just proved my point. When you get past the emotions and the excitement, you have it in you to control your abilities. You simply have to learn to focus. It'll come with time. And we have lots of that."

—⚡—

"What made you go through your change?" Khaki asked.

Xander lazily ran his fingers up and down her arm. "I was working narcotics in Kansas City when it happened," he said. "When I first transferred into the unit in late 2003, it was full of really good people. Unfortunately, most of them rotated out a few years later, and the people coming in… Well, they weren't really the same caliber. We went from a unit of cops who would do anything for each other to individuals looking out only for themselves. They started with skimming drugs and money, and it just went downhill from there.

Sleeping with the female CIs and junkies, taking bribes, even selling the crap we confiscated from the dealers."

"Why didn't you transfer out?"

He hesitated. It still hurt to think about how bad things had gotten in such a short period of time.

"I thought about it," he admitted. "But I was young and naive enough to think I could fix the situation if I stayed. Instead, all I did was watch the unit fall apart from the inside out."

"What about your partner?" Khaki asked.

He grimaced, glad she couldn't see his face. "He was a senior detective with lots of commendations and one hell of a reputation for getting the job done the right way. The guy was my frigging hero."

Xander stopped and swallowed hard, then cleared his voice. All this had been years ago. Time should have made the pain fade, but it hadn't.

"I expected him to step up and do something about the crap going on, but instead he started taking money to look the other way and spent more time sleeping with junkies than working."

"And you still thought you could fix the situation on your own?"

Xander sighed. "No. I knew I was in over my head by then. But by the time I finally decided to transfer out, the unit was in the middle of a big undercover operation and my supervisor asked me to hold off the transfer request until it was over. I agreed, thinking that another week or so wouldn't matter."

"Is that when it happened?"

He gently curled the end of her long, silky hair around his finger. "Yeah. We had two new gangs that had been trying to take over the city's drug trade. The plan was to take them both down at the same time. The idea was to use their greed and distrust of each other against them, making them rush into buying our drugs rather than letting the other gangs get them first. It would have been hard to pull off if everyone had had their heads screwed on straight, but with the cops we had, it was a disaster waiting to happen. We didn't find out until later, but the gangs knew exactly what we were planning. And rather than run, they decided to send a message to the entire KCPD by killing all of us."

Khaki inhaled sharply. "Oh God."

"I'd never been in anything remotely like what happened that night. It was a frigging bloodbath."

Xander didn't even know he'd shifted until he felt Khaki's hand on his arm. He glanced down to see that his claws were completely extended and his fingers were flexing. As if he was trying to rip out someone's throat.

"You don't have to say anything else," Khaki whispered, taking his hand in hers.

He forced his claws to retract, then took a deep breath. "My partner—the guy I practically used to worship—turned tail and ran. Some drug dealer shot him in the back before he could get ten feet. I got hit five times as I tried to drag him to safety, but it was too late. He died in my arms. I should have died too, but I didn't. That's when I changed. Gage found me a few weeks later. I was confused about what was happening to me, pissed off at the idea of being a cop, and ready for a career change, but then he told me he was building a team that would be tighter than any other law enforcement unit in existence, and I jumped at the offer to join SWAT. I wanted to work with people who put their teammates first and remembered why the hell they were doing this job in the first place."

Khaki's eyes filled with tears. "I guess I understand now why you were so adamant at first about not getting involved with me."

Xander gently wiped a tear from her cheek. "What do you mean?"

"I think that part of you was worried that if you let yourself get involved with me, you'd be doing the same thing all those other cops in Kansas City did—putting your own interests before the good of the team."

His first instinct was to deny that his past had anything to do with how he'd treated her, but then he stopped and thought about it. "Maybe," he finally said. "But all I ever wanted was to do right by you."

Khaki put her head back on his chest and snuggled close. "Don't ever worry about that. You definitely did. It may not have been the way the rules say it should be done, but for us, it's the right thing."

He smiled and pressed a kiss to her hair. "I know that now. Forgive me for being a slow learner?"

She scratched her nails across his abs, making him jump. "Of course. You're a guy—I expect it."

Xander folded one arm behind his head and relaxed, letting his other hand play in her hair. It was funny. He hadn't thought about that night back in KC in a long time, but now that he'd told Khaki what happened, he realized there'd been a weight sitting on his chest. It wasn't gone completely, and probably never would be, but it was lighter than it had been. And it was all thanks to the amazing woman lying next to him.

Chapter 12

"So, why do you need clothes again?" Xander asked as Khaki dug through her panty drawer.

They'd had this conversation already, when she'd mentioned she wanted to come over to her place and pick up a few things. If he had his way, she would stay naked the whole weekend. While that was definitely an appealing thought, it was rather unrealistic. They could spend only so many hours having sex.

"Why do I need clothes?" she said as she found the black lacy pair she'd been looking for. "Two words—burned eggs."

While she'd been making scrambled eggs in the nude this morning, he'd come up behind her, slipped his arms around her, and…well…one thing had led to another… and the eggs had turned into carbon.

"I suppose I can see your point," he acquiesced. "As long as you don't wear too much."

She turned, dangling the skimpy black panties from her fingers. "These work okay for you?"

Xander eyed the tiny scrap of fabric. "Maybe." He gave her a hungry look. "It might help me decide if you model them for me."

She'd promised herself that she wasn't going to let her libido get the best of her again—at least not for a few hours. But the moment Xander's eyes started to smolder, his amazing scent wafted in her direction, and she knew it was hopeless. Just the thought of parading around in front of him in nothing but a pair of tiny panties had her pulse quickening.

"Turn around," she insisted, pulling off her top, then unbuckling her belt. "Or you'll blow the whole effect."

"I don't think that's possible," he muttered, but turned around anyway. "I'm pretty sure we both know what effect seeing you in those things is going to have on me."

Khaki quickly stripped out of her clothes and wiggled into the panties. She turned to paw through her bra drawer, searching for something to complete the ensemble when the doorbell rang.

"If you're not expecting someone, I hope you plan on ignoring that," Xander growled.

Khaki was more than ready to agree, but the doorbell rang again…and again…and again.

"I'd better answer it." She grabbed her short robe and put it on. "It's probably my neighbor Emma."

Xander grumbled something she couldn't make out. "I'll give you exactly one minute, then I'm coming out—naked. So you better get rid of her fast."

Khaki laughed as she hurried into the living room. She was still trying to come up with some way to get rid of Emma when she looked through the peephole.

"Oh, crap!"

Xander was at her side in a flash, eyes blazing and claws extended. "What is it? Is that asshole Jeremy back? I'll fucking—"

Khaki turned and slapped a hand over his mouth. "Worse. It's Cooper, Max, and Becker!"

He stared at her in confusion as she took her hand

away. He lifted his nose a little and sniffed. "Shit," he whispered. "I can't smell anything over your... Well, over you. I didn't even hear them."

"What are we going to do?"

"Maybe they'll just leave?" he asked hopefully.

That thought was dashed when one of her new team-mates banged on the door.

"Hey, Khaki! It's us," Becker said. "Get your lazy butt out of bed and answer the door. No way are you lying around your first weekend off. We're taking you on a tour of Dallas."

She pushed Xander toward the bedroom, whisper-ing as they went. "I'll get rid of them, but you've got to hide."

He agreed with a quick nod and looked around her bedroom before heading for her closet. She didn't have a chance to tell him not to bother. He figured that out on his own when he opened it and saw that the tiny space wasn't even big enough for her minimal amount of clothes, much less a guy his size.

"Khaki!" Cooper shouted. "You okay in there? What's all the noise? Do you need help?"

"I'm fine," she called out. "I'll be right there."

Crap, crap, and double crap.

"The bathroom," she told Xander urgently, then realized that hiding him from sight only addressed half the problem. "Wait! Aren't they going to be able to smell you?"

"Shit, you're right," he muttered. "I'm not good at this clandestine stuff."

Neither was she. But they'd better get good at it—quick.

She grabbed Xander's arm and tugged him into the en suite bathroom, then turned on the shower and pointed at the bottles of shampoos and shower gels in the caddy hanging from the wall. "Dump one of those all over you."

He frowned. "Which one?"

"All of them."

Before he could ask anything else, she dashed into the living room and yanked open the door. Becker's eyes weren't the only ones that widened when they saw her. Cooper and Max looked just as shocked to see her standing in the open doorway in nothing but a short bathrobe.

"Sorry," she said. "I was just getting ready to take a bath."

"No problem," Becker said with a nod, still trying hard to not look anywhere he shouldn't. "But now that we're here, you want to skip the bath and go out with us instead?"

"We hate the idea of you hanging out by yourself the whole weekend," Cooper added. "The Cowboys have a home game this weekend, and since we know security, we can get in and watch them practice."

"Then maybe head out to the Mesquite Arena to catch some of the rodeo," Becker said. "Or go to the State Fair."

Khaki grimaced. If she didn't have Xander getting soggy in her shower, she would have jumped on their offer in a second.

"I'd love to, but I'm going to have to pass," she said. "I kind of made plans to spend the day pampering myself. It's been a really long week."

"Pamper yourself?" Becker glanced down to take in

what he had to assume was her naked body under the robe, then quickly snapped his head up again.

Khaki stifled a laugh. "Yeah, you know, light some candles, take a long soak in the tub, wash my hair, paint my toenails. Girlie stuff."

Max frowned. "You'd rather soak in a bathtub than hang out with us?"

"No, but… It's just that I really need some me time to chill out and destress a little. I'm really sorry, guys. Rain check?"

"Definitely," Cooper said. "And no need to apologize. Next time, we'll call first."

She grinned. "Sounds like a deal."

"Guess we'll let you get back to your bath," Becker said, the disappointment obvious on his face.

"Thanks for thinking about me," she said. "You don't know how much I appreciate it."

"Anytime, Khaki," Cooper said. "You're a member of the Pack now, and don't you forget it."

She was about to assure him that she wouldn't when he suddenly sniffed the air. "When was Xander here?"

Crap. Cooper must smell Xander's scent on her.

"Xander?" she echoed.

"Yeah." Cooper sniffed again. "I can smell him in your apartment."

Khaki's mind went completely blank as she scrambled for what to say. "Um…he stopped by earlier to drop off some training material he wanted me to go over—first-aid stuff. I haven't looked at it yet though."

"Oh." Becker snorted. "Sounds like him. No matter how fast you're learning, it's probably not fast enough for him."

Khaki let out the breath she'd been holding. "Guess not."

"See you on Monday," Becker said.

"Have a good weekend," Max told her.

They turned to leave, but Cooper stayed where he was, studying her with an intensity in his dark eyes that made her squirm. Khaki had no idea what was going on, but she could practically see the gears turning in his head, and she didn't like it.

"I should probably get back to my bath before it overflows," she said, hoping to nudge him on his way. "I left the water running."

"Yeah. Gotta take that long soak in the tub, right?"

She wasn't sure what he knew, but he knew something. She forced herself to smile. "Right. See you on Monday?"

She braced herself, expecting Cooper to call her out right there in front of the other guys, but instead he smiled and gave her a nod. "See you then."

Khaki stood in the doorway, watching them walk down the hall. They gave her a wave before getting in the elevator, and she waved back. She let out a sigh of relief. Apparently, her paranoia had been misplaced.

Locking the door, she raced into the bathroom and jerked the shower curtain back to see Xander standing there with a sexy grin on his face, shampoo in his hair, and shower gel slowly running down his naked body. He might smell like he'd been locked in a Bath & Body Works store during an earthquake, but he looked hot covered in all that soap.

She considered teasing him a bit more. She had promised him a big reveal after all. But after making him stand in the shower covered in fruit-scented shower gel for so long, she simply didn't have the heart. She dropped her bathrobe, then her panties, and climbed in the shower with him.

"Sorry it took me so long to get rid of them," she said as she helped him rinse off.

"Don't be. That was some quick thinking."

He got most of the soap out of his hair, then pulled her into his arms for a kiss. She moaned as she felt his erection press against her stomach.

"I think I owe you big for being so calm under pressure," he murmured as he kissed her again.

For half a second, Khaki considered telling him about the way Cooper had looked at her before he left, and her concerns that he might have figured something out. But as Xander's hard-on pulsed against her, she pushed that thought out of her mind.

"Speaking of owing me something big…" she said.

Eyes smoldering, he swung her up in his arms and stepped out of the tub to head for the bedroom.

"Xander, you're getting me all wet and gooey," she squealed.

He laughed again as he plopped her on the bed. "And I've just started."

"Are you sure it's okay to go out in public?" Khaki asked. "What if someone we know sees us? Won't they realize we're a couple?"

Xander grinned. "Becker and Cooper go out together all the time and no one thinks they're a couple."

She thumped him in the chest as they drove along

Interstate 30 toward Fort Worth. "Very funny. I'm serious. I just told the guys a couple hours ago that I'd be
spending the day pampering myself at home. What if
they see us?"

He stopped laughing. Khaki was right. This wasn't
something to joke about. And after the near miss at her
apartment, it was something they were going to have
to address.

He pulled her closer, rubbing his hand up and down
her arm. "Sorry. I didn't mean to make light of your concerns. But it's not like we can hide in our apartments for
the rest of our lives and hope no one ever knocks on the
door. This morning pretty much proved that's not going
to work. But Dallas is a big city. We can go out now and
then. We just have to be careful when we do. If we go to
places outside of the city and stay away from ones where
I know the guys like to hang out, we should be okay."

She glanced up at him, worry in her dark eyes. "And
if someone sees us, what do we do?"

Xander pulled off the interstate and turned onto U.S.
Route 377. There was an awesome Mexican restaurant
he'd found about a year ago down here. He'd never
mentioned it to the guys on the team, and it was too out
of the way for them to stumble across. It should be a
perfect place to have a quiet dinner with Khaki.

"If anyone sees us," he said, "we're just two cowork-
ers having dinner. We're in the same squad. It's expected
we'll go out occasionally."

Khaki nodded, but he could tell from the way she bit
her lip that she was still apprehensive about going out
in public. Until they pulled into the parking lot of the
small restaurant and she finally saw how nondescript

and out of the way it was. She sat up straight and looked around, some of the tension leaving her body when he drove around back and parked.

When they got inside, he asked for a table in the darkest corner of the restaurant, just to be safe. But as they ordered, Xander noticed Khaki throwing nervous glances at the doorway every few seconds.

"So," he said, leaning his forearms on the table. Maybe talking about something else would distract her. "Last night you got to hear about how I went through my first change. How about you? What happened?"

Khaki gave him a curious look. "I thought Sergeant Dixon already told you guys."

Xander shook his head as he tipped back his bottle of beer. "Not all of it. He told Mike and me that you'd run into some problems back in Washington with another cop you'd been seeing and were looking for a new start. He said you'd gotten in a shoot-out, but he didn't give us the details about why you were so eager to leave Lakefront. I'd like to hear about it, if it's something you're comfortable discussing."

She nodded but didn't say anything. Instead, she took a slow sip of her beer, then smiled at him. He loved that smile.

"What do you want to know?" she asked. "You already know about Jeremy, at least enough to know he was a jerk. I don't mind telling you more, if you really want to hear about my ex-boyfriend."

He grimaced. "Maybe we can just skim over those details. I'm more interested in why you became a cop and how you turned into a werewolf. So, let's start with the basics. Did you grow up in a family of cops?"

She laughed. "Far from it. I'm the only cop in my family. Mom is an interior designer, Dad's a financial advisor at a big investment firm in Chicago, and my sisters are in accounting, marketing, and sales."

"Huh. How on earth did you end up being a cop?" The waitress came over with a big basket of homemade tortilla chips with salsa on the side, and he and Khaki dug in as she told him that it was all because of career day in grade school.

"Dad came into my class when I was in the fifth grade and started talking about the power of compounding interest and how important bonds were to the economic growth of the greater Chicago community." She made a face. "I almost crawled under my desk in embarrassment. Then Scott McDaniel's mom came in wearing her Chicago PD dress blues, telling stories about busting burglars and car thieves, and I knew from that day I wanted to be a cop. I was so sure of it that I announced my career choice in front of everyone that night at dinner."

Xander chuckled, imagining a ten-year-old Khaki telling her parents she wasn't following in their footsteps. "That must have disappointed your mom and dad."

"Not really. My dad told me that after listening to Mrs. McDaniel, he wanted to be a cop when he grew up too." She laughed at the memory. "And my mom just wanted me to be happy. Although I think she secretly hoped that my dream of being a cop was merely a phase I was going through."

That was understandable. His own mom hadn't been crazy about the idea of him becoming a cop either. "How did you end up in Washington State? Why didn't you join the Chicago PD instead?"

She nibbled on another chip before answering. "I did try to join the CPD, but they weren't offering the entrance exam when I was looking for work. I was checking out some of the smaller towns nearby, hoping they might be hiring, when my sister, Kirsten, talked me into going out to Tacoma with her on a business trip. She knew I was bummed out about not getting into the police academy and thought it would cheer me up. She also spent a good portion of the trip trying to convince me to go back to school for accounting. I can barely balance my checkbook and she wanted me to be responsible for someone else's money. No, thank you." Khaki snorted. "So, while she was working, I went sightseeing. Long story short, I ran into some patrol officers from Lakefront who told me that their department was hiring. I filled out an application right then and there. Everything else is history."

Over dinner, Xander got the rest of the story, including why she'd started dating Jeremy, when she'd realized he was an asshole, and how bad everything had gone after she'd broken up with him. Although the jerk was out of Khaki's life now, Xander still wanted to rip him a new one for what he'd done to her.

"No one would answer your request for backup because they didn't want to get on this asshole's bad side?" he asked.

"I guess." She gave him a small smile as she started on her second enchilada. "It turned out okay, since that was the night I changed. If I hadn't, Sergeant Dixon never would have offered me a job and I never would have met you."

When she put it that way, Xander couldn't argue.

And while she might be okay with what happened, or at least pretended to be, he was pissed for her. Xander had a very satisfying vision of chasing the guy through the woods and ripping him to shreds. But even if he could, he knew Khaki wouldn't appreciate him fighting her battles. She'd stood up to the man even before she'd become a werewolf, and handled him just fine. Of course, that didn't make the image of him tearing out the guy's throat any less appealing.

Xander didn't want to spoil the rest of the night for her by talking about her jackass ex-boyfriend, so he steered the conversation back to more pleasant subjects—like what kind of training he still had in store for her over the next couple of weeks, and what the workload was going to be like now that she was off probationary status.

They also spent a lot of time talking about what they could do together outside of work. He told her about a few rodeos and sporting events he knew of that were outside of Dallas.

"They're small enough and far enough away that it should be safe for us to go there." He grinned. "Plus I think you'll really enjoy them."

Khaki casually slipped a hand under the table to rest on his thigh. The simple touch did all sorts of crazy things to his body, and he stifled a groan.

"I'm sure I will," she said. "But in case you haven't figured it out yet, it's not what we're doing that I enjoy; it's who I'm doing it with."

Nothing in her expression or tone indicated that she'd slid her hand up to caress his cock under the table. She had one hell of a poker face. But if she kept doing what she was doing, he wasn't so sure if he'd be able to stay so calm. His hard-on was already straining the buttons of his jeans.

"If that's the kind of entertainment you have in mind, maybe we should take care of the check and head back to my place," he suggested.

The nod she gave him might have been nonchalant, but the sexy smile curving her lips was anything but. He'd say it was downright devious.

"You don't feel like hanging around for dessert?" she asked, her fingers toying with the buttons that were keeping her from getting at his bare cock. "Because I was really looking forward to something special to end the dinner with a splash."

He slipped his hand under the table and grabbed hers, keeping her fingers from accomplishing their obvious mission. "If it's a splashy ending you're looking for, then we should definitely go back to my place."

Khaki laughed as he took out his wallet and tossed enough twenty-dollar bills on the table to cover the bill and tip.

"I don't know if I can wait that long," she said. "Maybe I can have dessert while you drive?"

Was she trying to kill him? The image of her giving him a blow job—or hell, even a hand job—made him so hard, it hurt. He bit back a growl and grabbed her hand, leading her out of the restaurant. Khaki was still laughing as they walked around back and hurried to his truck. Halfway there, he stopped and pulled her in for a quick kiss, then led her to his pickup.

Thinking about what she had planned for the drive back to his apartment had him so distracted he barely noticed when she suddenly stopped in her tracks. He heard her growl at the same time he sensed someone materializing from the shadows. He spun around, instinctively pushing her behind him.

A tall, blond guy dressed in a T-shirt and jeans was coming toward them. He wasn't carrying a weapon that Xander could see, but the fact that Khaki was practically exuding anger from every pore was more than enough reason for him to be concerned.

The guy stopped a few feet away, lip curling in a sneer as he looked at Khaki. "I thought it was bad enough that you were banging the SWAT commander to get the job. But now I find out you're screwing your squad leader too. Your friends back in Lakefront would be so proud."

That was all it took for Xander to realize who this guy was—Jeremy the jackass ex. Fury boiled in his gut. No way in hell was he going to let this asshole get away with saying that shit about Khaki. He was going to rip off the guy's head and shove it up his ass. Jeremy would be singing a completely different tune then.

Xander took a step toward Jeremy, but Khaki grabbed his shoulder. He felt the sting as her claws bit through the material of his T-shirt and sunk into the muscles underneath. She'd lost control and shifted again.

"That's right, bitch," Jeremy sneered. "You'd better control your pet caveman, unless you want to see him bleeding on the pavement."

Khaki snorted. "You seriously think I'm holding him back to protect him? Please. The last time you tried to get physical with anyone, it was with me, and I put you down like the loser you are in front of half the Lakefront PD."

Jeremy clenched his jaw, pissed off at the reminder. Khaki had hit a sensitive spot, for sure. Xander would have to remember to ask about it later.

"You bitch," her ex spat. "I'll—"

Jeremy must have thought demonstrating was better than any threat he could come up with because he lunged for Khaki.

Xander met him halfway, catching the fist Jeremy swung at him in one hand and crushing down on it as his other hand shot forward and wrapped around the man's throat, stopping his forward momentum. Xander lifted Jeremy up until his feet were off the ground—and held him there.

Jeremy tried to kick him in the knees, thighs, nuts, and anywhere else his booted feet could reach as he attempted to break the stranglehold Xander had on him. Xander squeezed a little tighter. Jeremy had said things about Khaki that made Xander madder than hell. Snapping Jeremy's neck would have been almost too good for him.

Xander felt Khaki's hand on his shoulder. She didn't dig her claws in this time.

"Put him down, Xander," she said softly.

He glanced over his shoulder at her. He could barely see the tips of her fangs, but they were out. Her eyes were still their usual beautiful brown, but he could tell she was on the edge of completely losing it. Even so, she was also aware enough to know killing Jeremy wasn't a good idea. Xander didn't really want to let Jeremy go just yet, but the guy's eyes were bulging and his face was turning blue. In another minute, he'd lose consciousness.

With a growl, Xander tossed Jeremy backward, watching in satisfaction as he slid across the parking lot a few feet. Khaki ran her hand down his shoulder to hold on to his arm. He wasn't sure whether it was because she wanted to hold him back or needed to steady herself so she wouldn't shift even more.

"Go back to Lakefront, Jeremy," she said. "We're over, and have been for a long time. I've moved on. You need to do the same."

Xander tensed as Jeremy crawled back to his feet. If the man came at Khaki again, Xander would end him and worry about the consequences later.

But Jeremy just spit on the ground in front of them, then wiped his mouth with the back of his hand. In the dark, Xander could see blood mixed with saliva. The stupid son of a bitch must have bitten his own tongue in the scuffle.

"You're not worth the effort. You never were," Jeremy said. "You can screw every member of your fucking SWAT team for all I care."

Giving them one more glare, Jeremy turned and stormed off without looking back. Xander didn't relax until the man got in his car and squealed out of the parking lot. Only then did he turn to Khaki. Her eyes might not have been glowing before, but they were bright green now. Her fangs and claws were completely extended too.

Shit.

"Jeremy must have seen us at my place and followed us here," she said.

"Well, he's gone now." Xander wrapped his arm around her. "Come on, let's go back to my place. We need to get you calmed down or you're going to be sleeping with those fangs and claws tonight."

Khaki didn't resist as he led her to his truck and helped her in. But he couldn't miss the way she kept looking behind them as they drove back to his apartment, as if she expected Jeremy to follow them and pick another fight. If her ex was stupid enough to do that, he deserved what he got.

———

Khaki's eyes were back to normal by the time they got to his apartment. Her claws and fangs were still partially extended though. The fact that she still couldn't control those aspects of her shift, on top of the run-in with Jeremy, seemed to infuriate her even more, which only made it harder to shift back.

Xander took her hand and led her into the living room. "Come sit on the floor with me."

"I don't need a lesson on how to shift," she protested, but sat down opposite him anyway. "I need to shift back."

"I know. Which is why we're going to do the same relaxation technique I taught you in reverse."

Khaki looked dubious but obediently closed her eyes when he told her to. He used the same running-through-the-woods exercise he'd used to get her eyes and claws to come out the first time, but instead of urging her to run faster, he softly talked her through the process of cooling down from a long run, slowly coming up onto two legs, and getting her breathing under control, then feeling the bright sunlight on her face. It took a little while, but after thirty minutes, her claws and fangs finally retracted.

"Why the hell is it taking me so long to pick up this shifting thing?" she growled so fiercely he thought her fangs and claws were going to pop out again. But she took a few deep breaths and got her inner werewolf back under control.

"Because right now, your abilities are at the whim of your emotions, and it's going to be that way for a while. Sometimes those emotions will bring on a shift when you don't want it, and sometimes they'll keep you from shifting when you want to. Until you learn to control your emotions, the wolf inside you will be in charge, not you."

She made a face at him. "You are aware that I'm a woman, right? News flash here, women aren't known for controlling their emotions. It tends to be the other way around."

"Maybe," he agreed. "But trust me, you'll get better at controlling your inner werewolf over time. It won't be long before shifting will be as easy as breathing for you."

Cupping her cheek, he leaned forward and gave her a kiss. When he sat back, she regarded him thoughtfully. He hoped her mind was headed the same place his was—one where clothing was optional.

"Speaking of controlling my inner werewolf," she said. "I heard some of the guys talking about a full shift. What does that mean?"

Clearly, they were going to be keeping their clothes on a little longer.

"It's when a werewolf pushes the shift so far, he—or she—completely assumes the shape of a wolf."

Khaki's eyes widened. "We can really do that?"

"Only some of us," he said. "While every werewolf can come to control the basics like claws, fangs, eyes, and strength, some are never able to achieve a full shift."

"Why not?"

"Because it has nothing to do with how long some-one's been a werewolf. A full shift is a matter of how totally a werewolf accepts their inner beast."

She blew out a breath, making her bangs flutter. "That leaves me out, I guess."

"Maybe not." He took her hand and squeezed it. "The important thing to remember is that being able to do a full shift doesn't mean a werewolf is any more valuable to the SWAT team or the Pack."

Khaki nodded, but Xander wasn't sure if she believed him.

"Can you do it?" she asked.

He hesitated, not sure if he should tell her the truth or not. He didn't want to make her even more bummed about not being able to do it herself. But she'd find out sooner or later.

"Yeah," he admitted. "But it took me years to figure it out, and I can only do it when I'm completely calm. Only Sergeant Dixon, Cooper, and Jayden can do it quickly—'on the fly' we call it. Most of us have to take our time, which is why it isn't something that serves much purpose in SWAT. But it's something we work on together regularly, and we'll help you try it too."

"Can you show me?" she asked. "Just so I can see what it looks like."

"I don't know if that's a good idea," he said. "It's freaky as hell to watch. There are some cracking and popping noises, not to mention some fur growing. That can be a little disconcerting the first time you see it. You sure you're up for something like that?"

"Definitely!"

She looked so excited that he couldn't say no.

"Okay. Just don't freak out when I'm halfway through and tell me to change back. It's not something I can turn on and off."

"I won't," she promised.

Xander stood, tugging her up with him. He moved the coffee table out of the way, then reached over his head to yank off his T-shirt.

Khaki's gaze caressed his bare chest, then settled on his hands, watching as he unbuttoned his jeans. "Not that I mind the view, but why are you taking off your clothes?"

He flashed her a grin. "You ever see a wolf wearing 501s?"

She laughed. "In that case, let me get comfortable." Sitting on the couch, she tucked her legs under her, then threw him a saucy look. "Okay, you can finish getting naked now."

Did she miss the part where he said he needed to be completely calm to do a full shift? Because the blatant desire in her eyes was turning him on like crazy.

Ignoring his rapidly hardening cock, he took off his jeans, then got down on his hands and knees and began taking long, steady breaths. He'd done this in front of the guys a lot of times and never felt nervous, but doing it in front of Khaki was different. She didn't say anything, but he could feel her gaze on him as he stretched his muscles, preparing for the shift.

He hadn't been kidding when he said a full shift

looked freaky. What he hadn't mentioned was that it felt a little freaky too. Transforming his muscles and bones into a different shape required the movement of a lot of stuff. It had felt bizarre and a little scary the first few times he'd shifted, but he'd done it enough to be comfortable with the strange sensations that came with a full shift.

When the bones of his hip and back started to break and pop out of place, he relaxed and breathed through it. Luckily, the same werewolf powers that made gunshots feel like bee stings prevented the breaking bones and tearing muscles from making him pass out from excruciating pain.

Even so, Xander didn't look at Khaki during the change. He didn't want her seeing his face twist and contort as he shifted from human to wolf. Just seeing the rest of his body go through that kind of a transformation was going to be traumatizing enough.

Khaki hadn't run screaming from the room yet. That had to be a good sign.

When he was done, Xander lifted his head and was shocked to see Khaki sitting on the floor beside him. He searched her face, but it was impossible to read her expression.

She slowly ran her hand down his flank. Her touch was tentative at first, then became more confident, her fingers burying themselves in his thick fur. Soon enough, she was running her hands all over him, caressing his fur, exploring his thick chest muscles with her fingers, using her sensitive nose to memorize every square inch of him.

When she got to his head, she went up on her knees

to grab his ears and tug him down for a closer look, her eyes full of amazement. He had an irresistible urge to lick her face with his big, wet tongue, but he controlled himself. She seemed to be comfortable with his full wolf form, but there was no reason to push it.

Gently holding him in place, she moved her face closer until her forehead was touching his much broader one. The position put them almost eye to eye and she stayed like that for a long time, looking at him in wonder.

"You have to teach me how to do this," she said softly. "Seriously, like right now."

Xander chuffed, the closest he could come to a laugh. He should have realized a woman like Khaki wouldn't be scared off by seeing him shift into a wolf. It would just make her want to try it herself.

He wished he had the ability to speak. If he could have, he would have told her that he'd teach her everything she wanted to learn. There was no reason to rush any of this. Now that he'd found his *One*, he wasn't ever letting her go.

Chapter 13

"OKAY," HALE SAID AS HE SHOWED HER HOW TO get a grip on his wrist and shoulder in preparation for a jujitsu-style body throw. "Remember to get your hip into my groin before you twist or you won't have the leverage to throw someone bigger than you without having to rely on your werewolf strength."

Khaki moved slowly through the motions of the martial arts move the team's resident black belt had been teaching them for the last hour. Xander and Trevor were in the office doing paperwork, but the rest of the squad was standing outside watching, already having taken their turn.

She eyed Hale skeptically. He easily had a good eight inches of height and about a hundred pounds of muscle on her. Nobody her size should be taking on a dude as big as he was without having access to werewolf muscles. "So, why can't I rely on my werewolf strength again?"

"Because you might have to take down a suspect where other people can see it," he told her. "It might not be fair, but if a man my size puts a big guy on the ground, it isn't likely to raise any eyebrows. But if a woman your size does it, seemingly by pure muscle—"

"It's going to attract unwanted attention," she finished.

"Exactly." He grinned. "So, let's see what you've got."

Khaki wrapped her hand around Hale's thick wrist the best she could and started the twisting takedown move he'd shown her. But when she came to the part where she was supposed to yank him over her hip and take him to the ground, he stood there like a freaking tree trunk and gave her a shove that sent her sprawling instead of him. That earned her a few laughs from the guys. Not that they laughed very hard since all of them were dirty from getting their asses whooped too.

"You have to use your butt to shove me off balance before you try to throw me, or it's never going to work," Hale said. "Try it again."

She climbed to her feet with a grumble and got back into position, but when she tried it again, she only ended up on her ass.

Hale offered a hand to help her up. "Let's team you up with somebody else and see if it works better." He glanced at the guys. "Becker, get over here."

Becker was at her side in a flash, making her—and everyone else—laugh.

"Be gentle," he said as she got a grip on his wrist and shoulder. "It's my first time."

"Somehow I have a hard time believing that."

Laughing, she shoved him off balance with her hip and executed the flip move. Becker was only a couple pounds lighter than Hale, but he didn't resist quite as much when she started to move. Maybe he was just better at being a practice dummy, or maybe he wasn't as experienced as Hale, but regardless, Becker went over her hip and landed in the dirt with a thud.

She'd done it! She'd put down a guy who outweighed

her by a hundred pounds without using her werewolf strength. She hadn't done it as smoothly as Hale did, and she fell over Becker in the process, but hey, he was on the ground.

The guys applauded as she climbed to her feet and helped Becker up. She was about to ask him if he wanted to try again when she realized he was looking at her strangely. Then he leaned forward and sniffed her. What the hell?

"Why does your uniform smell like Xander?" he asked.

She froze as Max, Alex, and Hale moved closer, apparently wanting to confirm it.

Crap. She was screwed. She and Xander were so busy showering separately to make sure their scents didn't linger on one another, they never even thought about it rubbing off on each other's clothes.

"Becker's right," Max said. "It smells like you and Xander have been rolling around on the floor together."

Actually they had, but neither of them had been wearing clothes at the time.

"It does?" Hale frowned as he leaned in to sniff her uniform top. "I can't smell anything."

"That's because your nose sucks, dude," Becker said, then looked at Khaki. "What, did you and Xander do your laundry together or something?"

Double crap. That was exactly what they'd done. She'd spent the night at his place and tossed her clothes in the washer with his without thinking about it.

The guys were looking at her expectantly, waiting for her to answer. The problem was, she didn't have a clue what to say.

She opened her mouth, not even sure what was going to come out, when Cooper spoke.

"You want to tell them, Khaki, or should I?"

Khaki's heart stopped. Cooper knew. She didn't know how, but he'd figured it out. And now, he was going to tell everyone.

"Um…"

She knew she should answer, but she wasn't quite sure what to say. How did you just come out and admit you were sleeping with your squad leader?

She was still trying to decide if it would be best to just rip the bandage off all at once or drop the bombshell in small, bite-size pieces when Cooper decided she was taking too long.

"Khaki was practicing takedown moves with Xander this morning before you guys got here," he said.

If she'd been at a loss about what to say before, she was absolutely speechless now. She hadn't done anything that even looked like martial arts training with Xander this morning. Wrestling, maybe.

He met her gaze, his dark eyes unreadable. "You might as well admit it. You were trying to get in some advance practice so you wouldn't embarrass yourself, right?"

Khaki had no idea why Cooper was covering for her and Xander, but she wasn't going to look a gift horse in the mouth.

"Um, yeah." She gave them a sheepish look. "I didn't even know how to take a fall, so I asked Xander for some tips. I didn't want to look like a complete idiot out here, at least any more of an idiot than I already do."

She held her breath, sure no one was going to believe

anything she'd said. But they all nodded, as if what she'd said made complete sense to them. Moments later, they were back in training mode, flipping and being flipped.

Khaki couldn't help looking at Cooper out of the corner of her eye every few seconds.

What the hell had just happened?

—∿∿—

It took her over an hour to find an excuse to get Xander by himself in a part of the compound where it was private enough to talk openly. But a run over to the small armory behind the maintenance and training building to pick up some new M4 magazines for the operations vehicle gave her a chance to tell him what had happened that morning.

"Are you sure he knows?" Xander asked.

His voice might have sounded calm as he dug through the cardboard box on the shelf and came out with four thirty-round magazines, but Khaki could hear his heart beating a mile a minute.

"No, but he was obviously lying about seeing the two of us practicing martial arts moves this morning," she said.

Xander grabbed another handful of magazines. "If he knows what we're doing, why the hell would he bother to come up with a lie to cover it up?"

Boots sounded on the concrete walkway outside, accompanied by a scent she knew all too well.

Cooper walked into the armory and closed the door. "I lied to cover your asses since you two are doing such a crappy job of it yourselves."

Khaki's first instinct was to deny everything, but it

was too late for that. She glanced at Xander. His body was tense as if he expected a fight. He exchanged looks with her before turning back to Cooper.

"How long have you known?"

"That you two were attracted to each other?" Cooper asked drily. "Or that you were sleeping together?"

Xander's eyes narrowed. "You knew something was going on between us before this morning?"

Cooper folded his arms across his chest. "Ever since your heart started beating like a crack addict running a marathon the second you set eyes on her that first day."

Khaki did a double take. She looked at Xander. "That happened?"

Xander didn't answer her. "There's got to be more to it than that," he said to Cooper.

Cooper leaned back against the counter separating the main room from the area with the gun safes and high-value cages. "First, there was your bizarre reaction to having Khaki on the squad. That wasn't like you at all. Then there was the way you snapped at her every time she made a little mistake. And let's not forget the way you shook your head any time you got too close to her, like you were trying to shake off her scent."

"I didn't do that," Xander snapped.

Cooper lifted a brow. "Sure you didn't. I could go on for an hour describing all the little stuff you two did to give yourselves away, but it didn't really all come together for me until I saw the way you two interacted down in those tunnels the other day."

"What do you mean?" Khaki asked.

Everything had changed that day, but she couldn't see how he could have possibly picked up on that.

"The level of instinctive trust you two had in each other was obvious," Cooper said. "I would have to be blind not to see it. And I'd have to be stupid to think that level of faith had magically materialized thanks to a few days of good training. You two were linked the second you met."

"But that just meant we had a connection," Xander pointed out. "How did you get from there to us sleeping together?"

Cooper smiled. "I picked up on the scents you two were putting off that night when we all went barhopping. I knew if you hadn't slept together yet, you were seriously thinking about it. But it wasn't until the guys and I stopped by Khaki's place the other day. When I mentioned I smelled your scent in her apartment, she came up with a lame lie about you stopping by to drop off training material. Then she told us she was going to take a bath when I could clearly hear the shower running. It wasn't hard to figure out that she was trying to hide your scent. That's when I knew for sure."

The muscle in Xander's jaw flexed. "Who else have you told?"

"No one." Cooper shrugged. "I figured if you two were willing to put your positions in the Pack at risk, it must be pretty serious between you."

"It is," she and Xander said at the same time.

"Then I'm not going to be the one to spill your secret," Cooper said. "But you have to know this is going to come out at some point. The other guys in the squad aren't stupid. If I figured it out, they will too. But it's not us you have to be worried about; it's Gage. And the thing that will piss him off more than you two having a relationship is the fact that you tried to hide it from him."

"It isn't like we have much of a choice," Khaki pointed out, although she knew he was right. It had been worse than naive to think she and Xander could hide this forever. "We know we need to tell him. Just not yet." The thought of walking into Sergeant Dixon's office and admitting she and Xander were sleeping together terrified her. "Maybe in a couple weeks, after he sees how well Xander and I are able to make this work."

Cooper shook his head. "A couple weeks? You know how crazy that is, right? I figured it out in a few days."

When he said it like that, Khaki realized just how impossible this was going to be. She loved what she'd found here in Dallas—both Xander and the Pack. The thought that she could lose both made her heart beat so fast her chest hurt.

She was so wrapped up in her sudden panic attack she didn't realize Xander had taken her hand until he spoke. "Hey. It's going to be okay."

Khaki tried to nod but couldn't manage it.

"Xander's right, so no freaking out," Cooper told her. "I said this was crazy, but I didn't say it was impossible. We do crazy every day. It shouldn't be that hard to figure out a way to keep this secret until you want to tell Gage. I'll do everything I can to help you guys and run interference when I can."

She blinked. "You will? Why would you stick your neck out like this for us, especially knowing how it's likely to turn out? Sergeant Dixon will be as pissed off at you as he is with us."

"You're a member of the Pack. It's what any of us

would do," he said, then grinned. "You may not realize it, but I'm a diehard romantic at heart, and you two make a hell of a cute couple."

Xander snorted. "Bullshit. You just like breaking rules whenever you get a chance and making life hard on Gage."

Cooper shrugged. "Maybe. I have to admit the thought of seeing him lose his mind when he finds out we were able to keep this from him does provide a certain level of motivation."

Khaki didn't care why Cooper was offering his help. She was glad to have an ally they could trust.

"Thank you," she said.

"You're welcome." Cooper's mouth edged up. "Don't worry. This is all going to work out."

Khaki knew it was insane, but she actually believed him.

They were heading for the door when Xander's cell phone rang. It was Becker saying the FBI had some tips they wanted the squad to check out.

"I am curious about something though," he said to Cooper after he hung up.

"What's that?"

"What does Khaki smell like to you?"

Khaki frowned. What kind of question was that?

But Cooper didn't seem as confused as she did. He shrugged. "She smells like a werewolf…a very feminine werewolf. Good, actually."

"Does she smell the same all the time?" Xander asked.

It was Cooper's turn to frown. "What do you mean?"

"How about the other day, when we did yoga," Xander asked. "What did she smell like then?"

Where exactly was Xander going with this?

Cooper's mouth quirked. "Oh, you mean when she gets aroused?"

Khaki blushed. "Oh God, you guys knew?"

"It's no big deal," Cooper said. "We can smell when all women get aroused. It's a smell that's hard to miss." He looked at Xander. "But in Khaki's case, it doesn't have that much of an effect on us lately."

Now Xander was the one who was confused. "What do you mean, it doesn't have that much of an effect on you *lately*?"

"She smelled really amazing when she first got here." Cooper gave her a sheepish look. "It got all the guys going. But after a couple days, the effect seemed to fade away. We thought it was because we were getting used to her, but now I think it's because she was already falling for you, Xander. I think your pheromones shifted so that the rest of us stopped getting smacked so hard with them."

"So the other day, during yoga…her scent didn't… drive you crazy?" Xander asked.

Khaki covered her face with her hands. Could this get any more embarrassing?

Cooper laughed again and shook his head. "Afraid not. Most of us were too busy trying to twist ourselves into pretzels."

That was a relief. Maybe now she wouldn't have to take twenty showers a day.

———

"So what kind of tip are we supposed to be checking out?" Alex asked from the backseat as Xander parked the SUV at the curb.

Xander cut the engine and opened the door. "An anonymous tip reported seeing several men carrying big black bags and what they thought might be weapons into a house rented by two women."

Khaki surveyed the neighborhood as she hopped down from the front seat. Judging from the dilapidated houses and cracked sidewalks, this part of Oak Tree had seen better days.

Alex snorted. "You're kidding, right? Big black bags and things that might be weapons?"

Xander came around the front to join her and Alex. "If it helps, the tipster said the women living there looked like they were really scared."

Khaki laughed at the look on Alex's face. She couldn't blame him. There had been three more meetings with the feds this week, and it was getting beyond old. Everyone had been sure the gang was going to hit the third, and supposedly last, bank over the weekend. The fact that they hadn't made most people think they'd already left town.

But the feds were keeping the task force together on the off chance that someone could come up with a lead that either pointed toward the next target, or at least gave them some idea who the hell these guys were. Khaki couldn't blame them. It wasn't like they had a choice. It was either stay in Dallas and hope to get lucky, or wait for the crew to strike another bank in some other city, then play catch-up. Just because everyone was working hard, didn't mean they were getting any closer to apprehending these guys. Outside of a list of potential banks that might be ripe for the picking and a collection of anonymous tips, they really didn't have anything. But

Sergeant Dixon wanted them to keep helping, so Khaki and the rest of the squad took turns running down the tips that came in.

They'd spent the last few hours driving all over the city, digging into dozens of useless tips that had come in to the hotline.

She fell into step beside Xander as he led the way up the cracked concrete walkway to the house. While it was in desperate need of repainting, there was nothing obviously suspicious.

"You two check out the back," Xander said. "I'll keep an eye on the front."

She checked the back of the house with Alex, but didn't see anything that made her werewolf senses tingle. When they came back to the front, Khaki walked onto the porch with Xander while Alex waited on the concrete walkway.

A harried woman with bleached blond hair answered their knock, opening the screen door just enough to slip her head out and give them a wary look.

"Can I help you?" she asked.

Xander did the talking while Khaki kept her senses alert. Xander was asking if the woman had seen any strange men in the neighborhood when Khaki picked up a scent she recognized. It took her a few moments to run through her mental database and pull up where she'd smelled it before.

Then it hit her—on the sidewalk that day during the bank robbery on Jackson Street.

She concentrated, trying to narrow it down even further. The scent was from the suspect she'd thrown against the wall.

Khaki threw Alex a quick look and flashed a two-fingered alert sign, then turned back to the woman in the doorway.

"Ma'am, is there someone else in the house with you?" she asked.

Khaki didn't know if the man was there or whether the scent was lingering on something he'd touched, but the question made the woman go pale.

"N-no. I'm alone," she said. "Look, I'm really busy. Could you come back later?"

Xander must have picked up on Khaki's concern because he put a hand on the door as the woman moved to close it. "Ma'am, are you in danger?" he asked softly. "Is there someone else in the house with you?"

Tears pooled in the woman's eyes and rolled down her cheeks even as she shook her head. "No. I'm fine. Really. Please just go."

Xander exchanged a look with Khaki, his hand coming up to rest on the butt of his holstered weapon. Khaki did the same.

"Ma'am, do you mind if my partners and I look inside?" he asked.

The woman shook her head, mumbling over and over that she couldn't come out. Xander took the woman's hand, gently urging her to come out onto the porch.

"You can't go in there," the woman hissed. "I'll get in so much trouble if you go in there."

Xander moved the woman to the side of the porch, then nodded to Khaki. She pulled her sidearm as she entered the house, Alex at her heels. The man's scent was much stronger, but a quick sniff confirmed he was gone.

Alex lowered his weapon at the same time she did, letting Xander know the house was clear before following her as she moved through each room, tracking the scent. His wasn't the only one lingering there. Khaki picked up the scent of the second bank robber in one of the bedrooms. From there it wasn't too hard to follow her nose to a pile of black duffel bags shoved in the back of the closet.

She unzipped the bag to reveal money—lots and lots of money. Alex was calling it in before Khaki even headed out to tell Xander what they'd found.

Xander was sitting on the bottom step of the porch, the woman sobbing against his shoulder. He looked up at Khaki.

"Anything?"

She nodded, dropping down to one knee in front of the woman. "Ma'am, we found some duffel bags filled with money in the bedroom closet."

The woman lifted her head from Xander's shoulder to look at her with red-rimmed eyes, but didn't say anything. The fear reflected there spoke volumes.

"You know who put those bags in the closet, don't you?" Khaki asked gently.

The woman nodded.

"Where are the men now, Shelly?" Xander asked.

Shelly shook her head. "I don't know."

"Did they say when they were coming back for the money?" he prompted.

"No." Shelly sniffed, wiping the tears from her cheek with the heel of her hand. "I didn't even know my boyfriend, Craig, and his buddies were robbing banks until Greta and I found the money. Craig and the other guys weren't too happy we found it, but promised they'd split the money with us if we kept our mouths shut." Another tear trickled down her cheek. "I know it was wrong, but I never had money, and there was so much of it… Greta told me that if we stayed with them, we'd end up in jail or dead. She said that if we called the FBI and told them which bank the guys were going to rob next, they'd arrest them and the two of us could run off to Mexico with all the money."

Shelly shook her head. "But it didn't work out that way. The guys came back from the bank job and over-heard Greta and I talking. They s-slit her throat right in front of me, then told me that they'd do the same thing to me and every member of my family if I didn't do what they said. When they find out you were here…"

Her voice trailed off, sobs wracking her body.

"We won't let anything happen to you, Shelly," Xander promised. "Do you know where Craig and the other guys are?"

It took a while to get anything else out of her because she spent more time crying than talking. But working together, Khaki and Xander finally got the information they needed out of the terrified woman. The crew was hitting the third and last bank in less than an hour. After that, the plan was for them to come back here and grab the rest of the money, then head to Mexico.

Two patrol cruisers pulled up as Shelly finished. Xander promised the woman again that she'd be safe, then handed her off to a female officer.

Khaki barely got in the backseat and clicked her seat belt in place before Alex pulled away from the curb and switched on the flashing lights. As they sped downtown to the bank, Xander called Thompson while Khaki pulled out her phone and got the rest of the squad up to speed, asking the guys to meet them.

By the time she hung up, Xander's conversation with Thompson had turned into a shouting match. After a lot of yelling back and forth, they finally came up with a plan. Since the bank robbers would probably follow the same MO that had worked so well before, Thompson and the rest of the feds would move in from the front of the bank, making sure that the suspects knew they were there. If the crew followed the script, they'd immediately head for their backup escape route, where she, Xander, and the rest of the squad would be waiting for them. If all went well, they'd catch the bank robbers completely by surprise and in no position to defend themselves.

There was only one problem. The whole plan depended on SWAT, the FBI, and the DPD reinforcements getting to the bank and setting up in time, during rush-hour traffic.

Xander kept his cell phone glued to one ear and the vehicle's radio in the other, trying to get all the moving parts to come together on the fly. Khaki used her cell to occasionally check on the status of the rest of the squad, when she wasn't checking the clock on the dash.

She, Xander, and Alex turned onto the street one block over from the main entrance of Suncrest Federal on Preston forty-two minutes later to hear the bank alarm ringing.

"Thompson and the feds just caught the crew as they were coming out the front entrance," Xander said, gesturing to Alex to position the SUV diagonally across an alley between two buildings. "Some of them turned around and went out the back. They should be heading our way any second."

Khaki hopped out of the SUV along with Xander and Alex, drawing her weapon and motioning for the people meandering down the street to get out of the area. She'd just herded the last civilian away when four men in ski masks came running out the back door into the alley. They all carried automatic weapons and black duffel bags that matched the ones Khaki had found in the house over in Oak Tree. The men skidded to a halt when they saw her, Xander, and Alex.

The suspects hesitated. Khaki tightened her grip on her Sig, ready to pull the trigger if the men tried to shoot their way out of the trap.

"Don't even try it," Xander warned, his weapon trained on them. "Your armored getaway vehicles won't be coming to get you because we've already arrested your drivers while they were waiting for you in the parking garage."

The four men looked at each other, then turned as one and started shooting.

The AR-15s they carried could fire a lot of rounds, but this time there weren't any cars and innocent civilians for the bank robbers to hide behind. This time, they were completely exposed.

Two went down immediately and the other two dropped their duffel bags and took off running.

Xander ran after them with a snarl. Khaki followed. If Xander was going to chase them down on foot, Khaki was going to stay with him to cover his back.

It was ridiculously easy to catch the two men, even when they threw down their empty weapons so they could run faster. She and Xander slammed them to the ground before they even reached the end of the block.

Out of the corner of her eye, Khaki saw Xander's suspect go limp as Xander twisted the man's arm behind his back. Her suspect—the man whose scent she recognized from the first bank robbery—must have decided he had a better chance of getting away since she was a woman. He clawed his way to his feet and tried to go for her weapon.

Khaki didn't even think. She simply grabbed the man's wrist like Hale had taught her, threw her hip into him, and flipped him to the pavement so hard his teeth clacked together. He didn't resist much after that. She rolled him onto his stomach and zip tied his wrists.

She stood, turning to smile at Xander when he was suddenly thrown violently backward. Three gaping, bloody holes appeared in his tactical vest as he hit the concrete. Khaki didn't even realize what had happened until the boom of a high-powered rifle echoed in her ears. She looked around wildly, trying to see where the shooter was when another round hit Xander.

Khaki's heart seized in her chest as she rushed over to Xander. Trying to stay out of the path of bullets, she grabbed his hands and dragged him across the pavement to a recessed doorway. She'd just reached the granite-edged corner when a bullet hit her in the left thigh. She ignored it, instead focusing on getting Xander out of the line of fire. Another round slammed into the stone wall just as she got him into the doorway. She dropped to the ground beside him, pulling him into her lap and cradling him there.

"Xander, are you okay?" she asked urgently. "Xander?"

He didn't answer, didn't even open his eyes. Was he even conscious? She slapped her hand down on his chest, shocked at all the blood soaking his shattered tactical vest. There was so much blood.

Alex rushed into the alcove, yelling in his radio for an ambulance and trying to give a location on the shooter at the same time. Then he was at her side, ripping off Xander's Kevlar vest and uniform shirt to reveal three bullet wounds.

Khaki watched numbly as Alex flipped Xander over.

"Shit," he muttered. "There's only one exit wound. The vest slowed the other two down. They're still inside him."

"But he can live through this, right?" she asked. "He's a werewolf. This won't kill him, right?"

But Alex refused to answer, flipping Xander back over and shoving his fingers into his chest, moving them around as he tried to find the bullets.

Khaki gently brushed Xander's hair back from his forehead. "Hang on, Xander. Please hang on." Tears spilled down her cheeks. "I love you, Xander. Do you hear me? I love you, dammit. Don't you dare give up!"

Alex looked at her sharply before focusing his attention on Xander again. Khaki knew she shouldn't have slipped up like that, but right then she was too terrified to care what Alex or anyone else heard her say.

Alex worked out one of the bullets, then went back in to look for the other. But after a few seconds, he slid his fingers out. Khaki thought it was so he could go at it from another angle, but he only kneeled beside her with a grim look on his face.

"What are you doing?" she said, trying to keep her voice calm—and failing. "You have to get the other bullet out!"

"I can't," he said. "The round hit some ribs and shattered them. There are bullet and bone fragments all over the place, and I'm worried some of them may be lodged in his heart. I could kill him if I go rooting around in there and do something wrong. He needs a doctor."

Khaki's heart was pounding in her chest like a drum. It felt like she couldn't breathe. But she squeezed Xander's hand and forced herself to get a grip, for his sake.

"What if a doctor figures out what he is?" she asked through her tears.

"We can't worry about that," Alex said. "If those fragments are lodged in the wall of his heart, and one of them tears through… Even a werewolf can bleed out from a wound like that."

"That's not going to happen," she said fiercely, as if she could make it true by a force of will.

"Not if we can stop it," Alex agreed.

Khaki sat there with Xander's head in her lap, smoothing his hair and telling him to keep fighting, that he was going to make it. She knew he could hear her. As long as she kept talking, he wouldn't give up.

It seemed like an eternity before the ambulance arrived and the two paramedics rolled in the stretcher. When they reached for Xander, she shooed them back with a growl and a glare. Khaki refused to watch the two paramedics struggle with Xander's two-hundred-and-forty pounds of muscle, not if jostling him could kill him. The medics didn't say a word as she and Alex carefully lifted him up and gently put him on the stretcher, nor did they complain when she climbed in the back of the ambulance with him, then knelt down out of the way and begged him to keep fighting.

Khaki looked up as the paramedic closed the back door of the ambulance to see Alex standing there with Xander's blood soaking his arms up to the elbows. Cooper, Becker, Max, Hale, and Trevor stood beside him, their faces etched with the same fear and concern.

Khaki looked down at Xander. She could hear his heart beating over the sounds of the monitors and sirens. His heartbeat was weak and irregular, but it was still there.

She squeezed his hand. Xander wasn't going to die. She wouldn't let him.

Khaki was still standing in the waiting area outside the trauma center when the rest of the squad arrived. She couldn't say how long she'd been rooted in that spot, staring at the doors that led to the operating room, but it felt like a lifetime. She vaguely remembered a doctor asking if she'd been shot. She'd looked down at the blood on her thigh and told him it wasn't hers. He'd left her alone after that.

Sergeant Dixon strode in right behind Cooper and the other guys, looking half-pissed, half-worried.

"What the hell happened?" he demanded.

"Cooper, Hale, Max, Becker, and I found the two getaway vehicles and took them down," Trevor said.

"At the same time, Xander, Alex, and Khaki caught four of the bank robbers as they were fleeing the rear of the bank."

"We had all four suspects cuffed when a sniper hit Xander with three rounds in the chest," Alex said, picking it up from there. "Whatever the sniper was shooting, it went right through Xander's Kevlar vest like it was nothing. One of the bullets fragmented too close to his heart for me to dig it out. I made the call to get him to the hospital."

Dixon nodded. "You did the right thing. What has me confused is why the sniper waited until after his guys had been arrested to start shooting."

Nobody had an answer to that. Until that moment, Khaki hadn't given a single thought to the sniper and why he'd done what he did.

"We had a helicopter conduct a sweep of the area where the sniper had been positioned moments after he shot Xander, but he was already gone," Trevor said. "We questioned the other bank robbers before the FBI took them into custody, and according to them, they didn't have a sniper with them. Whoever the guy is, it's going to take a lot for those assholes to give him up."

Dixon's mouth tightened. "We'll worry about that later. The only thing that matters right now is Xander." He looked at Alex. "How bad was he when you rode in with him? Was he conscious?"

Alex hesitated, giving her a quick look. "I didn't ride in with Xander. Khaki did."

The entire squad held their breath as Dixon turned his attention to her. "You rode in with Xander?"

She nodded.

Something flickered in Dixon's dark eyes, but it was gone too quickly for her to figure out what it was. "How bad was he?"

Khaki tried to report in the same calm, professional voice Trevor and Alex used. But the moment she opened her mouth, her throat locked up and she could barely get the words out.

"The…the surgeon came out a little while ago and said they had to open him up. The bullet fragments nicked a lot of vital areas, and a big piece is lodged in the wall of his heart. The doctor couldn't believe Xander even lived long enough to get him on the operating table. He said Xander was still holding on, but he…he warned me…us…to prepare for the worst."

Tears stung Khaki's eyes. She didn't bother to wipe them away when they ran down her cheeks. She'd been telling herself the doctor had been wrong, that he just didn't know how strong Xander was. But now, standing here in the middle of the hospital with its pungent antiseptic odor and the rest of the Pack around her, she wasn't sure about that.

No one said anything for a long time, and when Khaki finally lifted her head, it was to see Dixon regarding her with that same curious expression. She tried to wipe the tears away, aware that she was acting way too emotional about a fellow cop getting shot. But fresh tears fell, taking their place.

"Khaki, is there something going on between you and Xander that I should know about?" Dixon asked quietly.

She wanted to lie and say there wasn't, but with Xander lying on an operating table, she couldn't. It would feel like she was denying everything he meant to her. She blinked back another rush of tears and nodded.

Dixon swore. "What the hell were you two thinking?"

Khaki didn't answer. What could she say? That she knew being with Xander was wrong? That would be a lie. Falling in love with Xander wasn't wrong, and if that cost her the job, it was a small thing to give up to be with him.

Dixon remained silent, waiting for her to say something. One by one, the guys in the squad moved a little closer to her—first Cooper, then Becker and Max, followed by Alex, and finally Trevor and Hale. Their show of support made her start crying all over again.

"Okay, this isn't the time or the place to talk about this, Khaki," Dixon said. "But when Xander wakes up, we are going to talk about it."

Giving her one more disapproving look, he strode off and pulled out his phone. Khaki heard him talking to Mike on the other end, telling him to get some of the guys out to the bank on Preston and figure out who that shooter was.

Right then, she cared as much about the sniper as she did about her career. All that mattered was lying on an operating room table, fighting for his life. If Xander survived, she didn't need anything else. And if he didn't, she wouldn't care about anything else.

Chapter 14

XANDER WOKE WITH A JERK. THE SUDDEN MOVEMENT sent a harpoon of pain lancing through his chest. He opened his eyes, trying to figure out where he was and why he hurt, but that didn't help much when the room started to fade to black. He closed his eyes again, fighting the wave of darkness threatening to overwhelm him. It felt like he'd been hit by a damn freight train. *What the hell happened?*

He took slow, steady breaths, searching his memory. Things came back in a rush, playing through his head like a movie on fast-forward. He remembered getting shot in the chest outside the bank, remembered Khaki on her knees beside him, remembered her begging him to keep fighting and telling him that she loved him. Most of all, he remembered her bleeding.

She'd been shot too.

Gritting his teeth against the pain, Xander pushed himself up into a sitting position. Or tried to. He didn't get very far before a firm hand on his shoulder pushed him back down.

"Whoa, take it easy, babe."

Khaki's voice was soft in his ear, her breath warm where it caressed his cheek. Her scent enveloped him, taking away whatever pain he'd felt. He relaxed against the pillow and opened his eyes to see her leaning over him, relief in her gaze. He'd gladly volunteer to get shot in the chest once a week if it meant being able to wake up to her beautiful face for the rest of his life.

Thank God she was okay. He opened his mouth to ask her, just to make sure, but she gently shushed him.

"You've been out of it for a while," she said. "Take your time."

As long as he could do it while gazing at her, he was okay with that. He only hoped some doctor or nurse didn't interrupt them.

Now that he thought about it, the room didn't feel like a hospital. Or smell like one either. He was in a hospital bed with an IV tube stuck in one arm and a bunch of wires running from under his blanket to a monitor somewhere behind him. But everything else seemed…off.

The walls weren't the usual depressing institutional beige. The comfy chair by the window was real leather. And the partially drawn curtains looked expensive even to him, and he didn't know a damn thing about curtains.

He looked at Khaki. "Where am I?"

"You're in a private recovery center that Sergeant Dixon arranged for you," she said.

Xander's mouth fell open in shock, and Khaki laughed. While it was good to hear her laugh, Xander was having a hard time with the bombshell she'd dropped about being in a private recovery center.

"Gage already had this place set up for us?" he asked.

She reached out to gently brush his hair back from his forehead. "I don't know who he is, or how the boss knows him, but Sergeant Dixon got a doctor into the operating room before they started surgery. The guy's not a werewolf, but he knows what we are. He had you moved here two nights ago, so no one could see how fast you're healing but him."

Xander knew Gage had set up contingency plans over the years for almost everything imaginable, but this was amazing. How the hell had he found a human doctor willing to cover for a pack of werewolves?

"Two nights ago?" he asked.

Khaki nodded. "You were in surgery for five hours and you've been out of it ever since."

He was still processing that when tears brimmed in her eyes. "What's wrong?"

"Sergeant Dixon knows about us," she said. "He figured it out the moment he walked into the hospital and saw me in the waiting area. He hasn't said it yet, but I know he's going to move me to Mike's squad."

Tears overflowed her beautiful eyes and ran down her cheeks. Xander was torn between the overwhelming desire to pull her into his arms and kiss the tears away, and finding whoever had made his woman cry and tearing that person to pieces.

He took her hand and tugged Khaki to his chest. She snuggled against him, resting her head on his shoulder. He squeezed her tightly, kissing the top of her head and wishing he could comfort her. But he didn't know how to comfort a woman. He was an idiot when it came to things like that. But he had to try. He'd rather get shot a hundred times than hear Khaki cry.

"Shhh," he whispered. "It's going to be okay. We're not going to let Gage split us up."

Khaki pushed away from his chest, wiping the tears from her cheeks. "And how do we stop him from doing that, kidnap him?"

He chuckled, partly because Khaki could still joke at a time like this, and because the answer to their problem was so simple it was funny.

"No," he said. "We tell him the truth, that we'll both quit the team before we let him split us up."

Khaki's face softened like she was looking at a really cute puppy. But then she frowned. "Xander, that's absolutely the sweetest thing any man has ever said to me, but I can't let you do that. You wouldn't just be quitting the team; you'd be leaving your pack, a pack you've been part of for a long time. I'll put in for a transfer to somewhere else in the DPD."

He reached up and traced the outline of her jaw with his fingers. She was so beautiful. And he never wanted to be without her.

"Yes, they're my pack, but you're my mate," he said. "Being with you is more important to me. Either we both stay in the Pack, or neither of us does."

She looked at him as if she couldn't decide whether she wanted to smack him or kiss him. She chose the latter, leaning over to cup his face in her hand and kiss him in a way no other woman ever had.

"Are you sure?" she asked.

"I'm sure." Xander grinned. "I'd go back to working patrol if I could come home to you every night. Besides, it's not exactly like I'm making a big sacrifice. If it comes down to being with the woman I love or a bunch of sweaty, testosterone-laden werewolves who get in fights all the time, the decision is easy."

Khaki's mouth curved. "The woman you love, huh? That's not just the bullet wounds talking, is it?"

He shook his head. "I'm sorry I made you wait until

now to hear me say it, but I really do love you more than anything else in my life, including the Pack."

"I love you too," she whispered. "So much."

Tears formed again in her eyes, one glistening drop rolling down her perfect cheek and falling gently to his lips. The feel of it was shockingly powerful, like an earthquake he could only feel in his soul. He swore that he'd do anything to make sure he was worthy of Khaki's tears.

Xander opened his mouth to tell her that, but she silenced him with another kiss. "Not another word," she whispered. "You've said everything that needs to be said."

They sat there in silence, holding each other for a long time. Xander was content to stay just like that for the rest of the night, and probably would have if Khaki hadn't let out the cutest yawn he'd ever heard. He'd been so relieved to see that she was okay, he hadn't thought about how exhausting the past couple days must have been on her.

"How long has it been since you've slept?" he asked softly.

She shrugged. "I've napped a little here and there."

He tilted her chin up so he could see her face. "Define a little."

"Three nights ago, when we were together at your place."

No wonder she looked so tired. "I understand why you stayed, because I wouldn't have been able to leave your side either. But now that you know I'm going to be okay, I think you should go home and get some sleep."

She opened her mouth to complain, but he put a finger on her lips to shush her. "You'll need to be fresh when we face Gage, and now that I'm awake, that's probably going to be sooner than later."

"Okay," she said. "But only because I know you're going to be okay. And because your bed will remind me of you."

Khaki gave him another kiss that made him consider asking her to stay and jump in the hospital bed with him, but he caught himself. Khaki needed to get some sleep. And to be truthful, he did too. He was getting stronger by the minute, but when Gage showed up, Xander wanted to face him on his feet, not lying in this bed.

Khaki found Mac and the guys from her squad, along with Mike and a good portion of his guys waiting in the outer lobby. Thankfully, Sergeant Dixon wasn't with them. Xander needed rest and he wasn't going to get it with their boss around.

"How is he?" Mac asked.

Mac had been a rock for her over the last two days. Not only had she gone to Khaki's apartment and gotten clean clothes for her, but she'd brought her something to eat and big cups of coffee around the clock. Mac had also been keeping Gage away from her, something Khaki was extremely grateful for.

Khaki smiled. "He's awake, and he's going to be fine."

Everyone breathed a sigh of relief, and Khaki could feel the tension drain from the room. The guys had said all the right things, that Xander was a werewolf and that werewolves could recover from any injury that didn't kill them. But none of them had ever heard of a werewolf going in for open-heart surgery and being unconscious for two days either.

Mac pulled her in for a hug. "Thank God. I've been so worried."

"Me too," Khaki admitted. "But he's okay. He sent me home to get some sleep."

"Did you tell him that Gage knows about the two of you?" Cooper asked. "And that he probably isn't going to let you stay on the squad?"

Khaki nodded. "He knows, but it doesn't matter."

"Doesn't matter?" Mike echoed. "I don't have a problem with you on my squad, but I find it hard to believe Xander is going to be okay with that."

Khaki almost laughed. No, Xander definitely wasn't okay with that. "I appreciate the offer, Mike, but Xander wouldn't be able to handle it, and honestly, I doubt I would be able to either. We've decided the best thing would be for both of us to transfer out of SWAT."

While it was painful as hell to say the words, she knew it was the right thing to do.

"But you're not leaving the Pack, right?" Alex asked.

"I can't see how we have a choice," she said. "How can we be part of the Pack, but not in SWAT when they're one and the same? Even if we could, it would be too hard for everyone involved."

The mood in the waiting room, which had been so high just a few moments ago, turned dismal. Mac was on the verge of tears while Mike and some of the other guys stared down at the floor. The others just look pissed. Especially Cooper.

Khaki didn't want that. She and Xander had known

what they were getting into when they started sleeping with each other. It wasn't Sergeant Dixon's fault, and she didn't want the guys trying to take this out on him. It wouldn't solve anything and would likely only make matters worse.

She cleared her throat. "So, Mike, did you and your squad find out anything on the shooter?"

Mike looked surprised by her question. She didn't blame him. How could he know how many hours over the last couple of days she'd spent imagining all the things she was going to do to the person who'd shot Xander? And now that Xander was out of the woods, those thoughts were back. She wasn't the kind of person who believed in retribution, but that was before she'd held Xander in her arms while he'd fought for his life. Maybe it was her werewolf nature, but she wanted the person who'd hurt him to pay.

"Not much, I'm afraid," Mike admitted. "We've been working on the theory that the sniper was backup for the bank crew, but we've found absolutely nothing to support that. Most of the crew have lawyered up and the ones that haven't claim they don't know anything about the sniper. Even the girlfriend, Shelly, swears we have all of them accounted for. Diego and Zane are down in lockup trying to get anything they can from the guys we arrested, but I don't think they're going to. Gage has the DA's office going through their old cases to see if someone Xander put away has recently gotten out of prison. But that's going to be a long list. He's responsible for locking up a lot of criminals."

"Crap," Khaki muttered. If anyone could get anything out of the guys they arrested, it would be SWAT's two hostage negotiators, Diego Martinez and Zane Kendrick, but like Mike, she didn't hold out much hope. Maybe the DA's office would have better luck.

Khaki ran her hand through her hair. She didn't want to go back to Xander's apartment for a nap. She wanted to track down the shooter and tear him to shreds. Even standing here in the waiting room, she could feel the tingles at the tips of her fingers that meant her claws wanted to come out. She tried to use the calming techniques that Xander had taught her. Having her claws make an appearance in front of the guys probably wasn't a good idea, not if she hoped to have a chance to go after the shooter, whoever he was.

"What about the crime scene? Did you find anything there that might give us a clue who this sniper is?" she asked.

Mike shook his head. "We found which building the guy was on when he shot Xander, and while he left a good scent trail behind, that was all he left. No shell casings, no DNA, no fingerprints on the doors, nothing. The guy is a pro."

"You didn't recognize his scent?" she asked.

"No." Mike smiled wryly. "Maybe if any of us had your memory for scents it'd be possible. But to all of us, he just smelled like a guy."

She smiled back at Mike. He gave her an idea. "Maybe I should run out there and sniff around a little, see if I recognize the scent?"

"I thought you were going home to get some sleep?" Mac reminded her with a frown.

She was, but the chance to get a sniff of the guy who'd shot Xander before the scent faded away completely was too good to pass up. "I'll just run over and take a quick look around. I promise I'll take a nap after that."

Mike scowled at her. "I don't think it's a good idea for you to be running around the crime scene on your own. We assume Xander was the sniper's target, but the guy was shooting at you too."

"How about a couple of us go with her?" Becker suggested. "That way she can get a sniff of the suspect; then we can make sure she goes home for some rest."

Khaki wasn't too thrilled at the idea of having company, but she knew if she made a fuss, it was likely to make Mac and Mike so suspicious they would probably insist on going with her, so she nodded. She probably wasn't going to learn much at the crime scene that the others hadn't anyway.

It was dark by the time she parked her Mini beside Max's Camaro. In silence, he and Becker led her to the building where the shooter had been.

The building was an eight-story office complex with more than twenty businesses, including a lawyer, a few investment firms, and a real estate company.

"And no one saw a damn thing," Max grumbled as he held open the door for her.

Khaki followed Max and Becker up the stairs, relieved the two younger guys had been the only ones who'd come with her. For a moment back in the recovery center, she'd thought Xander's whole squad was going to accompany her. But then Cooper said something about wanting to be there when Sergeant Dixon showed up so he could tell their boss what a dick he was being. The rest of the guys had wanted to stay too. Some to give Gage a piece of their mind, some to keep Cooper from saying something that would get him in trouble too.

"The shooter slipped out the building through a fire exit without tripping the alarm," Becker told her as they stepped onto the roof.

Khaki was so caught up in the memories of Xander getting shot that she almost missed the faint but familiar scent clinging to the rooftop. When she finally realized what it was, she nearly stumbled over her own feet.

Jeremy.

"No way," she whispered, feeling the color draining from her face.

She shouldn't be surprised her asshole ex-boyfriend was the one who'd tried to kill Xander and her. It should have been obvious.

"Everything okay?" Max asked. "You smell something you recognize?"

Khaki hesitated. If she told Becker and Max the shooter had been her stalker ex-boyfriend, they'd almost certainly try and keep her from tracking him down and killing him. She shouldn't have had thoughts like that considering she was a cop, but ripping Jeremy to shreds was exactly what she wanted to do. Jeremy had followed her here from Washington, stalked her, harassed her, then shot the man she loved. Tearing him to pieces seemed the most rational thing in the world to her at that moment.

Her cell phone rang, making her jump. "It might be Xander," she mumbled as she pulled it out of her purse.

She glanced at the call display, expecting to see Xander's name, but all she saw was a phone number.

She thumbed the green button and turned away from the guys. "Calling to gloat?"

There was a snort of amusement on the other end of the line that made Khaki bite back a growl. "Not much to gloat about since it seems I didn't succeed in killing that caveman you call a boyfriend," Jeremy said. "I have to admit, he's one tough bastard. Although considering he's been unconscious for almost three days, it makes me wonder if it's just a matter of time."

She growled this time.

"Everything okay?" Becker asked from over by the edge of the roof.

She turned to tell him everything was fine, but Jeremy's voice interrupted. "I wouldn't say anything to those two cops with you. I'd hate to have to shoot them like I did your boyfriend. I don't think they'd survive a shot to the head at this distance."

Khaki tightened her grip on the phone, darting a quick look around at the nearby buildings. Jeremy might have been lying about being out there somewhere with a rifle, but she doubted it. He was obviously close enough to see she was with Becker and Max, which meant he was probably close enough to shoot them. And if he hit them in the head, they'd be dead.

She forced herself to smile and nod at Becker and Max, then turned her back on them, moving a little farther away. "If you didn't call to gloat, why did you call?"

"Because we need to talk," Jeremy said. "You haven't been answering your phone for the last few days."

She wanted to shout at him that she'd been too busy worrying about Xander, but she bit her tongue. She needed Jeremy to give her a clue where he was.

"So talk," she said.

"Not over the phone. This is a conversation we need to have in person."

Khaki laughed. She doubted they'd be doing a lot of talking. Jeremy intended to kill her. Then again, if he wanted her dead, he could have shot her with the rifle he was pointing in her direction. But no, a quick kill like that wouldn't be satisfying enough for him. Jeremy was the kind of sadistic bastard who'd want Khaki to see her death coming in slow motion.

And by meeting with him, she'd give him exactly what he wanted. But she was okay with that because she was going to get exactly what she wanted, too. A chance to punish the man who had tried to kill her mate.

The anger that rose up inside her was like nothing she'd ever experienced. She felt her fingertips burn and her jaws ache as her out-of-control claws and fangs extended fully. She had to struggle to control her voice as she answered Jeremy.

"Where do you want to meet?"

———ᴧᴧᴧ———

Xander didn't realize he'd dozed until movement beside his bed woke him. He opened his eyes, expecting to see Khaki, and was disappointed to find Gage standing there. Was it too much to hope he was dreaming? But then his team leader's scent finally filtered through his fuzzy head, confirming he wasn't.

He sat up straighter in bed, steeling himself for the coming confrontation. Gage had been his alpha and his best friend for a long time. He'd have been lying if he said walking away from the Pack and that friendship wasn't going to hurt.

But before Gage could tear into him, the door opened and a gray-haired man in a white coat came in. The doctor ignored the obvious tension in the room and walked over to the bed.

"Let's have a look at that wound," he said, gently pulling Xander's hospital gown aside.

Xander instinctively grabbed the man's wrist, pretty sure it was a bad idea to let a doctor get a look at his wounds. The man raised a brow, then looked at Gage.

"It's okay, Xander. Doctor Saunders knows what we are."

Khaki had told him about the doctor.

Xander released the man's wrist. After only being around the team's medics, it was weird having a human doctor poking around the rapidly developing scar tissue on his chest, but he put up with it. He spent most of the time eyeing Gage instead of paying attention to the doctor. His boss looked as if he was biting his tongue for the doctor's benefit, but just barely.

Saunders glanced at Gage. "He's recovering quite nicely. The wound is completely closed, which is remarkable when you think about it." He turned back to Xander, taking off the little sensors from his chest and hanging them over the monitoring equipment. "It's been nice meeting you, Corporal Riggs."

Xander nodded, never taking his eyes off Gage as the doctor quietly left the room.

"Dammit, Xander," Gage snarled. "What the hell were you thinking, sleeping with Khaki?"

A part of Xander wanted to explain, wanted his friend

to understand why he'd done what he'd done, but he knew it would be a waste of time. Gage had already made up his mind. Besides, even if he'd had a chance to do it all over again, he wouldn't have done anything differently.

"This wasn't about thinking," Xander said, surprised at how calm the words came out. "It was about doing what was right."

"Right? Are you frigging kidding me?" Gage's eyes flared gold. "You broke every rule in the department: sleeping with a subordinate; sleeping with a member of your squad; sleeping with a fellow officer; sleeping with a teammate!"

Xander ground his jaw. It took everything in him not to shout back at Gage. Not that it would have mattered. Clearly, his alpha wasn't done.

Gage shook his head. "You're lucky I don't suspend both of you."

Xander knew Gage was trying to intimidate him into falling back in line. It wasn't going to work. What he and Khaki had was complicated, but it wasn't wrong. And he'd be damned if he was going to let anyone—even his best friend and alpha—try to convince him otherwise.

"As of right now, Khaki is on Mike's squad," Gage said.

"Like hell she is," Xander growled, throwing back the sheet and pushing himself up. The move hurt, but not bad enough to make him stop.

Gage put a big hand on Xander's shoulder, shoving him back down. "You don't have a say in the matter."

Xander snarled, baring his teeth. If Gage wanted a fight, he was going to get one.

"He might not have a say in the matter, but I do."

Xander glanced over to see Mac standing in the doorway. Cooper, Hale, Trevor, and Alex flanked her on either side.

"Gage, you can't keep Khaki and Xander apart." Mac walked in the room, quickly followed by the others. Trevor closed the door firmly behind him, then stood guarding it. "She's *The One* for him."

It took a moment for Mac's words to sink in. "Wait a minute," Xander said. "How do you know Khaki is *The One* for me?"

"Because she told me." Mac's lips curved into a smile. "You've been the topic of conversation between us from the day she got here."

Gage's golden eyes narrowed. "Mackenzie, you knew Xander and Khaki were sleeping together?"

"Yes."

Ignoring the glower Gage sent her way, Mac came over and gave Xander a hug. Then she poked him in the shoulder. "You scared the hell out of us. Don't ever do that again."

"Mackenzie?" Gage growled. "You knew and didn't tell me?"

Mac turned and glared at Gage. "Isn't that what I just said? Honey, I wanted to tell you, but I couldn't because I knew how you'd react. Or maybe I should say overreact, which is what you're doing right now."

Gage clenched his jaw so hard Xander could hear his teeth grind. "Mackenzie, I don't expect you to understand, but Xander and Khaki can't be a couple and be on the same squad. It's against every rule in the book."

"Those are department rules," Cooper said, crossing

the room to stand in front of Gage. "We might be cops, but we're werewolves first. You know that sometimes you aren't going to be able to follow the book when it comes to the Pack, and this is one of those times."

The look Gage gave Cooper could have melted steel. "Let me frigging guess. You knew about Khaki and Xander too?"

Shit. There was no need for Cooper to get himself in hot water trying to cover for him and Khaki.

"Cooper," Xander warned, but Cooper ignored him, shrugging in that "whatever" kind of way that frequently got him in trouble.

"Yeah, I knew."

"You should have told me," Gage ground out.

"It wasn't my job to tell you," Cooper shot back.

The idiot probably would have said more, but luckily his cell phone rang before he could. He dug it out of his pocket and held it to his ear as he walked over to the far side of the room. "Cooper."

"Gage," Mac said, "I know you think you're doing what's best for the team, but in this case, Cooper's right. You can't apply all the department's rules to the Pack, especially this one. Khaki and Xander have to be together as much as you and I do."

"We don't work together," Gage pointed out.

"But if we did, would you want me on anyone's squad but yours?" When Gage didn't answer, she sighed. "Honey, if you try to split them up, you're going to lose both of them. They're ready to walk away from the Pack. Is that what you want?"

Gage looked at Xander in shock. Gage hadn't even considered he and Khaki would leave the Pack. Xander thought for a second that might sway his boss, but instead Gage's jaw tightened. He was going to call Xander's bluff.

Xander's chest constricted. He'd known it was going to come to this, which was why he'd talked to Khaki about it, but it was still tough to say it out loud and make it official. But putting it off wasn't going to make it hurt any less. He took a deep breath, ready to cut ties with Gage and the Pack once and for all when Cooper's angry words interrupted him.

"What the hell do you mean she gave you the slip?" Cooper demanded into his phone. "Khaki's driving a frigging Mini and you have a Camaro. How the hell could she lose you?"

Xander hadn't been paying attention to Cooper's conversation before, but at the mention of Khaki, he immediately tensed. On other end of the line, Max was saying something about her driving down an alley too narrow for him to fit through.

"She did it on purpose," Becker added. Clearly they were on speakerphone. "She was trying to shake us."

Xander could hear the squeal of tires in the background and knew that Max was driving fast after Khaki. But why?

"What's going on?" Gage demanded.

Cooper didn't answer. "Tell me exactly what you heard up on the roof," he said into the phone.

It took everything in Xander not to jump out of bed and grab the phone from Cooper. Something was wrong; he knew it.

Cooper cupped his hand over the phone and looked sharply at Xander. "You know somebody named Jeremy?"

"Fuck," Xander snarled.

Untangling his legs from the blanket, he leaped out of the bed and hurried over to the closet on legs that were a little unsteady but getting stronger by the second. He yanked open the closet door, praying someone had put his uniform in there. No uniform, but there were jeans, a T-shirt, boots, and a leather jacket.

He reached for the jeans when a heavy hand slammed the closet door on him. He turned to find Gage scowling at him.

"Is he talking about Jeremy Engler?"

Xander nodded and opened the door again. He grabbed the jeans and pulled them on, then yanked off the hospital gown and put on his T-shirt. He glanced at Gage as he shoved his feet into his boots and tied the laces.

"Engler confronted Khaki earlier in the week, begging her to go back to Lakefront with him. Then a few nights ago, he followed us to a restaurant. I roughed him up pretty good and I thought for sure he left town."

Gage frowned. "You thought a guy who was so obsessed with Khaki that he not only forced her out of her previous job, but followed her halfway across the country left town because you knocked him around?"

Xander tried to muster up some righteous anger but couldn't. Gage was right. He should have known better. "Do we need to discuss this now?"

Gage's jaw worked for a moment, but then he shook his head. "If Khaki deliberately gave Becker and Max the slip, that probably means she ID'd Jeremy as the shooter. Any idea what she might be up to?"

Xander was about to admit he wasn't sure, but Mac spoke before he could.

"She's going to go kill him. If Khaki thinks he tried to kill Xander, she'll want to tear him to pieces." Mac shook her head, her blue eyes a mix of consternation and worry. "I can't believe I have to tell this to a pack of werewolves."

Gage swore, then strode over to Cooper. He held his hand out for the phone. "Max, which way was she heading? Mesquite? No, I don't want you to try to find her. I want you to get Becker to a computer. I need him to track Khaki's cell phone signal. We need to stop her from doing something crazy."

Xander jerked open the door and walked out of the room. He was halfway down the hall before he realized he didn't know where the exit was. He looked around for a directional sign, found one, and headed that way. Gage was right behind him, still giving instructions to Becker and Max. Behind him, Trevor was on the phone with Mike, telling him to get his squad together and head toward Mesquite, while Mac and the others practically had to run to keep up. Xander's legs still felt a little weak and every step made his chest throb like hell, but he ignored the pain and kept moving.

He glanced over his shoulder at Gage. "Tell Becker I'll be with Alex, Hale, and Cooper. I want Khaki's location as soon as he has it."

Xander expected Gage to demand he sit this one out—as if that was going to happen—but his boss only nodded.

"I'll link up with Mike and bring in the cavalry," Gage said. "You find Khaki."

—⁓—

Khaki sat with her back against an old Honda Accord and tried to stop the blood pouring out of her stomach with her hand. It hurt.

Confronting Jeremy hadn't gone the way she'd planned, not even close. Then again, she hadn't really had a plan. She'd been going off pure animal rage. She should have realized Jeremy wanted to meet her at a deserted junkyard for a reason.

She didn't have her backup gun since she'd gone directly from the recovery center to the crime scene, then here, but she also hadn't thought she'd need one. She'd envisioned chasing Jeremy through a helter-skelter maze of rusted hunks of metal as he shouted in terror. She'd even deliberately parked her car a good half mile from the junkyard, wanting to make sure she didn't tip him off that she was there. The place had been as quiet as a church, and with only a few dingy pole-mounted streetlights throwing the place into shadows, she was sure she'd have no problem sneaking up on Jeremy.

But that hadn't happened. She'd just started weaving her way among the piles of old cars when she felt a stab of pain in her midsection. A moment later, the boom of a rifle echoed around her. No doubt it was the same rifle Jeremy had used to shoot Xander.

Khaki pressed her hand against her stomach harder, waiting for the initial wave of pain to pass and the worst of the bleeding to stop. She reached around behind her back with her free hand and felt the warm patch of blood there. The bullet had gone straight through. That was good. Alex had told her that werewolves healed faster when there was no foreign material in the wound.

Footsteps sounded on the gravel. Jeremy was coming to finish her off. Her heart pounded overtime, though whether it was because she was afraid he intended to shoot her again or anticipation at the thought of ripping out his throat, she wasn't sure.

She closed her eyes and willed her claws to extend, savoring the sensation of punishing Jeremy for all the crap he'd put her and Xander through.

But when she opened her eyes, her nails looked as human and unthreatening as always. Khaki growled in frustration and tried harder to shift as she heard Jeremy coming closer. Her fingers tingled in response, but her claws refused to come out. *Dammit!*

She kept pushing…right up until the moment another bullet smacked into the far side of the Honda she was hiding behind.

That's when she knew she had to move. She forced herself to her feet and hobbled toward the remains of an old pickup truck thirty feet away. She moved as fast as she could, but even though the pain was starting to lessen, it was still hard to stand up straight. Getting shot in the stomach was worse than getting stabbed there.

She made it to the truck just as Jeremy came around the side of the Honda. The sound of his mocking laughter made her grit her teeth, but she kept going. She had to bide her time until she could heal enough to turn the tables on him.

She moved silently past a truck and two more cars until she reached a fifty-five-gallon drum that reeked of old oil. She went down on one knee behind it, taking a moment to check her wound before peeking around it to keep an eye on Jeremy. She reached into her back pocket for her phone to call in the cavalry, but then remembered she'd left her phone in her purse, which was in her car…half a mile down the road. She hadn't wanted anything to distract her from what she'd been planning to do. Not her best idea. Like everything else about this trip out to a desolate junkyard, anger had clouded her thinking.

"You are one tough little bitch!" Jeremy shouted as she saw him kneel down and trace his fingers through the bloody patch of ground where she'd been hiding. Then he stood and turned in a slow circle looking for her. "But you've got nowhere to go now. You're sure as hell not scrambling back over that fence like you did coming in, not with how much you're bleeding."

As Khaki watched, Jeremy turned and started moving off to the right, as if he had no idea which way she'd headed. But that didn't keep him from trash talking.

"Why don't you come out and just let me finish this nice and fast? I promise I won't leave you flopping around on the ground like that SWAT boyfriend of yours. What's his name…Riggs? What did you ever see in him? You could have done so much better. Hell, you did do better—me."

She knew she should have kept quiet. Jeremy was only trying to get her to snap and say something to give her position away. She should have kept going the other way until her stomach closed up enough to allow her to move fast again. But the second he spoke Xander's name, the anger she felt burning inside her was worse than the bullet wound.

"When did you get so screwed up, Jeremy?" she shouted. "You stalked me all the way to Dallas, tried to kill the man I'm dating, tried to kill me. All because I dumped your ass and left the Lakefront PD?"

She knew she was stupid for exposing her location, and sure as hell, Jeremy spun in her direction and started shooting. The clank of the high-caliber rifle rounds hitting the metal drum forced her back to her feet.

Jeremy's boots thumped on the gravel behind her. But her stomach was starting to feel better, and she easily pulled away from him.

Then a random bullet bounced off the heavy bumper of a car as she ran past, clipping her right thigh and almost putting her on her ass again as it tore its way through her leg. Getting hit with the ricochet hurt worse than a straight shot, and she didn't even want to look down. She knew the damage was bad. Some of the bullet was still in her leg but Jeremy was coming fast and she didn't have time to check. She'd barely crawled under the rusted-out remains of an old clunker when Jeremy raced into the clearing.

Jeremy saw the blood on the ground. Khaki knew that Jeremy had spent a lot of time hunting in Canada and Alaska. He enjoyed tracking animals, especially after he'd shot them and they tried to run. He never let any of them get away from him alive.

She was a werewolf, but Jeremy was a monster. She was twice wounded and unable to get her inner animal to come out; he was armed and in his element. She'd seriously screwed up by coming here to face him alone.

Khaki peeked through the grass and weeds that grew around the car, trying to see if she'd left a trail of blood. She didn't see anything, even with her werewolf-enhanced vision. But still, she held her breath as Jeremy bent and searched the ground. After a moment, he looked up and swept the area with his gaze.

"You think all of this is about you leaving me, you stupid bitch?" Jeremy shouted into the night. "Was I pissed that you decided to leave town rather than stay with me? Hell yeah. Not as pissed as when you tricked me with that candy-ass martial arts move and put me on the floor of the bull pen in front of everyone before you left though. I almost shot you then. If there hadn't been a room full of cops around, I would have."

Jeremy crossed the clearing as he spoke, disappearing between two cars. Now that the nasty smells of the junkyard had faded into the background, she was able to pick out Jeremy's distinct scent and use it to help pinpoint his location. He was definitely moving away from her.

Khaki resisted the urge to immediately roll out from under the car and run the other way. She needed to calm down, figure out how badly she'd been hit, then come up with a plan. The hell with that. She needed to shift, now.

"But I calmed down after you left, especially after I realized that it was your loss and that I could move on to any woman I wanted," Jeremy continued. "Then a day later, Silver calls me into his office. He had internal affairs in there with him, and they started asking me about all kinds of bullshit about whether I harassed you, blackballed you, and convinced other officers not to respond to your calls for backup. They even asked whether I had lied on official police reports to make you look bad. I told them that was crap and that you were the one who'd been screwing up. That I'd tried to help you. But internal affairs pulled out statements and reports saying otherwise."

Khaki had only been half listening, more focused on her wounds. But that got her attention.

"All the people who claimed to be my friends turned on me!" Jeremy shouted. "They told internal affairs I almost got you killed, that I assaulted you, and that you left to get away from me. They didn't want to listen to a damn thing I said. They fucking suspended me, pending some bullshit ethics review. The union rep is telling me I'm never going to work in law enforcement again. Did you hear that, you bitch? You cost me my job. My reputation. My life!"

Khaki would have laughed if her leg hadn't hurt so much. She had no idea what kind of mental game of Twister Jeremy was playing that allowed him to blame his suspension and possible unemployment on her, but he was.

He was moving around the area in a circular search pattern now. Sooner or later he was going to stumble over a blood trail or a footprint, something that would lead him to her hiding place.

She closed her eyes and tried doing the mental exercises Xander had taught her so she could get her claws and fangs to come out, but it didn't work nearly as well as Xander's voice. After a few minutes, she was forced to give up again. The pain she was trying to find relief from was also preventing her from calming down enough to bring on a shift. It didn't help that she was worried about Jeremy finding her.

She slowly rolled out from under the car and crawled to her feet as quietly as she could, quickly looked for Jeremy and then slowly limped in the opposite direction, toward the big building in the center of the junkyard.

Her best bet now was to get inside and find a phone so she could call for help. She hated the idea of admitting to Dixon and the rest of the guys what she'd been planning to do to Jeremy, but she didn't have a choice now.

"Funny how things work out," Jeremy said from somewhere off to her left.

She immediately veered to the right. She was still heading for the building, but was willing to take a longer path to get there to avoid Jeremy.

"My original plan was to show up at your apartment and woo you into coming back to Lakefront with me. I figured if I could come back with you at my side all my problems would go away."

Jeremy suddenly started moving in her direction. Had he heard her? That wasn't possible. She moved a little more to the right and kept going, making sure to keep close to a car or some other piece of heavy metal—anything that would stop a bullet if she had to jump behind it.

"How the hell was I to know you'd go and sleep with the first Neanderthal who'd pull your panties down? You never were too bright. But then I saw in the news how you saved those snot-nosed kids from the bank robbers. I even saw the video clip. It pissed me off pretty good. No way in hell were you going to have a dream job here in Dallas while I filed for unemployment. That's when I decided to kill you and your SWAT boyfriend."

Khaki walked backward as she listened to Jeremy, hoping to keep a lock on exactly where he was. How could he casually talk about killing two fellow cops like that?

"But then your Corporal Riggs went and lived. Still

not sure how the hell that's even possible when I put three armor-piercing bullets through the center of his chest. I guess the Dallas PD can afford better Kevlar vests than Lakefront."

She was still backing toward the main building when the overwhelming scent of blood reached up and grabbed her attention from behind. But it was too late. She stumbled over something, jarring her leg so hard when she hit the ground she almost cried out.

She looked down and saw that she'd tripped over a man...and a dog. The man's arms were wrapped around the dog, and there were three bullet holes in the center of his back. As if he'd been trying to protect his dog from Jeremy. Based on the animal's still body and the amount of blood all over both of them, the man's efforts had been in vain. Rage surged through her. Damn him to hell. It was stupid to even think it, but why'd he have to shoot the dog?

Her jaws and fingers ached with the urge to rip Jeremy to shreds. But no matter how much she strained to get her fangs and claws to come out, they stubbornly stayed where they were. She was so focused on trying to shift she didn't realize Jeremy had worked his way closer until she heard him walking just on the other side of a row of minivans to her right. If she hadn't tripped over the man and his dog, Jeremy would have seen and killed her already.

Considering the fact that he was just about at the end of the row of soccer mom wagons, she guessed Jeremy was about to see—and kill—her soon.

～

It took Becker a while to call in with Khaki's location, and by the time he got to them, they'd gone nearly twenty miles too far to the east on U.S. Route 80. Swearing, Hale jerked his FJ Cruiser into the grassy median and did a U-turn, getting them heading back to I-635.

"Her cell phone is stationary about a half mile from a junkyard called Eastside Chop and Shop," Becker said over Alex's phone. "The area around there is mostly residential subdivisions, so the junkyard is probably where she's heading. And, Xander, her car hasn't moved for almost fifteen minutes."

Hale floored it without Xander having to ask.

Xander tried his best not to count the mile markers they zipped past. Even as fast as Hale drove, the poles still weren't going by fast enough.

"Khaki's going to be okay," Cooper said into the silence filling the vehicle. "She's tough and smart. She won't let Jeremy get the drop on her."

Xander wasn't so sure about that. Although Khaki was more than capable of taking care of herself, Jeremy was clearly a good shot with a sniper rifle. All it would take was one perfectly aimed shot and Khaki would find herself in serious trouble. And considering that Jeremy had lured her to that junkyard, an ambush wasn't out of the question.

But he was worried about more than just the possibility of Jeremy shooting her. What if Mac was right and Khaki had headed after her ex with the intention of killing him? Xander didn't want to think about Khaki doing something like that, but he knew how much she hated Jeremy. He'd made her life a living hell out in Washington. So bad that a fighter like her had left the state. The fact that Jeremy had come here to Dallas, where she was trying to create a new life for herself, and shot him in cold blood might be more than enough to push her over the edge and make her do something she'd regret for the rest of her life. She could even end up going to prison.

Xander refused to let his mind go down that path. Instead, he focused on all the things he hadn't had a chance to say to Khaki yet. She knew that she was *The One* for him, and he'd told her that he loved her, but that didn't seem like it was enough. He promised himself that he was going to spend two straight days telling Khaki how much he loved and needed her. Hell, if he had to, he'd use Google Translate to come up with twenty different ways to say it.

Alex's phone rang, echoing in the silence.

"Guys," Becker said when Alex put him on speaker. "You need to get to that junkyard now. We have multiple reports of shots being fired. Gage has gotten Deputy Chief Mason involved and they're calling for a perimeter to be established outside the area, but you need to hurry."

"We'll be there in two minutes," Hale said as he weaved in and out of traffic.

In the backseat, Alex pulled out his backup piece and checked the magazine. He and Hale were the only ones packing. Cooper's off-duty sidearm was sitting in a safe at the compound. That meant two 9 mms going up against a renegade cop who was carrying who knew how many weapons.

Alex offered Xander the 9 mm, but Xander shook his head. A handgun wasn't going to make a difference in this situation. He needed to find Khaki and get her away from Jeremy. That was his only goal at the moment.

Hale slid the SUV to a stop outside the junkyard's entrance. Xander would have preferred to keep going, but the gate was closed and it looked substantial enough to stop their vehicle cold if they tried to ram it.

Xander was out and testing the air for Khaki's scent before the Toyota stopped rocking back and forth. The wind direction wasn't helping, and even worse, the whole place reeked of gasoline and motor oil. He could pick up Khaki's scent on the air, but he couldn't pinpoint where she was in the large junkyard, or even a general direction.

"Spread out and find Khaki," Xander ordered. "Mike will be here in a few minutes with his fully equipped squad. We'll let him worry about taking care of Jeremy."

They nodded, scrambling over the ten-foot-high fence, then spreading out once inside. Out of the corner of his eye, Xander saw Cooper start to strip off his clothes and casually drop them to the ground. Cooper had obviously decided that searching the junkyard in his full wolf form was faster than doing it on two feet. Xander couldn't disagree. He'd love to change into a wolf right now, both because it would improve his senses and because he'd like nothing better than to kick Jeremy's ass in that form. But it wasn't practical at the moment. In his weakened state, it would take too long to accomplish a full shift and unfortunately, it would leave him without the ability to use his hands. He had no idea where Khaki might be. Being able to open a door might make the difference between her living and dying.

But just because he wasn't able to shift into wolf form or carry a weapon, that didn't mean he was defenseless. He let his body go into a partial shift, extending his claws and fangs as far as they would go, feeling the muscles of his arms, shoulders, and back ripple and twist as they bulked up. He wasn't looking for Jeremy, but if he ran across him, the asshole would find Xander more than a handful to deal with.

He moved quickly across the middle of the junkyard, straining both his nose and ears to get a bead on Khaki. He caught an occasional whiff of her scent, but it was fleeting and inconclusive. He wished he had Khaki's ability to separate out different scents. Then he'd be able to ignore all the harsh petroleum odors and focus on the one smell he cared about.

He was just passing an old, rusty drum of oil when he smelled a familiar scent. Even more than any other smell in the place, there was no missing the scent of Khaki's blood. He turned and ran in the direction it was coming from.

He found a splatter of blood on the ground, then more leading under the remains of an old car. He didn't have to stop and see if she was still there. She wasn't. He would have heard her heart beating if she was.

The trail of blood led him to a row of partially disassembled minivans, and he almost stumbled as he saw a dark shape on the ground ahead of him. *Oh God, no.* But the overwhelming scent of blood coming from the bodies didn't match Khaki's. She'd definitely been here, though. He could smell her.

"Xander!"

His heart thudded at the sound of Khaki's voice, and

he spun around just in time to see Jeremy standing fifty feet away aiming a rifle at him. Xander threw himself to the side, but it was too late. Jeremy fired, and Xander cartwheeled through the air.

Xander hit the ground hard, the air whooshing out of his lungs, and his chest throbbing like an elephant was stomping on it. He'd known his previous injuries were still healing and sapping a lot of his strength, but he didn't realize exactly what that meant until he tried to get to his feet and found his legs refusing to cooperate.

To his right, footsteps rapidly approached. For a moment, Xander thought it was Hale or Alex, but then he saw Jeremy come around the side of one of the minivans.

"What kind of fucking monster are you?" Jeremy eyed Xander like he'd stepped out of a horror movie, revulsion on his face. Then he lifted his rifle and pointed it at his head. "Whatever you are, I'm going to put you out of your misery for good this time."

Chapter 15

KHAKI HAD FOUND A HIDING PLACE INSIDE ONE OF the minivans moments before Jeremy came around the corner. She held her breath as he walked past her, only a few feet between them. If he'd turned and looked her way, he would have seen her. But he didn't, and as he slowly moved past her, she finally let herself breathe again. She didn't move, not even after he was out of sight. Instead, she stayed where she was and tried to push the sharp pain in her leg and the dull throb in her stomach to the edges of her perception.

But no matter how hard she focused, the calmness she needed to shift wouldn't come. It wasn't surprising, considering she had to keep half her attention on Jeremy. She was so wrapped up in trying to put herself in the forest scene Xander always used with her that she didn't realize Xander was actually there in the junkyard with her until his scent brought her back to reality.

She had no idea how Xander had gotten here, and she didn't care. All that mattered was that he was, and that she had to warn him about Jeremy.

As slowly and quietly as she could, she crawled out of her hiding place. The pain shooting through her leg made it hard to move quickly, but she managed to get to the open door of the minivan without sounding like a herd of escaped monkeys.

Khaki was about to congratulate herself when she

saw Jeremy standing on the far side of the row, staring at Xander like he'd seen a ghost. Although he was shocked to see Xander in the middle of the deserted junkyard, it didn't stop him from reacting with his perfect killer instincts.

Khaki was shouting Xander's name even as Jeremy raised his weapon. But it was too late.

She screamed as Xander jumped aside to avoid the shot, only to be smashed violently to the ground, where he lay motionless as Jeremy raced toward him.

She leaped out of the minivan but stumbled to her knees. Her leg had practically gone numb while hiding in the van and now it didn't want to move as fast as she needed it to. She lifted her head and saw Jeremy come to a stop in front of Xander and raise his rifle for a head shot. No matter how much damage Xander had survived before, she knew he would never survive that.

There were twenty long yards between her and Xander, and she'd never get there in time with her wounded leg not cooperating. She needed to shift now.

Khaki closed her eyes and tried to remember what Xander had taught her. Step one, stay calm and breathe. Which was nearly impossible knowing Jeremy was only a few seconds from shooting the man she loved.

She shoved that thought away and focused on the memory of Xander's soft, sexy voice as he talked her through that first werewolf lesson in his apartment. She remembered how calm he'd made her feel, how easily she'd shifted her eyes that night.

"Think of a wolf running through the forest, jumping over dead trees, leaping across a stream. Think about

the sun going down, your eyes widening to take in the dim light as your claws dig into the loose soil."

She blocked out everything else, thinking only of Xander's voice and how much she loved him.

Her heart slowed and she smiled as she remembered how it had felt when her claws had come out that night. She hadn't even been thinking about it when it happened. Because she'd been thinking about Xander.

When she thought about Xander now, everything finally clicked. She heard his smooth, confident voice telling her that she was the most beautiful woman—the most beautiful werewolf—in the world. That she didn't have to force herself to shift, but instead had to let herself do it. That she had to simply allow herself to be what she was supposed to be.

She heard Jeremy say he was going to put Xander out of his misery. But more than the words, she heard the gloating tone, knowing that the monster Jeremy had become reveled in killing Xander because he was important to her.

As if on command, she felt her claws slide out. With them came an overwhelming wave of confidence. She could do this; she knew it.

The change kept going and she felt her jaw flex as her fangs pushed their way out. The muscles of her arms, shoulders, neck, and back hummed as strength and power flowed through them. She felt an urge to keep going, to see how far her body would shift, but she didn't have the time. Xander would die right now if she didn't act.

She was up and running toward Xander before she even opened her eyes. When she did, everything around her was brighter and more alive, every smell and sound clearer and more defined. Even her emotions felt rawer and more electric.

Jeremy smirked as Xander got to his feet, no doubt letting him do so just for the thrill of putting him down. A fury unlike anything she'd ever felt tore through Khaki. With a growl, she launched herself the last five yards toward Jeremy, flying through the air like the graceful animal inside her.

Jeremy whirled at the sound, his eyes going wide. She hit him hard, the impact sending both of them rolling. Khaki was immediately on her feet, lunging at Jeremy with a savage fury as she ripped the rifle out of his hands and tossed it aside. She advanced on him with a snarl, baring her fangs so he'd know what was coming.

"You're a fucking freak like him!" he shouted in terror, scrambling away from her on his hands and feet. "I always knew there was something wrong with you."

Khaki glanced at Xander to see him standing now but heavily favoring one leg. Blood spread from a wound on his hip, staining his jeans.

The rage inside her built up even more. It was bad enough that this bastard had shot her twice, but he'd shot Xander again. Khaki couldn't let that go.

She turned to Jeremy as he backed up farther and farther. His shoulders thumped into one of the stripped-down minivans, forcing him to stop. He must have seen the rage on her face because he fumbled around in the dirt and weeds and came up with a three-foot-long piece of metal with sharp, twisted brackets mounted to the end.

Faster than she would have given him credit for, Jeremy was up and running at her. Seeing him coming at her with that homemade club set off something primal inside her. He swung at her head with the length of metal, but she caught it easily in her left hand, stopping its trajectory inches before it caved in her skull. At the same time, she brought her right hand up and wrapped her fingers around his throat, shoving him backward like he was nothing. She didn't stop until she'd slammed him into the minivan, then she ripped the club from his hand at the same time she lifted him off the ground.

Anger made it hard to see, but she had no doubt that everything would be better after she killed Jeremy. The mere sound of him choking was already a calming salve to the injuries she'd sustained at his hands.

She heard herself growling and knew she was going to choke the life right out of him. A little voice in the back of her head told her she shouldn't be doing this, that nothing would be better simply by killing him. But the animal part of her viciously dismissed that little voice.

Jeremy kicked with his feet, struggling against the grip she had on his throat, but Khaki barely even felt it.

She felt Xander's gentle hand on her shoulder though, as well as heard his soft voice in her ear. "Khaki, it's okay. We got him."

She knew she should release Jeremy, but she couldn't make her inner wolf obey.

Xander stepped closer. "Khaki, if you do this, you'll be the monster and the freak he claims you to be. Sweetheart, please."

Xander's words tamed the wolf inside her and as her anger slowly disappeared, Khaki released Jeremy and backed away. He dropped to his knees, coughing and gasping.

Khaki looked at Xander, feeling the last of her rage slip away. Her claws and fangs quickly followed. The realization that she'd almost killed a man who couldn't defend himself against her suddenly hit. Knowing she had that much anger and hatred inside her scared her, and she thanked God that Xander had been there to stop her.

She threw her arms around him and held on tightly, burying her face in his neck. "I'm so sorry."

"Shh," he whispered, his arms holding her close. "It's okay."

It was okay…now. She pulled back to kiss him when a shout behind her made her whirl in his arms just in time to see Jeremy coming at her with his makeshift weapon again. Except this time, she wasn't in a position to stop him from hitting her or Xander with it.

She shoved Xander away, hoping she could at least protect him, but he spun her in his arms like she was a toy, yanking her to the side and blocking the length of metal with his arm. Something cracked and Xander grunted, but he shrugged off the pain from the blow, then ripped the club from Jeremy's hand. Then he just as casually shoved her ex-boyfriend, knocking him on his ass.

Jeremy scrambled to his feet and lunged for the piece of metal again, but a deep growl from the side stopped him. Khaki looked over and saw Hale and Alex stride out from between two vehicles, gold eyes glinting, fangs flashing, and claws flexing. Then they stepped aside and made way for a huge wolf so tall he almost reached the other guys' chests. The wolf stopped and stared at Jeremy, his eyes glowing and his lips pulled back to expose a lot of long, sharp teeth. Khaki had never seen any of the other guys in full wolf form, but the beast's scent told her it was Cooper. She'd always thought of him as laid-back, but in wolf form he was intense.

All of them together must have been too much for Jeremy. He gave up on the piece of metal and instead took off running. Xander made a motion with his head and a moment later, Cooper, Hale, and Alex chased after Jeremy, their snarls and howls filling the night.

Sirens echoed in the distance as Xander pulled Khaki back in front of him and kissed her. She kissed him back even harder, so thankful he was okay, but then she cut the kiss short as she remembered the crack she'd heard when Jeremy hit him with that piece of metal.

"Your arm," she said, gently cradling his forearm and carefully checking for breaks.

"It's fine." Xander cupped her cheek. "Are you okay?"

She grimaced. "Jeremy shot me a couple times, but it's nothing that Alex or Trey can't stitch up. Otherwise, I'm fine."

Xander relaxed, but then frowned as the sounds of a struggle reached their ears from the other side of the junkyard.

"Do you think we're going to regret letting Jeremy live?" she asked quietly.

"Probably. But it was the right thing to do."

Khaki hoped Xander was right as they both limped their way toward the front of the junkyard and the unavoidable confrontation with Sergeant Dixon.

―⁘―

Xander insisted that Alex and Trey Duncan, the team's other medic, take care of Khaki's wounds first, but then

she watched along with the rest of her squad as they dug
around in Xander's hip for the pieces of Jeremy's .308
round that had broken up when it hit. She had no idea
how the two medics did it, but it was as if they had some
supernatural ability when it came to knowing where the
bullet fragments were.

Mike and most of his squad were still out clearing the
junkyard. Even though Jeremy was cuffed and safely
tucked away in the back of one of the SWAT team's
SUVs, Mike was a stickler for procedure...and the procedure in this case was to clear the entire area before
turning the scene over to the rest of the DPD.

Sergeant Dixon and Trevor were holding everyone—
including Deputy Chief Mason—at the outer perimeter.
That was good. If anyone saw the way Alex and Trey
were digging around in Xander with forceps and scal-
pels, it might be a bit hard to explain. It looked more like
torture than first aid.

The guys were just finishing up with Xander when
the sound of fast-moving feet dragged Khaki's attention
away from Xander. Jayden ran into the clearing, carrying a big, bloody dog limply in his arms.

"Alex, get over here. Trey, you too," the big man
shouted. "This dog is still alive."

Alex was up and running toward Jayden. Trey only
waited long enough to swipe most of the blood off
Xander's hip, and then he was gone too.

Khaki helped Xander get his jeans back on; then they
both gathered around with everyone else to watch as
Trey and Alex administered medical attention to the dog.

Tears pricked her eyes as she realized the dog she'd
thought was dead had been lying out there hurt the

whole time. She'd been sure Jeremy had killed the poor dog along with his owner.

But Alex and Trey were doing their best to make sure that didn't happen. As Trey got an IV started, Alex slid an air tube down the dog's throat and started working the squeeze bottle. Under all the blood, it was hard to see exactly how bad the pit bull mix was injured. It looked like all three bullets that had hit the dog's owner had hit the animal too, and she heard Alex say something about a collapsed lung. Could a dog, even one this big, survive that?

Khaki was so focused on the dog, she didn't realize Sergeant Dixon and Deputy Chief Mason had shown up until Alex and Trey were loading the dog into one of the SWAT trucks for an emergency ride to the nearest vet.

"I'm really looking forward to reading the official report on this one, Gage." Mason slowly surveyed the scene, then Xander's and Khaki's blood-soaked clothes. "As of this morning, all I knew was that Corporal Riggs would be recovering from major surgery at a private facility for several weeks. Yet, here we are twelve hours later, and I find out that Corporal Riggs was one of the first officers to respond to the scene where the man who tried to kill him was intending to murder a second SWAT officer. A man who is not only a suspended cop from Washington State, but is also Officer Blake's ex-boyfriend."

Gage opened his mouth to answer, but a ranting Jeremy cut him off.

"I'm telling you, they're monsters!" he shouted. "They have claws and fangs and these glowing eyes—"

The uniformed officer didn't even slow down as he

led Jeremy from the SWAT SUV to a patrol car. "Uh-huh. Tell it to your lawyer."

"A suspended cop who is apparently going for an insanity defense," Mason added.

Shaking his head, he walked off to talk to a DPD officer who was setting up crime scene tape around the perimeter. Khaki couldn't believe the deputy chief hadn't wanted a complete report right then and there, but she was glad he didn't because she wouldn't have been able to explain half the stuff that had happened, at least not to someone who wasn't a werewolf.

But Mason's departure had left them completely alone with Sergeant Dixon. Well, except for the rest of the Pack standing a few feet away. Unlike the deputy chief, Dixon looked pissed.

Xander took her hand, holding on protectively as Dixon frowned at them.

"It was bad enough that you two decided to get involved with each other, but since then your mistakes have gotten even worse," he said.

"Getting involved with Khaki wasn't a mistake," Xander growled, his eyes flaring.

Khaki tensed, ready to get between Xander and their commander. The rest of the team was standing off at a distance, ready to help her if things got out of hand. But they knew this was something that she, Xander, and their pack alpha were going to have to work through on their own.

"But I'll concede that I haven't made a lot of good decisions besides that one," Xander finished quietly.

Dixon glowered at Xander for a moment, then pinned Khaki with a look. "Xander told me that your psycho ex was in town since earlier this week. You never thought to mention that to me?"

Beside her, Xander flushed beneath his tan. Khaki knew he felt just as stupid as she did about ignoring the threat that Jeremy had represented. But Xander's pride wasn't going to let him admit that, and neither would hers.

"We thought we could handle it," Xander grated out, his jaw flexing. "It wasn't something we wanted to involve the Pack in."

Khaki expected Dixon to tear into Xander for even trying to justify what they'd done—or rather, failed to do—but instead he snorted.

"That didn't work out too well for any of us, did it?" Dixon asked. "Now there's a psychotic killer on his way to prison who knows we exist."

Khaki felt her legs weaken as all the air whooshed out of her lungs, and she tightened her grip on Xander's hand. She opened her mouth to tell Dixon that she never wanted Jeremy to learn about the Pack, but her boss cut her off.

"Were you planning to kill Jeremy when you came out here, Khaki?"

"Whether she did or not doesn't matter," Xander said before she could answer. "She didn't kill him, and that's what's important."

Dixon gave him a hard look. "I was asking Khaki."

Khaki squeezed Xander's hand. "It's okay," she said, then looked at Dixon. "I did come here to kill Jeremy. When I realized that he was the one who'd shot Xander, all I could think about was tearing him apart. I knew in my heart that if I didn't stop him, he'd come after Xander again, and I couldn't let him do that."

Dixon sighed. "I get that you had an overwhelming urge to protect Xander. Believe me, I get that. A few months ago when Mackenzie got kidnapped, I lost my mind. But when I went after the man who'd taken her, I went to get her back, not to kill him. In the end, the man ended up dead, but that was never my intent. Do you understand why that's an important distinction?"

"I do now. I realize I let my rage and fear control me." She gave him an embarrassed look. "I guess there's still a lot I need to learn about being a werewolf."

"But don't worry, Gage," Xander said. "You and the Pack won't have to be responsible for teaching her. We'll have our transfer requests on your desk in the morning."

Khaki braced herself, expecting Dixon to tell them he wanted them that night. But after staring off into the darkness for a long time, he shook his head.

"Don't waste your time. I'd only tear them up."

Khaki did a double take. Beside her, Xander looked as baffled as she did.

"Back at the hospital you were more than ready to let Khaki and me walk away," Xander said. "What changed?"

"I never said I wanted you out of the Pack." Dixon's mouth tightened. "I'm pissed at both of you, that's for sure. Not for falling for each other though. I know more than anyone you had no control over that. I'm mad because you two forgot that at the end of the day, no matter how bad things get, the Pack will always have your back—that I'll always have your back. If you had, maybe this situation with Jeremy wouldn't have gotten so out of hand. You'll be a member of the Pack forever, even when you screw up. What kind of hypocrite would

I be if I booted you out after everything I put the Pack through with Mackenzie? Besides, she'd kill me if I even tried it. But no more secrets. Understood?"

Khaki let out the breath she'd been holding. She turned to smile at Xander, but then realized he was still staring at Dixon intently.

"What about Khaki?" he asked. "Is she still on my squad? Because that's nonnegotiable."

Khaki tensed again. Standing twenty feet away, the other guys on the team stiffened as well.

"That depends," Dixon said, leveling his gaze at Xander. "Can you be her squad leader and her mate at the same time? Because that's nonnegotiable, too."

Crap. Just as it looked like everything was going to be perfect, reality intruded.

"Can you treat her like every other member of your squad when you're on duty?" Dixon asked. "Can you put her at risk when the mission calls for it? Can you let her do her job without you having to be there every minute to keep tabs on her? Because if you can't, she can't be on your squad. Regardless of what the other guys on your squad might say now, sooner or later, it'll cause problems. Can you really do what it takes be both her squad leader and her mate?"

Khaki's breath caught. Xander's jaw was so tight, she thought it might crack. He was going to say something he'd regret; she just knew it.

"He can do it because I won't have it any other way," she interrupted. "If I'm on his squad, I'll do my job just like the rest of the guys. If that puts me in danger, then that's the job. And if Xander tries to stop me, I'll transfer to Mike's squad on my own."

Xander wanted to argue, but when she frowned at him, he closed his mouth.

Khaki turned to Dixon. "That work for you, Sergeant?"

"That works for me." He glanced at Xander. "You okay with that?"

Xander scowled. "Do I have a choice?"

"No," she and Dixon said together.

Chapter 16

KHAKI LEANED BACK AGAINST THE PICNIC TABLE WITH Mac and her photographer from the newspaper, Zak Gibson, dining on Becker's incredible barbecue ribs and smoky bacon-stuffed burgers while watching the guys play volleyball in the big sand court that dominated the area behind the training-slash-maintenance building.

Mac sighed. "I never get tired of watching sweaty, muscular men playing around in the sand."

Khaki couldn't agree more. She'd played a few games but decided it was much more fun to watch sixteen shirtless men run around in the sand as they spiked the ball than it was to participate. Jeremy's sniper attack had left Xander with some seriously spectacular scars across his chest, something all the guys were quick to point out. Khaki had never thought much about the sex appeal of scars, but on Xander, they looked good.

"Should you be saying that out loud?" Zak asked in between bites of food. "Seeing as you're engaged to be married."

Mac laughed. "Probably not. But it's not my fault that I have a thing for sweaty, muscular men. It's a weakness we women have to deal with."

Khaki couldn't help laughing. She was insanely in love with Xander, but it was hard not looking at all that hunkiness running around out there.

Even Tuffie, the pit bull mix they'd saved from the

junkyard, was sitting there watching with her tongue out and a smile on her face—when she wasn't begging Becker for more food. Khaki couldn't blame Tuffie. Becker knew how to work the grill. His burgers were to die for, and he looked damn good wearing nothing but cargo shorts and an apron.

The dog still limped a little if she ran around too much, but she was doing well, and the vet was sure the dog would make a complete recovery. After all the work Alex and Trey had put into making sure the dog survived, it was a foregone conclusion that she'd come to live with the SWAT team. Tuffie spent her days at the compound, and each night, a different member of the team took her home. There was supposed to be a duty roster, but most nights she ended up going with Alex or Jayden, who had really bonded with Tuffie during her rehab.

Tuffie wasn't the only one getting along well. It had been about a month since all the craziness with Jeremy, and the rift between Sergeant Dixon and Xander had been pretty much repaired. Things had been a little tense between them for the first week or two, but after she and Xander ran a few incidents together, Dixon finally realized everything was going to work out. Xander still had a protective streak that Khaki had to constantly keep in check, but they made it work. The alternative wasn't something either of them wanted to think about.

Deputy Chief Mason showed up as the game was winding down. While the rest of the guys grabbed food, Dixon went over to talk to him.

Khaki forced herself not to eavesdrop. She'd been shocked when Mason hadn't called her and Xander in to give their statements. But the deputy chief never said a word to them. She wondered if he was one of those hide-your-head-in-the-sand types, but it didn't fit. The way he looked at them made her think he knew something was going on. He just never asked.

Mason's lack of apparent concern with the details of the case could have stemmed from the fact that the media had made Jeremy Engler out to be as nutty as a fruitcake. The ex-cop, who'd been dropped from the Lakefront PD like a hot potato, had carried on about the Dallas SWAT team being full of monsters the whole time he was in the local lockup. He'd even tried to bring it up during his arraignment, which had gotten him a seventy-two-hour visit to a mental facility for a psych evaluation. The media assumed the man was a stalker-turned-killer who was working an insanity defense. Regardless, no one paid attention to a single word he said.

As Xander came over to join her, Khaki couldn't help but listen in a little to Dixon's conversation. Mason wasn't talking about what had happened at the junkyard at all. Instead, he was saying something about crime picking up in the city thanks to the power vacuum being left behind after the death of the crime boss Walter Hardy. Mason predicted that crime would only get worse as other power players moved in and tried to take control.

Khaki was still considering what that would mean for the SWAT team when Mason changed the subject.

"You've done a good job bringing Blake in," Mason said to Gage. "She fits in with the rest of your team perfectly."

Xander leaned in close to her ear, whispering in a voice so low no one but she could hear it. "Wonder if Mason realizes exactly how perfectly you and I fit together?"

She laughed. "Maybe we should take a picture of that position we tried out the night before last so he can see how perfectly we fit. Well, how perfectly *you* fit at least."

Xander's eyes flared. His arousal teased her senses, making heat pool between her thighs. They'd been spending a lot of time together since they'd been outed, but all it took was one look from him and it was like the first time all over again—pure and immediate animal attraction.

"You are so bad," he whispered, sitting back.

For obvious reasons, they refrained from any PDA while on duty, but they were also careful to keep their hormones in check around the rest of the team. The guys were fine with the fact that she and Xander were a couple outside the job, and they claimed they barely noticed when she became aroused. Still, it was embarrassing to think of the whole team knowing about it every time she got all hot and bothered. But it was tough when almost anything about your man could set you off.

She sighed and took a deep breath, telling herself that all she really needed was a good dose of Xander's scent to make her happy. Well, maybe not all, but it would hold her over.

Xander wasn't dealing quite as well. There was still a glint in his eyes and while his yummy I-need-you-now scent was less intense than it had been, it still lingered in the air.

"Calm down, big boy," she told him softly. "You're just going to have to wait until later."

"Speaking of making me wait, where were you last night? I know you went out shopping with Mac, but I thought you'd come by after."

She smiled. "Things with Mac ran late. We stopped at Tiny's place, and his wife spent four hours finishing my tat. I figured you'd be asleep by then and didn't want to wake you up."

Xander's eyes flared. "It's done? Show me."

Khaki laughed at his eagerness. She'd gotten the outlining portion done last week, but had kept the work covered with a gauze bandage. She didn't want to spoil the big reveal when she finally showed him the ferocious, but still very feminine, wolf's head positioned perfectly in the middle of her lower back. She had no doubt it was going to drive Xander crazy, in a good way.

She was about to answer when she realized that the entire SWAT had stopped what they were doing to look at her. *Sheesh, talk about pressure.*

She looked at Xander. "Should I show everyone at the same time, or do you want to see it first?" The guys didn't even wait for Xander to answer. They all jogged over and crowded around her.

Xander's mouth edged up. "While the idea of a private showing is definitely intriguing, I think that in this case, everyone deserves to see it. We're a pack, after all."

She smiled coyly at the guys as she turned around and pulled up her shirt, showing off the tattoo on her lower back. They "oohed" and "ahhed" as soon as they saw it.

"That looks outstanding," Xander said, admiration in his voice as he lightly ran his finger over the tattoo.

The wolf head was a lot like the ones the guys had on their chests, but she'd had a few little additions to make it unique, and since she was the only female werewolf around, she figured that was okay.

"Um…exactly how far down does the wolf's ruff go?" Becker asked curiously. "Your shorts block the view."

She dropped her shirt and turned to pin him with a stern look. "Trust me, Becker, you are never going to know how far it goes."

Becker groaned in disappointment, but before Khaki could say anything else, the other guys began ribbing him about not having the imagination to even know what she was teasing him about.

"So how far does the ruff go?" Xander asked in a seriously sexy voice after the rest of the team went off to play another game of volleyball.

She smiled. "You'll just have to wait until we go home. Then you can put me in all kinds of interesting positions so you can find out for yourself."

The growl that vibrated from Xander's throat was music to her ears—and other parts farther south. Taking her hand, he dragged her toward the parking lot.

"Sorry we have to blow off the cookout," he said in a voice Khaki knew the other werewolves could easily hear. "But something suddenly popped up."

The guys laughed.

"How about you take a photo of the whole tattoo for us?" Becker asked as Xander opened the door of his truck and helped her in. "You need to throw us a bone every once in a while, at least until the rest of us find *The One*."

"Don't worry, Becker." Khaki grinned. "I'm sure your girl is out there somewhere. You just need to be ready when you find her."

Whatever Becker might have replied was cut off as Xander cranked his truck and sped out of the parking lot. Khaki scooted across the bench seat and snuggled close to him.

"You really think there's someone out there for each of the guys?" Xander asked as they headed for his place. "Even Becker?"

"I hope so," she murmured. "I'd hate to think that we and Sergeant Dixon might be the only members of the Pack lucky enough to find our *Ones*."

Xander didn't say anything to that, and when she looked at him, he was regarding her seriously.

"What?" she said.

"We really are lucky, aren't we?" he said. "Finding each other like we did?"

Khaki put her head back on his shoulder with a smile. "Yeah, we really are."

She'd had to go through a lot of ups and downs to get to this really good place. But the journey had definitely been worth it.

HERE'S A SNEAK PEEK AT BOOK THREE IN
PAIGE TYLER'S SIZZLING SWAT SERIES

In the Company

of Wolves

Dallas

EYES GLUED TO HIS BINOCULARS, OFFICER ERIC BECKER
surveyed the dimly lit warehouse across from the rooftop he was positioned on. It was four o'clock in the
morning and the place was about as quiet as you could
expect a major import/export warehouse located outside
the Dallas/Fort Worth Airport to be.

"Anything yet?" Xander Riggs queried softly through
Becker's earpiece.

Becker checked the heavy shadows along the west
side of the warehouse before answering his squad leader.

"Nothing yet. But they'll be here. This target is too
good to pass up."

"They'd better show," fellow SWAT officer Max
Lowry muttered over the internal communications channel. "I have a hundred dollars riding on it."

"Which I'll be more than happy to take off your hands when it turns out Becker is wrong," the team's resident medic-slash-sniper, Alex Trevino, added.

"Cut the chatter and stay alert," Xander growled.

Silence descended over the radio as Becker's teammates went back to watching their assigned sectors. Like him, they were positioned in a loose circle around the main warehouse either on rooftops or hidden inside trucks or shipping containers. The idea was to let the thieves slip past them and into the warehouse. Then Xander would give the word and they'd move in, trapping the bad guys in their net. Of course, the plan would only work if the thieves made an appearance. But Becker wasn't worried. He'd studied the ring's MO long enough to know they'd show. And soon. It was as quiet as it was going to get down there.

A secure and bonded freight forwarder like World Cargo was open for business 24-7, but there were always lulls in the workload, and the biggest one was right now, after the midnight rush and before the pace picked up again at sunrise. It might seem like the warehouse was deserted, but there were four security guards roaming the twelve-foot-high perimeter fence, with another stationed in an armored shack located just inside the gated entrance. Becker couldn't see them from his vantage point, but he knew there were two more guards inside the warehouse. It was risky leaving all the guards in place for this operation, but if they didn't, the thieves would know something was up.

Movement out of the corner of Becker's eye caught his attention, and he swung his binoculars to scan the long row of windows that covered the upper level of the warehouse. A moment later, a uniformed security guard walked past. That must have been what he'd seen.

Becker relaxed and swept his binoculars over the rest of his sector as he considered how the death of organized crime boss Walter Hardy had paved the way for these new thieves to move into the city and take over.

Hardy had been a major player in Dallas, but it wasn't until Sergeant Gage Dixon, the commander of the SWAT team, had gone all werewolf on the jackass and ripped out his throat that people really understood what kind of grip Hardy had maintained on almost every criminal enterprise in the city.

For a few blissful weeks following Hardy's death, violent crime rates had dropped to the lowest levels the city had seen in nearly forty years. Of course, that wasn't the reason Gage had killed the man. He'd ripped Hardy to pieces because the son of a bitch had been dumb enough to kidnap the woman the SWAT team's pack alpha werewolf had fallen in love with. Not a smart thing to do. The fringe benefits of the guy's sudden departure from the local gene pool should probably count as a public service.

Unfortunately, nature abhors a vacuum. Within a couple months, every violent offender with a gun and delusions of grandeur was making a play to take over control of the old man's territory. At first, the scumbags spent most of their time killing each other. Soon enough though, deals started being made, alliances started being formed, and it looked like Dallas was heading for a serious turf war.

But then a group of outsiders showed up and the shit really hit the fan. Normally, it would take a crew moving into a new territory months to take over, but these guys were organized, heavily armed, and ruthless beyond frigging belief. Within weeks, they'd put a serious dent in the local criminal leadership, wiping out a lot of people in the process. But if rumors were to be believed, this crew didn't have a huge army of gun-toting soldiers. Instead, they supposedly depended on a relatively small group of enforcers who were vicious and scary as hell.

When these enforcers weren't busy intimidating the crap out of every criminal in the city, they spent their free time stealing stuff. In the last week alone, they'd taken out two jewelry stores, an art gallery, and an electronics store that had cases upon cases of the newest iPhones sitting in secure storage—a week before the phone was due to hit the street. Combined with the other heists, these guys had pulled in nearly half a million in a week. They were good—and dangerous. According to the few witnesses who'd gotten a glimpse of the enforcers, they tended to carry some serious firepower. That's why Becker and the rest of his squad were here. Deputy Chief Mason was worried that when the Dallas PD finally caught up to these guys, there was going to be a lot of shooting. Luckily, Becker had some really sneaky ways of finding people like the ones they were after.

Becker was just musing over how easy it had been to create a search algorithm to predict the crew's next target based on the types of places they'd already hit when another shadowy movement through the warehouse's windows caught his attention. He swung his binoculars up, expecting to see the security guard again, but instead he saw a man dressed head-to-toe in black and carrying an MP5 submachine gun.

"Shit. They're already inside," he shouted into his mic.

Jumping to his feet, Becker headed for the rappelling rope coiled and waiting for a quick descent down the backside of the building. He wrapped the rope around the snap link attached to his harness, then tossed the other end over the side.

"How the hell did they get in there without us seeing them?" Xander demanded in his ear.

"They must have gone inside with one of the earlier shipments," Becker said as he stepped to the edge of the building and kicked himself backward into space.

The rope slid through his gloved hands as he sailed down from the third-floor roof in a single large bound. He ignored the heat in his hand, waiting until he was only a few feet above the ground before jerking his right hand behind his back and braking hard. His downward momentum immediately stopped. He hit the pavement, then ran toward the warehouse, sliding his M4 off his back at the same time.

"They've been waiting for the perfect time to slip out of hiding and take down the interior guards," he said.

"Should we try to warn them?" Khaki Blake, teammate and Xander's significant other, asked across the radio.

Becker could hear the sound of feet pounding on pavement in the background—the rest of the team running for their entry positions.

"Negative," Xander ordered. "The suspects could have the guards' radios."

Becker swore as he raced to the side entrance where he was supposed to meet up with fellow SWAT officer

and explosives expert Landry Cooper. They had no idea
how many bad guys were in the warehouse or where
they were. If the guards weren't already dead, that meant
the suspects now had two hostages they could use as
human shields to hide behind on their way out. That
made this operation a hell of a lot harder.

He absently heard Xander tell the on-scene commander to keep the rest of the Dallas PD officers at a
distance. Xander didn't want their fellow cops running
into the building shooting at everything that moved,
including SWAT.

Cooper was already waiting at the heavy metal security door when Becker got there. Cooper punched the
code into the cypher lock on the wall, then Becker led
the way in. He and Cooper hesitated as soon as they got
inside, both of them waiting for the rest of the squad to
signal they were ready to go.

That was when Becker realized there was something
really strange going on in the warehouse—so strange
that it took him a second to realize what had him pinging
all of a sudden.

"Shit," he muttered, finally recognizing the familiar
scent in the air. "We might have a problem, team. The
guys we're going up against are werewolves. Every one
of them."

There was stunned silence on the other end of the radio.

"You sure?" Xander asked.

"He's sure," Cooper answered before Becker could
say anything. "I smell them too."

Xander's curse was succinct over the radio.
"Everyone stay together and watch yourselves."

Becker didn't need to be told twice, and he doubted

anyone else did either. The idea of facing criminals who were just as strong, fast, and hard to take down as the SWAT team was more than enough to keep them on their toes.

He and Cooper moved slowly through the warehouse, checking behind every box and pallet as they covered each other. How the hell had another werewolf pack moved into Dallas without them realizing it?

He was still trying to come up with an answer when gunfire sounded from the far side of the warehouse.

"Contact!" the SWAT team's lead armorer, Trevor McCall, shouted over the radio. "Khaki and I are engaged with three of them, all heavily armed. They're definitely werewolves. I put four rounds into one of them and he's still going."

More automatic weapons fire came from somewhere off to the left of Becker, then even more from the right. Bullets ricocheted off the concrete floor and steel shelving units, punching holes in shipping crates and containers, and making it damn near impossible to figure out which direction the bad guys were shooting from.

"I'm pushing the exterior security guards and the rest of the DPD to the outside perimeter," Xander announced. "We can't let regular cops engage with these guys or it'll be a bloodbath. This is all on us."

"Roger that," Becker said.

"Incoming!" Cooper shouted.

Becker turned just in time to see two hulking figures dressed eerily similar to him and Cooper in black garb, tactical vests, and toting automatic weapons, which the bad guys were aiming in their direction.

Becker ducked behind the closest crate while Cooper

dove for cover behind another as bullets whizzed past them. Using the crate as a shield, Becker stuck the barrel of his M4 out and took aim. He hated the idea of killing fellow werewolves, but he didn't have a choice. This crew would take down him and every member of his pack without hesitation. It was pack against pack, and there was no question about what he had to do.

Becker put two rounds through the thug on the right, just above the top of his tactical vest. The werewolf stumbled back, but then charged forward with a growl, his eyes turning a vivid yellow-gold, his lip curling in a snarl, exposing his fangs.

Becker lifted his weapon a little higher and squeezed the trigger, putting three 5.56 mm ball rounds through the werewolf's forehead. That stopped him cold and he immediately went down. On the other side of the aisle, Cooper took out the second werewolf.

That left about a dozen more. And unlike their buddies, they quickly figured out he and Cooper were werewolves too. After that, their tactics changed. They came at him and Cooper from multiple directions at once, using their keen hearing and sense of smell to pinpoint their location. They even attacked from above, climbing on top of shelving units and trying to pin them down in crossfire.

In the two years he'd been with SWAT, Becker had never gone up against anyone who was even close to being a match for him and his pack. These guys were fast, and they were strong. But while they fought like berserkers, they didn't fight as a pack. That gave Becker and Cooper the advantage. When they put down yet another werewolf—this one fast and wiry, who'd climbed and hopped around on the shelving units like a frigging monkey—the rest of them turned tail and ran.

On the downside, that meant he and Cooper had to split up. It was dangerous, and Xander would have their asses for it, but it was worth the risk if they could take down this crew.

"I found the two guards," Khaki reported over the radio. "They're alive, but unconscious."

Xander said something in reply, but Becker didn't hear what it was because he was too busy trying to figure out the new scent his nose had just picked up. It was unmistakably werewolf, but unlike any werewolf he'd ever smelled before. It reminded him a little of Khaki, but sweeter.

He took a breath, then another and another until he was almost hyperventilating. Shit, he could barely hold up his weapon.

Becker shook his head, trying to clear it as he rounded the corner, and came face to face with a female werewolf so beautiful that all he could do was stop and stare. She stared back, her blue eyes as wide as saucers. Her heart beat a hundred miles an hour and there was blood splattered on the tactical vest she wore. Becker's heart lurched at the thought of her being hurt. But one sniff confirmed the blood wasn't hers. It belonged to one of the other werewolves with her.

He opened his mouth to order her to drop the MP5 she had aimed at him, but nothing would come out. It was like she'd robbed him of the ability to speak. But he had to get the weapon away from her. If she pulled the trigger, he'd be dead. Shooting her wasn't an option, though. And the idea of arresting her didn't make him feel any better.

Becker didn't consider if what he was about to do

was smart, but simply lowered his weapon and took his finger off the trigger, letting his M4 hang loosely against his chest by the strap over his shoulder. Then he slowly lifted both hands as if in surrender.

He'd done it to put her at ease, but her heart pounded even harder. Her eyes darted left and right, her ponytail swinging from side to side. And while she kept her weapon trained on him, at least her finger wasn't wrapped around the trigger now.

Becker reached up and switched off his mic, then pulled up the black ski mask hiding his face. When he finally managed to find his voice, he didn't want his teammates listening in.

"Relax and put down the gun," he said, keeping his voice soft and calm even though gunfire echoed in the rest of the warehouse. "We can work this out. No one else has to get hurt."

She didn't say anything or lower her weapon. She didn't run, either. That was progress, he supposed.

He was wondering if he should try a different tact when Xander's voice came across loud and clear over the radio in his ear. "They're bolting, so be careful. The ones left are going to fight like caged rats."

Becker didn't have to ask if the woman heard what Xander said. She was a werewolf like him, which meant she had the same exceptional hearing. If he needed further confirmation, the look of terror on her face would have been it. He couldn't blame her; her pack had just abandoned her.

Off to the right, the sounds of gunfire increased, and so did the howls. Boots thudded on the concrete floor, heading in their direction.

She looked around again, trying to see every direction at once. Her grip on her weapon tightened and she swung it at whoever was coming their way.

Oh hell, she was going to start shooting.

Swearing under his breath, Becker closed the distance between them and ripped the MP5 out of her hands, tossing it aside. She bared her fangs in a snarl, but before she could get the sound out, he slapped a hand over her mouth.

"Trust me," he said in her ear.

COMING DECEMBER 2015

Tajikistan

Angelo Rios glanced at his watch. The team needed to get moving or it'd take all day to get back to camp. Their A-team had been doing a recon sweep back and forth through the rugged terrain of southern Tajikistan when they heard about a small town near the mountain pass that had been hit hard by a recent storm. Repairing buildings damaged by high winds and torrential rain wasn't the kind of work Special Forces usually did, but Angelo and the new lieutenant, Brad Watson, figured it'd be an easy way to gain a little goodwill with the locals, which definitely was an SF mission.

He squeezed the last of the cheese onto a cracker from his MRE, meal-ready-to-eat, and shoved it in his mouth, then stuffed the empty wrapper into his rucksack and swung the pack over his shoulder. The rest of the team got the message and did the same.

"So, tell me this," Derek Mickens said as he tightened the straps on his own ruck. "What does that big bear shifter have that I don't?"

Angelo chuckled. The guys had been ribbing Derek ever since they heard his crush Kendra Carlsen—now MacBride—was having twins with her husband, Declan.

Angelo was about to point out that the DCO's resident bear shifter had seventy-five pounds of muscle and six inches on Derek, not to mention a face that didn't scare small children, when screams of terror from the far end of the village they'd just helped rebuild silenced the words in his mouth.

Angelo had his M4 in his hands and was running toward the sound even as the rest of the guys spread out behind him, checking for incoming threats. He rounded the corner of a dilapidated building and was heading down a dirt road lined with more crumbling buildings when a man covered in blood ran toward him. Two more men followed, fear clear in their eyes and blood staining their clothes.

At first Angelo thought it was an IED—an improvised explosive device—but that didn't make sense. He hadn't heard an explosion. He slowed down anyway, worried he was leading the team into an ambush.

One of the men pointed behind him, shouting something in Tajik. Angelo's grasp of the language was pretty good, but the man was speaking way too fast for him to make out what he was saying. Then he figured it out.

Monster.

He opened his mouth to ask where the "monster" was, but the man was already halfway down the road. Angelo picked up the pace only to skid to a stop in front of a mud-covered shack a few moments later. He knew he was in the right place because there was a guy who looked like he'd been sliced up by Freddy Krueger on the ground in front of it.

Angelo got a sinking feeling in his gut. He'd seen damage like this before.

He jumped over the dead guy and was through the door before he even thought about what he was doing. Thinking only slowed you down in situations like this anyway.

Angelo raised his M4, ready to pop the first threatening thing he saw. If he was right about what had attacked those men, it would take multiple shots to kill the thing.

But what he found stopped him cold in his tracks. Derek and Lieutenant Watson skidded to a stop right behind him.

There wasn't a square foot of wall space in the one-room shack that wasn't splattered with blood, and in the middle of it stood a pretty, dark-haired woman, gazing down at two dead men at her feet. Her shirt was on the floor beside them, one of her bra straps was torn, and her skirt was ripped. Her feet were bare and covered in dirt, and he thought there were tears on her cheeks, but he couldn't be sure since her long, dark hair hung down around her face almost to her waist.

Angelo felt a rage build inside him like nothing he'd ever felt before, and he was torn between staying where he was and going after the rest of the men who'd tried to rape her and killing them, too.

He glanced at her hands, hoping to find a knife there and praying he was wrong about what she was. But she didn't have any weapons. Unless you counted the wickedly sharp claws on each slender finger. And given the amount of blood in the room, those hands certainly qualified as weapons.

As if just realizing he was there, the woman lifted her head to look at him with glowing red eyes. She growled, baring her teeth and exposing some seriously long canines.

How the hell had a hybrid turned up in Tajikistan? More importantly, what the hell was he going to do with her?

"What the fuck is that thing?" the lieutenant asked hoarsely even as he raised his carbine and sighted in on the woman's chest.

The woman growled again, louder this time, and crouched down on all fours, like she was getting ready to pounce on them.

Shit. Things were about to get ugly.

But instead of leaping at them, her eyes darted around, like she was looking for a way past them. Unfortunately, they were blocking her access to the doors and windows, and she knew it. For some reason he couldn't explain, Angelo suddenly didn't see a hybrid monster like those he'd fought in Washington State and down in Costa Rica. He saw a woman who was scared as hell.

"Derek, get everyone outside and away from the building," Angelo ordered softly, never taking his eyes off the woman. "We're freaking her out."

"Freaking her out." Watson snorted. "Are you kidding me? She's the one freaking me out."

"Outside, LT," Angelo ordered again, more firmly this time. "Trust me on this one."

He knew the lieutenant wanted answers, but right now, he didn't have time to give him any. Behind him, Derek was herding the officer toward the door.

"LT, remember when we told you that you'd be seeing some weird shit in the field that they never mentioned in school?" Derek asked. "Well, that weird shit just started. But trust Angelo. He knows what he's doing. He's dealt with these things before."

Their voices faded as they moved outside.

The woman's eyes followed Derek and Watson until they disappeared from sight, then slid to Angelo. He slowly lowered his weapon and carefully set it on the floor. Then he raised his hands and spoke softly in Tajik.

"It's okay. You're safe now. No one is going to hurt you."

The red glow in her eyes flickered, then began to fade. Angelo let out the breath he'd been holding. Maybe he'd be able to get out of this situation without killing her. He couldn't explain why that mattered to him all of a sudden. She was a hybrid and clearly out of control. Many might consider killing her to be a mercy, and the only sure way to keep her from killing again.

But from what he'd seen, the woman had a pretty good reason to attack those men. And more importantly, Angelo knew for a fact that not every hybrid was beyond reach. Tanner Howland from the Department of Covert Operations was one of those. Not only had the former Army Ranger learned how to control the rages that defined his kind, he'd learned to harness that rage to save a lot of people down in Costa Rica several months back. Angelo was pretty sure he wouldn't be alive if it wasn't for that one particular hybrid. If Tanner could do it, who was he to say that this woman in front of him couldn't get herself under control too? She certainly seemed to be trying.

Angelo kept up his calm chatter, reassuring the woman that she was safe, and soon enough, her eyes turned to a normal, beautiful brown. There was still some anger there, but there was also confusion, maybe even hope.

Raised voices echoed outside, drowning out Angelo's soft words. The villagers had worked up their courage and come looking for blood. The woman's head snapped in that direction, and like a light switch being flipped, the veil of calmness that had descended on the female hybrid disappeared.

She tensed, and he watched her face as anger warred with what he could only describe as frustration mixed with honest-to-goodness fear. As each of those emotions ascended, her eyes changed from red to green to brown, over and over in a dizzying display like nothing he'd ever seen before.

But then, just as it seemed like she might have a chance, the internal struggle was over and the woman leaped at him.

Every instinct in Angelo's body screamed at him to lunge for his weapon, or at the very least to pull out his knife. But he ignored his instincts and instead set his feet for impact, blocking her slashing claws with his forearm, then ducking down and tackling her. It wasn't the nicest way to treat a woman, but considering the fact that she was trying to kill him, he decided she'd just have to forgive him.

He twisted at the last second, letting his shoulder take the impact. He'd planned to immediately roll his weight onto her, hoping to keep her from getting away by pinning her to the floor like a wrestler, but the hybrid didn't give him a chance. She spun in his grasp, trying to break his hold on her. He wrapped his arms around her, doing his best to trap her clawed hands safely against her breasts as he pulled her back down. She twisted in his arms again, trying to sink her teeth into his shoulder.

He hugged her tightly to his chest, whispering over and over that it would be okay, that she was safe, that no one would hurt her.

When she buried her face in his neck, he just about freaked, sure she was going to tear out his throat. He resisted the urge to shove her away and go for his gun, instead continuing to talk to her. Unbelievably, she didn't bite him. She kept struggling to free herself, though. But after a few moments, she went still, all the fight gone.

Angelo glanced down at her. Her cheek was resting against his chest, her eyes closed, and her fingers curled into the front of his uniform. He wasn't sure if she was asleep or had simply passed out from exhaustion. Either way, her breathing was rhythmic and even. The sight of her made his heart ache, and he gently brushed her hair back from her face. This close, he was finally able to see past all the dirt and blood. While he'd thought she was pretty when he first saw her, now he realized that she was absolutely beautiful—and vulnerable looking as all hell.

"Damn, Tex-Mex," Derek said from the doorway. "You're good with the ladies when you want to be."

Angelo didn't laugh. "Get on the satellite phone and call Landon. If you can't get him, try Ivy or Clayne. Tell them where we are and that we've stumbled on a hybrid. We need a priority airlift to get her out of here. And whatever you do, don't let LT get on the line to the battalion."

COMING SPRING 2016

Acknowledgments

I hope you had as much fun reading Xander and Khaki's story as I had writing it! When hubby and I were talking ideas for the second book in the SWAT series over Spicy Chicken at P.F. Chang's, we immediately knew we wanted to add a female werewolf to the team. The moment we broached the subject with all the guys on the team (not named Gage, of course!), everyone wanted to be *The One* for Khaki. But ultimately, we left the decision up to her. We think she made the right choice!

In addition to another big thank-you to my hubby, I want to also thank my agent, Bob Mecoy, for believing in me and encouraging me and being there when I need to talk, not to mention always having such great ideas; my editor, Cat Clyne, for loving this series and hot guys in tactical gear as much as I do; and all the other amazing people at Sourcebooks, including my publicist, Amelia, and their crazy-talented art department. I'm still drooling over this cover!

I also want to give a big thank-you to the men, women, and working dogs who protect and serve in police departments everywhere, as well as their families.

And because I could never leave my readers out, a huge thank-you to everyone who has read my books and Snoopy Danced right along with me with every new release. That includes the fantastic girls on my street team. You rock!

Hope you look forward to reading the other books in the SWAT series as much as I look forward to sharing them with you.

Happy reading!

About the Author

Paige Tyler is the *New York Times* and *USA Today* bestselling author of sexy, romantic suspense and paranormal romance. She and her very own military hero (also known as her husband) live on the beautiful Florida coast with their adorable fur baby (also known as their dog). Paige graduated with a degree in education, but decided to pursue her passion and write books about hunky alpha males and the kick-butt heroines who fall in love with them. Visit www.paigetylertheauthor.com.

She's also on Facebook, Twitter, Tumblr, Google+, Instagram, and Pinterest.

Her Perfect Mate

X-Ops

by Paige Tyler

New York Times and *USA Today* bestselling author

———

He's a high-octane Special Ops pro

When Special Forces Captain Landon Donovan is pulled from an op in Afghanistan, he is surprised to discover he's been hand-picked for a special assignment with the Department of Covert Operations (DCO), a secret division he's never heard of. Terrorists are kidnapping biologists and he and his partner have to stop them. But his new partner is a beautiful, sexy woman who looks like she couldn't hurt a fly—never mind take down a terrorist.

She's not your average Covert Operative

Ivy Halliwell is no kitten. She's a feline shifter, and more dangerous than she looks. She's worked with a string of hotheaded military guys who've underestimated her special skills in the past. But when she's partnered with special agent Donovan, a man sexy enough to make any girl purr, things begin to heat up…

———

Praise for *Her Perfect Mate*:

"A wild, hot, and sexy ride from beginning to end!"
—Terry Spear, *USA Today* bestselling author

For more Paige Tyler, visit:

www.sourcebooks.com

Her Lone Wolf

X-Ops

by Paige Tyler

New York Times and *USA Today* bestselling author

Leaving him was impossible…

It took everything she had for FBI Special Agent Danica Beckett to walk away from the man she loved. But if she wants to save his life, she has to keep her distance. Now, with a killer on the loose and the stakes higher than ever, the Department of Covert Ops is forcing these former lovers into an uneasy alliance…whether they like it or not.

Seeing her again is even worse

The last thing Clayne Buchanan wants is to be shackled to the woman who broke his heart. She gets under his skin in a way no one ever has and makes him want things he has no right to anymore. All he has to do is suffer through this case and he can be free of her for good. But when Clayne finds out why Danica left in the first place, everything he's tried to bury comes roaring back—and there's no way this wolf shifter is going to let her get away this time.

"Dangerously sexy and satisfying." —Virna DePaul, *New York Times* bestselling author of the Belladonna Agency series

For more Paige Tyler, visit:

www.sourcebooks.com

Her Wild Hero

X-Ops

by Paige Tyler

New York Times and *USA Today* bestselling author

───◦◦◦───

The third book in the hot, pulse-pounding paranormal romantic suspense X-Ops series from *New York Times* and *USA Today* bestselling author Paige Tyler.

───◦◦◦───

Department of Covert Operations training officer Kendra Carlsen has been begging her boss to let her go into the field for years. When he finally agrees to send her along on a training exercise in Costa Rica, she's thrilled.

Bear-shifter Declan MacBride, on the other hand, is anything but pleased. He's been crushing on Kendra since he started working at the DCO seven years ago. Spending two weeks in the same jungle with her is putting a serious strain on him.

When the team gets ambushed, Kendra and Declan are forced to depend on each other. But the bear-shifter soon discovers that fighting bloodthirsty enemies isn't nearly as hard as fighting his attraction to the beautiful woman he'll do anything to protect.

───◦◦◦───

Praise for *Her Perfect Mate:*

"Absolutely perfect. One of the best books I've read in years." —Kate Douglas, bestselling author of the Wolf Tales and Spirit Wild series

For more Paige Tyler, visit:

www.sourcebooks.com